Eugene

GIFT OF THE TIGER

EUGENE MCCREARY

ACKNOWLEDGEMENTS

I am greatly indebted to the late Graham Peck's *Two Kinds of Time,* his excellent, personal account of life inside China during World War II; to John G Martin, DVM, *Through Hell's Gate to Shanghai*; to Deng Ming-Dao, *Chronicles of Tao*; to John R Mabry's wonderful but partial translation, *The Little Book of the Tao Te Ching*; to Yoshimi Yoshiaki, *Comfort Women*; to Frederick Wakeman, Jr, *The Shanghai Badlands;* to Donovan Webster, *The Burma Road*; and to Ralph D Sawyer, trans., Sun Tzu's *The Complete Art of War;* and to Stephen Becker, *The Chinese Bandit.*

DEDICATION

I am deeply grateful to Rosemary, patient reader and astute critic, and to Jeff.

Note to Reader: this is a work of fiction. While rooted in real events, it is not strictly speaking historical fiction. Events and dates have been altered somewhat to fit the story. The characters, of course, are all fictitious .

CONTENTS

PROLOGUE

I asked the boy at the temple door, where his master had gone. "Somewhere on the mountain," he replied. "Gathering herbs. Hidden by the clouds. No one knows where." –Chinese poem.

Western China, 1926

Someone was stalking him.

In a fog-shrouded forest on the slopes of a mountain, Master Po Lin crouched low along a rock-strewn stream and cocked his ears. Silence reigned. Monkeys, birds, even insects seemed to have fled. Nothing broke the quiet except the gurgle at his feet and mist dripping off leaves. Uneasy, he moved on, picking his way up the watery stairway, a wraith in a cloud. The willows and maples tapering down to the watercourse withheld their usual welcome, standing hostile and withdrawn. His gray brows knit together.

"You may come out now," he called to the impenetrable brown-green hedge of bushes, ferns and branches, the sense of peril stronger. "I have important work to do and you have no business in this holy place."

Since early morning he had been clambering over fallen, uprooted trees and boulders swept down from the heights of the sacred mountain, by the winter's run-off, looking beneath rotted masses of vegetation for little nail-like fungi in the mouth of a particular moth's tiny mummified larvae, *ch'ung-tsao*, an antidote to opium poisoning and a balm for the aged villagers who lived

1

nearby. Suddenly his neck hairs stood. Danger was behind, just beyond the range of his peripheral vision.

"I am Po," he cried out. "I fear no man. And Emei Shan belongs to heaven. Do not anger it." His head snapped around. "Show yourself!"

The forest refused its secret. He had a premonition that some momentous act was about to occur when out of the dead calm a sudden breath of wind brought a high-pitched sound to his ears. It cut through the fog like an arrow. He ducked instinctively. The stalker? Up ahead? How? His question led to an animal track to his right that pierced the wall of vegetation along the stream. Curious, he decided to follow it. The trail zigzagged over matted weeds and grass for a short distance then faded beneath the trees. The sound grew louder and with each step drew him deeper and deeper within his *dantian*, the core of his being, commanding him to make haste. He wrapped his hand tightly around the bamboo walking stick and forged onward, sharp twigs and broken branches whipping his leather leggings.

At length the trail emptied onto a rough escarpment with a gradual downward slope, a natural amphitheater. High above and to the left, a spring cascaded over a steep stone raceway, spewing a fine mist over an ancient landslide—a chaos of boulders and misshapen dwarf trees—that clung to the precipice's edge on his right. Small patches of brush surrounded granite slabs as smooth as if a stonecutter had shaped them, but the only masons here had been wind, rain and snow. Across, opposite him, where the now much-diminished forest resumed, he believed he saw the trail continue. He reckoned he knew every inch of the mountain but he did not remember this place.

On a great block of granite near the clearing's center lay a yellow bundle, the source of the keening. Ah, he thought. Puzzle solved. A child left to die here on the Sacred Mountain. An old story. Times were always hard on the peasants. Tax collectors cheated them; landlords charged too much rent. Too many mouths to feed made female infants expendable. And yet why come this far, intent on infanticide? He drew near, unwrapped the golden silk that gleamed with an intricate, embroidered figure of a red dragon, and touched the infant — warm, abandoned less than a day. It ceased crying, gurgled and moved its limbs spasmodically. A mother loved this daughter, gave it a royal gown and set it out as a sacrifice to the gods.

"Let it be so," he said to himself, as he re-wrapped the swaddling cloth. "May her wishes be fulfilled."

Nevertheless the little one's beauty moved him — a perfect creature from the Tao, destined to be extinguished because she was a female. Senseless. In his wild youth he fought as a mercenary half-way across China and back, witness to enough useless slaughter for two lifetimes.

"I have come for medicine, not babies," he said aloud as if he needed to remind himself. "A Master does not take in foundlings. A monastery is not an orphanage."

On the far side of the clearing, the trees and low growth looked promising for fungi. He hoisted his pack, picked up his staff and headed to where the animal track

3

resumed, while the infant resumed its irritable bawling. He had not taken ten steps when the almost forgotten danger revealed itself, blocking the trail. No one had seen a tiger in this mountain range for untold years. Villagers spoke of legends, tales, the stuff of fantasy, but he could smell the fetid aroma of a wild animal. It snarled, baring four incisors that could tear off an arm or crush a skull with ease. He stood motionless until his amazement gave way to the sight a few paces from the beast. A woman in a shredded silk robe lay in the brambles. She had not been throttled the way tigers normally kill their prey. Blood stained her face but her eyelids fluttered.

His one encounter with a tiger was nearly forty years ago, in the mountains north of Xi'an, when, puffed up with arrogance, he foolishly tried to defend himself with a sword. The low branches of a convenient tree saved him. With nowhere to flee today, even his Qiongzhu stick, legendary for hardness that rivaled steel, would do him little good.

"So it was you," he murmured, "who hunted me." He rolled up his sleeve, revealing the tiger image burned into his forearm, the mark of all Shaolin priests. "I am one with you, *laohuo*. Why are you here?"

The Master advanced cautiously, drawn by an irresistible impulse to test himself once again. With each footstep, the conviction grew this was no ordinary being he opposed. The tiger blinked, dropped on its haunches in the brush and yawned. Eyes fastened on the unpredictable engine of death, he dragged the woman three paces, lifted her onto his shoulders and walked backwards. Death had hunted him often and in many guises but never like this.

A profound calm suffused him. If the end came, so be it. It would arise neither from hate nor greed. Heaven and earth were impartial. They allowed things to die. Those were the Sage's words.

When he reached the clearing, the child's wailing stopped and the tiger growled. He propped the woman against the stone altar. Her long black hair washed over a bruised face of chiseled beauty. Though in shock, she found the strength to roll her glazed eyes toward the child. The next instant she was dead. The infant seemed to sense the loss and once more resumed its wail. What was her story? he wondered as he placed her beside the babe, deeming it fit for them to die together. A farmer's wife? Her clothing's fineness said no. A warlord's concubine? In any case, she had paid a heavy price for her devotion. Sadness impelled him to touch the infant once more. It ceased its bawling.

"Good, little one. No use inviting death." He nodded at the trail. "It will come soon enough." He gloomily re-tightened the swaddling cloth, his mind buffeted with misgivings. "Who knows why Heaven allows things to happen? Not even the Sage can say for sure."

Satisfied he had done all he could, he left the clearing and retraced his way to the stream. He took pride in not being a stone Buddha, but children were out of the question. And a girl. It went against every tradition. Why was he thinking such thoughts?

After a few steps, his neck hairs raised again. What magic was this? His astonishment at the prospect of the massive beast blocking his way him gradually prompted him to a closer look. This tiger was much larger than the other and a male. The alternative — that the animal could be in two places at once — frightened him even more than the tail-twitching creature eyeing him. He breathed slowly.

"So. Death for me, along with the woman and child," he whispered. "Is that your edict, *laohuo*?"

Just when he had accepted his fate, the tiger snarled and a force beyond his conscious mind compelled him to turn and run. At any second he expected five hundred pounds on his back and vise-like teeth clamped on his neck. To his surprise he made it back to the slab and the infant where he sat to catch his breath. Anger and fear and laughter at his wild retreat bubbled up. All he had wanted from this walk was medicine. He reached over and again laid his hands on the golden cloth. The wailing stopped once more but simultaneously a muffled roar broke the silence from the way forward and from the way back. Flaming fur flashed at both ends of the glade. The babe cried. The tigers retreated into the thicket. He touched the infant. Silence, followed by another growl.

"So, child, it seems I either take you with me or we both die here. But I am old, too old to take up such a burden. How can it come to any good?"

A deafening roar answered him and shook him like a rag doll. The fog thickened momentarily, covering them like a blanket of incense. Almost as fast, it rose to allow a hint of sunlight on the natural temple. He marveled at the sight, inhaled slowly, and with a formal bow to each end of the clearing, lifted the infant in both hands and held it above his head in solemn offering to the energy in all creation.

"Forgive this block of wood, spirits of the Tao, for taking so long to recognize your message. This infant is your gift. I will treasure it."

His voice echoed against the mountainside. He dropped the babe into his sling and prepared to leave, casting a last somber eye at the dead woman.

"They thirst for life in the monastery," he announced to his tormentors, reflecting on life and death, yin and yang. "Indeed, China itself has lost its balance."

He tugged on his wisp of beard. To raise a girl-child would be an astonishing break with tradition. It would be necessary to conceal her identity, then, until the right time. The old, familiar tingle of danger made him pause, as if he were once more preparing for battle. Against what? The spirit tigers? The future? Accept the inevitable. Was that not the Tao's essence? The babe started to howl as he headed back.

"Sing your song, little one," he said. "If Heaven is willing you can protect us until we reach safety. If we make it to the bottom of the mountain, I'll take you to old Mai. She'll find a nursing mother."

The monastery would provide extra food and perform sacrifices to the gods for the family's prosperity. The Grand Master did not believe in superstitious nonsense but the *laobaixing*, the common people, needed rituals.

At last the forest came to a halt like the edge of a theater stage, a dark curtain of brush and leaves with the fog hovering above it all. A muffled growl told him he had been followed. These great guardians of China, what did they portend? The emperor gone. Rumors of war. Warlords. Too much yang. Clearly the Tao itself had touched him. A blessing or a curse — or both? Even Lao-tze could not answer such questions.

He listened again. No more growls — merely his own stomach clamoring for food, and the child had fallen asleep. The day had drawn to a close and still he had not eaten. He would gather fungi another day.

CHAPTER 1

To believe in the Tao is easy. To keep the Tao is difficult. – Chinese Proverb

Western China

"Do not be afraid to appear foolish," Zhe Zhao, the visiting master from Wushan, admonished the assembled monks and students of the Golden Sun Monastery. "All good arts, all great skills, begin with acting like a fool. May I have a volunteer to demonstrate?"

Heads turned but the virtuoso of the bamboo fighting staff was even then crossing the exercise yard to the ranks of novices, seated cross-legged on the ground in front of the dormitories to the right of the temple. Seventeen-year old Su Li bent low, avoiding any chance of eye contact.

"Do not choose me," she prayed in a voice barely audible to her own ears.

But the master's long rod tapped her shoulder. The touch startled her; the palm resting on her abdomen beneath her tunic fell away. The young woman, indistinguishable from her fellow male novices, at first refused to acknowledge the invitation, then felt another slight tap. She looked up into the eyes of the master. Hadn't she been fool enough? her flushed expression asked. And how did one repair, Master, folly previously committed? And how can such rashness lead to anything but disaster? And how does one escape the curse of

9

gender? But her unspoken questions were met only by the stocky Zhao's disconcerting smile and a slight, encouraging nod. His gesture of exceptional honor would be rude and humiliating to refuse. Nearly dizzy with sudden bitter anger she arose with a wobble.

Zhao ran his hand with a lover's touch over the rock-hard bamboo rod. "We Chinese hate to lose face but until you absorb my meaning your whole life will be mired in foolishness — the wrong kind."

A rhythmic music throbbed in the mercurial master as he leaped, somersaulted and vaulted across the yellow sand of the arena, bounded by the temple at one end, the refectory and dormitories on the sides, and the entry gate at the other end, sometimes comic, always supple. Even the resident orange-robed masters, who stood in a row of honor before the storehouses opposite the residence halls, clucked in approval while enthralled novices and disciples in white clapped with delight. Finally he paused, gave her a reassuring wink and nodded at the spare staff on the sand.

It did not matter what the others suspected, she decided. Or if she had given them reason. Today was a chance to prove it made no difference if she were female. Zhao nodded imperceptibly, as if he had heard every word. Loosening her shoulders, the lithe young woman, taller than most of the other novices, retrieved the bamboo from the yellow granite sand and bowed.

"Give me your best effort, young, ah, student."

He pulled out a white cloth from his sash and tied it around his eyes. The blindfold added to the comic aura of his performance yet at the same time evoked a sense of magic. The other students gasped in amazement but Su Li was not surprised. Wushan was the mother of martial arts and its masters legendary. Even a blind one could defeat a mere student. Resolved to do her best, she assumed a fighting stance: both hands on the staff shoulder width apart, elbows bent, knees flexed slightly, balanced on the balls of her feet. Zhao waited, relaxed.

She approached warily, at first probing where she believed her opponent would least expect, then shifted to a thrust straight at his chest. Feinting, she swung the staff wide, aiming at his ankles. Leaping, twisting, she whipped the bamboo rod back and forth, faster, faster; but with uncanny accuracy the sightless Zhao blocked each blow and hopped over the low swerves. His spinning cudgel drove her backward with ease and landed blows as if it had its own eyes. Minutes dragged like hours. At last he took pity, turned away and circled in a high-step dance.

Bruised from shoulder to ankles, dejected, out of breath, she dropped her arms and turned her back to her opponent. The spectators grew quiet, anticipating her concession. Zhao waited, head cocked, listening. She glanced at her mentor Po, whose opinion alone mattered to her, but he was conversing with a stranger at the temple porch.

Out of the embarrassing quiet, a raptor's harsh screech soared above the yard. A strange hawk perched on the temple roof and called once more. She looked up, surprised at a sudden ability to perceive the smallest

11

detail of the bird's extraordinary blue and gold plumage. As its fierce orbs bore into her, to her astonishment, it spoke.

I do not care about failures. Past mistakes and worries for the future do not intrude on me. I am who I am. Always here, always now. Be like me. Wu wei. Let go. Can you comprehend the Sage's words?

The message formed as images that arose from a hidden compartment, or from the silence — or from nowhere. Puzzled, she nodded at the bird then glanced around. The entire assembly was still watching her, just as they had seconds ago, but frozen in place. All at once, the knots of trying too hard vanished like morning fog as she stepped into the dimension of altered time. She closed her eyes, the touch of a smile on her lips. *A fool. Why not? Here and now.*

Conscious control fell away and her energy rose like a fountain. She attacked with full force, effortless and unhurried, the countless hours of running in the snow barefoot; of endless days of practice, often in rain, striking burlap sacks of rice and wooden posts until her hands cried out for mercy; tedious bouts of sweeping, cleaning, weeding, that all seemed at the time utterly pointless, coalesced into a locus of singular elegance and power. Her staff rotated in nearly invisible arcs, took on a life of its own, became an extension of her body, rocking and twirling from all directions, propelled by arching leaps, spins and somersaults in mystic counterpoint to Master Zhao's, the artistry of combat unfolding as if two superb dancers were responding alternately to the other's lead.

Behind her eyelids she could sense Zhao's moves as he must have perceived hers. Ever backwards she drove the masked master, both their poles a blur. The onlookers held their breaths. Such an extraordinary display of skill—from a student—would have overwhelmed any ordinary opponent.

At last they paused. Zhao lowered his staff; she turned and walked away. He took two steps toward her, the soft crunch of his bare feet on the sand the sole sound in the exercise yard. To the onlookers' surprise, Su Li whirled. In the same movement her own staff's upward sweep knocked Zhao's pole high into the air above him. Even the other masters gasped. Impossible. How could she know in which hand Zhao carried his cudgel? Her back had been toward him, her eyes closed.

When she opened them, smiled in triumph and turned to see if Po was watching, the here-and-now took flight. The blind-folded Master shouted "Ha!" and reached out to catch his cudgel as gravity pulled it back to earth. Like a cat he took one step to the right and in the same motion brought the staff behind her ankles. Her butt thudded to the sandy floor. Zhao whipped the cloth off and approached the crest-fallen Su Li. He helped her to her feet, where she returned a bow, red with humiliation.

"You see," he announced, "this student has come quite close to my meaning. Although it took a while."

He placed his hand on her shoulder with affection and whispered. "Take courage. Trust in yourself and the Tao."

Her head hung as she ran away from the assembly, aware the next hours promised to be the most difficult of her life.

Beneath the temple's portico, at the rectangular courtyard's southern border, Po stood next to his old mentor and friend, Wang, and spied his hawk, a black speck against a brilliant blue sky, riding the thermals far above sacred Emei Shan, where the monastery lay hidden on a substantial plateau, three-fourth of the way up its western shoulder, nearly encircled by towering spires. No one could explain how such a level space had formed this high up the mountain so many eons in the past, but a thousand years ago, monks had discovered it, despite its difficult access and the great precipice that plummeted from its perimeter, and declared it a sign of heaven's blessing for a site. Po Lin had presided over its residents for forty years, as Grand Master. The avatar he had summoned had served its purpose for now, he noted with satisfaction, as it soared beyond his vision's range. On such a day it might see the mountains of Tibet where he had visited as a young man.

"The young tree has good roots." Wang made an approving nod as Su Li disappeared.

"Your presence honors this poor disciple, my old master. You have been away too long. Your health remains vigorous for one so ancient," Po said.

"My hundred years are long past. If I live any longer, I may just turn into a bore like you." The bald-headed Wang supported himself on a walking stick. His eyes as always sparkled with dry humor. "Which I suppose is a great improvement over the rascal you once were."

Wang's hundred years was an ancient, oft-used metaphor for his own death. I hope, thought Po, it will not be soon, for as long as you live, I will never have to worry about taking myself too seriously.

"You were the one who created something worthwhile out this unworthy wretch."

Wang grimaced. "So little to work with."

"Zhao chose her right away. He perceived her potential. She shoots the bow and arrow as well as a Mongol. Do you realize, Wang, we have not had a bow master at the monastery for two hundred years?"

"Except you, Po. You are a bow master." He turned his head a fraction, tugged on the thin gray wisp at his chin. "It is not wise to make waves on a calm sea. Even a Grand Master cannot change nature's course."

"Your wisdom exceeds my feeble understanding, as always." Po noted his own tone sounded much too defensive. He thrust his hands inside his robe's wide sleeves.

The older man laughed at the false modesty. A bit taller than Po, he patted one of two great bronze lions that stood sentinel at the head of a granite staircase and peered up at the sky. "Nothing lasts forever."

"Except the Tao."

To their right, a master was training the youngest novices in the basic elements of *kung fu,* children of wealthy parents sent away with no place for them in the

15

household. Their shouts resounded after each practiced movement.

"Hmph! That's the trouble with wise men. They have all the answers to life's questions." Wang put a hand on Po's shoulder and stared into his eyes. "Perhaps not even the Tao lasts forever."

Po cast one last glance at the door where Su Li had vanished. She had come so far, so fast. At her age he had hurt so many people. No compassion. No yielding — until he met Wang. Lao-tze himself could have learned wisdom from the older man. Yet Po found himself resisting. Why?

"You have another orphan besides her. What was his name . . .? Han?"

"Their monastery names are *laohu nuer* and *long er*, tiger-daughter and dragon-son," Po said.

Wang's eyebrows arched. "Fit for gods' offspring." He snorted with disapproval at Po. "Where is he? A large, impulsive boy, I recall."

"Gone. To fight the invaders." Po paused. The notion he wanted to express eluded him. "Yang and yin." The words sounded feeble.

"Let her go, Po. I say no more."

Wang leaned on his bamboo walking stick and turned toward the garden. Po lingered. Above the mountain ridge, ranks of ragged clouds were flowing toward them, a vanguard of darker formations, an army massed for an invasion. *Clouds. Merely clouds. They would pass and disappear.* He turned and followed his old teacher.

In the wood lot behind the refectory she retched for the second time. Not even mind-control, the core of Po's teachings, prevented the hated ritual, when in the mornings her body insisted on reminding her of what she tried her best to ignore in the daily activities of monastic life. She wiped her mouth and with her shoe covered the detritus with dirt.

The whole monastery was familiar with the legend of how Grand Master Po had found a child seventeen years earlier, but none, she believed, knew she was not a male. At his insistence she had trained the same as the boys since he summoned her from her foster home when she was six, but though she dressed the same and had her scalp shaved, she lived apart in a tiny room near his own, an arrangement that protected her but generated no end of questions and ongoing resentment at her special relationship to the Master, until Po himself commanded there be no more comment on the matter.

But in the last year, something besides her body had changed. When Po increased his special lessons with her, teaching her more because she was smarter and cleverer, her fellow students cast even more hostile glances her way. Instructors attempted to humiliate her, trying to destroy her belief in herself.

She angrily flung the wood-splitting axe as hard as she could into a log. "Han, Han, Han," she sighed. "I miss you. You were the only one who would not betray me."

In her loneliness and misery, she revealed her secret to her best friend, tall, two years older, handsome, powerful in *wushu*, full of laughter — an orphan like her but so different from her own serious nature. An unfamiliar longing in her heart beckoned. Afterwards she brooded. Was coupling what the books call love? No master had ever given her instruction on sex — it was a forbidden topic in the monastery.

A barely recognized place inside her even now reveled in its mystery. Yet even if it had been love, was it not weakness on her part? For one day, one hour, one minute of all the days and times that might have been, fate — or bad luck — chose that particular one. Folly. How much longer could she keep pretending? And feigning what? That she was a male? Or that she was not with child?

"You must have known." she cried aloud wishing the impossible, that he could somehow hear her. "Why else would you leave? Because the sight of me sickened you? Or to escape your own guilt? Yet I would never blame you, Han. It was my fault."

But what to do and how she could not tell. Her mind could not find its way through the tunnels of confusion, ignorance, doubt. Nothing in her education explained what was happening to her or how the wheel of her universe had turned half-way, but then her whole life had been one mystery after another.

She was eight when she had first come into contact with the Tao's secrets. Po had taken her on one of his walks on the mountain. A sense of foreboding impelled her to hold his hand as they approached a clearing. A violent trembling overcame her and she threw her arms around the Master. In a display of affection he allowed himself only when they were alone, he picked her up and sat on a rock with her on his lap.

"This is where I found you and your mother, little tiger-daughter. The last thing she cared about was you. She paid the price so you could live."

And as he told her the story of that day, she clung to him and sobbed, trying to imagine the scene, frightened at the images of the fearsome animals and her dead mother. Yet, without fully realizing what was occurring, a great strength flowed into her from the Master, and a thread of gratitude wrapped itself around her *dantian*. In her mind she followed that filament to where it stretched back through him to her mother, to the two tigers, and to all things, so she need never fear, never deep within herself be afraid.

"But always remember this, child. The tigers were the parents of your spirit. You are their gift to the world."

Her mother had paid a price and now she would surely have to also. Did that mean she would never feel that same fearlessness again? Genuinely learn the message of the bird? Her life, once a stream of smooth flowing water, had turned muddy, as if someone had thrown a boulder into the middle. Meanwhile another conundrum, an unpleasant one, demanded her attention. Her hands lifted the undyed woolen tunic and gently

19

massaged her tender breasts. *Master Zhao's words are lost on me. I am a fool.*

CHAPTER 2

If I laugh at any mortal thing, 'tis that I may not weep –
Lord Byron
Burma, 1944

"The bastards are up there, Buzz. I can feel it."

But from the cockpit of the Dragon Lady, only a few scattered clouds streaked the blue sky. First Lieutenant James Ellison shifted his attention back to his landmark, now three hundred feet below, a tributary of the Irrawaddy River that started as a waterfall high up in Himalayan peaks and had cut the heart out of the Chindwin valley for eons. The silver-blue stream disappeared and reappeared again and again as it wound its way between sand bars and hills only to hide itself beneath the dense jungle canopy. The C-47's big Pratt and Whitney engines purred as they followed their elusive signpost.

"I still don't understand why you're always volunteering for these suicidal supply runs." 2nd Lt. Buzz Taylor shifted uncomfortably in a seat suitable for smaller men. "The goddam place is infested with Japs and look what they give you for a marker."

The co-pilot checked the map, now on his lap instead of the map table. Their usual radio man was in the stockade for starting a drunken brawl so Taylor had to assume double-duty as navigator.

"A white pagoda in the middle of the jungle? I'll never figure out these heathen religions."

21

"China. There're a lot of those in China," Ellison said, his mind elsewhere, marveling at the strength of water, its endurance, its patience, its indifference to things human, immune to time. "There're Zeroes up there. Mark my words."

"China? Wait a minute, I see it. The drop site shouldn't be much farther —"

From somewhere below them a bullet tore through the cockpit's floor on out the roof. More shells pinged off the wings and fuselage.

"Good God!" Taylor gaped with astonishment at the hole two inches from his foot. "Jap patrol. Can't see 'em, though."

Ellison pushed the throttle, increasing the airspeed, bullets trailing them like angry, buzzing hornets. "That's the trouble," he grumbled out loud. "If you fly too low, you risk a hundred bullet holes and it just takes one to knock out an engine. But too high and a Zero can spot your shadow and make minced-meat out of you."

"Yep. The jungle's a graveyard all right." Taylor nodded wisely at the bromide. "But nobody escapes a Zero. Better hug the jungle than get blasted out of the sky."

"At least it doesn't torture or rape or kidnap." *I should know. Should have done more, much more that day.* He glanced upward again, the narcotic of danger unable to banish the usual ghosts of frustration. Still nothing but blue above.

"China? Aren't your parents missionaries in China?" Taylor asked. "I was in Bible college studying to be a missionary before I enlisted."

"*Were* missionaries. Keep an eye out, for chrissake. We should be there by now."

He looked over his shoulder to check the fuselage where two crewmen—the kickers—were scrambling to stack crates and sacks as close to the cargo door as possible. The C-47 was simply a DC-3 passenger plane converted for wartime use, the Army's workhorse hauler. Its door had been removed to allow easier drops of supplies which lay inside the plane's belly, a skeletal rib cage of bare aluminum supports and plywood flooring, like huge undigested bits of food.

"Looks as if the Nightclub Act is about ready," Ellison said.

"You mean the 'Brothers Singh,' right? You know, my friend, that's just godawful." Taylor strangled a laugh.

"They look like brothers to you? All Sikhs have the same last name, knuckle-head." Ellison thumbed over his shoulder. "They hate the Japanese. Even more than they despise the Brits." He chuckled. "Kindred spirits. All Scots detest the limeys. It's pounded into you from the time you can talk."

The turbaned Sikhs, Corporal G. Singh and Corporal B. Singh hailed from His Majesty's Army in India, Sixth Rajputs. Govinder, a dark chocolate-brown fireplug of a man, tossed hundred pound sacks of grain like pillows against the opposite wall, babbling non-stop to his gray-bearded companion, sometimes in Hindi, sometimes in English, while the taciturn, light-brown-skinned Brian lifted wooden ammunition crates into place like a patient work elephant. They had crammed the boxes with their small parachutes in front of the door frame, the first to go. The rest—mule feed and salt, medical supplies, rice and beans, double bagged in burlap—the men would shove and kick out on the second pass when speed and the need for escape were critical.

"I don't like the looks of that weather front pushing down from the north," Taylor said. "Coming fast. We might have to abort if visibility becomes a problem. We don't want to crash into a mountain on the way back."

"Quit being a chicken-shit." Ellison sighed. "I know all about that," he mumbled to himself.

The Dragon Lady yawed, banked right and headed south following the defile of a narrow, green valley. The cleared drop-site appeared below off the right wing tip. The space measured no more than a hundred and fifty yards long and twenty yards wide.

"Bollocks," he said, hitting the rudder pedal. "That's not much bigger than my back garden."

"Back garden?" Taylor made a face. "What're you talking about?"

"Back yard. How they say it in Scotland, ye ken. My mother was from Edinburgh." *And now held by the Japs, somewhere in China.*

"You have a back yard?"

Ellison raised his eyebrows over a wide grin. "Once upon a time. In a little village." He laughed softly. *Hers. It was hers. And I will find her.*

"Good grief. How about let's get serious here?" Taylor rolled his eyes.

The C-47 finished its wide arc and levelled out above tree-top level, its target the site of an abandoned village, now less than a dozen decaying huts sprouted amidst rotted tree stumps and a swath of mostly low-growth vegetation.

"Okay, you guys. Start the show!" Taylor yelled back to the kickers.

Ten seconds before they hit the clearing, G. Singh, lying on his back, propelled the crates out the door with both feet while his strapping coworker replaced them with new ones. The plane's balance shifted as hundreds of pounds of materiel—rifles, ammunition, mortars, explosives, grenades—disgorged itself under parachutes of green, red, yellow, blue and white, color-coded to match the contents.

"There's the OSS unit, our guys." Ellison's heart sank.

On the ground, dozens of half-starved figures with rags for uniforms—a few even were naked, suffering from dysentery—bolted from the jungle. One group took positions at the far end of the drop zone, firing their carbines at the Japanese patrol hidden deep in the brush. The others sprinted for the crates as they drifted to the jungle floor like great lazy feathers. The ragtag guerilla outfits—official and unofficial—who infiltrated deep behind the lines to harass Japanese forces, lived in the jungles for months on end and depended on supply drops like his for food, medicine, and ammunition. A frantic few waved and pointed to the sky while the C-47 made the same banking turn as before. What was that about? Ellison wondered.

"God, they look like escapees from an asylum," Taylor said.

"I spent a week with an outfit like that six months ago. A band of Kachin scouts rescued me after a crash. How'd we do?"

"Looks maybe two or three got caught in the trees. One broke open. Guess the chute got screwed up. Ammo scattered everywhere." He held up his hand, intent on the radio head set. "I'm trying to —." Bullets began to ping the cockpit walls. Taylor ducked reflexively. "Shit, we need to get out of here. The weather front's just about to dump on us. The clearance's too small to make a low pass anyway."

"Out of here? Without dropping the food? Bugger you! Those poor orphans haven't been anywhere near home for months. Hell, years." *Like me. I don't even have a home.* He pushed on the throttle.

"But Captain Dalby's orders. He doesn't want to lose any more planes."

"Fuck that pissant. Bloody tax man."

"I heard he was an accountant. Whatever. Isn't it enough you're already in his doghouse?" Taylor shook his head.

"See anything?" Ellison asked.

Taylor glanced down then up. "God help us. Three black birds up there." His voice quivered. "Vultures must've been circling, waiting for us."

"That's what those blokes on the ground were trying to warn me about. Too late to stop now. Fuck it all. Got to do it."

Ellison completed the wide loop, again lined up the Dragon Lady, lowered the elevators and decreased his airspeed, his target just above the curtain of trees. The guerillas on the jungle floor stood out starkly, their wild, flowing hair and bearded, sun-burned faces beneath floppy hats. The C-47's belly grazed the top of the canopy as oversize bean bags fell to the green earth below. Abruptly the fighters on the ground started to run toward the jungle. Bullets from behind the Dragon Lady ripped into the engine cowling. A tiny mist of fuel trailed behind it. Ellison's heart raced. A Zero. Right on his tail.

"Don't puke out on me now, you drunken broad," he roared while the last food bags cascaded in long, sweeping parabolic arcs. Now what? The Zero would have no problem mimicking him.

"James!" Taylor covered his head with his arms.

The pilot whipped his head around to see the end of the drop-zone tunnel sealed off with solid green forest. Too late to pull up.

A voice in his head told him, *You're going to die.*

CHAPTER 3

Reversal is the movement of the Tao — Lao-tze

"Don't spill anything," snapped the chief cook, above the clatter of dishes and the roar of fires. "I took special care to prepare these just as he likes them."

Massive arms glistening with sweat, the leathery-skinned Xi scowled at Su Li as he circled through the chaos of burlap sacks, storage crocks, poles, pulleys, and various stoves and ovens. The busy emperor who made no allowance for mistakes paused to stir bean sprouts in a sizzling tub-sized wok with a wooden spoon as big as a small spade, all the while issuing commands to his young assistants who washed and cleaned the dried food, chopped fresh vegetables stored in reed baskets or prepared them for pickling. A novice about ten years old, about to wilt in the room's heat, stood precarious guard over rice boiling in a large pot near his mate who was rolling flour on a wood table into a pillow-sized ball of dough to make noodles, snarling in turn at an even younger boy adding firewood to the stone ovens.

"This humble student apologizes," she said nervously and bowed.

Many monks looked down on the irascible, sharp-tongued perfectionist and his crew as a less worthy calling, though some said Xi knew the Master before he became a monk. Bothered by such condescension, she had asked Po about it. Enlightenment, he told her, could be found in cooking as easily as meditation or martial arts. Serving the Grand Master's meals had been her honor for the past two years. She steadied herself and placed the porcelain dishes on the wicker tray. A soup with bean curd, sautéed vegetables with nuts, rice and a steamed bun sent a heady aroma that aggravated the hollow sensation in her stomach. She covered the food and hurried to Po's chamber.

Outside the door, she called, "Master! It is I," held her breath and entered.

Dressed in his blue robe, Po knelt at a narrow teakwood table, head bent in concentration over a scroll of shining mulberry-bark paper, in his hand an ornate, carved ivory brush of fox-hair bristles, a plum-colored ink stone and two ink sticks on the table's front left corner. Renowned for his poetry, he often composed before he ate the evening meal. Once he had explained to her a poem should appear as graceful as it sounded. Po had a keen appreciation of all things beautiful, natural or man-made, a skill he had nurtured in her, consistent with his reputation as a maverick. Once considered the greatest martial arts practitioner in all China and in his prime, the older monks said, a powerfully built and imposing man, Po went his own path without challenge; and it filled her with pride and gratitude that his eccentricities allowed her to accompany him; indeed, they were why she was alive at all.

"Please place the food on the other table, tiger-daughter," he said without looking up, his deft, elegant strokes transforming the white background into figures of beauty.

On that very table, under his guidance, she practiced over and over drawing the character *yong*, eternity, because it contained all eight basic strokes of calligraphy. She uncovered the tray and laid out the dishes, but when she set the chopsticks in their brass holder, she knocked it over.

He looked her over with a curious expression. "You have paid your respects to Master Wang?"

How many times had she studied in the simple room so familiar to her? And yet had she really looked at it, absorbed what it told her about this sometimes distant, sometimes warm, always demanding mentor she regarded as a father? The knot in her abdomen warned her this evening might be her last opportunity. Besides the tables, the only furniture was a thin straw-filled mattress on a low wood bed frame tucked in one corner next to a carved chest for his ceremonial robes. He allowed himself two indulgences — one, a window which overlooked the garden where he spent much of his time; the other, a painting by Muqi Fachang, an artist of the Chan period, very old and revered, its brilliant ink depicting a tiny hermit on a mountainside beneath the stars. On the wall opposite, a mighty bow almost as tall as the man himself was slung over a peg with a leather quiver of arrows, a legacy of his career as an officer in the Imperial guards.

"Tiger-daughter?"

"Oh. I have, Master. He is kind."

"Ummm." He made a few more strokes, then set the brushes aside. "Ahh." He said with a satisfied smile, reviewing his work.

Po used occasions when they were alone to listen to her questions and to instruct her in his esoteric blend of Taoism and Buddhism. She would leave his room or the garden, her heart soaring, ready to burst into song. But eternity? She turned the concept over in her mind. This evening the idea was as reassuring as an endless winter.

He traded the teak's polished grain for the pine's simplicity and a stone jug of water. "You wielded the staff with skill today. Master Zhao was impressed. Your other studies progress satisfactorily, I presume?"

"Well, Master, thank you." He had been watching after all. She hid her delight with a bow. "But I have a question." She paused.

"Ask."

"Life is precious, is it not?"

"Of course, tiger-daughter. We in the Shaolin and Taoist traditions treasure life. We avoid violence and taking life. This you comprehend — we have spoken of it many times. Yet life is not to be clung to at any cost." He took a bite. "How one lives makes all the difference."

"And death?"

His piercing eyes glanced at her with a thin quizzical smile on an oval face. A short gray beard hung from his chin. No one could say for sure how old he was but rumors spoke of offspring from his years in the emperor's court. Po seldom spoke of that past to her except to depict soldiers as ruthless animals.

"Death? It is precious also. Life and death arise mutually. Like yin and yang, you cannot have one without the other, though there are many who try to live as if it were not true." He sipped some water. "Any more questions?" Outside a peacock's call echoed, lamenting the end of another day.

"Master, something is happening to my body."

He lowered his chopsticks, turned once again to face her.

"You recall for the past two years I have had my bleeding times," she went on, "the times that remind me I am a . . . . " Her lip curled up in disgust. "For four months though I have had no blood."

"Are you telling me you are ill, tiger-daughter?"

"I wish I were ill, Master." She bowed, unable to meet his eyes. "I fear I am with child."

His face betrayed no emotion. He rose and placed both hands on her shoulders. "How can this be?"

She did not reply.

"I see." He walked to the window and gazed out at the twilight, motionless. Su Li grew anxious. The peacock voiced his lonely cry once more.

"I do not know what to do, Master."

He turned around and without looking at her resumed his seat at his calligraphy table, took up the brush, dipped it in the ink stone, and began to draw the strokes in strong graceful sweeps. "Leave me. You must go to the west face tonight and meditate. Come to me tomorrow." She took a step to clear the unfinished meal. "Someone else will attend to it."

His voice lashed like a cold north wind. She cowered, put the knife-edge of her palm to her chest in a farewell salute, bowed and backed from the room.

CHAPTER 4

Bring me my chariot of fire – William Blake

An impenetrable wall of tropical forest rose up to smite the Dragon Lady, but the warning voice had triggered a hitherto unknown calm center in Ellison's mind. It fixed his attention dead ahead, reducing the indecipherable puzzle of life versus death to two enormous trees that leaned in opposite directions like sides of a gigantic sling shot.

Time slowed to a crawl, the V expanded to twice its size in his visual perception, and a wordless command in his brain told him to turn the yoke, all the while dimly aware that Taylor had covered his face with his hands and was whimpering, "Dear God. Dear God. Dear God." The ailerons responded. The plane wobbled, lurched, and rolled ninety degrees onto its side, a fat lady from the circus trying her best to ape an acrobat. Its left wing sliced through the bamboo below. Enormous leaves whipped against the cockpit window. The lower propeller buzz-sawed through twigs and branches. She shuddered in protest, threatened to stall out, but the Dragon Lady squeezed through the slingshot. Ellison instantly righted her, pushed the throttles and gunned for altitude, vines trailing from the wings. Seconds later a fireball erupted twenty yards behind them as the Zero, intent on his kill, crashed head-on into the mahoganies. Both wings sheared off when the plane's fuselage rocketed through.

"You got him, you son of a gun! Holy cow! Holy cow!" Taylor jumped up and hit his head on the ceiling. "I didn't think this broad could wiggle her ass like that."

Ellison's heart pumped with excitement. They were going to make it. Possibly he wouldn't have to piss in his pants or use that offensive relief tube. Now if he could —. From nowhere bullets ripped through the cockpit's roof. One tore by an inch from his head. Another drove Taylor into his seat.

"I'm hit! Oh, God!" he yelled. " Shit!"

"Bad?"

White with fear, Taylor held his hand up, covered with blood from a wound on his thigh.

"Give me your scarf!"

Ellison grabbed the co-pilot's muffler, tied it in a tight knot over the hole in his friend's pants while Taylor kept an unsteady hand on the yoke. *Doesn't look that bad. You won't die from that bullet, Buzz. Just don't faint. I didn't bring any smelling salts.* He finished the tourniquet and resumed control. The port engine began to smoke. The Dragon Lady decided to foxtrot like a drunken whore. What next? He forgot to wear his dancing shoes. Hydraulic pressure was low. A leak? C-47's were always leaking something. The controls did not want to respond. That might be a wee bit of a problem. No rubber bands or hair pins in sight. Beads of sweat dripped onto his sleeve.

"We got company," Taylor croaked. "Again!"

Two Zeroes closed on the Dragon Lady, one on either side. The one on the right cruised just thirty yards away, close enough for Ellison and Taylor to make out the pilot's face. The enemy flier grinned, ran a finger across his neck.

Taylor pressed his own middle finger against the cockpit glass. "We're not gonna' make it, are we?" His voice cracked.

"Time to say your prayers, Buzz," Ellison said. A wan smile covered the churning inside. "Better yet, get your buddy Moses on the radio. Maybe he can part the Red Sea again." Billowing gray cumulus clouds floating over the valley gave him an idea. "I'm going to buy us time."

Ellison pulled back on the wheel to lift the elevators and the weaponless Dragon Lady clambered upward at full throttle. The engines chugged like some overweight matron running to catch a bus, but the maneuver left the startled Zero pilots behind and below, still on a level course. The sky transitioned into a fleecy, gray world that blotted out sun, sky and fighters. Inside the gigantic cloud-room Ellison could only rely on the artificial horizon and compass. What does a bird do, when it can't see a flipping thing, he wondered, and has two hawks on its tail? Thirty-five caliber bullets rained an answer from above. The port engine caught fire.

"Cut the fuel supply!" he yelled. Don't panic, James boy, he told himself.

Taylor threw the switch. The flames snuffed out. Taylor re-started the engine. From within the cloud, a Zero dove right past the plane's nose, firing blind. For a tenth of a second, the two aircraft were nose to belly. Ellison pulled up just as the enemy disappeared. *Blind man's bluff. Both of us.* The Dragon Lady creaked and groaned and clawed her way up five hundred feet and banked left, toward what he remembered as the bulk of the cloud near the valley's ridge line. After twenty seconds he realized his miscalculation when his plane and a Zero emerged side by side in a macabre formation. The Japanese pilot looked as surprised as Ellison.

"I screwed up!" he roared.

"Yeah, but now there's just one," Taylor said, his face a pale mask. He adjusted the scarf around the wound. "I think the bleeding's stopped."

In the next instant they were hidden again, inside the bowels of another massive raincloud. Ellison turned out of his seat, reached for his Browning M1911A1 .45 handgun in its holster on a hook behind him.

"Can you take over? Just keep her steady and straight on for a while?" he asked.

"I think so. Why?"

"Goin' in back. For a smoke."

Taylor looked askance. "But . . . but you don't smoke."

In the fuselage the stoic kickers squatted along one wall. G. Singh hunkered low, expressionless, eyes fixed on the hole where the door used to be. Ellison lurched his way past them as the plane rocked in the turbulence.

"Do we pray to Shiva or Vishnu now, Corporal?" he shouted over the deafening engine noise and wind that roared by at hurricane speed. Since his father's death, Ellison swore by the deity of whatever country he happened to be in. Any old god willing to lend a hand right now would be most welcome.

B. Singh's face was a stony mask. "All the gods, Leftenant. All of them."

Ellison leaned into the door opening, checked his magazine, planted his feet wide, unsure of what he might discover when the visible world returned. A nimbus of light grew in the ambient atmosphere as the cloud fragmented. Through wisps of fog he caught glimpses of the Zero. The black vulture had fallen ten yards behind, leveled off even with the cargo door. In a few seconds both planes would leak out of the cloud. His own heartbeat more turbulent than the air, Ellison propped his automatic against the airframe's reassuring aluminum to steady his shaking hands and aimed in the Zero's direction. Calm down, man, he ordered himself, held his breath, relaxed his arm muscles and waited. For once he was glad he had spent those hours practicing at the garbage dump, against sticks of bamboo and the occasional pack of jackals. The aircraft's wings swayed like a see-saw, threatening to pitch him out the door.

"Steady, Buzz. Steady," he muttered.

The planes abruptly materialized in full sunlight, the enemy no more than twenty yards away a little lower than his vantage point. For two long seconds the blinded Japanese pilot made no moves. Meanwhile the Dragon Lady lost her fear and held firm. Ellison squeezed off two rounds. The first shattered the cockpit windshield. The Zero's wing tip rose to turn just as the second bullet tore into the pilot's helmet. The man slumped forward while the fighter, nose pointed to the jungle, accelerated into a delirious spiral of death.

Ellison staggered for a second at the door, his two hands clutching the gun, the air outside spinning in all directions. The C-47 shook from side to side, lifted, then without warning pitched and plunged sharper than a hobby horse on a carousel. Almost as soon, it caught an updraft. He lost his balance, unable to catch himself, the terror of falling to his death paralyzing him. Come to me, you poor adrift soul, the jungle seemed to say as he tottered at the opening when from nowhere huge hands seized him and set him safely down in the fuselage.

"Best watch your step, Leftenant." B. Singh's yellow teeth showed through a grim smile.

Ellison steadied himself. "Aye, Corporal. Wouldn't want to stumble, would we now?" He managed a weak laugh, mustered the energy to salute, before staggering to the cockpit on rubber legs.

"I'll be a monkey's uncle," said Taylor, shaking his head. "I bet there's never been a Zero or anything else brought down by a .45. Son of a bitch! You got two of 'em, James."

"Vishnu smiled on us again." Ellison slumped into his seat once more. "But we're not out of it yet. There were three of them." He looked up, expecting to see another Zero ready to pounce. "Hey, something doesn't make sense. It's hightailing like a scared sparrow." Out of the sun two P-47's barreled into his line of vision. Ellison pumped his fist. "Go, you limey bastards!" The Allied fighters peeled off in hot pursuit of the enemy, disappearing into an anvil cloud.

"God bless us!" Taylor leaned over to watch the show. "They came!" The two P-47's dipped their wings in salute, broke into a long acrobatic circle, and finished with a barrel roll, before disappearing over the southern horizon. "I called it in on the radio. Wasn't sure they'd make it in time."

"Arrogant Brits," groused Ellison. "Thank you, Shiva." He laughed and winked at Taylor.

"You mean God, James. God was with us." Taylor nodded with self-righteous assurance. "Thought we were going to lose both engines. Praise the Lord."

"No, not God" Ellison said. "Good old American engineering. My RAF uncle — my mother's brother — once told me these buckets of bolts were the most reliable airplanes ever built. Nothing else would have a chance. Not with all these holes."

Taylor agreed. "Reliable is good."

"Right," Ellison said softly. "Like keeping your promises." *Well, at least I'm trying.*

As the adrenaline wore off, the shock of almost dying submerged itself in the struggle to pilot the damaged plane. They just might be able to limp back to Hell's Gate, the Ledo Pass, Dinjan. He glanced over his watch at the fuel gauge. Check. The Dragon Lady climbed higher until distant ridges came into view, where massive cumulonimbus formations heralded the weather system's front edge dumping cauldrons of rain mixed with lightning and hail. Right around him, the downpour had tapered off allowing golden sunlight to burst through mounds of fleecy clouds separated from the band of moisture.

"I think it was God," Taylor persisted.

"Horseshit," Ellison mumbled below the roar of the engines. His co-pilot believed existence was a battle of evil against good, black and white, the war against Japan merely another skirmish in the endless contest between God's forces and the devil's. Yet he was quite adept at fixing things — equipment, jeeps, radios, whatever needed repairs — and eager to explain how they worked, including life, which rankled Ellison no end. But all in all, a reliable bloke, like the Douglas C-47. Reliable. The word struck a deep chord. Besides, most men craved something to cling to, especially in a war.

"Praise the Lord? You mean, as luck would have it, Providence was on our side." Ellison laughed unable to resist the barb. "And my lucky charm." He patted the sleeve of his flight jacket and twisted so Taylor could see the special insignia of the Flying Tigers stitched across the back. "A gift from Uncle Roger." He turned to his co-pilot. "But Providence sure wasn't on those dead soldiers' side, was it?"

Taylor paused before he replied. "It was their time, James. And not ours. God knows why."

Hah. Reverend Abraham Ellison would have spouted some bullshit like that. Still, he should have been there with his father, not in a field with Lian. He imagined that whenever he completed a wild assignment the old man in his mythical heaven forgave him. But his mother? How could he have been so pathetically weak?

He had crumpled to the ground, dazed by a rifle butt to the back of his head. By the time he opened his eyes, the column of soldiers and prisoners had formed up, ready to depart, when a noise came from the house of the *Fung Shieh-hua*, the wealthiest landowner in the little village northwest of Shanghai. His mother, a nurse and teacher whom his missionary father had wooed and wed at a Presbyterian divinity college in Edinburgh, used the building as an infirmary and school. The Japanese lieutenant gestured and sent his sergeant to investigate. He emerged with an angry Mary Ellison in tow, her blue frock half-ripped off. She fought like a fury, raining blows on the man's head until he pinioned her, slammed her to the earth and kicked her as if she were a dog. James struggled to his knees, spitting blood, desperate to help her, but a foot in the back smashed him flat on the earth.

"Hey what was that stuff about China? You want to go and visit your parents? I bet your Dad would be proud."

"Murdered by the Japs. Six years ago."

Taylor winced. "Shit, I'm sorry, Ellison. Me and my big mouth." Taylor contemplated his gaffe for a moment. "What happened to your mother?"

Ellison grinned. "I thought Baptists weren't supposed to curse."

"Go ahead. Cast your atheistic scorn on my religion. You're a bad influence on me, you damned Scot. Bad!" Taylor had a smile on his face. "God will forgive you, though." He looked back at the kickers who were having a smoke. "Some pilots are already flying routes to Kunming, you know. If you hadn't pissed off Dalby . . . . Buzzing the control tower? What the heck were you thinking?"

"God will forgive me. That's nice to know. I could use some forgiveness."

"You know what?" said the co-pilot. "I wish I was still playing linebacker. Tackling running backs is a lot safer than getting shot in the leg. God, this thing hurts. Hope I don't pass out. Hey, you should get a medal for what you did today."

The co-pilot's words blended into the noise of the engines. Forgiveness — what there was of it — lay far to the north on the other side of the Himalayas. Today, maybe, he had proved something. He tightened his grip on the yoke and for the next hour the memories and doubts vanished as he struggled to fly his battered chariot of fire.

CHAPTER 5

Going to hell as fast as an arrow – Zen saying

There was a place the monks called the Great Leap.

A small door near the main gate opened onto a rock-strewn plateau scattered with stunted junipers and tufts of hardy wildflowers. This last extent of the monastery's natural formation ended in a cliff that wound its way around the western face of the mountain. Beneath the sun's last rays reflecting off the cloud patterns, always lingering around the peaks of Emei Shan, she picked her way across the bleak landscape.

Ever since she could remember, she had dreamed the same dream: the Master took her for a walk in the garden where they sat on a bench. He put his arm around her, told her he was her real father. As she got older, his approval anchored the inner peace that guided her daily life. She sought to imitate him, be like him. How bitterly, utterly ridiculous that seemed to her as the sky's orange and purple faded into a shroud of twilight.

The trail appeared where the plateau pinched to a close, a rough track of jumbled rocks and small boulders that grew ever narrower. A steep face of granite soared to her right and a sheer drop-off plunged sharply to her left, but she hurried onward with reckless haste, heedless of the danger, afraid darkness would fall before she reached her end point with the ominous-sounding name.

The pathway ended at a chasm. A smooth granite façade on her right, ascending upward to the crest, formed a gentle horizontal arc that curved around to the gorge's other side where the path resumed, a natural chute, like the inside of a tilted, hollowed out half-cylinder. Erosion and ice had expanded a crack in the stone and sent a hillside's worth of rock to the depths below. In miraculous fashion, ancient engineers had found a way to stretch chains across the gulf and anchor them. Boards as wide as a man had been fastened to the underpinning chains; a thinner one acted as a handrail. With the last rays of light winking out of the sky, Su Li hesitated, took a deep breath, suddenly and alarmingly aware Po's command would involve much more than an evening of meditation. The iron links creaked and swayed as she took her first cautious steps. Nauseous, ever dizzier at the sight of an unfathomable drop, she stopped in mid-span, paralyzed.

As the wind picked up, the bridge twisted like a wild horse. Her knees buckled. Her throat filled with bile. She spat out the bitter, foul taste and clutched the thin handrail until it hurt. Her legs refused to budge, while her mind raced, trying to find the motivation to go forward. Each novice who desired to pass the training came here before his final initiation. This was her first test alone, no Master to watch, no one to give encouragement.

A message from the deepest well of her being, deeper even than the life within her womb, spoke to her. "You are not a weakling," said the calm, female voice. "You have the strength of yin. A true sage has the power to walk on air."

"I can cross over this simple bridge," she told the phantom voice.

The gale responded with a howl. Undaunted, she let go of the handrail, tilting and swinging on the narrow board platform like a sure-footed sailor amidships in a storm-tossed sea, up one wave, down another. For a time, cool air streamed across her brow and her bare soles skimmed over the boards; she became one with the wind's whistle, a bird making its way by the Pole Star's faint light.

This is easier than I expected. As soon as the words formed she stumbled.

CHAPTER 6

A fool that persists in his folly will become wise – William Blake

Dinjan Air Base, India

"We've got a hero here, Captain. Damn few of 'em in this armpit of the world."

Ellison sat upright from a cocoon of woolgathering, picking at his food, and responding mechanically to the wisecracks of his messmates. He was having a hard time emptying his mind of the enemy pilot—the first man he had ever killed. His fellow mates in the officers' mess hall by now stood at attention. Startled, he fumbled to his feet. Somebody important was talking, talking about him.

Colonel Jack LaFarge, base commander, and Captain Russell Dalby, the diminutive CO of the 10TH Air Combat Cargo Squadron, stood next to his table. Ellison saluted and blinked in the harsh light of the carbon arc lamps that hung from naked steel beams of the concrete block building.

"Unheard of. Two Zeroes. I mean, Christ." The paunchy senior officer shouted his words over the clatter of the evening meal. A dozen tables erupted in applause in the cavernous hall. La Farge, who carried his weight on a six-foot-four inch frame, signaled for quiet, a wide grin on his fleshy face, his heavy hand a vise on Ellison's shoulder.

"At ease, men," the Colonel ordered. "This man deserves some leave, Captain. Before we crank the China operation up a notch," he continued. "I need men like him. The Army Air Force needs men like him." Ellison came on full alert, gripped the edge of the metal table at the mention of China.

"Leave?" Dalby whined. "But he's always breaking the rules — ."

La Farge glared, waved his hand to shut him up. Besides his rank, the Colonel's physical bulk made it easy to dominate his subordinates, Dalby in particular. "Does that suit you, Lieutenant?"

"Just fine, sir. The Colonel mentioned China. I — ."

"We want to keep you here, Lieutenant," Dalby said with a grimace, showing his perfect teeth.

Ellison suppressed an impulse to punch him. By some miracle, blind luck and the Army's moronic efficiency landed him in a job perfectly suited to his talents — keeping rein on a herd of young men who cared less about his notions of discipline. Like Ellison and the rest of them, Dalby had no flying experience before the war. Up your nose with a rubber hose, you little shit, Ellison thought. You have no idea what's at stake here. The Colonel's words changed everything.

"Captain, I want somebody from *Stars and Stripes* to interview him. Pronto. Hell, even Vinegar Joe Stilwell's gonna want to know about it. Maybe give this man a medal. Yeah, a fucking medal." He nodded in agreement with his own conclusion. LaFarge was a mid-fifties plodding bureaucrat intent on riding out the war until retirement.

"Yes, sir," muttered Dalby.

"And make sure this soldier gets that leave." Intent on his set-piece, the superior officer wagged a finger at his subordinate, not oblivious to the Captain's animosity but not giving a shit, then turned back to Ellison. "Well done, son—even if you are half British." He chuckled.

"Scots. But thank you, sir." Ellison arched his brows at Taylor with a what-the-hell-have-you-done look. Stilwell? A medal? He needed a medal like a hole in the head. LaFarge towed Dalby away to another set of tables.

Taylor leaned over to him. "Listen, my friend, if you want to get to China, you've got to stop taking these crazy risks. God can bail you out just so many times." He paused, grabbing his friend's arm. "Thanks, though. You saved my life. And the lives of those guys on the ground."

Startled, Ellison glared at him. "I don't even know what happened to her." But Taylor, already turned away, was laughing at a joke by another pilot. "And I'm not sure I have the guts to find out," he said softly, mainly to himself. "I'm no bloody hero."

Five minutes after the superior officers moved on, Ellison slinked from the mess hall, unable to stomach the attention any longer. Outside, the rain had paused and a faint moon pierced the overcast. He walked though oil-slicked puddles, past rank after rank of jeeps and transport trucks, parked neatly in rows. China. She might be a thousand miles away but wherever she was, she was alive. The Dragon Lady could take him; and there the crazy broad was, with other C-47s lined up on concrete aprons, ready for tomorrow's missions. On the opposite side, perpendicular to the long central tarmac he passed dozens of warehouses filled with supplies for the allied forces, then the concrete batch plant, its conveyor belts and steel towers ghost-like as fog settled low to the ground.

As frustrating as being stuck in India was, his very presence in the exotic subcontinent struck him as little short of miraculous. It had taken a year for the missionary organization that sponsored his father to extract him from Shanghai after his father's death. He arrived in San Francisco by steamer, then caught a train to Davenport, Iowa to live with his paternal grandparents. They arranged for him to attend the state university at Ames. He hated college and the provincial mid-western United States. Cornfields ad infinitum only aggravated his restlessness. Throughout, he maintained correspondence with his mother's brother, Roger Stuart, an attache´ to Lord Louis Mountbatten, the Supreme Allied Commander in Southeast Asia. When America declared war against Japan, Stuart urged him to enlist in the Air Force and promised to pull strings to get him stationed in Assam, the base closest to China. Stuart, forthright in his pessimism, knew his nephew would never be satisfied until he found out what happened to Mary Ellison. That was more than a year ago.

But tonight, a first glimmer of real hope, hope he had come close to losing as the months went by. The Army's bureaucracy, pettiness like Dalby's, each day's tedium — except when he was flying over the jungles — were grinding down the edge of his fervor, but a major push into China would give him a chance to at least enter the country again, sharpen his commitment. After that, the plan was murky, but something would pop up. It had to.

Saving lives? Well, Buzz, I wasn't so good at that six years ago. Sure, I was only seventeen. They had guns. What could I have done? He had asked himself that question a thousand times. He reached the perimeter fence where outside the dense undergrowth of trees and bushes threatened, impenetrable, dangerous, as far as he was able to go and as far as his thoughts could take him. Raindrops started to fall. He shuffled on, trying to stay out of the mud, when he noticed a dim light ahead. It glowed in the low-hanging mist like a magical orb floating in the ether, but he soon realized it was a naked bulb held by a conduit arching above the door to a godown. To his surprise Brian Singh was leaning against the wall, smoking a cigarette. He met Singh upon his arrival in Assam and they had become friendly. The light-skinned northerner was likely a far-flung descendant of Alexander the Great's army, Ellison figured, his more immediate sire, a long-dead British soldier from the Raj.

"Thank you for saving my rear end out there, Corporal."

"Calcutta." Singh's unsettling eyes reflected all the mysteries in his strange country.

"What?"

"You read books. No good. Find a woman. Here." Singh handed him a folded paper. Dumbfounded, Ellison glanced at it, stuffed it into his shirt pocket. By then Singh had disappeared around a corner.

Mystified, he continued to meander around the vast air base, bull-dozed out of an old tea plantation, once a staging area for fighters and bombers in the early years of the war but now mainly a logistics depot for Burma and China. By the time he returned to his room in the *basha*, the long single story bamboo dormitory that housed the pilots of the Army Air Transport Command, the northeast India monsoon had resumed its steady drumbeat on the thatched roof. Taylor, in the bunk on the opposite wall, stirred, grunted, rolled over. The big drops thudded like bullets, like those from the Zero, like the first bullets he ever heard. Those people, those friends, gone. He lit a kerosene lamp on a tiny rattan table beneath a leaky window, ran his finger over a framed, wrinkled photograph of a smiling young mother and father who dandled their infant son, thankful to have the picture, to remind him how they looked. It would be so easy to let go, give it up. But how could he live with himself, knowing she might still be alive, knowing he might have done more?

The caustic smell of smoke threatened to choke him. He coughed and roused himself. At one end of the square, a bucket brigade doused fires on houses the Japanese had torched as they left. The remaining women sobbed or wailed in grief. Men stood paralyzed or walked aimlessly, traumatized. One older woman sat on a flat stone, rocking a crying grandchild in her arms, the rest of her kin killed or taken.

"Where's my mother?" he cried. "Mother!"

No one paid attention, too traumatized by their own anguish. A dazed survivor wandered by, a man James recognized from Sunday services. "God has punished me. God has punished me," he repeated, weeping.

James grabbed his shoulder. "Where's my mother, dammit?"

The traumatized man's face flickered from grief to disbelief. His eyes wandered away. "The soldiers tied her. Hands and feet. Threw her over the horse's back. A sack of grain." He was on the verge of sanity. "God has punished me."

"Make sense, man. What are you talking about?"

He pointed at two bodies, a woman and a little girl.

James rubbed his eyes. "I'm so sorry. Which way did they go?"

He tore along the road to where it meandered through fields of rapeseed, the hoof prints and bicycle tire tracks still fresh, but the raiders had disappeared over the horizon. Out of breath, he stumbled and stared for a long time at the empty skyline.

He replaced the photograph, checked under his bed where he stashed his father's old fiddle and case in a piece of parachute silk next to his trunk, inspected his mattress for snakes and spiders, and thumbed through a dog-eared coy of the *Bhagavad Gita* for a few minutes before he turned off the lantern. He lay in his bunk with his clothes on, his mind suspended in the zone between sleep and wakefulness. Out in the darkness a blast echoed above the rain now falling in soft, slow drips. He sat upright. For a few seconds the report silenced the raucous chorus of creatures engaged in their nocturnal symphony. Somebody at the latrine found a python in the shitter. Or one of those Green Kraits, the Ten Step Snake. Anybody with any sense always took his sidearm and flashlight to the jakes. The jungle surrounded the base, patient, ever ready to take back what belonged to it. It would endure long after the war was over. One thing at least to be grateful for. He loved living this close to it. Many nights he sensed large animals on the prowl a dozen yards away, seen rhino footprints in the mud, heard a wild elephant's trumpet, a tiger's roar.

He took out the scrap of paper Singh had given him. What did it mean, Calcutta? He lay back, his hands clasped behind his head on the pillow, his doubts revolving and echoing in his brain, staring at the ceiling as if it held an answer, but the rain lulled him to sleep before one arose.

CHAPTER 7

Heaven's net is wide, yet nothing is lost – Chinese proverb

She was not plummeting to her death. That was the first coherent thought that burst through the miasma of fear. Somehow she had latched onto one support chain where two of the wooden treads had gone missing; still, her legs dangled over the yawning void, a fiend from hell who threatened to seize her and drag her to its depths. She snapped her head up.

"Aieee!" she screamed, her body twisting worse than a rag on a clothes line.

Terror whipped her mind with visions of falling, falling, falling forever. The wind rocked the bridge, its sole aim to rip her hands free. It succeeded with one.

Her sole lifeline, one aching arm, was ready to pull from its socket when the mysterious hawk appeared and hovered above her, its gold plumage a torch in the darkness. Its wavering screech, though it sounded like it might have come from under water, pierced her inner tumult, allowing its message to once more echo in her brain.

"Yes, I hear you," she sputtered, tears squirting from her eyes, "but I can't this time."

She choked on a sob. The raptor called louder, more insistent, a challenge to her self-pity, and once again her spirit was able to find the bright flame of courage the Master had revealed to her so many years ago. She gritted her teeth and stared straight into the abyss.

"I reject such an unworthy death." She hurled the words at the shapeless wraith of fear, waiting expectantly, hungrily below.

The chain was a snake determined to break free of her grasp, but with a previously unknown strength, the arm that held her life flexed upwards until the opposite hand reached the chain. With a desperate, fierce thrust, one knee swung up onto the boards and with their last ounce of strength, her arms dragged her lower body all the way up until she lay prone, her fingers clutching the wooden steps until they ached. Her mind, whipped raw by fear, gradually nursed its way back to relief. I am alive, she thought, vowing to never again take that simple, self-evident truth for granted. At last, she marshalled the courage to crawl inch by unsteady inch the rest of the way across the gorge, collapsing at the far end.

After a time she mustered the strength to confront the gloom of the mountaintop. Faint merciless starlight barely penetrated the haze in the air, but slowly her eyes became accustomed to the dark. She groped her way along the track with cautious, hesitant steps until it ended at a carved out chamber of rock worn smooth by centuries of wind and rain, head-high and open to the elements, the place of meditation. Its exposed side fronted on the same chasm she had just crossed as it circled its way around the mountain. She pondered whether the cubicle, which sheltered her from the wind, was man-made or a strange natural formation. Whatever its origins, lines of ominous energy pulsed within, vibrating through the soles of her feet. Han had told her about unworthy students who sat in this very spot at the edge of Emei Shan, weak souls who did not return from their combat with the site's power. They leaped to their deaths because their hearts were not pure.

The memory made her shiver. Drained, she slumped to the stone floor, its solidity a bond to a sense of self about to evanesce. She sat, knees crossed in the lotus position, eyes closed. By degrees she became aware of her breath, but something was wrong. Like the throb of a great war drum, a sound began to reverberate from within the mountain's core and to echo off the encircling barrier. Or was it her own blood, her pulse pounding in her ears? Whatever its source, her entire body resonated to the hammer blows. Demons of doubt filled the rests between the beats and called to her over and over: *come, come, come.*

The stone enclosure became alive and hostile. The drumbeats forced her to her feet and propelled her to the edge. She resisted at first but her legs moved as if she had lost control of them. An overwhelming urge to leap outward seized her soul. Yes, she berated herself, this is how it had to be. What she deserved, for being impure. She should have guessed this vile thing inside would disqualify her. It is why the spirits were pushing her to jump. The Master sent her here to discover if she was worth saving. She had failed.

Clouds blocked the feeble starlight. Numbness in her feet was spreading to her other extremities. Resolved, she stepped forward to confront the pit of hopelessness, ready to spring outwards, but when she opened her eyes

Han's image hovered before her, a ghostly figure within the heavy mist, its arms extended, palms up. It spoke.

"But you are not like those others, Su Li. That will never happen to you. You're the purest, most beautiful person ever to live on Emei Shan."

She reached out and groaned. "Han? Is that you?" Tears fell. "How wrong you are!"

The image pointed downward. Her eyes followed, her feet aware of a vibration that emanated not from the walls but from the rock floor, a force directly beneath pulling her body backwards. When she looked again, Han's likeness had vanished, but the new energy lingered and caressed her like a sighing breeze. With a moan, she surrendered to its lullaby and sank back on the cold reassuring stones. The pangs of guilt melted away with a gentle wind that stroked her forehead. The haze cleared. The stars shone brighter. Engulfed with relief, she clasped her knees tight to her chest, grateful for the certainty she would not kill herself, not this night.

CHAPTER 8

To see a world in a grain of sand, and the universe in a wildflower – William Blake

Six years earlier.

Black and white feathers flashed against the blue sky on a quiet summer day, the magpies' raucous caws protesting the unwelcome crackling sounds that disturbed their feeding. Far below in a millet field, the seventeen-year old James unwound a girl in his arm, hoisted himself on his elbows above the stalks and looked around, irritated. Someone setting off firecrackers? Why? On a Sunday? He shrugged. Her dark eyes beckoned.

"You are beautiful. And I love you. Even if my father believes I'm headed for hell." He ran his fingertip from her chin to her navel. "I don't believe in hell, anyway," he laughed and continued in English even though she didn't understand. "If God is as good as my father says he is, he wouldn't send people to hell." She put a finger to her uncomprehending lips and pulled his fair-skinned body against hers. "My mother doesn't care we're here," he said, reverting to Chinese. "'Love is love. That's a' there is to it,' she would say." He smiled at the idea: his mother — wise and tolerant and lovely, unlike his father.

Only their second time together like this, the girl let herself smile, still fearful, he knew, even though they had known each other since he was seven. To hell with Dad, he thought, and laughed inwardly at the irony.

More explosions, louder this time, followed by screams and shouts. "The savages are coming! The Japanese!"

Alarmed, he rolled to his side and sat upright. A half dozen frantic farmers were fleeing madly across the bridge. Gunshots, not firecrackers. Further down the dirt track, a platoon of soldiers were on the march led by an officer on horseback with the flag of the Rising Sun in his saddle boot. James clamped a hand over the girl's mouth and buried her deep inside the millet. Muffled footsteps and the clip-clop of horse hooves passed not fifty paces away. The officer snarled an order. James peeked above the stalks to see the last of the patrol quick-marching into the village, a non-commissioned officer bringing up the rear on a bicycle. A prescient, icy fear clutched his chest, that he might never see her this way again, so honest, so innocent. He pulled her close, soft breasts against his skin, before releasing her.

"Put on your clothes."

She shook off the chaff clinging to her back and threw on her tunic and trousers. "But what does it mean?" Her eyes asked for reassurance.

"God alone knows," he mumbled. "My father said they wouldn't come this far south." From inside the village a shriek of pure terror arced above a crescendo of barking dogs. No, he seethed. No! No! No! He threw on his own clothes.

"Stay close," he ordered and tore across the mantle of knee-high stalks in the direction of the soldiers. She followed as well as she could, struggling to braid her hair.

When he no longer heard her footsteps he stopped to turn around. "Stay close, I told you!" She winced at his angry words. "I'm going to protect you," he said though he shook inside. "This has got to be a mistake."

They sprinted along the dirt footpath, past irrigation wheels and brick kilns, wispy smoke rising from holes in their domes. On straw mats, layers of the harvest's grain dried golden in the sun. Before they reached the old stone bridge, shots rang out. They stopped, breathing hard. Now he was truly frightened. He snatched her hand as they raced barefoot across wood planks, smoothed by travelers for 500 years. In a narrow muddy alley, they pressed against the wall of a brick house, shaken by more shots from the marauders. A huge black hog bolted past them, its chain still attached to its mud-caked iron anchor post. The girl clamped her hands over her mouth to suppress a scream. I have to protect her, he reminded himself. He wanted to cry and be brave at the same time and momentarily jammed his knuckles into his eye sockets, unwilling to see what he knew was around the corner.

As he and Lian hid and watched, people were weeping, pleading, fleeing and shouting, helpless and bewildered, while Japanese soldiers conducted their business with ruthless efficiency. Two hauled an hysterical mother and her teen-age daughter by their hair, like animals to the slaughterhouse, toward a long rope attached to the saddle of an officer's horse. Other soldiers were kicking in doors of tile-roofed houses to drag out any more women they could find. The captives' hands were bound to the main line. Across from the granary, a soldier was raping a mother while his comrade waited his turn. Her panicky children were bawling on the steps while their father angrily tried to pull the rapist off his wife. The second soldier shot him. Alongside the wall of the blacksmith's shop, the Red Spears, guardsmen of the village, slumped in a heap. Some of them had been his father's converts. Their red-tasseled hoes and pruning hooks, pathetic weapons of defense, lay broken alongside the bodies. Beneath a window a bayoneted dog sprawled with its entrails attracting flies.

CHAPTER 9

This arises. That becomes – Buddha

She found Po alone in the garden behind the monks' sleeping quarters, seated on a granite bench with a carved dragon's head at one end, a lion's at the other, the enigmatic bird perched on his shoulder, contemplating the small stream that meandered through the center. The garden had always been her favorite place, not only for its innate loveliness but because here Po instructed her on Chinese culture.

At the rear of the monastery grounds, it nestled up against the mountainside which to the visitor's eye appeared to be an extension of the garden itself. Under the Master's supervision, the area had been renovated, sectioned off from the vegetable plots and enclosed years before – a waist-high wall of rough-hewn stones marked its more or less elliptical perimeter – and was a manifestation of his peculiar, even unique commitment among Taoist masters to the necessity of beauty in all activities. Some said his creation had been inspired by his time at the Emperor's court.

"Quiet your heart and let your eyes behold, tiger-daughter," he said.

She concentrated hard, terrified the scene before her might from now on exist only in her memory. On the side opposite the Master, rocks chosen for shape and texture had been placed to create the illusion of a miniature mountain range, a small scale version of the mount upon whose shoulder the garden rested. The gurgling creek,

63

lined with iridescent moss-covered rocks, tumbled over man-made waterfalls into a pond before continuing to the fields. Sculpted pines, plum trees and stands of bamboo mimicked the forests on the eastern slopes of Emei Shan where Po had found Su Li. Shrubs and plots of medicinal herbs and plants arranged in accordance with *feng shui* principles formed geometrical patterns that aligned with the Five Elements so that the effect was a balance of artificial and natural. The arched wooden bridge that spanned the water, the ancient stone lanterns along the path to the Buddha's shrine, but above all the flowers, especially the rhododendrons, chrysanthemums and white-petalled roses, called to her. *Remember me,* they said. *I love this garden,* she replied.

"I have taught you all I can. Therefore you must leave. Tonight."

"No!" she cried, realizing there would be no talk of father and daughter — ever. Her whole body shivered, dreams of the future evaporating like morning dew. "Master, forgive me for speaking. I am sorry for my mistake." Her face drew up in anguish. "I realize I cannot remain in this condition. But I will dispose of this thing inside me. No one will know and I will work harder and progress as before. I want nothing else but to be a Shaolin monk. To stay here. With you."

He looked at her in angry disbelief. "No! You will not take this life. Do you forget what you have learned? How you yourself were rescued? You will accept your fate. Your destiny."

A wave of panic swept over her. "But," she stammered, "this is my home." Tears welled at the edges of her eyes. "You are . . . I hoped . . . ."

He waved his hand. "Who did this to you? I ask you once more."

She remained defiant, silent. The stream gurgled. The hawk shifted its feet. *I love this garden.* The thought persisted. Yet the garden's essential yin — like her own female principle — continued to elude her. It did not strive to make or do, yet nothing was left undone while she on the other hand tried and tried to surmount the monastery's all-pervasive male energy.

"I see. In any case, I intend to find the culprit." His head shook in dismay.

"Where will I go?" she sighed.

"Wherever the Tao leads. I cannot see your way."

"What will I take with me?"

"Everything you have learned here." He gestured at the landscape. "Pay attention, tiger-daughter. When the light fails, go to the temple. It will reveal what you must do."

She bowed. "My shame must not be made public."

"You *have* brought shame to me!" His brows narrowed in anger. "And to yourself." His face hardened. "You must eat bitterness from here on."

She winced, the finality of his words a physical blow, a cut deeper than any weapon. "I understand," she said.

"No!" he thundered. "You do *not* understand. Even I do not comprehend." The startled look on her face brought him up short. He heaved a sigh. "Will you remember my instructions?"

"Yes, Master." Tears came now. *I love this garden.* The certitude was her only refuge in a storm-tossed, mind-engulfing ocean of sorrow.

"And those I just mentioned."

She nodded.

"Now go."

She paused and glanced around one last time. *I love this garden.* Here the Tao became real. She could touch it, smell it, see it, the perpetual rhythm of death and life, decay and renewal, order and chaos, pulsing, vibrating, spinning onward without beginning, without end, not generated by some mythical gods or god but of itself so, *tzu-jan.* Everything she had done up until that moment, her entire essence as a person, was summed up in an undeveloped, muddled, and discordant love that made the garden a revelation and a reproach. Without that love, without at least the memory of it, her lungs could not draw air, her heart could not beat. She saluted with an open palm to her chest, choked on a sob and turned to leave, but before she reached the bridge, she sensed his presence. He spun her around, placed his hand on her wet cheek.

"Be like this water. As Lao-tze said, nothing in the world is softer than it or weaker, but the strong cannot overpower it. It endures."

Then she was gone.

The stream flowed in front of Po as if an answer to an undiscovered question might arise from its depths. Water symbolized the essence of Tao. It always sought the path of least resistance. Downstream, the past, gone, seen and understood, clear to him, but upstream, the future, was unknowable. He was powerless to see her way. Nor his own. The Tao's message those years ago on the mountain, did he mistake it? Was there some way other than banishment? One thing was certain, he realized with astonishment, the pregnancy was an indisputable sign that confirmed Wang's warning. *She needs to depart, for her own sake*, the rivulet whispered to him. Despite his conviction that in some manner this wrongful act might in the end come right, Po found in his heart an unexpected, powerful spasm of sadness, more acute because he was unwilling to express it. She had passed the first test, the test of life, far from easy. Now the second, the test of power. Was she ready? Do not fail, tiger-daughter, he prayed, closed his eyes and exhaled slowly. *I am an old man, too old.*

Later that night, rain fell as Su Li climbed the steps to the temple, the largest structure in the monastery, on a man-made hill in the now-deserted grounds. As the Master instructed, she said good-bye to no one. She carried only the iron chains of sadness. Sluggish feet moved toward the door, reluctant to pass through a portal that allowed no return. Beyond lay a little-known land, a future impossible to guess. She had accompanied Po to towns and villages near the mountain but had minimal contact with their inhabitants. The women with their distended stomachs about to breach repelled her, bawling, needy children their disagreeable result. Brutish men lorded over tiny empires of wives, concubines, slaves. Their lives struck her as ignorant, ugly, at times pathetic; death, disease, starvation fell on them as quickly as a summer rain or winter snow. They lived and died without ever knowing why. She herself was destined for that kind of life, it now appeared. Though she had learned how to read and write, though Po had instructed her in Chinese history and geography, none of that would teach her how to find food, travel safely, or handle the evil men called money.

Alone, anxious, she pulled open one huge door to the temple and slid inside. Dozens of candles blazed in racks set along the walls; incense burned in iron braziers, sculpted into animal shapes. The inner architecture with its columns and great ridge beam gave the illusion that the space floated above the earth and reminded the worshipper no mortal object, not even a temple, was permanent. As if she needed a reminder this night, she thought bitterly.

At the very back of the nave, beneath an overhead arch of wood filigree lattice, stood three statues on a high altar — Lao-tze on the left side, Amida Buddha to the right, and in the middle the Original Being — the Pure Ones. The life-size figures had always frightened her as a child, not hostile but cool and distant. Unlovable, that was the word that came to mind. Tonight they appeared just as unsympathetic, the peace they represented a world apart from her inner turmoil. They focused their sightless eyes on a strange marker composed of different colored and shaped tiles set within the otherwise green-tiled floor. It drew her with irresistible force, as if the holy images themselves were exerting power over her. When she reached the mystic geometry, its energy prompted her to look to her left. A corridor led to a cunningly-wrought iron portcullis. As she approached, the grid of iron bars rose by itself, opening to a small, circular room with walls of smooth stone.

As soon as she passed into the narrow chamber the portcullis descended. She whirled, tried to pull it back up but it refused to budge. She looked around for an exit. The blocks of the walls had been cut so precisely their joints were imperceptible. There had to be one, she thought. Calm yourself. Look more carefully. There, on the opposite side, ornate carvings traced a tiny, almost indiscernible outline. To reach it she had to squeeze past a saucer-shaped stone table holding an iron brazier filled with glowing charcoal. Left over from the day's ceremony, she surmised. This was the testing room. The Master had told her every monk must undergo the ordeal of the marks.

After wiggling by the stand that all but filled the narrow space, she discovered the door had no handle. Frantic fingers swept the wall for a hidden lift or lever, a block that needed to be pushed. Panic crept higher. Was it merely an illusion? Was she trapped? Was it some cruel test she was powerless to comprehend? There had to be a way, she was sure, to open it. She glanced around the cubicle, drawn to the ominous red eye of the coals. On one side of the squat fiery container was the figure of a dragon embossed on the metal, on the other a tiger. Glowing white-hot, they writhed as if alive. She understood the truth now of what she always regarded as student rumors — to grasp the bucket by the forearms was how Shaolin priests acquired the symbols of their calling.

But no, these cannot be for me. I am unworthy. Yet the Master's instructions led to this point. *He thinks I could be worthy. He arranged it. Help me! Someone! Tell me what to do.* Part of her wanted to cry out but instead she wiped a few tears. The moisture harkened her back to the Master's teachings about the strength of water, yin, a woman's, hers. The entirety of her training lay before her. Now it was her turn. He believed in her. She would not dishonor him — or herself.

She summoned her courage, stood before the bucket of coals and pulled up her sleeves. Smoke filled her nostrils, heightening her awareness like a drug. Her central nervous system vibrated in rhythm with the glowing mystic creatures. Knees bent, she held out her forearms, took a breath, and pressed skin to metal.

The cells in her body exploded with agony. The breath rushed from her lungs. Every drop of moisture flushed out of her pores. Her eyes begged to weep but there was no fluid left. Her mouth screamed but had no air to exhale, locked in an O of torment. Release, let go, fail, die, every nerve pleaded, but the iron brazier bound her forearms as if it were an extension of her body. In the next instant, a bolt of energy rooted in the floor electrified her feet, then pumped strength from the rock back up the channels of her *chi*. The fire within turned to ice even as her scorched forearms lifted the brazier off the table. The hidden door swung open. Wind and rain poured in. On the verge of collapse she held on for another second in animal-like defiance. Her throat uttered a snarl, a triumphant roar as she released the brazier, before lurching outside into a storm.

"Unhhhhhhhh."

Wha . . .? What was that? A creature? A dream? Fire. Yes, without flame. Something burned. "Unhhhhhh." *That noise again. Whatever you are, go away.* The pain tried to smother her but she forced her eyes to open.

Another groan. The sound came from her own throat. From head to ankles, her traumatized body flowed by degrees into full consciousness. Face down, she pushed up to her hands and knees then slumped back into a pool of rainwater. On the second attempt she levered herself to a sitting position and attempted to wrap her arms around her knees. With a gasp she dropped them and gingerly raised her sleeves. On her forearms the brazier's images glowed like dying embers. She was not dreaming. She eased herself to her feet and held her arms wide to let the cool morning air flow around them.

She was Shaolin. Forever. She managed a forlorn smile. Nobody but the Master would know. Someday, maybe, she might redeem herself and thank him for the honor. Someday. With a sigh she pieced together how she succeeded in exiting the testing room. She must have

71

staggered out, fallen and lay all night in the rain. Dawn's pink light creeping above the peak, she walked over and placed her palms flat against the stone. Utterly smooth. No door.

At last she gathered herself and sat on a low boulder. Next to it lay a tooled leather case, a pouch, a sack. The long sheath held arrows and a bow, old and exquisite, much like the Master's. Her heart wanted to break at the memories of those lessons with Po as her hands ran over it end to end. Enough. A gift, not something to weep over, foolish girl, she admonished herself. Inside the rough burlap, someone had put food—dried fruit, cooked rice, beans, a tiny clay pot. Xi, the cook? She untied the pouch and drew out an ivory and onyx medallion, the yin/yang disc, encircled by a silver ring. With reverence she draped the symbol of power around her neck, certain she would never remove it.

She nearly missed one last item, a man's cap. Ah, she must continue the charade. A lone woman on the road invited rape or murder, but the other route—a woman disguised as a man—meant a cruel death if discovered. That prospect did not trouble her; she had acted the part of a male long enough for it to be second nature.

As the light grew brighter, a deep, rich wave of sound from the temple's massive bell swept over her, then on and on out to the farthest edge of the mountain's peaks. This morning she and Huang were to have swung the massive rough-hewn timber and thumped the three meter tall inverted cup of bronze that hung from the pavilion's rafters and columns, to call the residents to a new day. They would file to the temple for morning prayers and the Master would instruct them. The bell sounded once more. She had never heard its music outside the walls and imagined its pure vibrations might reach out to infinity, for its music was the same as the universe's, an eternal harmonic reverberation. Her body's cells pulsated in sympathy, and for as long as the bell's voice rang out it reminded her she too was part of that majestic chorus.

When the echo died, her own dissonance-filled private universe clamored for attention. Time to leave. Yet everything had happened so fast. Two mornings ago she had sparred with Master Zhao! An outcast and a Shaolin. It defied comprehension. Misery coursed through her veins again.

To the north she could see the footbridge and the Great Leap, the fearsome precipice where she had almost killed herself. Suddenly, right below her, just as the sun peeked above the mountain top, a golden circle formed on the white cloud layer. It shimmered and scintillated in rainbow-colored bars in all directions, the *Fo-guang*, Buddha's glory, a vision of eternity. Her hand shielded her eyes from the brilliance.

On this morning the sign of Emei Shan's holiness brought her no solace; the omen was not meant for her. The Master was right to cast her out. Marks on arms did not make one worthy. She must eat bitterness then see if she could follow the Tao. With the bow case slung over slumped shoulders, she tied the food sack at her rope belt. Deadened with sorrow, she shuffled toward a secret place at the lip of the cliff, paused, put the cap on firmly, and, with a thin chain as a handrail, backed down the steps cut into the rock and never looked up.

CHAPTER 10

Where shift in strange democracy, the million masks of God — Chesterton

"Damn it, Ellison. I dunno why I let you guys pull me around by the nose. Even if I do got a kinda big schnozzola," complained 2nd Lieutenant Frank Mazzetti as he, Ellison and Taylor rounded a corner onto one of the strangest streets on the planet. "Holy shit!" Mazzetti, who joined the squadron three months earlier fresh from the Jersey shore, had jumped at the chance to come along. He had been dealing blackjack at a casino before he was drafted

"Welcome to Calcutta!" Ellison whooped with manic delight.

It had taken a month before he could snag a transport shuttle for his leave. In Calcutta he hoped to find life in its rawest forms, far from rules, orders, promises even. He needed to not remember for a while, but just in case, he had brought along the paper Singh had given him.

The men elbowed their way through an open-air bazaar. Like most streets in India, it served less as a thoroughfare than as a gathering place, a crammed concourse where a thousand life-threads wove a dense, chaotic, half-raveled tapestry. Up and down the road dingy one and two-story shops with stalls spilled out on both sides. In between, myriad small-statured, brown-skinned women and men, some in European-style suits and carrying umbrellas, others, naked to the waist,

75

pushed and shoved against each other, conducted business, constructed ramshackle homes, struck up conversation — engaged in all possible human activities, including relieving themselves, except sex. Even sex was not far off — a dozen steps away, behind tacky signs above doors where pimps beckoned.

Humans were not the only mammals with business in the humid, pungent air. A small eddy in the river of humanity swirled around the tail end of a sacred cow defecating five feet away. As soon as she finished and moved on, the void filled with people. In front of the shops, heaps of garbage disappeared beneath a flock of vicious buzzards. Nature abhors a vacuum, Ellison concluded.

"Jesus H. Christ. Are we on Mars?" asked the short and slim Italian.

"Gomorrah." Taylor snickered. He walked with a slight limp from his wound.

"Criminently, if you just wanted a lay, I coulda' found you a couple of those limey officers' wives back at the hotel.".

"What's the matter? You don't want to mingle with the natives? Hell, your skin's almost as brown as theirs." Ellison felt unfettered, fortified by the dark beer in the bottles they carried.

"Hey, you son of a bitchin' Brit. That's a fuckin' insult."

Ellison swigged his beer. "Nay, Frank. Brown is beautiful. The color of the earth. You're beautiful, you ugly shit. And I'm not a limey. I'm Scots." He patted

Mazzetti's cheek, the liquor a buzz on his brain. "Even Taylor, here, with all his moralistic manure, is lovely. Like this stuff." Laughing, he pointed at a cow pie Mazzetti had just stepped in.

"Aw, fuck!" Mazzetti tried to rub the mess off his shoe on the ancient cobbles.

"Where we headed?" asked Taylor.

"A tavern, I think, but who knows?" Ellison winked.

Singh's address was supposedly a hang-out for Japanese spies on the prowl for information from unwary soldiers who patronized it. What the hell, Ellison figured, he might by some miracle discover where the Japs held their prisoners. And if he met this mystery woman, well, whores were often a good source of info. At worst she could tell his fortune.

"God, this place stinks." Mazzetti whipped out a handkerchief to cover his nose. Men were urinating not ten feet away, in the open.

"Tut, tut, my good man. Let's not offend our hosts." Ellison laughed.

Along the sidewalk, vendors shouted their wares in a Babel of languages and dialects — rugs, sorry looking vegetables and fruits, pots and pans, European watches stolen from the British occupiers, chickens and monkeys in cages, anything that could catch a potential customer's eye. Charmers played on their little wooden pipes to tempt cobras from open baskets. Women with gaudy, painted faces brushed against the soldiers, their intentions obvious. Other women in tattered saris, containers on their heads filled with food, towed children in rags; they ignored the foreigners, the daily business of survival their sole focus. Above the din the tinkling of tiny bells never ceased, like a permanent case of tinnitus.

"Watch your wallet," Ellison said. "Keep it in your front pocket. See those blackguards?" He tilted his head at three thugs who had shadowed them.

"Cripes, those aren't your average Atlantic City pickpockets." Mazzetti scowled. "I'd feel better with my .45."

"Going to hell. The whole bunch. Pagans." Taylor gestured at a broken-down building where scantily clad women leaned from second story windows.

Ellison stopped and laughed, shaking his head in disbelief at his friend's utter certitude about divine intentions. "Going to hell? This *is* hell."

"I'll drink to that," said Mazzetti. "Though I seen worse on the boardwalk."

"Mud in your eye." Ellison lifted his hand to drink but found it empty, certain it once held a bottle. "Correction. Hell is a step up from this place."

"At least hell doesn't have these fucking cows," Mazzetti griped, as another brahma sauntered by, to reveal in its wake a fakir, naked on a bed of nails. The men stopped to join the crowd that had gathered. "What shit is this? Where're his clothes?"

"They say they want nothing from this world. Even you'll admit, my friend, there's something admirable about that." With a grin, Ellison started to unbutton his shirt.

"Jesus, you red-haired lunatic. Stop already." Mazzetti grabbed hold of him. "Take it easy."

Taylor knit his brow. "Man alive, this is way off limits."

Almost delirious, Ellison ignored his friends and jostled through the milling crowd when he spied a small cleared space where a loose mass of arms and legs was lumped together on the cobblestones. A white-bearded old man sat crumpled on the pavement next to a precarious box of broken pieces of wood, his dwelling. His legs, thin as branches, protruded at hideous angles. One withered arm hung from a thin shoulder tenuously connected to his sunken chest. A brass bowl lay between his fractured feet. Aha, Ellison thought, exactly what he was after. But he noticed right away the cripple had more room than anyone else; and his ravaged face — crooked teeth set amongst bloody gums — was smiling. An initial impulse to vomit metamorphosed into a sudden urge to bawl his heart out like a child.

"Step right up, ladies and gentlemen. Where else can you behold humanity at its finest? Flesh and bone." Ellison strutted like a carnival barker, patted the old man's bald head. "The very stuff of existence."

"For Chrissake' He's filthy," Mazzetti said. "Ugh!"

Ellison knelt to eye level. The man kept on smiling. His eyes. Did they conceal a wisdom deep inside or was this an idiot's grin? he asked himself.

"It's a punishment, James. From God. A punishment." Taylor's voice trailed off to a murmur. "That's got to be it — ."

Ellison cut him off with an angry scowl. "So how did you sin, old man, that God hated you so?"

"James." Taylor tugged on his sleeve. "This isn't like you."

"Were you a murderer in your former life? Or a pedophile? Speak man!" His mouth twisted in anger. "If you know something, say it, damn you!" He seized a bony arm.

"What're you doing? Leave him be." Taylor gripped Ellison's shoulder. "What the heck is wrong with you?"

Ellison blinked as if he had awakened from a nightmare. He patted Taylor's hand and turned back to the cripple. "I'm sorry, ancient one." So ashamed at himself he was unwilling to look directly into the beggar's eyes, he reached into his pants pocket, pulled out his coins, turned to his buddies. They handed over what they had and he put the money into the begging bowl. The man's eyes opened wider; his head nodded rapidly. He pointed a bony finger.

A sign above a two-story structure sided with boards whose paint had long ago peeled off and whose front was scarred with windows too dirty to let light in or out, read *The Golden Horde*. Ellison took the scrap of paper from his shirt pocket. His mouth opened in astonishment. "How . . . ?"

He sped away toward the dive, zig-zagging through eddies of pedestrians swirling past him. Mazzetti and Taylor scrambled to catch up. Before they reached the café doors, a mustachioed Hindu in a black cut-off shirt and tattooed arms threw them a menacing look before slithering away.

"Wasn't that one of those gorillas?" Mazzetti said.

"Dalby warned us there'd be Jap spies and sympathizers all over the place," Taylor pleaded. "James . . . ."

But Ellison was by then inside.

In the smoke-filled room, thieves, hired assassins, drug sellers, pimps — the whole spectrum of India's criminal underclass — sat at round wooden tables or stood at the bar, plying their trade in English, Urdu, or Hindi. Like a boiling mud pot, quarrels and brawls erupted then vanished under greasy chandeliers with yellow oil lamps. Two tall men in turbans — Sikhs, with huge biceps — patrolled the room to make sure the patrons adhered to at least minimal standards of behavior. Made-up whores, lips painted a fiery red, plied the floor, before disappearing up the stairs with customers. At one table, sergeants from the Indian army played cards. At another, British officers with weeks-old beards and wild unkempt hair were drinking tankards of brown ale and telling bawdy jokes to their companions, four small dark-skinned soldiers smoking pipes.

Ellison's fascination with the Ghurkas was interrupted by an itching on the back of his neck. Someone's eyes were on him. There, at the bottom of the stairs, he was sure it was Singh's mystery woman. Like a maharani, she paraded through the crowded tavern as if the occupants were her servants. She radiated light in the dusky room, from an inner sun that blazed as bright as the yellow sari on her brown skin. It blinded every man there. No one dared touch her.

"I'll get us another beer," he announced and headed for the bar for a better look, positive she was still watching him. He ordered a round from a swarthy bartender with a thick beard but when he turned he couldn't see her.

"Looking for someone, soldier?"

He spun to his left, brushed against her, catching his breath at the electric sensation. A red traditional veil, fastened behind her forehead, covered straight, jet black hair that flowed to her waist. Her dark eyes narrowed beneath long lashes, brows daubed with purple. Set above a rounded nose with tiny nostrils, they compelled obedience. She was the most exquisite creature he had ever beheld.

"What's wrong? You've never seen a woman?" Her musical voiced was a clipped, Hindi version of British English, the smile on her face mocking, seductive. His tongue thickened. Her perfume, a combination of jasmine and citrus, hit his brain like a drug.

Ellison pulled himself together, swallowed hard. "I was, ah, told by a friend, ah, you could maybe tell my future. Umm, and other things." He smiled, embarrassed. "I mean—."

"I know what you mean." She turned to leave. He took hold of her arm to stop her, unable to restrain himself. No one in the room existed except her. She looked at his hand with an how-dare-you expression.

"Wait, please," he pleaded, letting go. "What do you know about—?"

A smile of amusement crossed her face. "More than you . . . ."

Shouts from a card game distracted him and made him miss the rest of what she said. By the time he turned around she had reached the doorway, pausing to cast a seductive glance at him, a dare. Ellison tore after her.

"Hey, where the hell you goin'?" Mazzetti barred his way.

Ellison spied her over his friend's shoulder walking toward a ramshackle building guarded by two Punjabis across the street. "I have to go! Now!" He fetched his wallet, stuffed a few bills into his pants and handed it to the Italian.

"James," pleaded Taylor, "those OSS guys over there told me she's the queen of this whole circus. This hell you talked about. Don't do this."

"As bad as kissing a cobra, man," Mazzetti said.

"She's a fortune teller, lads," He wouldn't tell them the real reason he was interested. He wasn't sure himself.

"If she's a fortune teller, I'm Heddy Lamarr," scoffed Mazzetti.

Ellison tore himself away from his dismayed friends. "I'm gonna lose track of her, dammit!"

"At least take this." Mazzetti offered him a pack of condoms.

Ellison waved him off. "If I'm not out in an hour, come and get me." He plunged into the river of humanity in the street. "Half an hour."

CHAPTER 11

It is easier to get to heaven than to reach Szechuan –
Chinese poem

Throughout the day light rain pummeled the grassy slopes of the steep, dirt and gravel road that wound north from Chengdu out of the Szechuan basin. War, famine, and omnipresent gangs of raiders had slowed travel on this remote mountain switch-back to a trickle. She hiked in a daze, heedless of danger and oblivious to the impending storm despite the warnings her body issued in the form of unsettling stabs of pain. She ignored the constant nausea, the tenderness of her breasts, the swelling abdomen, single-mindedly intent on putting distance between her past and her future. That she was alone, vulnerable, had no significance, nor that any village or town lay within many *li.* It was a day that mirrored each one the past months, of deadened hope and raw open-sored mourning.

Evening's gloom threatened to dissolve into dark and expose her to the weather when she at last took thought for her well-being. Faint traces of a track led away from the road to dense undergrowth beneath a rocky outcropping, a vacated den. Drenched, too weak to move her limbs any further, she collapsed on the limestone cleft while the rain continued to press her. You will attend to what is about to happen, it demanded, for happen it will. There was no alternative but to submit, and, like a wounded animal weakened by exhaustion and the sharp ache in her womb, she leaned back against the stone and waited. And waited. The pangs came on with a sharpness and speed that surprised her. When they reached their peak, she arched her head to the darkness and let out a cry.

"Aieeeee."

The sound should have awakened the dead; but muted by the raindrops, it carried no more weight than a whimper, powerless to enliven the small lump of flesh on the gravel between her out-spread legs. Her pregnancy had come to an end with shocking, sudden brutality, a cruel mockery of her attempts to block the process from her mind or pretend it was not real. She fumbled for the afterbirth, pulled it out and slumped against the rock wall, unable to move or think for hours.

A slow drizzle prompted consciousness to once more worm its way through veins and organs and nerves. At least the rain would wash away the blood. So, when it ended, she would leave this pile of folly for the carrion eaters, as she herself would one day be consumed. For that was all that nature was, a never ending feast of eat or be eaten and her first true taste of it was foul and rancid. Now on to the war. Become a guerilla. Kill Japanese. Ignore the Master's commands about violence. Or find death in a manner not unlike the lifeless mass that was once a part of her. The night's absolute black compressed her despair to a white hot point. She opened her eyes. *Nothing. I am in darkness. The price to pay will not be this easy.*

In seconds she was asleep as the rain mingled with her tears in the mud.

CHAPTER 12

Bring me the arrows of desire – Blake

He burst into an empty hallway on the first floor, tore up a flimsy staircase and paused on the landing, then reached for a porcelain knob; it turned under its own power. The door opened to what he could only describe as a temple dedicated to sensuality.

Tapestries in bright gold and reds decorated the walls, embroidered with erotic scenes from Hindu mythology. Orange, green and yellow silk scarves hung from the ceiling, swaying from the lazy heat of scented candles. In quarter-size statues carved from sandalwood, others from stone, men and women and fantastical beings he didn't recognize were wrapped around each other in contorted sexual positions, writhing on ornate tables. Tiger skin rugs lay scattered on a spotless wood floor. In the smoky light, the shrine's high priestess presided before an altar to his right. Dark, luxurious hair cascaded to her waist over a scarlet cloak that ended above her bare feet. Palms together, she was praying before a black marble statue of a man-like figure and a woman entwined. Incense burned from braziers on either side.

"I have never allowed a foreigner in this room before."

A diaphanous veil covered her countenance. She stepped from the dais and gestured imperiously. Her scent set his brain whirling like a narcotic. Her aura pulsed against his senses. He resisted an impulse to worship her, bow down and kiss her feet as an incarnation of the goddess in the statue.

"Why are you here?"

The question rammed a cold spike of fear into his gut. "Sorry, I think I made a mistake." He turned to leave. To his amazement she now stood between him and the exit, hand against his chest.

"I can turn you over to the Japanese." She laughed. "Or worse." He made a move to go around her, push her aside, but his arms had no strength. Her palm propelled him deeper into the center of the room, one irresistible shove after another. "Show me your money." The voice changed, now cynical, matter of fact. "Let's get on with it."

He started to pull the bills from his pocket before realizing what she meant. "No! That's *not* what I'm after. I was hoping . . ." He clung to a life raft in a drowning pool of confusion.

"That's what all men want." Her eyes taunted him.

He sensed she was testing him. "Not me. I'm here to . . . ." He managed a small laugh that was little more than an exhaled breath and stepped back. "I dinna know why I'm here,"

Cynicism elided into a musical snicker. "You are afraid of me." She pushed him against a stool and onto a velvet cushion. "You should be terrified. You have no notion what you've stumbled into."

He hesitated, desperate to say something coherent. "Uh, can you teach me *Tantra*?" He blurted the words out and immediately thought: What the bloody hell am I doing? She had bewitched him.

She scrutinized him up and down as she lit a small brass incense burner. *"Tantra?"* The music in her voice transformed into suspicion. "Who told you there was even such a thing?"

"A book. I, ah, can't remember." How idiotic, he thought, but the sensation in his groin, a reservoir of desire, grew harder.

She noticed his crotch, laughed at his embarrassment and put her hands on her hips. "You Westerners already know everything."

"Almost. Not quite." At long last something that sounded like him.

She cocked her head, as if pleased by his answer. "Men are pathetic, predictable creatures." Her eyes narrowed. "How can someone scarcely a man learn *tantra? Tantra* is dangerous." A haughty smile crossed her lips before she lifted her veil as if it were an initiation into a sacred mystery.

He inhaled; his eyes widened. Her uncovered face radiated splendor brighter than an evening star. He didn't believe in gods and goddesses yet once again adoring her seemed the only appropriate response. The skeptical, cynical net he had cast over his world suddenly appeared as little better than a child's toy. The scarves and tapestries whirled by his vision in a spinning kaleidoscope of colors.

Satisfied with the effect, she dropped the veil once more. "There. I have given you enough. Now go, before you regret it." She turned away again.

"No, please." He drew in a breath, full of incense, exhaled, fought the dizziness. "I would ken more, if you were willing to teach me." He was captured but didn't care anymore. All he wanted was to follow the thread to its end.

She drew herself up to her full height and held in front of her the black figurine of the god and goddess. "Shakti and Shiva, creator and destroyer. Bringer of life, bringer of death."

His mouth hung open. The figures seemed to writhe in pleasure yet at the same time to be blissfully detached. "I know some things about death," he said, finally tearing his gaze from the hypnotic statue.

Her smile mocked him. "It is life you do not grasp." She gestured. Embarrassed but unable to resist her unspoken command, he dropped his trousers.

"As I said. Predictable." She laughed. "You are thinking, how can enlightenment come from someone you believe to be a common whore? If you have the courage to obey me, you will see."

She gripped his shoulders and straddled his thighs, the cloak draped over his lap. "Adepts call *tantra* 'Becoming the Tiger.' I am the tiger, the inexplicable truth you seek. Do you understand?" He nodded though it sounded like something between a witch's spell and a philosophy textbook. "Breathe deeply. Do not move."

His hands had a fiery urge to caress her, take her. He could hear his heart pound when without warning she sat on his lap and swallowed him. An electric current shot from his toes to his teeth then back again. A burning fuse nearing a stick of dynamite, he wanted to shout, to thrust, to explode but she uttered an incantation in a strange language that relaxed him. He took a slow breath; a wave of surrender swept up his spine as bare legs wrapped around his waist and ankles crossed behind his back.

Her eyelids narrowed into a trance, her lips a small oval. His groin was a reservoir of molten magma, an energy stream flowing up and out his skull. He floated above their coupling in the starry ether with hawk-like vision, bound in a spell he did not want to resist, to stay this way forever, wrapped in a divine embrace, safe inside a goddess. No war, no quests, no promises. Beyond good, beyond evil. Shiva.

Mazzetti checked his watch, glad it was still on his wrist. A guy could lose a dick in this hell-hole if he wasn't careful. Which was almost certainly what that whore was doing to the damned Scotch fool, he figured. It had been more than thirty minutes and the Hindus were glowering at him and Taylor as if they didn't belong there.

"Hey, Buzz, let's blow this place. He's had plenty of time." They rose to leave. "Not that I wouldn't mind getting a piece of that myself. Such a broad. But, you know, a switch blade. What's inside can cut your balls off. Give you a little present to take to the doctor."

Outside, they discovered they had lost their bearings. Too much to drink, the crowd, the light—they couldn't remember which door Ellison had entered. Meanwhile a street urchin was pulling on Taylor's sleeve—dark, curly hair, rags for clothes, big brown eyes. "American," he kept saying. Taylor pushed him away. The boy persisted. "Your friend. You must come."

Mazzetti took out a rupee. "What the fuck did you say?"

Someone was trying to kill him. Ellison at first believed he was having a nightmare until his crumbling awareness dissolved into an explosion on his skull and a bombardment of blows on the rest of his body. He threw his hands up to protect his face and clutched at consciousness, afraid if he blacked out he would die. Two small men with billy clubs were beating on him, cursing in Hindi. A third—the one with the moustache who followed him in the street—was tying his ankles with a cord. Anger at his own foolhardiness and a savage instinct to survive swept away the last cobwebs in his head.

Damn the bitch, he cursed, jerked his knees up to his waist, freed his lower body, rolled to the left and whacked his knee hard against the big man's nose. The thug yelped and fell. Surprised, the other two paused long enough for him to spin free, whip off the thongs and confront them. It was not the same room, he vaguely realized, bare, smaller, and with a single window that let in a sliver of afternoon sunlight. Backing into a corner he grabbed a

91

rickety chair and brandished it as a weapon, the adrenaline now pumping full bore to block out the throb in his skull.

Two of his angry attackers wore red bandanas around their foreheads and had tattoos on their arms. The other, biggest one, thin-faced but built as powerful as a rugby player, pulled out a long knife and laughed at the soldier. "Japs pay well for you, foreign. Not dead. Cut is okay. Ha, ha!" He nodded at Ellison's bloody head.

He held the chair like a shield. If they came at once he had no chance, but he hoped they were as ignorant as they looked. The smaller two hung back even as the hulk lunged for him with a knife. He swung the chair with all his strength, smashed the thug's hand and knocked the blade across the room. The man howled while his mates charged and slammed Ellison to the floor. He punched, shoved and kicked like a demon, stronger and much bigger than they, but by then the rugger straddled his chest, hands around his neck, and crashed his head on Ellison's forehead. The shock wave reverberated in his cranium but he fought as fierce as a snake-bit mongoose to keep from blacking out. The other two backed off, shouting with hatred and encouragement. With the rugger's head ready to crush him again, Ellison rammed a finger into an eyeball. The henchman roared, spinning up and away and covered his eye. The others jumped back into the one vocation they were good at, thumping their billy clubs on his chest. He was losing the energy to fight back when, with a splintering crash, the door exploded inward. Taylor and Mazzetti staggered in.

"Up yours, you motherfuckers," Mazzetti whooped, his whiny voice never sounding so sweet. The Italian weighed in with a stave of wood and smacked the two smaller goons on their heads while Taylor went after the big man now bent over in agony. Someone gave a whistle outside and the three assailants scrambled through the door, one leading the half-blinded giant. Mazzetti flailed at him one last time.

"For God's sake, man. You okay?" Taylor grabbed his friend around the waist to keep him from collapsing. Ellison tried to mumble a response but the adrenaline had drained out. His legs were rubber as he slumped onto the chair.

"Course he's not okay." Mazzetti was all of a sudden the mother hen. "He's nearly buck naked and beat to shit. Wipe that blood off and let's get the hell outta here."

The bumpy ride back to Dum Dum airfield was torture to Ellison's bruised ribs, banging on and off against the jerricans that shared his space in the back of the jeep. On the foothills of the mountains, fields of green bushes — tea plantations of northern India — stretched to the horizon, all owned by the British occupiers. From time to time the men passed a mahout and his work elephant dragging logs by a heavy chain for a construction project, and always on the road, the beggars, the beggars and the naked, white-painted lepers, the lowest of the low, shouting "Bakshees."

"I owe you lads. Thanks."

"Welcome," said Taylor. "But you should thank the little kid who told us where you were."

"Kid?"

"Street brat," said Mazzetti. "Outside the bar. Said you were in danger. Japanese agents. Couldn't tell what he was saying at first."

"How?" He struggled to put the pieces together but the potholes in the road and the jeep's minimal suspension knocking on his battered rib cage made it hard to think.

"The cripple told him where to find you. The kid called him the rajah of the street. I asked him how he knew. He said the ancient one knows whatever happens on this street. Good investment, that donation." Mazzetti chuckled. "Anyway, he said a beautiful maharani had talked to the old panhandler. Then the geezer sent the brat."

"Maharani?"

"Kid was talking so fast. I dunno. Shook? Shack? Something like that. Buzz?"

"Shakti, sounded to me," shouted Taylor over the engine's growl. "Yeah, that's what her name's supposed to be."

"Hey, Scotch boy," Mazzetti said, "bet she stole your money."

Shakti. He had no clue as to the identity of the exotic woman he had almost worshipped. He shut his eyes and tried to ignore the jeep's side-splitting rumble; he wanted to bask in her memory. A countenance as comely as a goddess would not steal; it was beneath her, surely. He opened his eyes and reached into his pocket for the money. Shit. Wrong as usual. So, just a sophisticated set-up. He felt something else, a scrap of paper. He drew it out and unfolded the tiny diamond shape. Through the dried blood inside his nose he recognized the scent. *The tiger must travel to Shanghai.* He shrugged, folded the piece the way he found it.

"Those bastards could have cut your dick off, you darn idiot," Taylor said.

"I think they were going to, my friend." He stuffed the paper in his pocket. It made no sense.

"Hey, Mr. Hero. Was it worth it? Or maybe I should say, was she worth it?" Mazzetti winked.

His head throbbed — proof the answer was "no." So what the hell had just happened to him? He squeezed his eyes shut and let her luminous countenance fill his inner sight. A sense of loss seized him worse than a physical ache. He craved to return and ask what the note meant, what the vision of infinity signified. Its memory was fading, but the heat signature remained, its embers still glowing. When his eyes opened again, far to the north, an evening haze hung over the barely visible mountains, symbol of the daunting task he had set for himself; yet the woman had shown him how to soar. *Hell yes, she was worth it.* He smiled inwardly. *This must be how Buzz feels about God.* But his instinctual incredulity could not deny the conviction in every drop of his blood that he would someday cross over those sky-reaching peaks and fulfill his promise to himself.

The jeep lurched for the ten thousandth time on the pot-holed road. He groaned. "I learned one lesson, though."

"Such as?" Mazzetti asked.

"Tigers are dangerous fucking animals."

He couldn't help grinning. No way his buddies could get it. Hell, even he didn't understand. Not actually. For one thing, the room he first entered had vanished or else he had been moved to different room altogether, but he had no memory of that. Then there was this itch in his brain that he had been told something important, something really important, but he had no notion of what it was. Another figment of his imagination, he figured. If it weren't for his ribs and that feeling in his balls, he'd have bet the whole thing was a drug.

Mazzetti roared. "You gotta' be shitting me!" For a minute it looked as if he might cry. "Listen, Jimmie boy, next time you go Walter Winchell about getting laid, ask me first. I'll tell you the shtick. For free."

CHAPTER 13

I go to encounter for the millionth time the reality of experience – James Joyce

Eastern China

"You have arrived."

The words came from . . . nowhere. On the opposite side of the otherwise empty glade a tree towered above a low stone house like a sentinel. On closer inspection, the willow, more than thirty feet tall, was a pitiful specimen, bent and misshapen. Its massive limbs twisted back on themselves. Scattered clumps of leaves tufted its branches and the shaggy bark peeled off like a sick animal's diseased coat. The house formed a fit partner with its swayed roof and out-of-plumb walls. If one collapsed, the other must surely fall, but their bond possessed a mystic power, and for the second time, Su Li, standing where the forest abruptly stopped, felt the energy of place, though far older than anything she could imagine.

Once again her whole being tingled with dread that her life was about to change. She blinked three times. Was the light slanting low in the evening sun playing tricks on her? For from out of the soil itself, a form took shape in the grassy open space. Not there a moment ago, she was sure, next to a creek a little man sat in the lotus posture, motionless, skin, robe, all as gray as the tree's bark or the house's stones, his scalp hairless and stretched. Even with his back to her, she knew the figure was as ancient and timeworn as the tree and house. Had a wood spirit emerged from the old tree or had she stepped into a fairy tale? She shook off the fantasy and drew near. The man's eyes were closed.

"Aged one, forgive me. Was it you who spoke to me? If so you have mistaken me for someone else. True, I have come on a long journey, but—."

"You've been sent. I've been waiting." He blinked his eyes at last. "Hmm. I didn't expect, well, a woman."

The old man penetrated her masquerade so easily it unnerved her. In the months since the stillbirth, she had wandered north first out of the Szechwan basin, then east on the single railroad in northern China from Paochi to near Luoyang, pulled by a psychic magnetism toward the enemy lines, a hunger for the purifying fire of danger. During the long months, experience, her new master, had taught harsh lessons about a woman's plight in China. Still, the cap and disguise deceived most. She had not been assaulted or killed, like so many other hapless women she had chanced upon, cast adrift by the war. Her countrymen's scorn for females as well as the subservience of women themselves appalled her. Master Po failed to tell her of such outrages. Yet these formed only a small swirl of what she witnessed along the river of misery that stretched across the country—starvation, disease, malformed children, legions of orphans, myriads clinging to the very edge of simple existence juxtaposed to those desperately attempting to maintain a pitiful semblance of normal life. Despite the risks, her heart, once deadened with remorse, had pushed up new shoots as the days and the distance from Emei Shan receded.

"But, holy one, I . . . ."

With astonishing quickness the little man sprang up and grabbed her wrist. His other hand rolled up her sleeve to reveal the tiger scar. He nodded. "Even after all this time, the Tao surprises me." He released her, picked up a knotty staff and pointed to the house. "Without looking out of that window, you can know the ways of heaven. I'll bet you didn't know that, monk, did you?" He laughed.

She did not believe in spirits, she reminded herself.

The wizened monk winked his eye slowly with mock sagacity, his face a burlesque of a serious grimace. "Neither do I!"

He doubled over in a gale of hilarity. Still chuckling to himself, he touched her head with his staff then aimed it at the stone house, the gray skin of his hand an extension of the robe he wore. A boy six or seven years old, dressed in simple clothes, emerged and walked toward them. To her surprise, the hermit put a tender arm around his shoulder.

"He will replace that which was lost." He smiled through gap-toothed lips, holding up a hand to halt her protest. "You're a priest, are you not? You will protect him now. As for me, my job's over and I'm off to die." He looked up at the clouds. "Before it rains. Not that it matters." He cackled at his own joke.

She shuddered. The boy walked over and hugged her waist. She stiffened. A warm energy flowed from his touch, the same kind that saved her on the night of her trial on the precipice. Her hands rested on his hair. The unconscious action startled her.

The hermit nodded in approval. "You will stay as I did, until someone comes."

"Are you Bodhidharma, Master, the holy saint? Is this all that is left of the Young Forest Temple?" She blurted the words out like a school girl, embarrassed as soon as she uttered them. A scholar she met on the train recounted a legend that a long line of wizards watched over a certain enchanted spot not far from a particular village. Just a fable, he said, an amusing myth. Nevertheless she decided to try to find it.

The sage burst into another fit of laughter as if the sun broke through the clouds. "I haven't had so much amusement in a hundred years." Tears rolled down his cheeks. He tried his best to appear stern. "Listen, priest. Learn to become a mother. That's all the advice I can give you." He turned and vanished into the somber trees behind the house before she could call out, his laugh echoing in her ears.

Mother! She glared at the boy and shoved him away. Memories of the miscarriage nauseated her. Motherhood had cursed her, cost her the one home she knew, ripped her from the one parent she had. She was a warrior-priest, not a mother. She intended to be a lone guerilla and fight the Japanese, like Han and other monks who had left the monastery to join in the fight against the invaders. Her sole reason for living was to prove herself worthy of the priesthood Po bestowed on her so he would take her back, but first she had to atone for her sin. She believed the fire of war could in some way purify her. Now out of nowhere a eccentric old recluse—who might have been an evil spirit — wanted to hand her a solemn duty, to care for a child. Madness!

"I cannot do this!" she shouted at the mute landscape.

She explored the tree-lined perimeter of the glade, haunted by the charismatic boy and the hermit's commands. That such oaks and maples even existed and had not been cut for firewood, she gradually realized, meant that people nearby feared the spot as magical. That would provide a degree of protection, and the house was better than living out in the open, as she had for so many months. The creek flowed into a shallow river a short walk away, plenty of water. The old tree offered shade. It might be a refuge, at least for a while. Wait, she told herself, derailing her train of thought. What was she thinking? Such ideas made the crazy man's prediction inevitable. Surely the Tao had not led her here. To stay in this forsaken place until she was old, as he foretold? Never able to see the Master again? Her knees wobbled at that possibility and she clutched at the tai chi disk.

The talisman calmed her sufficiently to look once more at the child who sat next to the brook quietly watching her, a young version of the old man. She drew near, hesitated, and finally parked herself on the grass in front of him, a hard scowl on her face. He challenged her displeasure with a calm, unafraid demeanor. She dipped her hand into the rivulet then pulled it out as if she had touched boiling water. *Such a son could have been mine if . . . . The insight shook her like an earthquake. She called on all her mind-control to stop trembling. The child's bright, alert eyes bound her own in mutual scrutiny. She exhaled.

So, boy. I am to be your mother — and your father, I suppose. I who have neither but lost the next best thing. Very well. The Tao brought me here and one opposes the Tao at one's peril. Yet I hate this horrid place.

He reached out to touch her hand and smiled as if she said the words aloud. Her heart raced with fear and wonder.

CHAPTER 14
A good man keeps his promises – Lao-tze

Myitkyina, Burma

It was an anniversary, of sorts.

Long after Taylor and Sgt. Reilly, the radioman, had disembarked, Ellison, reluctant to exit the Dragon Lady, brooded in the cockpit, staring at a forlorn wind sock drooping with tropical humidity on a pole at the runway's end. Under new orders, they had landed an hour ago at a strategic jungle-infested outpost in north Burma with a load of pipes for a fuel line. It was one year exactly since La Farge touted giving him a medal. Nothing had happened. Typical Army. And sure enough, in the meantime flights to China had ramped up big time, hundreds every day. Leaving him in this shit-hole called Burma. He couldn't go on this way, no good to anybody, especially himself. Pipes, for chrissake!

The base was as ugly as his mood. Except for the concrete tarmac, tropical rains had turned most of it into a lake of mud. After years of bombardment and strafing by bombers and fighter planes, the Allies secured a bitter victory at Myitkyina that took ten weeks and exacted heavy casualties on both sides. For the time being, the combined Allied forces under American command, were using its airfield for their forward staging areas to carry the fight into southern Burma and reconstruct the land route into China over the damaged Burma Road. Units from the Air Combat Cargo Squadron, the C-47 Skytrains, ferried supplies for months in preparation for the push. Pipes!

Bulldozers were scraping open a new section of jungle while work crews filled holes in the main runway, damaged by bombs and artillery shells from Japanese incursions. The last time he saw those dozers, they were Tinker Toys, cut up by acetylene torches into parts small enough to fit into planes like his. Now, savvy mechanics had reconstructed them and they worked. A modern marvel, he mused. If only he could put his own mess together half that well. Maybe it was time to give it up. The war was too damn a maze, full of twists and turns, and he was just one more little piss-ant, not that different from Dalby. That was the trouble with promises.

He was ten that humid day when Chen the farmer hauled him before her, angry because he had been playing with his bullock. She knit her brows. "How many times ha' I told ye?"

"I won't do it again, Mother. Really. I promise."

She shook her head in dismay, that look on her face, half-way between a smile of affection and a stern rebuke. She had a way of reassuring him while driving home the proper dose of remorse.

"Jamie, my dear bairn, ye should nae make promises ye dinna intend to keep. Please apologize to Chen."

He loved that old ox. He sighed and drew out of his shirt pocket the scrap of paper with the cryptic message from India. Shanghai? Tiger? Bollocks. On the verge of tearing it up and tossing it, he folded it instead and put it back, a repeat of the same ritual each time he flew a sortie over the past year.

Off to the side of the runway, temporary structures, some made of boards and sheet metal but mostly canvas tents, centered on a wooden control tower and a larger field hospital where medics treated seriously injured Allied soldiers. The bombings had destroyed or inflicted severe damage to most of the support buildings — warehouses, barracks — built by the Japanese who had occupied the base for more than two years. Piles of spare parts and ammo littered the landing zone, blown from their packing crates by mortar rounds from the enemy. A half dozen aircraft crammed together on the narrow tarmac looked as if they would never fly again, covered with dents and bullet holes, some with flat tires. Optimistic flight crews were busy repairing them. Chinese troops camped in the open around the perimeter, huddled against the weather. From the number of bandages he counted, hundreds lay wounded, stretched on bare earth, nothing over their heads.

A bulldozer revved alongside the plane; its engine's deep growl broke the reverie and he shambled out of the cockpit.

He caught up with Taylor in a wood and bamboo building that once served as headquarters for the Japanese commander. They passed orderlies and officers at work in an outer room and entered the office of Col. Jackson Lear, the commanding officer, puffing on a Cuban cigar behind a mahogany desk with a stack of papers on top, in back of him an oil-cloth wall map of Burma and southwest China. Salt and pepper hair, nearing sixty, with intense eyes that missed nothing, he snatched a cane hanging on his chair and shuffled by the paper mess. His brown Army tunic was a garden of battle medals on the left; on the right side the Croix de Guerre. No soldier-bureaucrat, Lear had fought in the Great War. An impressive man, a hero, Ellison realized.

"I've been expecting you two. Tomorrow you fly to Kunming —."

Ellison's jaw dropped. "Kunming! You mean in China?"

Lear, as tall as Ellison, frowned at the interruption. "You think Kunming's in North Dakota, Lieutenant?"

"Nay, sir. I apologize, sir." His heart pounded.

"Orders from General Stilwell himself. Seems he got wind of your exploits, Lieutenant. Wants to award you a medal in person. He's in China for the next month. I guess he figures the folks back home need some good news. They like to hear about heroes." He shrugged, puffed his cigar, and leaned on his cane as he circled the desk.

Dumbstruck, Ellison gawked at his superior. "Stilwell?" Suddenly he remembered. "Oh, sorry, sir."

"We're fighting a war, Ellison." Lear allowed a trace of irritation in his voice. "These things take time." He glanced at Taylor as if to reassure himself at least one other person in the room wasn't a moron. "You're to meet a Major Harris there. He'll have further instructions. Here's your manifest." He handed them their orders for the morning's flight. "You're flying a few dozen wounded soldiers back to China. I wish to hell I was going with you. I'm too old to be in this damn war. Dismissed."

Ellison heard simply one word — *China.*

CHAPTER 15

The Sage is always ready to help, so no one is left behind. Always there to see that no one is abandoned. This is called being clothed in the light. — Lao-tze.

A village, Henan Province

It was an anniversary, of sorts.

Two years and a day after her arrival at the old house, Su Li and her adopted son were wending their way toward the village, the paths through the countryside moist under their feet from last night's rain. High cirrus clouds were feathery arches over fields belonging to Sung, the village's wealthiest landowner and her protector. At her suggestion he had removed the stone walls that divided them into small sections. The result—increased production for the man who had befriended her and to whom she owed her tenuous way of life.

A crowd had gathered outside Sung's house on the day she first entered the village.

"What is happening?" she demanded.

The stupid peasants gaped at her. "Sung's son is ill. His only son," someone said finally. "They think he may die."

"Where's the doctor?" she asked.

"In this forsaken place?"

She understood right away what the situation required from her training in traditional medicines at the monastery. The Tao was revealing her role.

"I am a scholar, a healer. From a distant land," she announced in a loud voice and haughtily plowed her way through the confused crowd. Inside, the amulet and the signs of her priesthood convinced the distraught father to allow her to minister to his son. By the next afternoon, the child was cured of fever. As payment, Sung promised not to reveal her Shaolin markings and to support her. From then on she was known as Lao.

Only outcasts or hermits lived alone in China. The villagers vacillated about which category Su Li fit into, as she herself did, but day by day her competence and wisdom wove her into their lives as teacher, healer and sometimes protector. She traded her mastery in medicine for food and other necessities, while knowledge of her skills spread to surrounding villages. Harvests have improved since you arrived, the farmers liked to say whenever she visited the village. You have brought us good fortune. She would smile at them benevolently, aware of the irony. Luck, indeed, but just as well not to tell them that. They had barely recovered from the famine that swept Henan three years ago. The peasants' ambivalent acceptance mattered little to her, though. One misstep and Qiu, Sung's rival, would have them all at her throat despite everything she had done.

The risk of death compelled her to maintain her disguise and the constant danger of discovery lurked like an assassin in the shadows. She kept her hair cut close like the other peasant farmers and dressed as a field hand — padded tunic and trousers and in winter a knee-length cotton coat — and always wore her cap or more often the conical straw hat used by the farmers, her small breasts bound tight against her chest. The legends that a magician once occupied the hidden dale allowed her to live undisturbed; moreover she suspected that behind their overt respect, the villagers and their families feared her.

Hunger for the Master's forgiveness haunted evenings when there was time for contemplation. To pick up the broken pieces of her true self, to become what her heart believed she was meant to be, were ideals she could not reconcile with the grudgingly acknowledged fulfillments of daily life. She dreamed of the Golden Sun each night. During the day, there was the boy.

"I saw it yesterday, Mother," he said, before running ahead and splashing through the puddles. Hui was the name she gave him. He claimed he didn't know his birth name and that the hermit always called him *erzi* — son.

The morning sun scattered its rays on a sparkling green mantle of spring millet while in the distance men pulled a single plow through crumbly loess, like mules or bullocks. Few large animals remained. The Japanese confiscated them or the hungry villagers slaughtered them for food. Irrigation ditches, brimming with yesterday's rainfall, lined fields of dead sunflowers where blackbirds pecked for stray seeds from the autumn's harvest. Higher up on the distant peaks a light dusting of snow formed a white crown, not yet melted by the weak sun.

On this day she rejoiced in the sky for the first time since she had arrived, willing to absorb its blessing, a measure of her reluctant acquiescence to her lot. Hui returned to her side after charging ahead, absorbed in a game he made up, his gray winter coat mud-stained from jumping first on two feet then on one. The child looked forward to the visits when she allowed him to play with other children. They had agreed he could call her *mama* — mother — in private. To the rest of the world, she was his father. He regarded the hermit as his true father but refused to speak of where he in fact came from or his birth parents.

"I hope you completed your studies," she replied, not really paying attention.

She had purchased books on her rare trips to larger towns and taught him how to read and write. She tried her best to be a parent, though most often she felt like an older sister. Yet she was his master as well, and instructed him in as much of Po's knowledge as he was prepared to comprehend and trained him in martial arts. A quick student, his growing mastery gave her pride in him and herself.

"That animal in the woods," he insisted.

Any normal woman would count herself blessed by the gods with such a son, she knew. Yet his physical presence reminded her each day of her loss. How could she ever truly love him? She was not his mother and did not belong here. Such thoughts made her ashamed, especially when she suspected he was weighing her emotions in the balance of his precocious judgment. He had an uncanny ability to hear her thoughts sometimes, sense her feelings all the time, even though most often he kept such knowledge to himself. She could tell when he was masking it; his eyelids would flutter rapidly. No doubt such awareness made him uncomfortable; it doubled her own unease, for not only must she be mindful of what she said out loud but even what she was thinking whenever he was nearby.

One time he told her, "I know you do not want to be my mother. But someday you will be glad you are." How had he known? she had asked herself a hundred times.

Yet his inner self was closed to her, a tiny furnace of personal energy that burned with its own secret fuel in a cave hidden within his heart. Although it had taken her over a year, with close observation of village children and shaky memories of the monastery's young students, she had at last accepted the undeniable fact that he was a boy and had given up on probing his mystery. There was root and dirt, air and water in that truth, sometimes delightful, sometimes frustrating. She resolved to pay attention to the simple things and ignore his unsettling powers.

His forehead was earnest, his mouth drooping with sorrow. "You are sad again, Mother."

She stared at him in stunned disbelief.

"Please, listen to me?"

"What?" She managed to smile at the annoyance in his voice and impulsively hugged him.

"It was real. And close, this time. Beyond the line of trees."

"This time?" A faint tickle of alarm trickled through her stomach. The disk around her neck grow colder. "You have seen it before?"

He nodded. "When the Japanese barbarians came through last time."

"And how is it you see such things, my son?"

"My spirit father taught me. He showed me how to know what people think, too."

A chill coursed through her body. "Oh, and this watcher, does it say the barbarians are coming?" She smiled to hide her alarm.

"No. It just watches. I saw it after you arrived."

She stopped. What was this? Her eyebrows arched in suspicion. He kept hopping, unaware. "And what does this imaginary friend look like?"

"It's a tiger. You know how tigers look." He snarled and took a great leap over a ditch.

"How many times need I remind you not to tell such fables!" Her words masked a growing anxiety. Long ignored inklings came back to her — sightings over the months, at the extremes of her peripheral vision. She had dismissed them as illusions, products of her desperation. Nonetheless she reached inside her shirt for her yin/yang disc. "Come, we must go. I have no time today for your fairy tales. I have sick people to attend to."

"It means something important is going to happen." He stopped and turned, all at once deadly serious.

She froze, senses alert, clapped a hand over his mouth and whispered fiercely, "Listen!"

Hui glanced around. Her hand dropped away. "I don't hear anything."

"Just so."

CHAPTER 16

Before I met the Buddha, mountains were simply mountains, and rivers merely rivers. After I studied long in his teachings, the mountains were no longer mountains, the rivers no longer rivers. But when I had truly understood and reached the Abode of Peace, the mountains were simply mountains again, the rivers simply rivers –Buddhist saying.

The morning after their meeting with Lear, Ellison threw the prime boost start switch and fired up the Dragon Lady's engines. He and Taylor checked the gauges, flipped the remaining switches on and off – Taylor grumbling, "I haven't seen any two of these darn planes with the same layout. Makes the engineer in me want to puke." – made sure the tail wheel was unlocked, eased forward on the two throttle levers, and taxied out of the parking carrels to the main runway, ready for takeoff. Gooney Birds lined up behind him were headed for newly liberated airfields in north Burma. Others, like his own, carried loads over the Hump, the eastern end of the Himalayas, into China itself. The crew chief gave the signal and the gangly camouflage-green Dragon Lady lumbered down the airstrip.

Halfway to take-off, two dark-skinned figures, wearing the white *dhotis* of the local villagers who worked at the base, sprinted across the runway directly in front of the C-47, their arms raised to the sky.

"Jesus, God Almighty," Taylor shouted as the perpendiculars crossed and the men disappeared beneath the propellers.

Out the cockpit Ellison glanced backward to his left. The workers stood at the tarmac's edge, waving to him and laughing. He gave the thumbs up and poured on the throttle. The C-47 gathered air speed while her reinforced honey-comb wings vibrated between the differences in pressure and slowly ascended above the jungle.

"The physics of flight never cease to astound me, you know?" Ellison said.

"What the heck was that about?" Taylor's face was white.

"Huh? Oh, that. Good luck. They think it wards off evil spirits."

"You ever hit one?"

Ellison shook his head. "Seen it, though. 'T'ain't pretty."

"Shit, I'll never understand these people."

Ellison checked his compass and came around to the desired bearing. "Ever lit candles in a church?"

"Hell, no! Catholic superstition?"

"Well, you've probably done some such. Promised God something."

"I dunno. What's your point?"

"Same thing. It's a bribe. To get one up on the universe." Taylor sometimes reminded him too much of his father. "They're not so different from us."

"Bullshit. To risk your life."

"So it's a big bribe." Ellison laughed.

"You ever make a promise like that?"

Still on his knees, he locked his gaze long and hard at the empty horizon, beyond which the Japanese patrol was taking away his mother and the girl he loved. Finally he stood and raised a clenched fist above his head.

"I promise you, Mother, Lian. I'll find you." His words rang out over the fields in a savage parody of his father in the pulpit. "I swear I will kill them all. I swear it!" He shook his fist and shouted to the heavens. "Not by you. Because if you exist you're evil." He picked up a rock. "No. I swear like the Chinese. By the ancestors. And by the sky and the earth. I swear." He flung the stone as high as he could. Then another. And another. Over and over.

"Not to God. To myself."

Taylor pondered that idea for a while. "Maybe that's just as good."

Ellison turned in amazement to his friend. "But will you please grab that big red handle and retract the landing gear?" The Dragon Lady climbed above the Himalayan foothills, before levelling out at fifteen thousand feet, well above her rated altitude, cruising at one hundred ninety miles per hour. "Finally behaving yourself, you dizzy broad," he said, absently surveying the gauges and switches. "Unlike last week when she scared the shit out of me."

"Unpredictable, that's the DL," Taylor agreed, giving a playful pat to the displays in front of him.

"I was dating this doll I met at Iowa State. Take you soaring higher than an eagle or leave you wondering what the hell you do next. Sarah? I think that was her name. Those days seemed as if they never happened. But yeah, that little dark-haired beauty was a wee bit terrifying. Like the good ol' DL." He laughed. "From up here, that phase of my life seems almost childish."

Taylor finally looked over at him. "You seem to stumble into women like that." Ellison gave him a what-the-hell-are-you-talking-about frown. "That Calcutta floozy, for instance."

"You ever hear about the oracle at Delphi? The Greeks used to bring gifts to her for her predictions."

"You learn that in college?"

"From my mother."

He turned his attention to the manifest. On this run they carried wounded Chinese soldiers and a half dozen regulars to help their comrades on and off the aircraft. He and Taylor were the sole vestiges of authority, without a radioman once again. The injured slept on the plywood floor, curled up beneath thin woolen blankets, intent on the warmest, least uncomfortable position possible.

"Half of those blokes will be dead before we even reach Kunming." He tilted his head backward.

Taylor looked up from the map he was studying. "When they get there?"

"Oh, off to this spanking new hospital. Clean. Sanitary. Surgeons trained in amputating limbs. Lots of nurses. The best medicine known to science."

"Right." Taylor rolled his eyes.

With the Dragon Lady purring contentedly, white peaks of the mighty Himalayan range soon came into majestic view. To the east, the mountains tapered down into China proper, Laos and Viet Nam. Many of the world's great rivers had their source in the Himalaya's massive glaciers—the Yangtze, Mekong, Red, Salween, even the Irrawaddy, which Ellison knew well. To the west, the gigantic massifs of the core beckoned, serene, cloud-capped, the top of the world.

"Even an emperor would be chastened by that sight," he said, pointing his finger. Once the peaks had symbolized the obstacles to his quest; now he soared over them, filled with excitement.

"Right," said Taylor dryly. "That's why they call it the Aluminum Trail."

Dozens of C-47s had disappeared in this vast wildness. Engines had failed or they had not gained enough altitude and crashed into the mountainside, and the weather was the most treacherous on earth. But for the time being each man contemplated the view in silent awe, dangers forgotten.

Ellison gestured. "*Tien tong men,* in Chinese. The Gate of Heaven."

"I gotta admit, it's pretty humbling."

"You asked me once what I believed."

"Mountains? You believe in mountains?"

"Don't be so damned literal. This isn't the Bible," Ellison said.

"I agree, they're magnificent. But they're just mountains."

119

"That's the point."

"Know what? You've been different ever since we were in Calcutta." Taylor was silent for a few seconds, mulling over some idea. "Okay, you believe in mountains." He was eager to sink his chops into this one. "Those poor guys back there? How do they fit?" Behind them in the fuselage, shouts were erupting.

"Tell you in a minute," Ellison said. "Doesn't sound right."

He unbuckled and twisted out of his seat. At least he spoke Chinese and the passengers carried no weapons. The American transport command did not allow an armed Chinese soldier in its planes. In any case the Chinese seldom issued firearms to their own men unless faced with an imminent engagement. The first thing he noticed was that the hatch dogs securing the door were unlatched and it was leaning against the wall, the fuselage open to the atmosphere. *Who the fuck?* He was furious. The culprits, the escort troops, were gambling and trading insults, most of them directed at one who squatted on his haunches. Even the wounded had roused themselves, despite the cold. The racket subsided before the young soldier threw the dice.

"You lose, Lu," someone shouted.

The youth came erect, his face frozen in terror. No more than seventeen, Ellison reckoned, his own age when the Japs massacred his village. The other gamblers circled the loser, yelling and gesturing at the door. When he wouldn't—or couldn't—move they rushed him.

Alarmed, Ellison yelled at them. "What's going on here? Break it—."

The C-47 suddenly pitched downward and he lost his balance. By the time the Dragon Lady righted herself and he was able to keep himself upright, the other soldiers had lifted the losing player by his arms and legs. The desperate man writhed as violently as a wild animal, bawling and pleading. In the next instant they threw their comrade out the opening.

"No!" Ellison shouted. "No! No! No!"

He leaped toward the door opening, tossing aside the smaller Chinese like children to see the soldier plummet to the snow-capped peaks a thousand feet below. Spellbound, he gripped the doorframe so tight his fingers hurt. The wind roared by like a level five hurricane. He wrapped his aviator's scarf around his face until the figure disappeared. Finally, he turned to the others.

"You killed him, you bloody, fucking bastards." The slow, deliberate English words masked the volcano within.

The dumbfounded soldiers eyed him; a couple had a crooked grin. One pointed to the door—he wanted permission to replace it. He swore to himself in disbelief and reeled to the cockpit.

"What was that about?" Taylor asked.

"Fucking Chinese," he muttered, seething with incomprehensible grief at what he had witnessed.

He drew out his .45 automatic from his belt looped on a hook on the firewall and stalked back into the fuselage. The soldiers were smoking cigarettes. He picked up the dice and threw them out the door, leveled the gun and fired after them. The men stiffened.

"All right, you sons of bitches. I don't really care if you kill each other, but not on my watch. I can bloody kill you, but you can't."

He shouted in English above the wind's roar, on the brink of succumbing to a mad primal urge to shoot them, as if their death could obliterate the insanity from minutes ago. The frightened soldiers cowered before his anger, eyeing the gun. He filled his lungs with a long, slow breath of the dry, cold air pouring in from the outside.

"Sit!" he yelled in Chinese. His finger stabbed at the floor. "And don't get up for the rest of this flight. Or I'll shoot you."

They cringed and headed for the rear of the plane, as far from him as they could get. The open mouth of the doorway mocked him like the maw of a monster from hell. He fired another angry shot through the opening, a futile attempt to slay the obscenity. The cold finally propelled him to holster the gun in his belt and secure the door. Still shaking, he glowered around the hold, searching for a clue to the madness he witnessed. A Chinese officer had levered himself to an upright position against the opposite wall. His arm hung in a sling; a wide blood-stained bandage circled his throat.

"You saw the whole thing, didn't you?" He came over and squatted next to the wounded soldier. The captain slowly closed his eyes as if even blinking was an agony. "So what the hell happened? Did he cheat?"

"He lost." The officer's voice was sandpaper on wood, his larynx damaged. "The loser has to jump out. If he doesn't, they throw him out."

"You've got to be kidding me," Ellison said in English. Of course. Now it made sense. He laughed bitterly. How could he not see it? You lost at dice, you got thrown from a plane. You rolled six instead of seven and your life was done. Your village was in the wrong place at the wrong time and your father got killed, your mother kidnapped. Perfect sense. His head hurt.

"Why the hell would anyone play a game like that?"

The captain coughed, took a shallow breath. "They have nothing. Forced to be soldiers. They play for the most valuable thing they have."

"So that's what life is? A game."

The captain shrugged and slumped over.

"My God, I'm sorry." He grabbed a blanket and a canteen. "Here, let me help you." He held the limp man's head in the crook of his arm, tried to pour water down his throat. "You're going to make it. A couple more hours."

He was dead. An immense sorrow suffused Ellison, as intense as the day his father was murdered, for the dead man, for himself, and for all the wrongs of a senseless world at war.

Father. James' skull still rung from the blow by the rifle-butt as awareness clawed its way back to an awful dread of what he had seen before blacking out, what he knew was so but would not accept. He crawled across the hard-packed earth to the dead man, cradled his head in

123

his hands and stroked his brow, frantic to discover a pulse, a flicker of the eyes, anything.

"Live. Live, please," he cried over and over, as tears streamed down his cheeks while he pounded on the lifeless chest with his fists. At last his arms fell limp. Eyes closed, he rocked back on his heels and fumbled in a broken voice snatches of songs his father sang on Sunday to his flock. "Oh God, our help in ages past," he croaked, stopped and turned to the sky. "Why did you do this to him?"

The Chinese soldier's head still resting in a tender embrace, Ellison sat on the plywood flooring, rocking back and forth, humming and wondering. Maybe he had not lived in China enough to appreciate the captain's words. Did they signify life was the ultimate value? Or that life had no value, as his father had argued Chinese culture believed. Abraham Ellison, who had often proclaimed his willingness to give his life for Jesus, had in fact died to defend his wife. And the brutal irony occurred to him, the son, who had tried to be as unlike his father as he could, that he was imitating the minister on a mission of his own in defense of Mary Ellison. Another stupid game? And whose was better, his or the dice? Did any of it matter? The mindless drone of the engines mingled with his hum. The Dragon Lady rolled from one side to the next, summoning him from his insoluble debate.

He dragged the corpse over near the door. This man's body would never be returned to his home village or town—if anyone knew or cared. Thrown in a common grave, if he got lucky. Or burnt. Ellison at least intended to honor him. He spun the hold-downs on the cargo door once more and set it aside. Outside the white peaks beckoned. For the briefest of seconds, he had an impulse to jump, to join the army of death, the true umpire of this lunatic game, but caught himself long enough to become aware of the captain's lifeless eyes.

"I'm not Shiva," he shouted at the maelstrom whistling past the open door.

The skies cleared and the sun shone red and gold on the mountain peaks. The air was cold enough to freeze flesh. His fingers were tingling. His mind stumbled through scraps of half-remembered bits and pieces of words that might fit. His mother had always recited poems to her sick patients.

"Oh Captain, my Captain, your fearful trip is done," he murmured. Aye, she would have said something like that, some hopelessly romantic poem. He flung the body to the wind, his own bribe, ultimately, to the Gate of Heaven.

"The prize we sought is won," he said softly. The memory brought a smile through a few tears that trickled down his face. Not yet. Not yet. But soon.

CHAPTER 17

There is no beauty in victory. That would be to rejoice in killing people. No one who delights in slaughter will ever find satisfaction in this world. – Lao-tze.

The Japanese had extended their foraging expeditions deeper into China as their occupied territories expanded into Henan and the counties near Su Li's village. At the outset they claimed to be liberators and promised better times under their rule; they even provided grain for the starving thousands. Many towns who sided with them in due course became enslaved, for the "devil dwarves," after initial cordiality, grew more and more rapacious, seized whatever they pleased and slaughtered all protestors. To them, the Chinese were insects to be stomped on or exterminated. In the past six months, the frequency of the raids had diminished — something about the war, she imagined, had changed, prompting the barbarians to withdraw some troops; but still they came and with equal ferocity.

Sung and some others had resisted the invaders' overtures and had suffered for it, but, after much cajoling and preparation, she had taught the farmers to hide their grain and their families, so when the troops came, they looked destitute, with mostly the old or ill or crippled present, while the rest hid in a wide network of caves and tunnels. Most of the time her stratagems worked, true to Po's instructions to avoid violence whenever possible; patrols passing through usually ignored the village, intent on richer prizes. But for the plan to succeed the skittish villagers had to play their part. A minimal number of the able-bodied needed to be visible, working in the fields or doing chores, otherwise the scavenging squads became suspicious.

The voices Su Li and Hui heard, after they sprinted to the first houses on the outer edge of the village, were not Chinese. The silence was broken only by sharp commands in a foreign tongue. The foolish, frightened peasants had disappeared. Now the Japanese were on the hunt. She motioned for Hui to stay still while she edged along the house's side wall to get a better view. Six Japanese infantrymen were probing house by empty house, after loot or slave labor. An impatient officer was goading them. If they found the tunnels, they would execute everyone. Even if they did not, they would burn or steal anything of value. She stole back to the waiting boy.

"Hui," she whispered, "return home. Do not let anyone see you. We are in grave danger. Run!"

The child darted back toward the fields just as a soldier, detached from the main group, emerged from an alley. The startled infantryman hesitated, shouted something in his language, then brought his rifle to his shoulder, still unaware of her bearing down on him like a silent tsunami. Instinctual maternal fear had awakened the muscle memory of years of practice in martial arts, sweeping aside for a moment the terror for her son's life. Before he could aim, the blow landed just below where his rib cage divided, a point of nearly instant death. He crumpled but managed to fire off a wild round.

She quivered at the sight of the dead man, aware her life had altered irrevocably. *Wushu* had been a mental discipline at the monastery as much as a physical one, yet it combined both elements much as a graceful dance or acrobatics, but she practiced against other students, rarely against one of the older monks. The idea she would have to use martial arts to fight and kill would have struck her as absurd.

In a dreamy, almost child-like wonder, she reached for the soldier's bayonet lying on the ground, then brandished it as if it were an old, familiar tool. Immediately the weapon's heft and the proximity of danger saturated her consciousness, pumping an I-can-defeat-them-all intoxication that swept away her qualms. Was she not tiger-daughter? Fearless, cunning? The student who had nearly defeated Master Zhao? The memory gave her pause. She had seen drunken fools who felt invincible. To proceed cautiously was not to err. True, the Master spoke of tales where Shaolin warriors walked through walls, even flew, but she was not one of those. The present danger was no story. It was life and death and she little more than a girl. Only stealth and guile, not magical power, could assist her.

The shot had alerted the invaders. Orders were being shouted. The troops would not rest until they found who killed their comrade, then torture her and burn everything. A quick reconnoiter told her the rest of the soldiers had fanned out in a search. That was good. Easier to isolate them and lay an ambush.

She took a position inside the entrance to an unsearched house — the furniture had not been smashed. Dishes and uneaten food still lay upon the table. The bayonet felt clumsy, unbalanced, unlike the sabers she had trained with but serviceable. It would kill. The idea, at first unsettling, lent her confidence. Cautious footsteps. Just outside. Voices, muffled. A rifle snout through the doorway. With one hand she jerked the carbine downward. The man tumbled headfirst as her blade swept across his throat before the second soldier barged in, saw her and fired. The bullet tore along her buttock, seared the flesh like a red-hot poker but she ignored the pain and whirled. The desperate soldier was pulling the bolt back as the bayonet plunged into his chest.

When she shoved the dying man aside, the blade snapped off its handle. Now what? No weapon. Find something, Shaolin, anything, she chided herself, leaving the house. As she raced past a shed she snatched a hoe then leaped onto the roof. Shouts from the enemy meant they had found the bodies. They would be more cautious but had not started to burn. They wanted her alive.

Silent as her namesake, she swept from one rooftop to the next, alert for footsteps. It did not take long, right below her, inching ahead, bent low, his weapon ready. She gathered herself and pounced, the impact driving the soldier to the ground. He struggled to his knees, desperate to shake her off his back but she whipped the hoe around his neck, yanked hard and broke his windpipe.

When she came erect a blunt metal object rammed into her back with such force she couldn't breathe. She doubled over, gasped, clutched her side, and turned around with excruciating effort. A bespectacled soldier, carbine aimed at her heart, motioned for her to rise. She lifted her hands to comply. Shouting like a lunatic, he pointed at his dead comrade and jammed the barrel into her chest and stomach again. Ribs ripped by pain, she sagged back to her knees. The rifle butt slammed into her forehead, arching her upper body backwards onto the ground alongside the dead man. She groaned, at the edge of consciousness, holding up a feeble arm to protect her head while her free hand swept across the dirt, frantic to find a weapon. It scrabbled over the dead soldier's belt, fumbled at the canvas strap, desperate to release the catch.

I cannot. I cannot . . . . Her last ounce of strength was seeping into the soil.

The touch of the knife opened a reservoir of willpower. *I will not die this way.* Through the miasma of agony, her weakened left arm deflected the rifle from its next thrust and startled the soldier, now off balance and vulnerable. Behind his glasses, his eyes gaped wide in disbelief while his hands groped the deep gash in his belly. She rolled to her knees, lungs billowing in quick, fiery breaths, her mouth full of stomach-churning fluids. A bullet whined overhead as she lurched off, the simple act of standing upright a torment. A second one grazed her calf. She pitched sideways, falling and spinning and hurling the knife at a soldier taking aim. The blade tore into his heart.

Back on her feet, blood oozing from the wounds in her leg and hip, she limped behind a bamboo barn, sank backwards in the filth of a pigsty and waited, feigning death. The last infantryman, a stubbly beard on his chin, found her, probed with his bayonet to see if she were alive, raised it to finish her. Her hand darted up, grabbed his belt, and pulled the startled man toward her. A wood stake rammed into his mouth before he hit the muck.

Steel bands of weariness bound her limbs. Her breath came in deep lugs. Gore and muck covered her clothes. She bled from half a dozen different wounds and bruises. Her temples throbbed with a pulse-bursting roar, yet enough adrenaline was still pumping through her blood to mask the hurt. Satisfied she was safe, she examined the dead soldier. How small he was. No wonder the Master had called them "little people." Were there more?

"Please, let it be over," she cried out loud, her mind numbed. The sight of her hands—dirty killer hands—made her want to vomit.

A pistol hammer clicked right behind her ear.

The unreliable Nambu's hammer hit home with a metallic snap. She spun so fast the surprised officer had barely enough chance to squeeze the trigger. The gun fired this time but the bullet burrowed into the mud. With both hands she wrenched its barrel toward his elbow. A second wild round managed to erupt before the weapon dropped from his broken wrist. A typhoon of *kung fu* punches thundered on his face and chest. Desperate, he

131

slumped to one knee, reaching for his sword, but with a whirling kick that channeled her whole body's energy, her foot shattered his shoulder. He uttered a curse and clutched his arm.

She stood above him, eyes locked in mutual hate. "Do you surrender, devil?"

"You filthy piece of shit. Rot in your Chinese hell!" he spat in broken Chinese and made a useless lunge for his pistol.

On and on she rained punches, even after he lay unconscious, impelled by an animalistic terror at how close she had come to dying and a quivering rage that her own carelessness let it happen. A metallic glint caught her eye. She reached for the pistol, held it to his head. The report snapped her out of the berserk trance.

"No! No! No!" she howled, recoiling in revulsion at the gun.

She heaved the abomination as far as she could throw it and staggered in a mind-dulled circle around the dead man, the back of her hand against her brow. This was not victory. This was defeat. A nightmare. She groaned. To fight, to slay, to kill—worse than a barbarian? She had become as foul as any ditch water. She had killed people, murdered a man in blind fury. Not maimed them, injured, them, or disarmed them, but killed them. Yet was there any other choice? They would have killed her and her son, slaughtered the innocent, destroyed their livelihoods. If ever she needed the Master's wisdom, she craved it now. Eyes blurred with blood and tears, she lifted the disk, in hopes that it might give her solace but its carvings were as obliterated by muck as her own life's moral clarity. Her tunic stuck to the flesh wound in her side where the bleeding had stopped. The calf wound still oozed and she walked with a limp. Shoulders slumped, she turned from the corpse and hobbled toward the village center. The empty dwellings were like tombs.

"Come out," she called. "The devils are all dead!"

A dozen people climbed back out of the tunnels and showed themselves. To their bewildered faces she looked as frightful as a demon, her visage a fearsome mask of mud and blood.

"I must go to my son." She gestured at them in disgust.

Dusk fell and the moon rose over the slow, laborious crawl home. Where the fields ended, she halted by a shallow cistern and took an inventory of her hurts. Fiery, tiny volcanoes of pain flared everywhere on her skin; her wounds were bleeding but her bones were bruised, not broken, insignificant compared to the sickness in her heart. She splashed water on her face, afraid her appearance would frighten Hui. Later when her son met her he trembled, burst into tears and wrapped his arms around her in a fierce hug. The pressure on her wound made her wince but she returned the embrace fervently, never more glad for his presence.

She was barely able to summon the strength to reassure the terrified look on his face. "The village is safe. But I must take care of myself. Finish the chores and prepare for sleep while I go down to the river and bathe."

With a blanket, bandages and her medicine pouch, she drew near the reeds that grew along the bank. When she stripped off the dirty trousers and blood-stained tunic her wounds opened again. In the moonlight, she examined them. Not serious but they needed a good cleaning and later, treatment. Her pulse hammered through the gashes on her forehead like a drum beat.

Naked, she waded in up to her waist and raised her face to the moon, letting it bathe her battered body with its light, in mystic union with its reflection on the water's surface. She dipped her hand in it. Moonlight on Emei Shan, she remembered, had been magical to a young girl. That girl no longer existed.

"Master, if I have done evil . . ." she moaned. "I do not know any more." She wanted to weep, to find release from the final loss of her innocence.

She plunged her head beneath the shallows near the bank over and over. Each time her spirit grew stronger, the freezing water anesthetizing her wounds. She had slain that last soldier out of rage. That was a grievous wrong even though he would have gladly killed her. One more burden of regret to carry. She scrubbed her skin as if the effort might wash away all the sad mistakes of her life, and bit by bit the physical cleanness nurtured a growing, tentative sense of self-approval. She had done well, saved lives. That truth must be weighed in the balance also. The Master might not completely approve but he would empathize. Still, a deep unease flared up faster than a fish breaking water. She was now bound to this place more than ever. The Tao intended her to grow old here, as the hermit did. Once a prospect worse than death, she breathed a sigh of acceptance when a noise distracted her. A shadow flitted among the reeds. She clutched at the disk and called out.

"Who is there? Hui? Is that you?"

No answer except the slight wind that soughed through the trees. Yet she was certain she heard a sound, saw something. An animal? Here? Impossible, yet a creature *was* moving. Her vision strained to penetrate the shadows. For an instant, yellow orbs peered from the brush. Or did they? She shivered, torn between terror and awe, and stared hard once again, listening for the slightest crackle of leaves. Nothing. Merely the breeze. Whatever was there had stolen away, but its energy lingered, settling over her, a warm protective force-field that enclosed her injured body, seeped in, and soothed it all the way to her soles. The river flowed past her like a blessing from the earth. At last, a profound weariness overwhelmed her. Time to go home, to sleep.

CHAPTER 18

To have time on your side is a great ally because you have no control over it – Sun Tzu

Kunming, China

Ellison lingered while a squad of Chinese soldiers unloaded the Dragon Lady's human cargo and transferred it to a couple of flat-bed trucks. No one noticed or cared two passengers were missing. No one would grieve for a simple soldier or a certain captain. It was not the Chinese way. But I will, he said to himself and gave a salute.

The sun was dropping behind distant peaks as he wandered away between a squadron of B-29 bombers parked on their hardstands alongside the enormous airfield, the forward staging area of the Army Air Force and the operations hub for all of western China. Jeeps and trucks sped around the sprawling base delivering supplies and people. Huge supply dumps dotted the cleared perimeter—stacks of bombs, ammunition for machine guns, recycled parachutes, crates of replacement parts for trucks and planes and endless arrays of fifty gallon drums of gasoline—delivered by aircraft such as his own or the newer C-87's from Chabua. Further on, tents, Quonset huts and more permanent concrete block buildings housed the growing American military might.

Thousands of Chinese from the local *hsien* had assembled for ninety-day stints to construct the last 9,000 foot runway. Workers had earlier removed topsoil, dumped in piles nearby. Now, in an endless stream of wheelbarrows and pole baskets, crews laid and compacted a layer of cobblestones hauled from a riverbed five miles away. The laborers provided their own food, carts and tools—shovels, hoes, rakes. A quarter of the total, which had reached almost half a million at one time, remained. The closest thing to a human ant colony imaginable, he reckoned.

At the far end, hundreds of coolies strained along the horns of a wooden yoke attached to each side of a huge cylindrical rock. The roller weighed tons, with a diameter taller than a man. Chanting a work song, they lugged it over the cobblestones to compact the base rock. Not far from him, piles of gravel mushroomed where thousands of women and children with small hammers chipped away at larger rocks to make crushed stone that other workers mixed with mud and slurry for the runway's foundation, the Chinese version of concrete. The whole operation labored under the supervision of Chinese engineers and local village leaders.

As if bulldozers had never been invented, he marveled. The Great Wall must have been built the same way. Awe and admiration for the Chinese people swept over him. Nothing was powerful enough to defeat this country except itself. Eminently practical, its citizens were capable of grand deeds with whatever was at hand. Their swollen numbers and ingenuity were able to turn weaknesses into strength.

In a messy little office in headquarters, Major Robert Harris was tall, clean cut and bored, his pressed uniform impeccable, a West Point officer slightly older than Ellison on the upward arc of his career.

"Your orders are in there," he tossed a manila folder across a gray metal desk. "We're starting negotiations for a northern prisoner exchange with the Nips. They've agreed to meet us in Zhengzhou. You and Taylor will fly our team and ten token prisoners to Chungking, where someone else will take over." He leaned back in his chair. "You know where Zhengzhou is?"

His imagination leaped halfway across China. He could almost believe that a power or force was drawing him eastward despite the war's enmity. Is this what they call destiny? he asked himself. Or what Buzz called Providence? As luck would have it . . . .

"North. In Henan province, as I recall," he managed to respond coherently.

"I heard you were half Chinese?" Harris had a supercilious smirk.

"Nay, sir. Scot, sir. I'm half Scot."

"Yeah, I thought I detected an accent. You should fix that if you want to go anywhere in the Army, by the way. Anyway, Commies are involved too. They've been fighting the Japs north of the Yellow River." His tiny interest in the junior officer had faded.

"Was there anything more, sir?"

Harris looked up, annoyed. "Oh, the medal, you mean." He opened a folder on his desk, shuffled perfunctorily through a stack of papers, then handed Ellison a sealed manila envelope with his name typewritten on it. "General Stilwell left for the States last week. Said he was sorry he couldn't award it to you in person. Told me to give this to you and to wish you luck." Harris resumed thumbing through his paperwork, signaling the interview was over. "Anything else?" he asked without looking up.

Ellison paused at the door and turned. "I've got a question, sir. Have you ever fired a gun? Seen a man die? Or even been in combat?"

Harris snapped to his feet. "Are you some kind of smart-ass? I'll have you up on charges if you're not out of here in two seconds!"

Outside, his heart hammered. He was getting closer. No thanks to dicks like Harris. He saluted with his middle finger at the building then drifted over to a beehive-shaped hill of crushed rock near the runway, sat on a crate and breathed deeply of evening air grown colder. The women had stopped their work and were preparing meals for their families. Thousands of wooden tripods had appeared with pots of rice or soup hanging from the neck over small fires. A little bird of a girl, perhaps the same age as Lian when he had first come to China, wandered over near him. She squatted on her haunches, pecked at some rocks and soberly banged them together to make noise. When the ragamuffin looked his way, Ellison smiled. She smiled back. He ripped open the envelope.

"Lieutenant Ellison,

Please accept this Silver Star on behalf of the government of the United States. From Col. LaFarge I have heard many good things about your courage as well as the tragic loss of your family. Perhaps, while you are in China, you will be able to locate your mother, if indeed she is still alive. I hope, for your sake, she is. That would make a great story for the folks back home. Unofficial sources tell me a few top Japanese generals have routinely kept European and American hostages as their concubines. General Okamura, the Chief of Staff in Shanghai, is reported to be much taken with Western women. Good news and bad news, I suppose. I trust this letter and this introduction from the Generalissimo Chiang Kai Shek will help in your inquiries. Well done, Lieutenant. We need more soldiers like you.

Sincerely,

Joseph Stilwell, Lt. General, US Army."

He held up the shiny medal, then examined the official looking document with Chiang Kai Shek's seal — something about the bearer being entitled to special consideration from any military personnel in the Chinese forces. Somehow Vinegar Joe found out and was willing to help. It was there, between the lines. Now, for Shanghai. Whoa! In the heart of Japanese occupied China? Good to mull that one over. Just a little. He laughed inwardly, reached into his shirt pocket and unfolded the paper from Calcutta. Mary Ellison was alive. If there was anything certain in this world his mother would find a way to survive. She was too strong, her presence too stunning not to be noticed, treasured. That red hair.

Sunday afternoons. After his father's sermons, when he removed his collar, rolled up his sleeves, tuned up his fiddle and became the person his child could love. Mary Stuart Ellison whirling in the square, dancing the Highland Fling, not caring the swords were bamboo sticks, her hair flying in flaming brands. She had always claimed descent from the house of Stuart. Her son was sure of it, for in his eyes she was Queen Mary. She used to say he looked like her own father. Said they both got the red hair from him.

He folded the documents, put them inside his jacket pocket, and stared at the exhausted Chinese women. All at once the image of the young soldier falling to his death filled his inner sight. The boy could have been a son to one of these families. What must it be like to fall with no parachute? Parachute! His body went rigid. It came together like parts of a machine that make no sense individually, but when you connect them, the device works. He needed to check things out — flight plan, topography, battle lines. Chiang's letter could make it happen. It wasn't logical; it wasn't rational. Someone like himself would say it was crazy, impossible, but it just might work.

The little girl tottered over right next to him, twittering and humming a song to herself. When he looked up, she was gawking at him. "What are you doing, big hairy?" Her bare legs and feet were thin and dirty beneath a dress not much more than a rag. Her nose ran snot but her wide, brown eyes were unafraid.

"When I was little, I had a friend like you, wee one. But you're prettier," he said.

"Me? How does a big hairy know someone like me? Where is she?"

"I don't know."

"Can you find her?"

"I don't know."

"You don't know much, big hairy."

"You think so?" he said in English and laughed. He stood up to leave. "Here, would you like this?" He held out the medal but the girl had by that time returned to the anthill of workers.

CHAPTER 19

For others to approve of me is easy. To approve of myself is hard – Zen saying

The night of the battle, Su Li stretched out on the floor mat next to the sleeping boy. Although the river sang its nocturnal lullaby, sleep eluded her; wounds and bruises protested every position. By and by she surrendered, sat with her legs crossed, and focused her awareness on the *kang's* dying fire. She threw a stick on it. Embers flared up a cloud of sparks. The hypnotic flicker of orange and yellow, red and black summoned her into the past. In heat and flame, visions took shape – Po, Han, a woman's likeness. The face was blurred but she knew who it had to be. The image threatened to dissolve into the smoke. She willed it to stay.

Mother? Who were you? Why did you abandon me? I have so many questions. The Master said the same destiny that brought you to Emei Shan flows through me. But my fate will be worse than yours, my mother. To fight this hopeless war against the Japanese invaders until they destroy me. For my curse is to be a woman and yet not a woman.

The vision vanished. She exhaled sorrowfully. Once, the Master had told her she was fortunate to study the truth of *wan wu*, the ten thousand things, because few women ever aspire to such knowledge. Hah, she thought resentfully. To know she was different meant she could never be one with her own culture. The Master revealed too much. And too little. To die as an outcast. That would be her fate.

143

She lay her battered body on its side, again trying to find the least uncomfortable arrangement of her limbs. Memories of the mortal clash with the Japanese haunted her. She fixed her attention on the fire once more to banish them. It danced, appeared and disappeared, interspersing orange, red and white, and beckoned once more.

She was once again in Master Po's room. He was unaware of her presence, his back turned. She spoke as if from afar. "I no longer fear death, my Master. It tried to seduce me. It held me in its arms and I almost succumbed to its embrace. But I chose life. I have used what you taught me to protect the innocent. Healed the sick and injured. Mothered this child as the holy man commanded. Are not these worthy of a Shaolin? Have I not eaten sufficient bitterness? Speak to me, O Master! I want to come home.

The tiny flame winked out. The yin/yang disk lay cold and silent on her chest but in the distance an airplane droned.

CHAPTER 20

Seek as if your hair is on fire and you're looking for water – Zen saying

Chungking, the same night

The prisoner exchange flight to Zhengzhou lifted off hours behind schedule but headquarters had alerted the Japanese Air Command. The delay gave Ellison extra time to prepare. He lied and cajoled and bribed the pilots with cigarettes, flashing his letter from Stilwell so the signature showed. He was on a secret mission, not allowed to say anything more. The flight jockeys, seeing he was one of them, winked and shrugged and sneaked him on board before the other passengers. This C-47 was configured like its original, the DC-3, with a standard door, seats and windows. The negotiating team — a civilian diplomat and two army brass — conferred in adjacent rows about the final details of the exchange protocol while toward the rear the manacled Japanese officers tried to sleep.

During the trip he hunched against a wall in a seat nearest the door, well apart from the others. Zhengzhou was not Shanghai but it was seven hundred miles closer than Kunming. His pack contained C-rations, extra clips of ammo for the .45 Browning, and money and opium in the med kit. The drug-filled packets could be exchanged for anything, in particular one's life. His Flying Tigers jacket had a US flag stitched into the lining and a small replica of the Chinese flag sewn on the sleeve so if he were captured by friendlies he wouldn't be shot. Inside in a zipped pocket were Chiang's and Stilwell's letters and a map of the area. At long last he had a direction. He might be able to enlist the local Chinese general's aid, disguise himself as a foreign advisor and sneak behind the front with guerillas or resistance fighters. His language skills would get him by. He could buy allies to get to Shanghai.

The hardest part had been saying good-bye to Taylor. It happened after mess, when they were returning to sleeping quarters.

He had pulled his co-pilot aside. "Let's walk for a while." They veered off toward the planes parked on the apron. He found words harder to come by than he expected. "I need a favor. Take care of my father's fiddle, will you?" He laughed half-heartedly to cover his anxiety.

"What the heck are you talking about?"

"I think you're ready to be a full pilot. Maybe you'll get assigned to one of those new transports they're bringing in," Ellison said.

Taylor was getting frustrated. "Quit screwing with me, James."

Once more Ellison hesitated. "I won't be flying back with you, Buzz. This mission—."

"Mission?" Taylor rolled his eyes in a completely incredulous look.

"From General Stilwell."

"Stilwell!" Taylor's jaw dropped. "You gotta be shitting me. Cut it out, James. What's going on?"

"I can't. There're some things in my life I've got to fix. As best as I can. You can relate to that, Buzz."

Taylor walked a bit further. Ellison suspected his friend was working his way through the variables. The light went on. "That bitch in Calcutta, she put this notion into you, didn't she?" He frowned. "You're making a helluva leap of faith." After a few seconds, he nodded a little. "I get it. I think. Okay." He extended his closed hand with a faint smile; in it was his silver coin allotment. Ellison had a broad grin, took the money and shook his friend's hand. "I'm gonna pray for you. And hold onto that fiddle until we meet again."

"Thanks, Buzz. I'll need all the help I can get."

Night deepened as the DC-3 approached the flood plain of the Yellow River, another hour to the Jap lines, but no sooner had he gone over the plan once more in his mind than doubts about its viability began to nag him. Zhengzhou was Japanese-controlled; agents and spies were everywhere. It would be dangerous, likely impossible to connect with the Chinese underground. The more he thought about it, the less he liked the odds, the more absurd his so-called plan sounded. Here he was, a lowly lieutenant, traipsing up to a probably corrupt and certainly overwhelmed Chinese official asking him to provide aid and support for what? A breezy trip hundreds of miles south to Shanghai to rescue some big nose red-haired captive? A woman to boot? Oh, yes, and would you like your dumplings steamed or fried? But eluding detection in a major city on his own had a snowball's chance in hell of working. So a little town might make for a better start, some inconspicuous place in the countryside.

He patted the parachute he had brought along. Just snatched it up without thinking, really, happy something in his brain was working right. Instinct, he supposed. That same instinct told him to jump right away. By this time everybody else except the pilots was asleep. He double-checked the chute for any defects, inserted his arms through the straps, looped the pack over his neck and unlatched the door.

Deep shadows from a dim half-moon blurred the landscape below except for a dark rise that loomed on the horizon. The wind howled louder than a horde of demons. The men inside stirred. This was it. Good riddance to the Dalbys and Harrisses. He said a prayer of thanks to the dead Chinese soldier and to the mystic Hindu woman—she was not a bitch, Buzz, he thought one last time—opened the door just enough to squeeze through, then gave himself to the spirits of the middle air.

CHAPTER 21

The Sage works anonymously. She achieves great things but does not wait around for praise – Lao-tze

She couldn't trust them. As the sun rose high above the eastern hills, Su Li reluctantly lugged herself across the fields back to the village to ensure the farmers had removed any trace of the devil dwarves. They expected her guidance. Sung in particular looked to her for direction. The wounds in her hip and calf pulsed as if a torturer probed them with a knife. She walked with a slight limp and used a bamboo staff, but she was stronger and had called on secret healing practices the monks taught her, Taoist teachings that seemed like magic to outsiders, ways the mind commanded the body's functions. Her strong spirit responded to these and to the ritual ablution in the river.

When she reached the center of the hamlet, she rolled her eyes in exasperation. Many still had not returned from their hideouts. Those who had milled aimlessly, too demoralized to do more than gape in bewilderment at the pile of putrid Japanese corpses.

"Master Lao, we have been awaiting your commands."

Sung greeted her with relief. He came from a moderately wealthy family and had been educated by a tutor. Su Li relied on his intelligence, but today he was beside himself and anxious. He ignored Qiu Xiquan, the second richest man in the village, who had mustered a group of obsequious supporters, and called to the others. "Come gather round. Master Lao is here."

She leaned on the walking stick and waited until the agitated villagers quieted. Silent fear clung to their eyes. The men awaited reassurance from her despite her youth. Most regarded her as a spirit in human form. She no longer tried to deny their credulity for it made the work easier.

"The first thing you must do is find those in the tunnels or in the forest and tell them it is safe to return."

"What do you mean safe? The Japanese will come again. Next time in greater force," said Qiu, long an advocate of appeasement as a way to supplant Sung as the *Fung Shieh-hua*. "Not even your formidable skill can defeat that many."

"The invaders became suspicious when they saw no one. You disobeyed my instructions."

"Sung was away when the barbarians came. Visiting his daughter. Qiu told us to hide," a man hollered. "He said they were coming to kill us."

"It is high time we stopped this charade," the jealous Qiu interjected, two wives and one concubine, with heads bowed, attending him. He wore his best brocade coat, arms crossed and hands concealed in the wide sleeves, and strutted back and forth like a rooster with his hens. "We must stop listening to this outcast." He sneered the words at Su Li while pulling on his droopy mustache. "It is time to make overtures to the Japanese."

"No!" Sung responded firmly. "Master Lao has helped us for nearly two years now and we have lost few lives to the fighting. I trust his wisdom." Though affluent by village standards, he dressed simply and had one wife. The poorer farmers respected him for his integrity; he was a true follower of Confucius' teachings. "He cured my son. And he has healed you and your children."

The tide turned against Qiu. Furious, he ground his teeth and stalked off with his harem in tow.

"Gather the others," Su Li said. "Then collect all that is left of the barbarians. Weapons, uniforms, anything. Bury it and burn their bodies out in the fields. Plow under the ashes. The Japanese will indeed return. But they do not know where their patrol went or where it disappeared. Other villages are not far. They will look there also. When they visit us again, it will be as before — they will see mainly the old, the helpless, the sick. And we will have a few baskets of grain ready for them. Do you understand?"

"*Gung ho!*" cried Sung.

Work together. Indeed, she was thinking, as she hobbled back to her house. The thunder of artillery rumbled across the sky. The farmhands in their winter gardens lifted their heads in fear. An omen? Even a Shaolin could trick devils only so many times.

CHAPTER 22

Weapons are the tools of fear – Lao-tze
The same day.

Howitzers. If that's reveille I'm a monkey's uncle, thought Ellison, the distant thunder shaking him awake. His trajectory had carried him onto a rise in wooded foothills where the parachute caught in the branches of a tree. Too dark and too high to attempt a descent, he decided to hang there until dawn. The night had lashed him with an arctic wind and wolves howled to the west. Worst of all was a dimly-remembered dream of his father on the edge of his wakefulness. Like a continuously adjusted artillery barrage zeroing in on its target, his still fuzzy mind alternated between memory and fantasy, trying to fix on some center of truth, while another part of his consciousness kept wondering why a dream about the old man here, why now?

Sundays had always started with church, held outdoors in the threshing square. In the midst of Abraham Ellison's little flock, he customarily sat by his mother during the sermon while the minister explained God's intentions for each of them. But on Saturdays and often during the week, his father worked along with the farmers, clearing rocks, planting, harvesting, while he, Lian and other children sometimes helped but mostly played games. In hindsight, he realized Abraham Ellison, raised on a farm, was sharing what he himself had learned from his own father about growing food.

It must have been frustrating to try to change farming practices a thousand years old, he thought. For all his moralistic crap, his father cared about those people. But dreams were for sissies, he used to say. Right.

From his vantage point — he estimated it about a hundred feet higher than the plains — he could see a sliver of the Yellow River far to the north where it made a great bend to the east then south, the River of Sorrows, the *Huang He*, where Chinese civilization arose. Closer in, a small river cut through deltas of yellow-brown loess extending to the horizon under a green mantle of millet seedlings, the Luoyang plains. Even closer, he fancied he could see flags flying above a Japanese fort. Somewhere between here and the tributary, there would be a hamlet or a small town where he could orient himself, locate the enemy lines and the position of any Chinese defenders or guerillas. By the time he flexed his half-frozen limbs and got the blood pumping, the barrage stopped; he found his knife, cut the chute bindings, and shimmied down the last ten feet of the trunk. His legs demanded a few knee-bends. Still troubled by bits and pieces of the dream, he hoisted his pack, checked the terrain, and headed in the general direction of the artillery rounds.

He had no sooner quickened his stride when a rustle in the undergrowth put him on guard. A peasant woman popped up from the bushes, her hair streaked with gray and twisted in a conical shape. Around her neck a chain necklace hung above a cotton coat and a blue apron, torn from brambles. She gawked slack-jawed, as if her worst nightmare had materialized.

153

He called out in Chinese. "Don't be afraid." Not a muscle moved, as if she were part of the forest itself. "I'm a traveler." She slowly lifted her hands over her head. "No, no. I won't hurt you. I'm an ally, a friend. Of China." He was unsure if she understood anything he was saying.

Her eyes opened even wider. He gestured encouragingly. At last the wary woman moved from her cover and approached, a frightened, doubtful look on her face. Fingers tweaked his nose and touched his hair, as if to reassure herself they were real.

"You are a big nose. I did not believe such as you existed." Her mouth hung open once more. "And you speak our language!"

Ellison laughed. "Yes. A foreigner. I need your help."

The crone stood transfixed for a while then found her voice. "Ah, you are a sorcerer. Please do not cast a spell on me."

He paused, frustrated. "Not if you lead me to your village."

She scrutinized him a minute longer; reassured at last, she motioned him to follow her through the sparse tangle of fallen branches and brush. At the tree line where the stony foothills ended, she bent an arthritic finger toward tiled rooftops a mile away. On a dirt track a man was hurrying in their direction. The crone stepped onto the footpath.

"Qiu, is it safe to return?"

The man stopped and came over to them. "Have you not heard, dim-witted slave? The *gao ming*," he said the last two words derisively, "has slain the soldiers and says it is thus. But, old Ping, who is this?" His eyes shifted to the soldier, as if he had not noticed but Ellison was certain he had.

"Ellison. Lieutenant James Ellison." He held out his hand but the richly dressed man ignored it.

"You are a foreigner from the West? A soldier. Hmmm. I have heard of your kind. I have been to towns. Even to Luoyang. I am an educated man. I know about such as you." Qiu examined him with care. "You speak Chinese, eh?" His eyes narrowed. "Do the Japanese know you are here?"

Ellison did not like his attitude. Too many questions. "I could use directions, honorable sir."

The man waved in dismissal. "I have business." He left without another word but kept turning his head around to look at them.

"The Japanese must have left," Ping said.

"Japanese?" Ellison was startled.

"They came two days ago. The second time this year." She gave him a gap-toothed grimace. "Last time they killed two of us. So this time we hid. It is not what the wise one taught us," she said. "Qiu ordered us to. Do not pay attention to him. He wouldn't recognize a wizard if the gods themselves showed him one."

Ping led him through a field where men were digging pits. Naked bodies lay heaped beside them. He guessed there had been a plague or an outbreak of disease and began to doubt whether his plan to seek a rural location was such a good idea after all. Up ahead, copses of fruit trees bordered a village, clumps of brick homes, each with small plots in back, demarcated by walls of stones, where cabbages and beans and peas flourished. Here and there, low gnarled oaks shaded the bare ground.

An urchin playing with his spinning toy was the first to see them. He ran away from them, shouting his lungs out. Ping and Ellison marched into the center of a village that seemed to have existed for centuries, about forty old stone and wood buildings strung out along rolling hills, the lanes between them packed dirt. Word of his arrival spread and a crowd gathered around the well in the center. Even the field workers in their thick jackets laid down their tools to see the stranger. Old men with long stringy beards and wild thin hair emerged from the narrow alleys between the houses, excited at the spectacle. The women held back, frightened, gawking at him with disbelief while Ping regaled them with her tale, making certain they understood she had found and taken possession of an item of great importance. When he displayed the miniature Chinese flag and greeted them in their own language, they jumped backward as if he had uttered an incantation. Everyone wanted to touch his red hair to make sure he was real. It baffled them.

The hubbub subsided when a dignified older man in a neat black cap emerged from the crowd. He made a slight bow at Ellison. "I am Sung. Head of this village."

He returned the bow. "Honorable sir, I am a traveler in need. A soldier from one of China's allies."

"Allies may be bought and sold. Friends are beyond price."

"Indeed. I count myself more than a friend of China, my adopted motherland."

Sung followed raised bows with a slight bow. "You speak Chinese well enough. If you are a friend of China, I am pleased to welcome you."

Ellison let out a breath of relief. "You honor me, Master Sung. I am a pilot who —."

Sung held up his hand, then gestured toward the bodies Ellison had passed. "After we are done we will listen to your story." He clapped his hands. "We have work to do," he shouted. "Return to the digging."

"How did these men die?" Ellison asked Ping as the others returned to their grisly burial detail or scoured the little town of any evidence of the invaders.

"Sung says the wise one killed them."

"Wise one?" He could feel his visceral skepticism of anyone claiming to be "wise" putting him on alert but kept his misgivings to himself.

"He is very powerful. A spirit from the ancient gods. So I believe anyway." Ping had seen one of her friends and drew Ellison along to show him off. "He might be able to help you. Sung will tell you where he lives and what to do. Sung approves of the wise one."

His anxiety deepened.

CHAPTER 23

How you do anything is how you do everything – Zen saying

"I cannot do it." Hui wriggled with impatience.

She glanced out the corner of her eye at the stranger. Tall and fair-skinned. From the Western armies. She had never been this close to one. Like most Chinese, she shared an innate hostility to soldiers and shuddered. Better a flood, better a plague of locusts, better a drought than an army, whether Japanese or Chinese. Natural disasters did not disembowel pregnant women, bury people to their necks with heads coated with honey to attract ants, decapitate rows of them for mere sport. To die of old age was the stuff of legend in China, it happened so seldom anymore. Soldiers. She wanted to spit in the man's face.

At least he was alone. Perhaps he was a mercenary attached to the routed Chinese army, cut off from his unit, and had by chance stumbled across her refuge. He would soon see nothing worthwhile and move on. She decided to continue and knelt at eye level to adjust the boy's grip on the bow. Hui had a way of testing her discipline. At times she indulged him; at other times, she was as harsh as any master. Both emotions came to a head during the archery lesson.

She was twelve that day, when she first asked the Master to try his personal bow. They were training beneath a long, open-sided pavilion, built outside the monastery walls for weapons practice, where she took instruction every week. Her last growth spurt left her almost as tall as he was. She hit the target each time with the smaller-sized bow.

"Master, I am hungry for more," she said.

"Who am I to say you are not ready for a fuller portion?" he replied with an amused smile.

She took the magnificent weapon, and as he must have known, was able to draw it only half way and handed it back, red-faced. She realized then for the first time his method of teaching her the most important lessons, those on how one must live each day, was to allow her to learn from experience.

"Who knows what the limits of human effort are?" he continued. "Men and women are capable of far more than they can imagine."

He took the bow, went to a position well wide of the pavilion where he started to run and shoot, perpendicular to the target. Before he stopped on the other side, a volley of six arrows pierced the center of the target at the same time.

Her eyes widened. "Someday, I will shoot like that, my dear Master."

"I believe it, tiger-daughter."

"Let the arrow fall like a piece of ripe fruit from a tree or a petal from a flower." The same words Po had used with her a hundred times.

"But I hit the target." Hui peeked at the stranger.

"Yes. That is true. A good start, my son."

The child was probing her, trying to read her thoughts, a power she sensed from their first meeting and had experienced many times since. She threw up a mental wall and warned him to stop. The soldier could not be allowed to interrupt the lesson. Her hand passed before the boy's face to regain his attention.

"The manner of an act is as important as the outcome."

"It is too hard to do what you say."

"All worthwhile endeavors are difficult at first," she replied sharply. "You learned that from the spirit-father, surely." The stranger stood motionless, a puzzle. His respectful silence was disconcerting. A tickling suspicion grew that his presence was not an accident. "Remember the proper address," she said in a low voice. She wore her tan ceremonial robe with a large stylized hand painted on the back and her customary black skull cap. She had no fear the foreigner could see through her disguise but the boy might blurt out a clue. To keep his adopted mother's identity secret was more a game to him than a life or death necessity, yet he was wise far beyond his years and in any case she had no choice but to trust him.

Hui nocked an arrow and drew the bowstring to his cheek. It took all his strength, his hands and arms quivering from the strain. Still on one knee at his side, she touched his elbow. He relaxed his grip and released the arrow.

"See? When you become one with the bow, the effort becomes effortless. That is what I learned at your age, from my Master."

The boy smiled with pleasure, lowered the bow, unable to resist his curiosity, and turned to the man. The child's mouth opened wide with astonishment. The soldier bowed slightly and grinned.

"Hui, pay attention!" she commanded. "The lesson is not finished."

"Effortless effort? What is that?" he complained. "I don't understand. Show me, father."

Before she could respond he ran to the tree where her own larger, intricately carved bow was leaning against the trunk. A copy of Po's own ancient and mighty weapon, throughout her journey east she had disguised it or hidden it from potential thieves. Torn between the desire to discipline the boy and the need to show him what she meant, she took the weapon and the quiver with an exaggerated glower. By an instinct that eluded her, the boy had maneuvered the situation to obtain what he wanted. She bristled at his frequent stratagems yet they amused and delighted her as well, in ways she did not entirely appreciate.

"Please, my esteemed father."

"Hui!" The old hermit had spoiled him. Discipline would have to be increased. Later. For now she had no choice.

She strung the compound bow. Despite the evening shadows, she could see with utter clarity the white circle painted on a pine tree a good fifty paces away. It shone in her mind's eye as bright as a lantern, two or three times as large as it truly was. She took an arrow from the quiver on her belt, nocked it and drew it back, settling into a trance-like focus. The arrow hovered, a near perfect stasis of tension within a triangular axis of wood and sinew, then sped away faster than an eye-blink. When she lowered the bow, Hui was holding the foreign soldier's hand.

"Come and see, *kao pi tzuh.*" The child grinned mischievously. In the next instant he was skipping along the pathway toward the target, the soldier in tow.

After a long day of incessant introductions and explanations in the village, Ellison had decided he needed to meet the "wise one." Sung's directions took him along a beaten path toward a shallow river whose water flowed from a cleft in the mountains then curved around a narrow stretch of land that separated it from the village. Mostly the terrain differed in striking ways from the flat land and meandering stream he had known as a boy. Here the households stretched along a bluff above the water. To the east lay its main source of livelihood where steps cut into ancient limestone accessed cultivated plots on hillsides, terraced level after level by retaining walls of hewn stones, now crowned by an orange halo of evening sunlight.

Among the reeds along the bank, women washed their clothes, pounding them on rocks as if they hated cloth. Farther back, dyers had left strips of blue cotton spread on pea gravel to dry. Elsewhere old men collected tobacco to season on straw mats in the weak winter sun. They gaped in disbelief as he passed. Further on he paused near a fish dam—interlocked triangles of wood and bamboo slats — where fishermen in sampans directed black cormorants with tethers around their long necks to dive for fish. The leashes kept them from swallowing the fish. When the birds caught one, the men pulled them back into the boats and retrieved the fish from their gorged throats.

The sun was setting. Tired and worried about where he might stay the night, he veered away from the water on a faint track that took him through a copse of trees, and finally into a glade where a gnarled willow with huge twisted branches towered over a stone slab-roofed house. In front, someone had laid out a garden studded with peas, beets and cabbage in an intricate geometrical design. Hardy shrubs marked each point of the compass. He called out. No one answered but he heard voices in the rear and went to investigate. Ten paces beyond the back of the house, an archery lesson was under way at the head of an irregular alley that extended into the scrub forest. A man in a ceremonial robe was teaching a small boy how to shoot. Ellison stood still and observed, certain the bowman had noticed him though not acknowledged his presence. The whole scene resembled a tale from some ancient Chinese fable.

It sounded strange to hear himself called "high nose" by the child, the light mocking phrase for a foreigner. At the end of the practice range they found one waist-high target, empty. Ellison nodded, unwilling to embarrass the strange archer whose puzzling face was a smooth-skinned mask, both hard and soft, with a curious androgynous tendency to shift shapes. A large gash with a scab marred the forehead along with bruises elsewhere on the face, evidence of a fight. The eyes impressed him the most. He had not seen such penetrating eyes since Calcutta.

"Not this target, high nose. That one."

The arrow had landed dead center in a circle just above head height. Ellison was astonished. Impossible. It had to be luck.

"You wonder about my father's sight? He can see better than anyone," the boy said. "I am Hui." He bowed.

"And I am James." Ellison returned the bow. "Lieutenant James." The boy had read his mind. What the heck? he marveled.

"This is James, Father."

"Forgive my intrusion, honored sir." Ellison turned to the archer, projecting his best imitation of Chinese manners. "But the honorable Sung sent me. I am looking for Master Lao."

The strange teacher lowered the bow. "There is no Master —."

"Do it again, *baba*," the boy interrupted and tugged at his sleeve. Irritated, the parent waved him away but the child persisted. "As the Master taught you. So that I might learn better. Please." His eyes twinkled with mischief.

"Please excuse my son's manners. He has not yet learned how to wait."

"I would be honored to see a further demonstration of your skill," Ellison said.

In the hazy twilight, the target was well-nigh invisible. Feet wide apart, the archer drew an arrow, the robe's soft colors blending with the dusky light, a blurred outline that might vanish at any time. Ellison noticed the eyes narrowed to slits, all sensory awareness concentrated in a tight beam. In the space of a breath, the nock was at an ear and the arrow gone as if it had not even been aimed. Twice as fast another flew in the same way, each unhurried movement executed with such fluidity they seemed a single motion. The trio walked down the aisle of trees to examine the results.

"There is no *Master* Lao," the archer announced without turning.

"But they said, the wise one they spoke of . . . ." The sight before him cut him short. The most recent arrows protruded on either side of the first one, touching at the target's center. The archer reached up, pulled them out and returned them to the quiver while the boy beamed.

"See. I told you he could do it. My father is the best."

"Quiet! You have misbehaved enough for three days. Run along and prepare tea." The excited boy skipped ahead like a fairy in the falling darkness.

"Your skill exceeds that of mere mortals."

"A wise man sees as children do, with the eyes of wonder. As for me, I am not yet wise. I have seen my Master — the one who taught me — split the first arrow with the second, and the second with the third. Blindfolded. Because he had perfect peace within."

"I don't believe that's possible," Ellison blurted. "Even for a Master. Do you have perfect peace?" *Oh, shit.* "Pardon me, master archer. It is an unworthy visitor who instructs his host."

"And what would you know about peace, soldier?" The bowman's pace quickened before he could answer.

He persisted and caught up in front of the house. "Why do the villagers call you Master Lao?"

"*Lao Pei Hsing?*"

"Old hundred names. The common people."

"You must not address me as 'Master.' I am not worthy of such a title."

He held out his hand. "Lieutenant James Ellison, US Army Air Force."

The archer ignored his offer and instead motioned in the direction of the village. "The farmers are children. Despised by those in authority in China. So they have no one to help them. The enemy lines are east and across the river. Patrols cross to barter for supplies. Mostly they rob and destroy and rape. Sometimes Chinese traitors come with them to tempt the ignorant with opium. I have taught the villagers to resist its lure."

"They are surviving better than most I've heard about."

"You see the ancient tree there? Its wood is too twisted for furniture and too pithy for burning. Its leaves offer nothing useful and its seeds are bitter. Thus men have let it stand. I have shown them how to appear like the tree. When the government controlled this territory, few county or provincial officials came here, even the police. They deemed it too poor and unimportant for their attention. Which simply meant the morsels we offered were too tasteless and too small to fill the appetite of their corruption. I convinced old hundred names this condition was an advantage, not a thing to be lamented, similar to the old tree. Even the Japanese leave us relatively alone."

"I see," he said.

"Not completely alone." The face, turned steely once again, motioned toward the door.

The house consisted of two rooms, a lattice of bamboo and cloth between them, one for sleeping, the other for everything else. In the main room Hui had stoked the fire in the stone cooking hearth along one wall against the night's cold. A rough wood table and benches for meals stood in the center over a floor of rushes. Thick green tea in porcelain cups mingled its aroma with oil from a lamp. On the opposite wall below a shuttered window, a smaller table was stacked with leather-bound books, old scrolls, loose papers, and various writing instruments. Growing up, Ellison had never applied himself to written Chinese. The language had no phonetic alphabet, and the number of ideographs, which were symbols and not sounds, seemed daunting; so while his limited reading knowledge prevented him from recognizing the names of the volumes, their mere presence astonished him. The child sat on a wood stool at the rough desk, brush in hand, absorbed in some kind of writing. The walls were decorated with long poems in exquisite calligraphy. Each item in the room was neat and clean with an overarching sense of propriety. He had stumbled upon a tiny school in the middle of nowhere. It reminded him of his mother.

His host, who had disappeared into the bedroom, emerged again, changed into a simple tunic and trousers of undyed cotton; around his neck hung a thin cord with the tai chi disk. He motioned Ellison to sit before proceeding to serve clay bowls with noodles and vegetables filled from an iron pot hung over the hearth along with a wooden platter of dried persimmons.

"Hui. Come."

The boy sat next to Ellison who removed his commissary hat. When Hui saw the red hair, his mouth hung open; his parent raised a single finger to silence what was coming next. He squirmed but bowed his head, chastened. A nod and both of them took a bite with chopsticks and chewed. They took a long time to swallow.

"We give honor to the food by chewing it without haste." The curious look on Ellison's face received an answer. "My Master once said enlightenment is to eat when you are hungry and sleep when you are tired."

"How is that different from what people do every day? I guess I still don't know your name."

To Ellison the simple beauty of the medallion embodied the mystery of his host. He studied the face before him, found it impossible to guess its age. With a fine nose and thin lips, it would be counted handsome in certain cultures — or even beautiful. The realization made him uncomfortable.

"Honor the food, soldier."

The command settled the dispute. They finished the meal in silence. When they were done, a lifted hand signaled the boy to clear the dishes and return to his writing table. "Now, foreign soldier, what has brought you here?"

The memories swelled so intensely Ellison was afraid he might choke. He gathered his thoughts and in swift order brought the story of the past five years up to the present. "I have learned the Japanese took many women captives to this eastern front. I want to find out, once and for all. Even if they're dead. Though I believe my mother is alive. In Shanghai, likely." He waited for a response. "Master Sung said you might be able to help me." The eyes looked past him. "I'm not sure how to find them but I won't give up. Even if I die trying." Minutes passed. Not a sound came from the aloof archer. *Fuck this. I'm getting nowhere.* Frustrated, he gritted his teeth, got up and walked out.

Under the dawn-like flood of a full moon Ellison followed the creek to where it flowed into the river. A bit of a self-righteous prick, he thought. Not likely to get any help here. Yet there was something about this person, some force. He couldn't quite figure it out. The place was almost spooky with energy. In the moonlight, the slow current sparkled like a diamond-studded belt.

An embroidered shape on the back of his jacket that seemed to glow with its own light compelled Su Li to follow him out the door.

"The symbol on your coat," she called to him.

He stopped and turned. "My good luck charm? *Fei hu.*"

Her legs quivered. Her ears rang. It took all her mind control to regain her composure. "What is a flying tiger?" She spoke the words slowly and deliberately.

The soldier explained the story of Claire Chennault's band of pilots, the first to carry China's air war to the Japanese, and how his uncle had given him the jacket, that this particular insignia was not the same as the true tiger shark on the planes but a special one, a tiger with wings. The words were unfamiliar to her and made no sense. Her head swam and she could not focus. The scar on her forearm was warm.

The Tao appears in many forms, the Master had once told her. For you, tiger-daughter, it prefers the form of strength and courage, *laohuo.* Her heart rate quickened, aware the image was drawing her toward it, toward him. He was not her idea of a soldier. She was still surprised at how she found herself earlier wanting, needing to explain, even to boast to this strange soldier who represented the power of an alien culture, of her accomplishments.

Yet his manners and use of proverbs, though acceptable, did nothing to placate her. In fact, her countrymen's mode of speaking in platitudes that hid one's true intent was a cultural habit she had come to despise. One reason to suspect him. Moreover the tiger sign was a borrowed one. It did not prove he had courage or wisdom. She owed Sung this, to listen to the man. After that she intended to send him where soldiers always return, slaughter and death.

"So, you have lost your parents, *laowai!*" She snapped at him, exasperated at her ambivalence. "So have I. So have many. You expect me to feel sorry for you?"

"I expect nothing. I made a vow. It was called Plum Blossom Village," he whispered, looking at his boots. "I was supposed to be helping him. Plum Blossom — ."

"Return to your army and kill people," she interrupted.

He lashed out in sudden fury. "Like those dead Japanese soldiers I saw?"

She involuntarily clenched her fist. *You would deserve it if I punished you, foreigner. Not even a Chinese could comprehend what I have endured, the price I paid for those deaths.* She breathed deeply. "Tigers cannot fly. Even old hundred names knows that much."

"Your son has no mother, I see."

His words sprang out of the night like a surprise attack, ripping into her solar plexus. A mix of anger and dread stirred her adrenaline. "I am his mother . . . I mean, I have to be his mother. And his father. And his teacher. But he is not mine."

She motioned in dismissal, dismayed at an unaccustomed openness that left her vulnerable to his feints and probes, aware that in articulating the knot of her present life — the deception of daily life as a man, the torment of guilt, her troubled relationship with the boy — she herself had exposed its fragility as insubstantial as moonlight.

An owl hooted among the trees. Night birds twittered and a fish broke water but the sounds simply deepened the enveloping silence. Near their feet, whirlpools eddied toward and away from the bank, while the moon, high above the evening star, cast a wobbly reflection on the water's surface, its light a ladder that connected the earth to the heavens. The soldier followed its path from the sky, knelt, cupped his hands in the water and lifted them out as if he meant to catch hold of the moment. His fingers separated and the water flowed through them.

"You know, I think if I stayed in this place long enough, the madness in this insane world would somehow make sense." He shook the water from his fingers. "You are fortunate to live here."

She stared at him in disbelief.

"The peace you mentioned," he went on, "if a man could —."

"There is no peace here!" Her words pierced the silence, loud and discordant.

The soldier looked up sharply. The moonlight turned his features a silvery mask. He scooped up more water, this time with one hand. "When did you lose your parents?"

The hairs on the back of her neck stood up; her skin tingled. Mere questions, words, yet they produced an actual physical discomfort in her abdomen as if he had thrown a series of punches. The soldier let the water run through his fingers once more. He was not trying to catch it after all, she realized. He understood it must pass through, like time itself. It dawned on her, the look on his face. This man had also confronted death. Conquered his fear of it. Was he using some kind of mental *wu shu* against her or had he cast some spell on her?

"To travel to Shanghai is a fool's errand," she said, arms folded tight against her chest. "I have no power to help you in this."

"Guess I'll be on my way, in that case." He stood to face her. "You obviously hate soldiers."

"I have no love for Westerners." Her eyes hurled daggers. She turned on her heel back to the house.

Ellison froze. He had heard such words before, from the woman in Calcutta. About to give up, now he knew he had found the right place, dangerous or not. The boy met them at the door.

"I wish to show the soldier what I've been working on, Father."

His parent, standing before the fire, ignored the remark.

"Lieutenant James . . . ." Hui tried hard to pronounce the words while he reached beneath a pile of rice paper rolls, produced a dog-eared book with a faded cover and held it for Ellison to see. He could not believe the title: *The Palmer Correspondence School Method of Handwriting,* the same workbook his mother had used for him growing up. Another omen? The boy offered up a sheaf of papers. On the lines he had written English words as precise and as graceful as the originals in the book

"My spirit-father — an old man, I mean — acquired the book from smugglers. Have I done well?"

Ellison traced his fingertip over the script. "This is very fine, Hui." He tousled the boy's hair.

"Thank you, high nose." The boy beamed.

"Listen, my friend, you must stop calling me that."

"May I call you *chenghongse toufa*?"

"Orange hair? I prefer *laoda*. Old Big. How about that?"

"I will call you *kui wei*," the boy responded with a shy smile.

"Big and Tall? A lot better." He turned to the boy's parent. "But does he read this? Does he know English?"

The boy's parent, now interested, shook his head. "No. He wants to learn though. I know ten or twelve words from my trips to Luoyang but cannot read your language."

"It will honor me to teach him some basics, if you will permit it and if he is willing."

"Yes!" exclaimed the boy with excitement. "Please, father."

An impulse to frown gave way to a grudging smile. "Very well. I am going to bed. Tomorrow after I conclude my business in the village we will decide what to do with you, soldier." She turned to withdraw into the other room through a curtained opening. "You are welcome to stay here this night."

The lamp burned low. Hui, tired with the lessons, put his head on his arms and fell asleep. Ellison carried him into the sleeping room and laid him on a mat next to his parent. Unwilling to sleep himself, he went outside to stare at the stars that shone with crystalline brilliance. He could make out some of the same constellations he learned as a boy, the white tiger, the azure dragon, the vermilion bird, and the black tortoise, his favorite. His work with the child brought back his mother's lessons with him.

A great loneliness swept over him, memories of his stern father, withdrawn and unapproachable, like this Master Lao. So few good times father and son had shared. Softer images of his mother drifted through his mind. He tried to recall how beautiful she was but her likeness had grown hazy. He recalled that day, though, five years ago, clearer than any in his life.

An earthquake of anger shook Abraham Ellison when he saw his wife on the ground kicked and humiliated. He tossed off his puny Japanese guards like dolls and grabbed a knife from the belt of the dead farmer at his feet. "Leave her be, you spawn of Satan!" he roared, lumbering toward the sergeant's back.

A bullet slammed into the big man's body. He staggered but lumbered on, blood spurting from the wound in his back. The Japanese lieutenant fired once more but his father's onslaught descended on the soldier like an angry bear. The knife plunged up to the hilt into the man's chest before his father collapsed.

James watched it happen in a daze, his vision still double from the rifle-stock blow to his head. He struggled upright but his skull reverberated louder than a temple bell. One thought wandered to the next. He took two unsteady steps before collapsing into unconsciousness, a marionette whose strings had been cut.

Since that time savagery had become the way of the world. He went inside and lay on a reed mat near the hearth, his pack for a pillow. There was a measure of refuge in this little dwelling. The moon, the earth beneath him, the river hummed with its truth. For the first time in a long while he slept a dreamless sleep.

CHAPTER 24

I hear and I forget. I see and I remember. I do and I understand – Chinese proverb

"Left foot kick! Higher next time. Align elbow to knee. Say it, Hui. Louder!"

Balanced on one foot, the boy shot his leg straight out from his mid-section. "Align elbow to knee."

"Align fist to heart! Strike harder."

Hui whirled and brought the edge of his palm down on a sack of dirt, propped on a tree stump. "Align fist to heart," he shouted.

"Align heart to mind," Su Li commanded, demonstrating a punch that started from her ear then exploded toward an imaginary opponent's chest. "Concentrate, Hui. Keep your balance. That's right. Now do it again!"

"Align heart to mind!" he cried. In the soft light of dawn, the boy struggled to imitate his parent, part of their morning routine to practice martial arts. He paused to catch his breath after his third try. "Won't we wake the Big Tall, Mother?"

"Pay attention! We must finish soon, then go to the village." She had to make sure the farmers erased any vestige of the Japanese and understood what needed to be done next time. It was necessary to emphasize to Sung that any more mistakes would be fatal. The lessons, like her son's, had to be repeated over and over.

"Without meditating?"

"Meditate while walking, Hui. It is good discipline."

177

"Can I play with Lin Bao, Mother?"

"Once again. Left foot kick! Align mind to breath!"

Afterwards, they walked along the river toward the village. Hui ran ahead, skipping and hopping with two feet over the puddles and ditches. She smiled in approval. He was real, she thought. The people she helped were actual families. Emei Shan and the monastery were a dream. No more than a dream. And she needed to stop clinging to false hope. The Master did not approve of clinging; he called it a Buddhist word, *trishna*. Yes, she must cast off this *trishna*.

She had allowed herself to become a foster mother in the first place as a kind of penance, in hopes that Po might forgive her, but such a trade-off was not true acceptance of the Tao. Life's river did not flow backward. Hui hurtled into her arms and hugged her. She returned the embrace. He made her existence bearable. No, more than bearable. Her son had the potential to be a true man, as Lao-tze called his ideal person. Even a great man, a leader of others. This soldier was a distraction. His presence meant nothing. He needed to depart tomorrow.

"Stand up, foreigner. You must come outside now."

Someone was shaking him. A groggy Ellison recognized the thin, goateed face and the blue felt hat — Qiu, the bloke at the edge of the forest, the suspicious one.

"What? What do you want? Where's Master Lao?"

"No concern of yours. We will deal with him and his brat later. But an important person outside wants to see you."

He stumbled out and rubbed his eyes in disbelief. Six Japanese infantrymen, their soft caps half-circled by dust flaps, had their rifles trained on him. Behind them a Japanese officer sat astride a horse.

"Goddamn you son of a bitch!" Ellison whirled to retrieve his gun but the traitor blocked his way. He whacked Qiu in the face and shoved him aside but not before the troops closed in to block the door. He hammered one but two more latched onto his arms while a third rammed his back with a rifle butt.

"You're not gonna take me!" Ellison punched and kicked anything he could reach but there were too many. A shot whistled overhead. The officer's pistol was aimed at him. He raised his hands above his head. The soldiers slammed him against the wall, expecting their lieutenant to execute the prisoner.

"Tell them, Qiu, if that's your name, I'm a downed American pilot and expect to be treated under the Geneva Convention."

"They say you are a spy, big nose," Qiu scowled. "And will be treated as such."

"I'm not a spy!" Ellison shouted, twisting to break free. "Tell them!"

But the treacherous landlord wiped his bloody lip and sneered. "He says you will tell them what they want to know. Then be put to death. The penalty for spies is death." Preening himself in his stitched green coat, Qiu clucked with self-importance, his hands concealed inside his large sleeves.

"I'm a pilot!" Ellison roared. "A pilot."

The officer, who took the measure of his prisoner with stony, hostile eyes, snapped an order to his men. A soldier pounded him in the gut with a gunstock and he staggered to his knees. The Japanese bound his hands in front and circled his neck with a rope then jerked him upright. Another soldier looped it around the saddle pommel while Qiu looked on, amused. Ellison cast a hate-filled glower at the Chinese traitor as the patrol marched away. He was as helpless as his father had been.

The minister's floppy black hat was plowing above and through the pandemonium toward the Japanese officer who had dismounted from his horse. "You can't do this," the son of Iowa farmers bellowed. "I'm a man of God, and these people are under my protection." The officer lowered his sword as if he understood, glared at the minister then turned away. Abraham Ellison spun him around. "I'm an American citizen. Do you hear me, you godless heathen?" he yelled, inches from the impassive officer. "And I will report this to our embassy."

The lieutenant, with an aristocratic face and a thin mustache, nodded a command to his soldiers who seized the taller man. He drew his riding crop and lashed Ellison's cheek again and again until his thick beard dripped with blood. Somebody help him, James called out silently, paralyzed with fear. God. Anybody. His earlier, mocking comments about his father sounded foolish.

Su Li and the child waved to farmers already in their fields hoeing weeds or spreading manure from a honey cart, but Hui was pulling on her sleeve. She stopped and noticed the troubled look on the boy's face.

"Why do you dislike this foreign soldier, *mama*?" he asked, his free hand tugging at the collar of his winter coat. She ignored him. "I like him." Hui covered his eyes with his hands and peeked through his fingers as if they could shield him from her displeasure.

She resumed walking. "He is a foreigner and a soldier."

"He is the one," Hui said gravely. "He must be."

She paused, attentive at last. "Who? And what, my son?"

"The one you've been waiting for, my Mother."

The remark startled her. "What? I never told you I was waiting for anyone."

He began to play an imaginary game with his hands as if he were no longer interested. "The old one. My first teacher and father. He foretold somebody would come, didn't he?"

She snapped her head, remembering the ghostly robe on a skeleton of a body. The ancient's words had baffled her: "You will stay as I did, until someone comes."

"Do not be impudent! If I were waiting — which I am not — it would not be for a foreign devil."

His playing stopped. Head bowed, he took her hand while they resumed their walk. "I beg your forgiveness, but he is no devil, Mother. And he has the sign of the spirit animal, *laohuo*. Like the one on your arm. The one who watches us. His hair is the same."

"I forbid you to speak to me in that manner!" Now angry, Su Li yanked him forward. "Superstitions." He winced. Tears rolled down his cheek. Stunned at her anger, she knelt to embrace him. Her fault, she thought, not the child's that she was no longer welcome at Emei Shan. It was past time to stop blaming him. "Since when does a son teach his mother?" she said softly. Her pulse beat with wonder. Impossible. It cannot be. Yet, as she held him close, filled with gratitude and a love she dare not acknowledge, a tiny door of hope opened, a door she was convinced she had closed for good.

Sullen, unhappy, the child lingered outside when they returned, his jaw set. "Will you at least help him, *mama*?" he asked.

"I have forbidden you to speak of this matter. I cannot. Even if I wanted to. Which I do not. I have obligations to those whom I protect," she continued, irritated that she felt compelled to explain herself to a child, even an extraordinary one, who had no business even commenting on her plight. But the soldier was nowhere in sight. Departed on his own? No, something else. Some evil had happened on this ground. There. Horse hooves. Footprints. Soldiers. Japanese.

"Forgive me, mother," he said. "I—."

She touched her finger to her lips.

CHAPTER 25

Bring me my bow of burning gold – William Blake

What was worse than having no hope? Torture? Torture for sure, though hopelessness was a kind of torture. Death? Maybe not. Hopelessness was a sort of living death; so, worse in that it went on and on for who knew how long whereas when you die, it's over, once and for all. He would get to experience all three if his captors had their way. Death would be welcome; he would seek it out, do his best to ensure it occurred before torture. No more time for self-pity, even if he had come further than he imagined he could. Even if he had been blindsided, thwarted by some jealous, greedy bastard who had nothing to do with what was important.

But he had to stop this daydreaming, this ridiculous attempt to grade the levels of despair and find comfort in it, or at least make the time pass, for he needed to focus on each step. Twice he had stumbled on rocks that jutted out beneath a thin layer of sandy soil. Immediately the lieutenant, who rode at the column's head and usually kept his mount at a slow but steady pace, spurred the horse's flanks. For agonizing yards the animal dragged him over the stony ground like a log while he clutched the rope with both hands. He thought his neck would snap. Focus meant ignoring the mass of cuts and bruises the ground and the guards had inflicted on his body and the burning sensation in his throat. Focus meant fixing on the lieutenant's sword that hung from his belt. The last time he had seen such a weapon, it had cut off the head of Lian's father. It wouldn't happen to him, he vowed to himself. He would die first and take the bastard with him.

A low overcast descended on the column. The men veered inland through scrub forest and thickets after taking a turn away from an ill-defined path that ambled near the river's bank. From time to time he tilted his head back and opened his mouth to catch moisture from the intermittent drizzle. No stops for food; no one offered water. The soldiers plodded in silence, accustomed to hardship and afraid of their superior's anger, their steps muffled by the fog.

As daylight faded, the lieutenant led the troop into a rough circle of trampled waist-high brush and grasses surrounded by a thick wall of trees. A cook was preparing food over an earthen fire pit. Under the watchful eyes of guards, a few conscripts from nearby villages were arranging baskets of vegetables suspended at the ends of long bamboo poles. Other hostages piled burlap sacks of grain near four mules tethered to trees, all the results of the day's foraging missions by other parts of the platoon.

A soldier moved to take the horse's reins to tether it with the mules, but the lieutenant, who had dismounted, cursed him for forgetting to release the prisoner's rope from the saddle. The soldier froze, cowered in fear under the blow from the flat edge of his superior's sword. In short order, two soldiers slammed Ellison on his back, spread-eagled, drove wooden stakes in the ground and tied one wrist to each of them. He did not resist, content to save his strength. Tomorrow when they untied him, he would grab the nearest gun and go down fighting. No way was he going to their torture chambers. Hopelessness be damned.

After their meal, the infantrymen, fifteen in all, stowed their tin mess cups in their packs and laid out blankets for sleep. By and by two came over to him, smoking cigarettes. They kicked his ribs and legs over and over and eventually pissed on him. He thought he would black out when a shot whined above the men. Out of his tent and pistol in hand, the officer spat harsh commands at the soldiers who shrank back to their bivouac. He inspected the remainder of his troops then after a few minutes withdrew into the tent.

Across the campsite the Chinese peasants huddled close to the mules and slept. One soldier guarded them. A second stood watch at the point where the column had entered. A third squatted near the larger trail that led southeast, their route the next day. The rest lay beneath blankets near the fire, exhausted from the day's hard march. Night thickened. Voices ebbed to whispers, then to silence. Hungry and thirsty, he closed his eyes. He had failed his mother and Lian, failed himself. A profound weariness overtook him and he drifted off into a troubled sleep.

He was a boy running through fields he did not recognize, covered with broom, furze and wild flowers. A Chinese girl ran ahead, picking flowers and putting them in a basket. Now and again she looked at him but her features were not Chinese but Hindi. She spoke but her words were incomprehensible. Her voice sounded like an owl. The next time she turned back to him, she hooted.

He woke from the dream. In the dying fire's light, the sentries dozed at their posts at either end of the camp. Across from him, the prisoners snored, packed together like a pile of firewood. His head rolled to the left. The soldier at the north edge had vanished. Ellison blinked, afraid he was disoriented. No, he was sure of it. The guard was there a second ago when he awoke. Relieving himself? Yet he had looked sound asleep. He turned his head to the right. A wiry filament curled around the neck of the other sentry who was slumped against a tree, his hands reaching for his throat until the forest sucked him in. He strained to check on the third and final guard, the one near the farmers, awake now. Before the man could call out an arrow rammed between his teeth and out the back of his skull.

The body slumped over onto the peasants who stirred and cried out. Groggy soldiers tore off their blankets, reached for their Arisaka 38 rifles, rolled to their knees, their sergeant shouting orders. Two arrows pierced two more necks in succession. The bewildered defenders fired blind volleys in the general direction of the arrows in a futile attempt to hit something.

From the opposite side, shiny objects hurtled across the campsite and lodged in the backs of two more Japanese. They jumped to their feet and howled, reaching in vain for the poisoned stars, staggered like drunks then crumpled. Panic-stricken, the remaining troops continued to shoot wildly at the shadows. A mule, wounded by a stray bullet, brayed louder than a demon unleashed from hell, prompting the Chinese prisoners to shriek even louder. The lieutenant, now out of his tent, fired his gun into the air; his shout, barely heard above the chaotic chorus of mules, dying and wounded soldiers and screaming conscripts, ordered the rest of his men to flatten on the ground while he kicked dirt on the fire. An arrow sank into his shoulder.

Silence. No one moved, the sole sound an intermittent bellow from the wounded mule. As the seconds passed, faint moonlight filtered through the cloud cover. An owl hooted. Its mate echoed the call. Three quick serpent-hiss exhalations came from a different location than before, the arrow points flashing in the moonlight, almost too fast to see, preceding three cries of agony. Then the glint of two more spinning stars. Bedlam erupted once more. The mules brayed at the top of their lungs. Mad with fear, the horse whinnied, bucked, snapped its tether and galloped into the brush. Shouts erupted. Angry, frantic outbursts among the soldiers were punctuated by their commander's heated voice. Ellison could make out punches, then footsteps running toward the south trail. The invisible attackers were too much for the superstitious foot soldiers, the last of them now racing for their lives. The lieutenant fired off two more rounds, not at the unseen enemy; he was shooting at his own men. Silence.

Visible now under the thinning overcast, the wraith-like officer, crouched over with a pistol in his good hand, cocked his head from side to side and backed in a circle.

From the void a shadow wrapped him up from behind, bound him, and threw him to the ground. Out of the darkness a torch flashed and descended into the fire pit and a pyramid of flames blazed. A black clad figure, bow slung over his shoulder and a quiver of arrows strapped to the waist, bent to cut Ellison's bonds.

"Who are you?" he croaked through parched lips. The hood lifted. "Lao?" He rubbed his limbs to restore his circulation. "Water. Could I have water?" The archer retrieved a canteen, handed it to him.

"Lie quiet until I come back." His rescuer trotted over to the terrified peasants and cut them loose, giving them instructions. Some of the freed hostages started to strip the bodies of their uniforms and gear and to pile it in a heap. Others loaded each naked corpse on the mules.

"What are they doing?" he asked between deep breaths.

"We must not leave any sign of the enemy. The barbarians must never know what became of them."

"What about those who escaped?"

"They did not escape." The eyes were as hard as steel. "We must take these corpses back to the river."

"Wait. Let me go with you."

"No." The archer laughed harshly. "Stay here. Better not to witness what happens there. There is food by the fire."

Trailed by the peasants who led the mules and carried the dead soldiers' equipment, the black-clad figure disappeared into the trees, leaving the camp stripped bare except for the plunder laid along the perimeter and the groaning Japanese officer bound on the grass. Ellison crawled over to the fire and found dried strips of fish, leathery like jerky. As he chewed he tried to make sense out of what he had seen. It had happened so fast, in such dim light, it seemed like a nightmare. He held his scarred wrists up, touched the cuts on his cheek and shuddered.

Hours later the bowman emerged from the thicket along with the farmers and the unburdened mules. They tied the sacks onto the animals and hoisted the bearing baskets with their long staffs onto their shoulders. The trussed Japanese officer was folded over the rump of a mule.

"You didn't take him to the river," said Ellison.

"He is not dead. Yet."

Led by a torch bearer, the ragged line of released prisoners retraced their trek back to their villages. Meanwhile Lao knelt to examine his injuries. Fingers probed the raw wounds on his face and neck. He stiffened but found the touch much softer than expected. Gentle hands rubbed a healing salve on his torn flesh.

"I owe you my life," he rasped. "Forgive me for the trouble I have caused you."

"Not you. The traitor." The face hardened.

A movement caught his eye. Another black-clothed form stepped into the clearing from behind a tree, likely the fighter who had thrown the darts from the other end. He removed his hood. The archer, unaware, continued to apply salves to Ellison's bleeding face, but he was mesmerized by the figure, a tall, muscular Chinese man. Their eyes locked.

"What are you looking at?"

He pointed with his chin. "Over there. The man who threw the *si xing* — the death stars."

His liberator dropped the salve and walked to where Ellison had indicated, lingered a while, whispering something, but the ghost fighter had disappeared. Finally he returned to scatter the fire's last coals and spread the ashes out with branches.

"You are mistaken," The bowman appeared agitated and twice more glanced over at the forest.

I might have been seeing things, Ellison admitted. It was a night not to be believed. But, on second thought, he was positive. A person who helped save his life had vanished. Arrows, death stars, two shadows of destruction, an armed Jap platoon wiped out. This is the twentieth century, he had to remind himself.

"We must go! Now!"

"I'm ready." His legs wobbled.

The fighter caught him around the waist. "You are too weak. I will carry you."

Ellison recoiled. "Hell, no. I can walk on my own."

"You will slow us. The Chinese are used to carrying foreigners."

The sarcasm was not lost on him. "I will not be a burden to anyone."

A grunt in response. "Hold on to the back of my shirt."

The scudding clouds played hide and seek with the moonlight but his guide moved through the murky brush and trees as if it were high noon. His own eyes eventually became accustomed enough to the dark so as time passed he stumbled much less over the rocks and exposed roots. His companion set a grueling pace. Sweat poured off his brow and beneath his shirt, even though the air was cold. His thrashed, bruised body rebelled at the effort but he had no time to dwell on it. Keep going. Stay on your feet. The words became a mantra. Finally they rested. At the limit of his endurance, he sank down and leaned against a bamboo trunk, other trees and large rocks dim outlines rising out of the ground.

"Why did you come after me?"

"A matter of honor. You are my guest." His shadowy rescuer, hardly visible on a stump, handed him a leather flask of water. "Even if you Westerners are the reason China has been brought so low." The accusation surprised him but he was too exhausted to reply. "I will carry you now. You cannot walk any longer."

Ellison took a swallow, handed the flask back and heaved himself up, managing a crooked grin. "Not by all the fires of P'ing T'ing!"

Despite herself Su Li smiled at his reference to the god of fire. How would a Western soldier know anything about Chinese gods? she marveled.

Hours later, they trudged over a rocky rise above the forest floor. Pin-pricks of light danced off the river's surface, tiny diamonds that announced the sun's appearance in the east. She had set a fast pace in a heartless challenge to push the soldier to his limits. The fool deserved it for not taking her offer to carry him. If he had, she would be done with him, despise him for being weak, send him away. His hand clung to her tunic. Trying to impress her. *Surrender, soldier,* she fumed. *Allow your weary limbs to crumble.* He had already lasted longer than she expected.

At last he faltered, pitched into her and wrapped his arms around her to steady himself. His physical immediacy jolted her nerves. Her body tingled at his touch, despite her efforts to deny it. Puzzled, alarmed, she swallowed hard, unwrapped his arms, and looked intently at the weary man.

"You have courage, soldier," she mouthed so he did not hear. She was acting like a child and could not inflict her pique on him any longer. She exhaled in resignation "Come. Let me carry you. We can nearly see the house, beyond that bend where the bamboo grows and I see you cannot continue without help."

He struggled up with a crooked smile, took a step, wobbled, fell to his knees. She held out her hand. He tried to push her away but she lifted him and draped his arm over her shoulders. His scent, the feel of his body next to hers brought sensations and long suppressed emotions that confounded her as she helped him limp the last hundred paces. Once inside the house, he crumpled to the floor. She rolled him onto a mat and stared at him.

My life here is finished. She recoiled as if the idea had wormed its way up into her skull from the sleeping man.

She shook her head vehemently. That was absurd. Her imagination. Give this up? Because of a Western soldier? Because some animal urge was making her react like a foolish woman? She performed her duty. Now he had to leave.

CHAPTER 26

Of the thirty-six ways of escape, the best is to run away –
Chinese proverb

"Han?" Su Li called out.

He was gathering his weapons and stowing them in his carry sack when she startled him. Without a sound he drew back farther behind the line of trees, invisible from the Japanese campsite, unwilling to reveal his presence, still ashamed after all this time at his role in her plight.

Two months before Su Li's banishment, he had left the monastery to fight with the resistance. At first he and a dozen fellow monks fought west of Peking in loose alliance with the Communists, but relations soured. The warrior monks came to realize what hypocritical fanatics the Communists were and spread out either on their own as solitary guerillas or in small groups. He and his band were rovers, seizing opportunity to kill Japanese officials and officers whenever they could, scavenging food along the way. Sometimes they met and temporarily joined up with other former monks. A year had passed when one of them had a message for him from Po. The Master had a special request to seek out Su Li. Through the network of temples Po believed he had learned approximately where his former student had settled.

Over the past year he heard tales of a magician or holy man who possessed a special way of healing and protecting villagers, but no one could tell who this shadowy figure was or exactly where he was located. So he decided to find the truth to the rumors and moved his followers closer to the sources of the reports even as attacks and reprisals in Henan grew more vicious. Two days ago news of a Japanese patrol that had disappeared under mysterious circumstances reached him. The incident smelled of Shaolin. He found the village, its inhabitants reluctant to talk, but an old voluble woman regaled him with stories of the "wise one" who was father to a young boy and also of a foreign sorcerer with red hair.

At nightfall, he spied the child alone at the house, noticed the signs of a struggle and raced after Su Li. The owl call and the encircling tactics were part of their training together at the monastery. He ambushed and executed the three soldiers who fled from the fight and quietly awaited her return, longing to see her.

"Han? I know you are there."

He remembered how sharp her vision was and feared he had lingered too long. He could not look at her any longer or his heart would break. He turned into the darkness and with sadness in his soul cast one last message at her, hoping her mind would capture it: *You must return and make your peace with Da Shi. Before it is too late.*

CHAPTER 27

Whereof one cannot speak, thereof one must be silent —
Wittgenstein

Ellison came awake, groggy with exhaustion, and blinked until his eyes adjusted to the darkness. He sat up, aware first of the reed mat and hard earth beneath him. Through the window he could see the glow of a waning moon. He had slept the whole day. Dirty in body and soul, he needed to wash.

Outside in the chill air he stripped off his mud-caked clothes, tied them into a bundle and wrapped a blanket around his body. Twenty yards to the west the river's soft susurration beckoned. He followed the sound, stumbling through brush, disoriented by the deep shadows cast by the moon. After pushing his way through a screen of trees, he stopped short among the reeds, a few paces from the bank. In the dappled moonlight a silhouette was bending over in the shallows.

If I lived in ancient China, I would take that for a spirit. Mystified he looked more closely. If that was a spirit, it had pretty nice hips. Back toward him, it was washing. The figure glanced at him as if it knew all along he was there. Their eyes met. Unperturbed, it turned away and continued to wash. It — she — was Master Lao . . . but . . . was a woman. He gaped in amazement before covering his mid-section with the blanket.

At last she emerged from the shallows, her breasts straddling the yin/yang disk, picked up her own clothes and walked by him as if he were one of the trees. He waded into the lazy current, hoping the temperature differential would confirm he was hallucinating, that he had not just seen a human being change from one shape to another. He sloshed his shirt and trousers in the stream, wrung them out, set them on the bank, and washed himself, oblivious to the cold, unable to reconcile what he had just discovered with the events of the past two days.

And what did he see? Besides a woman who took out a Jap patrol? He put a knuckle to his forehead and closed his eyes. Before long, his body began to shiver. Back in the house, he moved the sleeping mat nearer the room where the woman and the boy slept, drawn by the *kang*'s heat but even more by her aura, palpable, disconcerting. He shifted to get more comfortable, grunted at the effort, but grateful for the earth's solidity beneath him.

What came next? He had no idea. His so-called plan had completely collapsed and likely never had a—he wanted to say "Chinaman's" — chance, but thought better of it. That was something Buzz Taylor might say, or Mazzetti. Neither of those blokes would believe what he had witnessed. But there would be a tomorrow, whereas yesterday he was sure there would not be. Thanks to him—her, he thought. And he was wrong about another thing. He—she—was not a prick. He laughed at himself, lying awake and staring at the roof until the moon faded from the sky.

The next morning, after their daybreak routine of meditation and martial arts practice, Su Li left Hui with the foreigner, who was still sleeping, and went to the village to report Qiu's treachery. Sung vowed to punish the traitor. On the way home her mind roiled with thoughts of last night's unexpected meeting at the river. It had the shape, the smell of Tao. An energy had passed between them. Something had watered a dormant flower with roots between her thighs, thrilling and alarming at the same time; and she recognized another unsettling insight that night before she fell asleep. This soldier possessed yin, the female principle. More yin than any man she had ever met. More even than the Master. When she arrived at the house, the boy had struck flint to stone and started a fire with bundles of straw in the oven. Water in a copper pot—a gift from Sung—was soon boiling. They made a meal of rice and barley gruel topped with a bit of honey from a honeycomb.

"Eat," she said, without a hint of the trepidation racing through her veins. They ate in tense silence and avoided each other's eyes.

After they finished the soldier rose to close his pack, ready to leave. "I think it's time for me to go."

"The blind man cannot see the sunrise. The deaf man cannot hear the songbird." She gauged his reaction.

He looked at her, paused. "Yet together they can accomplish much."

"I cannot help you, soldier."

"Fine." He hoisted the pack. "I owe you my life, whoever you are. For that there are no adequate words. But I wanted to say before I go, you should take this child to a special teacher. Maybe somebody such as your own master. I mean, you have done an excellent job, but . . . ."

Her pulse throbbed in her eardrums and his voice trailed off. She sat thunderstruck, keenly aware that her flimsy walls of defense had just been shaken to their foundation by an unexpected possibility, a completely different reason to return to the Golden Sun than the one she clung to so fiercely. The links in her life's broken chain—the old hermit's prophecy, the sign she never expected; her son's visions and his attraction to the Westerner; the unspoken message at the Japanese camp—joined together in a bond of sadness and excitement. The Tao was leading her back to the Master to resolve the consequences of her acts—all her actions. The long period of waiting, of despair—more than two years that seemed far longer—was drawing to an end. For good or ill, there was no way to judge. He was almost out the door. The tiger symbol on his jacket seemed to burst into flames.

"Wait!" she commanded.

He stopped.

"Sit. You have less patience than my son." He returned to the bench. "I cannot help but there is a person who can," she continued in a quieter tone. "One man who has the power to find out if your mother or your friend is alive or not. And if they are, tell you how to rescue them."

"Who, Mistress Lao . . . or whatever your name is?"

"You may call me Su Li, the name given me by the man I refer to, Grand Master Po." *Tiger-daughter,* her secret monastery name, was reserved only for Po himself.

"My apologies, Mistress Su Li. I do not wish to trouble you any further. Tell me where he is and I will find him."

"Stop this charade, soldier. You no longer want my help now that you know I am a woman." She lifted her chin.

"With respect, that knowledge makes my admiration greater." He bowed.

She made a disdainful sound. He sounded too like a Chinese, full of half-meant praise, but the expression on his face exhibited the shape of truth. "A beggar is not received in the court of the emperor. You cannot find him alone. And if you could he would not meet you. I will take you to him. Though it may be he will not see even me."

As for the stranger's quest, though an honorable one, Su Li cared little for it, nor would the Master help him. Beside the point in any case. She was returning for the boy's sake, who was rapidly moving beyond her wisdom. He belonged with the Master. She might even be forgiven. If their return helped the man, so be it. As far as she was concerned, he was no more than a vessel, a sign.

"Thank you," he said. "I am honored."

"Do not thank me yet." She said gruffly. "We will depart tomorrow morning.

CHAPTER 28

If you do not change direction, you may end up where you are heading – Lao-tze

Sung and his son came that evening to report Qiu had fled. "The Japanese will return," he warned her, "to take vengeance." War had taken its toll on the sober, upright village leader; his hair had turned grayer and worry furrows creased his brow.

"My presence poses a danger," she said gravely. "If they do, tell them the foreign soldier was aided by guerillas who went north. We intend to go south. At the very least, our flight should draw any pursuit away from our people."

"It is farewell, therefore." Sung's eyes grew misty. "Lin, say good-bye to Master Lao, who saved your life."

The boy stepped forward and bowed low. "Thank you, honorable sir. We will not forget you."

She touched his head. "You have been a good friend to my son, Lin." She turned to the father. "There are resistance fighters in the area. One is named Han. Send word that you are in need of him. Your plea will reach him, I believe. And he will help you."

"Zhang and Chen have told me they have spoken to a strange man in the last few days, a man who has asked about you. Could that be him?" Sung asked.

Su Li paused, a complicated churn of memories clamoring for her attention. "It may be. Protect our families, my noble friend."

"As best this humble spirit can. But I will miss you." He and Lin turned to go but as he left she heard him say softly, "Daughter of Lao-tze."

Before sunrise the next day, she buried her bow — her second most valued possession — at the end of the archery range. She dug a shallow grave with a spade near the practice tree.

"Good-bye, symbol of my best self. We have travelled far together, but from now on I must act the slave and leave you behind, in the care of the earth, from which we both arise."

She covered it with dirt and leaves and returned to the house, pausing outside to consider her time since she came upon the old hermit. Compassion — the Buddha's mantra — helping one's fellow humans, even saving lives, these lessons were mere words in the monastery. Here, her flesh and bones and spirit learned them by actions. The weather-beaten stones and the bent, misshapen tree lent their patient attention to her acknowledgement.

"I have become a better Shaolin, old friends, but only by leaving, do I recognize this. And it saddens me, even though I have hated you and this place too often. You have protected me and the boy. I was still a child myself when I came here. Now I am a woman. May your spirit help me bear this fate. So the Tao has determined and brought this foreign soldier here to force me to accept its ways."

That insight bothered her most as she drew a bucket from the creek and watered her garden for the last time.

The plot of vegetables and flowers, arranged in rows and layers, prompted sharp memories of the Golden Sun. How she loved those gardens. Things useful must also be beautiful, so the Master had taught her. "Why should I be surprised," she told the flowers, "the Tao sent this big nose, any more than the old wise one was amazed by me? The future will be what it is and my life here will enable me to endure it."

Later, she closed the old door for the last time. The air hovered chill and motionless above their departure, suspended over the meadows in a thin mist distilled from the dew. Shafts of sunlight slanted through the evanescing fog like golden spikes striking the brown earth. The trio wound their way along the track where Ellison met Ping a few days earlier. Stubborn peasants plowed in fields pock-marked by bomb craters and artillery shells, eager to plant crops despite a dangerous, uncertain future. Most paid no attention to the travelers.

"My plan is to head southwest. There is a long-forgotten cut through the hills," she said. "From there we can connect with the rail line to Xi'an and to Paochi. With your silver, soldier, we may find transport over the mountain passes to Chungking."

"Maybe I can report in there," Ellison said, "and fix my AWOL status. Or get shot as a deserter." He laughed.

"AWOL?" She tried to pronounce the word.

"Never mind."

When they approached a bend in the rutted dirt track, Hui stopped to stare longingly at the only place he had called home. He cast a reproachful glance at his foster mother, then resumed his march alongside Ellison, clinging sorrowfully to the soldier's hand. Beyond the next rise they lost sight of the village.

Ellison noticed the child's plight. "Try saying these English words, Hui. My. Name. Is. Hui."

Hui repeated the words.

Ellison touched his chest with his finger. "My. Name. Is. James."

Once again, Hui mouthed the English words. Ellison smiled and tousled his hair. "Good," he reverted to Chinese. "Do you want to continue?"

"Yes, Big Tall. I like these words."

And so as they walked, the Westerner spent his time practicing English with Hui. He was patient, a good teacher, she admitted. The lessons fascinated her. She deliberately hung behind and mouthed the words along with her son, strange noises, as if from another world, without music — or at least without a music she could appreciate; but Hui could. The sounds delighted him. He soon put his homesickness out of his mind.

Their journey, paralleling the river's contours, found more and more fields untended, plowed up by exploded munitions. They encountered no other travelers but smoke rose in the distance. In the afternoon they came upon a small settlement reduced to smoldering ruins. Even the dogs had disappeared, eaten by starving survivors. Three women and an old man scratched through the ashes for vestiges of their former lives.

"Kill all, burn all, destroy all. The Japanese way of making war," she said viciously. "I have tended the sick in what used to be this town."

Completely still, the soldier looked intently at the rubble for a long time, his face turned away.

"Soldier?" she called at last, twenty paces ahead.

Their route was supposed to lead them across a bridge over a narrow section of river then on to a pass that opened onto the railroad line but as they drew near a forlorn void opened where once there had been an exquisite low arch. The long center span, torn from its foundations, lay nearly submerged, jutting from the middle of the river, a huge fish out of its watery element, dead. Jagged chunks of once perfectly-cut stones were scattered on both banks and in the shallows. The moorings at either end had bowed beneath their own weight and tilted into the mud. Without the span's support, they had collapsed.

She ran her hand over a foundation block, her face contorted in fury. "I loved this bridge. It was a treasure." She choked on the words. "I sometimes came this far when I traveled to see the sick. I would sit here and simply meditate on it for hours. It has arched over this neck of the river for more than a thousand years. The master builder Li Chun built one other like it."

Ellison walked with the boy to the water's edge and examined the wrecked blocks of masonry. "Explosives. They blew it up." He surveyed the rest of the tumble of hewn stone. "I see what you mean. The workmanship."

"Did the Japanese do this?" she asked.

205

"Your own soldiers. Kuomintang. Scorched earth policy."

She looked at him without comprehension.

"Destroy anything the enemy might use."

"Even if it means whatever makes your own land worthwhile? You soldiers sicken me!" Anger boiling below the surface the whole day burst from her heart, at the war, at the foreigner. Like her own life, her country was torn apart. "That bridge was worth ten thousand soldiers."

Nobody spoke for minutes after her tirade.

"So how do we cross?" Ellison finally asked, looking around.

His question was answered by a blood-curdling yell that shattered the quiet afternoon. A horde of men swarmed out of a cave on a hill that overlooked the bend where the road flowed into the bridge. Armed with knives, swords, even hoes and shovels, they swooped down the slope, their crazed faces howling with desperation.

"Starving farmers. Cannibals." She answered the puzzled expression on Ellison's face. "Hui!" she cried. The boy was running toward her as fast as he could. "You have a gun?" she asked, her face drawn with tension. "We will need it to hold these wolves off. I am not certain I can do it alone."

Ellison drew the .45 from his pack and pushed the boy behind him. The bandits were a good fifty yards away. They slowed and fanned out, threatening to encircle their quarry and push them up against the river to cut off any escape.

"Take him. Run," he said. "Before they surround us."

Su Li wavered. She doubted even the two of them could hold off this many and to fight would put Hui in grave danger. The soldier was offering to protect her and her adopted son. But to leave him to die? There was no good choice. She raced to the frightened child, snatched him up with one arm and sprinted back along the path they had just traversed. The startled wild men did not pursue her, the foreigner their true prey.

Ellison was encircled except for the river. The Browning rested steady in his hand this time, no drunken Dragon Lady to knock him off balance. A brief glance to the north told him Su Li and Hui were safe. The ragged mob advanced with cautious steps. Some had lost limbs or were covered with ulcers and pus-oozing sores. Many cackled and hopped up and down in an insane war dance. Beasts who wanted to tear him limb from limb, crazy with starvation, they were generating the collective frenzy to charge, but the dark threat of the .45 held them in check a while longer.

One seemed to be the leader, larger than the rest with wild hair and beard and an eye missing. Like a Cyclops, scar tissue had covered the opening. He raised his arm. A signal? Ellison thought, with a calm that surprised him. Well, here's a fucking signal. He took aim and squeezed off a round. The bullet exploded into the man's chest and lifted his body off the ground. The others ducked, retreated. Minutes later their macabre war dance resumed, a pack of hyenas howling themselves into a fury. How long before they realized if they rushed all at once, they had him? He weighed his chances as he backed right up to the river's edge. He was not a strong enough swimmer to make it across and could no longer see Su Li and Hui. The water lapped over his boots.

At last Su Li set the boy down. The outlaws were well upstream, but she was unsure of what to do. Would the crazy men kill the soldier and then come after them?

"Mother, look," Hui said and pointed to two men in a sampan, just offshore.

She called out to the fishermen. "We need your help."

The men ignored her.

"Help the soldier, Mama!" Hui's eyes blurted tears. "Don't let them kill him, please!"

She hesitated. It would be wrong to abandon someone who had put his trust in her, not if there were any other way. Besides, she was responsible for him. "We—the man back there by the bridge. He can pay!"

No response.

"He has a pack full of money," she cried. It got their attention.

"Silver!" One man called out. "No Kuomintang money."

"Yes, yes. Don't let the outlaws steal it all." The two fishermen responded as if motion was an effort.

"Opium," she yelled and pulled out a packet Ellison had given her in case they were separated. She waved it at them. "He has plenty of it." When they realized what she held in her hand, they glanced at each other and began poling toward shore. "Hurry! Hurry!" She snatched Hui in her arms and waded out toward the boat.

Ellison fired two more rounds. Two more bandits fell but death held little fear for creatures half-dead. He guessed there were eighteen or so left and he would run out of ammunition before he could reach the extra clips in his backpack.

"You won't get me you bastards," he shouted, and splashed further into the river, the bottom growing squishy beneath his feet. They advanced warily, half-crazed eyes intent on their prey. He doubted they could swim at all. So when it came to it, he would take to the river; death from drowning was better than falling into their clutches. He stumbled on a rock and lost his balance but caught himself on his knees just as they rushed him. He got off another shot. A ragged man fell a yard from the bank, so close the blood spattered his jacket. The weapon still held a power over the herd which halted its mad charge and retreated again, furious, taunting, gesturing at him with threats of every variety of horrible death.

"Soldier!" Su Li was directly behind him. Ten yards out in the river she beckoned from a sampan with two fishermen and the boy. "Swim!"

Ellison scrambled to his feet and plowed deeper into the current, stuffing the gun into his pack. Before the water reached his waist he tossed it to Su Li and swam for his life. Their prey about to escape, the feral pack of men howled and stampeded. One of the bandits who wielded a rusty sickle charged in after him, hacking away wildly before he tripped and disappeared below the surface but was able to latch onto a boot before Ellison could escape. He kicked furiously but the hand would not dislodge and the man's weight was pulling him under. Ellison held his breath, eyes open. He could see the raider was panicking, his mouth agape, taking in water. The clumsy weapon dropped but his other hand still held an ankle. Ellison brought his leg up and drove his heel against the smaller man's neck. The remaining air in the drowning bandit's lungs bubbled out while he clutched at his throat and dropped toward the bottom. In a minute of furious stroking Ellison reached the sampan and held on to the side next to a wicker basket that held its catch. His chest heaved with exhaustion. Su Li and a fisherman pulled him aboard.

"No tricks," the man growled.

Ellison's body shivered but they had saved the pack--the money, the opium, Stilwell's letters, his gun, even his hat—all safe. On the receding bank, the furious jackals cursed and threw rocks at the boat, but his rescuers did not look much more promising, dressed in ragged brown pants and shirts of woven reeds, little more than wild beasts themselves. One sat in the bow, scrawny and fidgety. The other, taller than Su Li but misshapen, with a sloped shoulder from a break never properly healed, poled the flimsy wooden boat forward. Now and then he took a drink from a clay jug of *ta chu*, raw grain liquor. His breath smelled rotten, even from the boat's other end.

They kept eyeing him but Ellison gave it little thought until Su Li leaned over and whispered. "They will betray us when we reach the other side."

After the boat lurched onto the gravelly bank the two boatmen stood apart, talking low. A dripping wet Ellison knelt and reached inside the lining of his drenched jacket without taking his eyes off his rescuers. The silver coins were still there. He checked his backpack, felt his .45. Su Li gathered the other two rucksacks, hers and the boy's, which held their food and cooking utensils. She turned her head for a second. With surprising speed the bigger man whipped out a knife and seized the boy, the blade at his throat.

"You will give us all the opium and silver, red-haired foreigner. Or we will slay the boy. And your slave." He gestured at Su Li.

Ellison chose his words with care. "What's that to me? I can buy a hundred more like them."

He debated whether to draw the gun, glancing at Su Li for guidance but her eyes were riveted on Hui who held his captor's wrist with no sign of panic, alert for the slightest opening. The fisherman hesitated, the knife pressed against the boy's neck. Ellison could almost hear the rusty wheels in the dim-witted brain clicking and grinding against one another while his comrade babbled incoherently. The knot of tension in his stomach

211

tightened, his fingers wrapping tighter around the pistols' handle. Su Li's eyes grew wide and she shook her head. He made a slight, reluctant nod and instead found the med kit and the drugs but kept the Browning near the flap.

"See this?" Ellison held up two packets. "I have enough opium for an emperor. It's yours. Release the child."

The boatman was vacillating and lowered the knife while his partner took another drink of the liquor, chattering and cavorting like a squirrel, waving a pitted blade and egging on the slower-witted one. "Slit the boy's throat," he yapped into the bigger man's ear, "and then kill the rest."

The tall one squinted, suspicious. "Let me see what else you have, big hairy."

All at once Hui dug his heels in and leaned backwards, upsetting the clumsy man's balance. In the same instant with a martial arts technique he twisted the fisherman's arm up and outward. The man howled while Hui ducked and rolled. Ellison dropped the pack and fired. A bullet ripped into the fisherman's shoulder and spun him around. Almost as fast, Su Li pounced on the weasel-like one, hammering a savage blow that knocked the knife out of his grasp. Screeching in pain, he stumbled and fled to the boat while his wounded comrade limped off into the brush.

Ellison's impulse was to finish them. Instead he lowered the weapon. The boy rushed to him and threw his arms around his waist. The pilot returned the hug then turned to Su Li. She was frowning. Their eyes met. He shrugged.

CHAPTER 29

All things rely on the Tao for their life, and it does not refuse them – Lao-tze

"This is a sin against God." His father was bellowing, struggling against his captors, but the Japanese officer dismissed him like an irritating insect, seized the nearest terrified farmer, threw him to his knees and raised his sword. The girl shrieked and bolted from James' arms. "In the name of Jesus," the minister pleaded as the blade descended. The head of Lian's father fell in the dust. The body slumped to the ground where blood gushed into a brief puddle before it disappeared into the earth.

"Father!" she cried and ran to the dead man. Two soldiers caught her and started dragging her toward the other captives. "James, help me!"

He erupted from his hiding place. "Let her go, damn you!"

"No, son!" his father shouted. Abraham Ellison heaved against the soldiers who still pinned his arms.

He hesitated, torn between his father's command and his desire to help the girl. Then his head snapped forward as a rifle butt crashed against the back of his neck and he crumpled to the ground.

The valley of the shadow of death. His father liked to use those words in his sermons. As a boy he didn't know what they meant — most of the time they sounded frightening — but the barren, karst canyon Ellison and his companions had marched through that day struck him as

214

a good approximation, devoid of life as far as he could tell and strewn with sinkholes and sharp outcroppings that constantly blocked their way. Higher up near the rim, as if trying to escape the ruthless sterility of the canyon floor, pines and firs had drilled roots into solid limestone, a tribute to life's tenacity he was grateful to see. Now and then flocks of black and white Siberian cranes or Muscovy ducks soared farther above this forsaken wilderness.

He wished life were that easy. But even as his own gloomy mood thickened, nearly horizontal shafts of evening sunlight sliced through a notch in the crest illuminating images of Buddhas and bodhisattvas, unnoticed by him before, carved in niches high on sheer rock walls. The holy men had stood sentinel for centuries, long before the sides of the canyon had collapsed, their crimson and ochre facades softened by erosion. Today, he imagined, they looked down with disapproval at a culture devastated by war and corruption. But several of the saints were smiling, their hands raised in blessing.

"You know," he said with a whimsical smile, "I've seen that gesture dozens of times at shrines in India, Burma, and as a boy in China but I never bothered to ask what it signified. So what is the Buddha telling us?"

Su Li paused and pointed at one of the larger figures. Its features, though sheltered beneath an overhang, had faded with the ravages of rain and wind. "Have no fear," she said.

"Sounds like good advice."

He nodded more gravely than he meant for what he wanted to do was laugh out loud. Fear of failure was his constant companion. It followed him just beyond his peripheral vision no matter where he went, and his current guide only added to the menace. She was leading him Buddha knew where and he really didn't know a damn thing about her except she hated him. On the other hand she had saved his life. And that night at the river with the apparition of her bathing, an energy had been exchanged and now bound him to her in a way he didn't understand. He wanted, needed to resist, to keep focused, but the more she hurled her hostility at him, the more intrigued he found himself, the more he admired her in an odd sort of way, even as the memory of her naked body kept drowning out her words. The tickle in his groin grew to his consternation, but it collapsed right away when a hand squeezed his. He glanced at the child. To his astonishment Hui was making the same sign as the saints with his free hand. *He thinks I can learn the Buddha's lesson.* Ellison smiled weakly. *We'll see.*

"An itinerant monk who passed along this very route visited our house once and told me about it," Su Li said. "Centuries ago it was a shortcut for imperial armies headed west to the Great Wall and a tributary of the Silk Road that led to Xi'an. He said a mighty army had been ambushed here by rebel troops."

"Ah. That explains some of these rocks. Though I think maybe an earthquake dislodged those big ones."

"The monk said the dead soldiers' spirits revisit the battle often. The memories of their passage are now the breezes that haunt the night." She laughed softly. "A fine tale, is it not so?"

A mostly cleared space opened up where traces of the original road remained. A few dead, misshapen trees gave testimony water had flowed in that spot sometime in the past. Beneath their feet, patches of quack grass along with clumps of mountain sorrel suddenly appeared, waging a hard-fought battle for subsistence with the spikey, knife-like spears of porous limestone in the arid, harsh pocket. He brightened at the meager sign of hope. The trio stopped to pitch camp near one of the mammoth gray boulders, eroded from outcroppings higher up, like a giant's building block heedlessly tossed aside.

Hui gathered dead wood. Su Li lit a fire with matches from Ellison's pack while he walked along the face of the boulder. "I think these stones could scour the blackest soul clean," he said mostly to himself, running his palm over the chalky face. "And what are those markers?" He pointed to a small pile of stones two feet high. Without the pyramidal cairns marking the route every four hundred yards or so, the track, overburdened with rubble and blocked by countless rockslides, would have been invisible.

"Road posts. Buddhist monks made them centuries ago—even before Lao-tze—when they spread the teachings of the Buddha throughout China. They walked for days without pause. To a Buddhist, humans are transformed simply by walking, each step and breath. The stones are called *Xuan Zeng*. I have seen them elsewhere in the mountains."

"Buddhist, Taoist. What's the difference — except the color of their robes, I mean?"

"They are similar — though you might not guess from the actions of many of their followers. Master Po in his own manner has tried to unite both." She chewed on noodles then continued. "True Buddhists do not fight. Even haste is a form of violence in their view." She squatted across from Ellison while Hui spread out his blanket. The child yawned and lay down. In seconds he was asleep.

Su Li leaned back on her heels warming her hands with the blaze. The day's events troubled her. All foreigners treated the Chinese like animals — except this one. "You could have killed that vermin fisherman back there," she said.

But the soldier was absorbed in the hypnotizing dance of fire. Today he had risked his own life to save the child's. Hui loved him, she realized. What surprised her more was how that affection relieved her burden as a mother, but there was something more perplexing. The soldier drew her spirit toward him — and indeed her body, she had to admit. She had been aware of his pull from the first but dismissed it as an animal-like distraction unworthy of a Shaolin. Her goal was the Master's forgiveness. Although life in the monastery was impossible, she might live close by and take up once again her studies of the Tao away from confusing emotions.

"Where did you learn martial arts?" he asked.

"I am taking you there. The Monastery of the Golden Sun."

He knit his brow. "I've been wondering about that. We're going in the wrong direction. My mother is east, behind the lines. The goddess said . . ."

"Goddess?"

"Never mind. I need to get to Shanghai. This will take too long."

"You have a better plan? Besides, one does not simply go to Shanghai." She shrugged. "Even I know that much."

He shrugged back.

"Anyway how can you be certain it is wrong?"

"I'm certain," he laughed out loud, "about nothing."

"The beginning of wisdom."

"Not after Calcutta. And especially not after meeting you." His last words were a soft exhalation.

She paused, not positive she heard him correctly. "I do not know if the Master will welcome me," she said in a shaky voice.

"So you were a monk?" he asked.

The question's abruptness startled her. She knelt up straight and opened her arms wide so the tunic's sleeves dropped below her elbows. The dragon and tiger scars flared red in the firelight. He looked intently at them, then at her, but she turned away, embarrassed at her impulsive display of pride, convinced in any case he would not appreciate it. She vacillated between weeping in despair and shouting with joy while at the same time an exhilarating relief engulfed her.

"A Shaolin. I'm impressed."

She squatted again, covering her surprise and pleasure with indifference. "You know of Chinese religion?"

He laughed softly and tossed a few sticks on the fire. "Why did you leave? I didn't think priests were women or reared children. Or got involved in wars."

She studied him while he gazed into the flames. Questions, always questions. Strange, reddish-orange hair. Hungry blue eyes with a yellow-flecked oval around them. A thin face by Chinese standards. Every attribute about him confounded her.

"Each person follows the Tao in their own way."

"Or not, as the case may be."

The stars wheeled above her as seductively brilliant and indifferent as the fire. "Many of the younger monks decided to fight this evil, I mean these Japanese invaders. They slay many, many barbarians."

He seemed uninterested.

"There are always evils in the world. Some, one must tolerate. Others must be opposed," she went on.

He looked at her. "How do you figure out which is which?"

She held her palms up. Some questions had no answers.

The soldier looked down at his boots. "You think Lian is alive? And my mother? Am I a fool?"

"Will the sun shine tomorrow?" Su Li gathered up their bit of gear, preoccupied. "As for your mother, we will see. But this Lian is dead," she announced matter-offactly. "A Chinese woman is worthless. You are prepared for that?"

"Worthless," he said dully but his eyes blazed in anger at her.

"Less than an ox or a mule."

He turned away and did not respond.

"After all this time you cling to her memory?" she persisted.

"You wouldn't understand," he muttered.

"You are one great block-head, soldier. Like this stone. Like most Chinese. One owes nothing to the dead."

"To her, I do." He adjusted a branch on the fire's edge, nudging it into the hotter center.

"You cannot change the world. And you cannot change yourself."

"I'm ready to go to sleep."

"Such folly."

He smiled. "And you? You did not become a guerilla army. You raised this child the old man left with you instead."

"Because I am a block-head like the rest!" Her voice was as sharp as the rocks and shattered the stillness like a cascade of stones. "I am satisfied with the burden I must bear." No answer, she realized, and not true. How could she explain what eluded even her own grasp? The mountains did not care, nor this soldier, this stranger from a culture so different. So why try? Yet she continued. "That is the Tao, the Way. I have tried to follow it." She bowed her head. "I did — do — what I can. What I must."

"Isn't that what we all do?"

Both of them sat motionless. The dark was absolute beyond the halo of light from the fire. The faint hiss of burning wood broke a silence that weighed like a heavy cloud. Memories of an earlier time when the spirit of stone sought to ensnare her passed before her mind's eye. The flames beckoned to enter their depths.

She was walking in the twilight through this same rock-strewn defile when all at once an army of dead soldiers surrounded her. The ancient warriors arose out of the rocks and took her by surprise, their ghostly visages fierce and angry. They encircled her and stepped closer, swords drawn, battle axes ready. There was no escape, no way to defend herself. The ranks parted and their general, dressed in black armor, rode up on a gleaming ebony horse and lifted his arm in signal for them to stop. The stallion snorted and pawed the earth, its nostrils puffing smoke. Towering over her, the commander lifted his helmet visor. Incandescent eyes burned into her soul. They were Ellison's.

"You yearn for forgiveness, monk. Who can give it to you?"

"I seek it from my Master," she replied haughtily.

He laughed and taunted her, an echo from hell. "No. It is not he who must forgive you."

She wanted to leap on the horse and kill him but fiery eyes mocked her and the voice laughed once more. The general waved his hand and the soldiers vanished. The horse reared on its hind legs, ready to race away.

"Wait!" she cried, now terrified. "Who, then?"

His pupils were points of blue fire. "You know the answer to that." He kicked his spurs. The horse galloped away with thunderous hooves. And she was alone, naked.

A breeze of frigid air snapped her out of the trance. She shivered. The night was bitter cold. She pulled the *pugai* blanket from her pack and spread it out next to her exhausted son. "Sleep over here, by Hui," she said.

Ellison spread his blanket by the sleeping child. He stroked the cropped hair, then tucked the boy's cover around his neck. "You have a remarkable son. You must love him very much."

"Yes, I . . . ." *Should love him more.* She finished the idea silently, lying on her back, looking at the stars. Should. The idea was not Taoist training. One's deeds led to consequences. Her life was living proof of that truth. One adjusted one's actions accordingly. The foundation of inner harmony was to accept the universe as it is was. And still she continued to fail. The stars cared not what side won the war, who lived or who died, or if she returned to the Master again. They inhabited a realm of perfect clarity.

"I am a woman and I am unworthy," she whispered, thinking her companion was asleep.

The soldier raised himself on an elbow. "You are wrong, Su Li. You are the one of worthiest persons I have ever met."

She clutched the tai chi disk as if it had the power to defend her ideal citadel of detachment, balance. She sensed its prospect sliding out of reach each day she was near the soldier. His approval called her to believe in herself as she once had. An image arose in her mind, unbidden. The soldier had his arms around her. She yearned to bury herself in the warmth, the comfort there.

"You know nothing," she hissed and turned over on her side. For a long time she stared into the darkness, wondering if the spirit soldiers were awake, watching.

CHAPTER 30

Be genuine; embrace simplicity. Put others first.
Desire little. – Lao-tze

"Look!" Ellison exclaimed.

After a hard trek through the foothills, the tired, dusty travelers crested a hill above a wide basin, an extension of the flood plain of the Yellow River. In the distance a vast expanse of loess extended to alluvial fans that supplied the *Hung He* with its sediment. Closer in, a colony of ants appeared to be on the move, but the procession stretching in both directions to the horizon was instead a mass migration of human beings. They streamed west, swarming over the old railroad track that terminated in Luoyang and cutting a ribbon through the plains. They spilled over both sides of the track berm, swamping the road alongside, like a stream when heavy rains push the water beyond its banks.

"Something's happened to the city." He raised his hand to his eyebrows and squinted. To the east, faint plumes of smoke spiraled at the limit of his vision. "Some new offensive? The Chinese garrison must've fled. Now the whole city's evacuating. Unbelievable."

"Where . . . who are those people, Big Tall?" Hui asked, eyes wide with wonder.

Su Li moved to put a reassuring arm around his shoulder but he was clinging to the soldier's hand. She seized the child's arm and tried to pull him to her but the boy resisted. Ellison noticed the expression on her face, as if she were afraid he was planning to steal her son from her, and gently placed the boy's hand in hers. In the meantime the sight of the migrating masses overwhelmed their attention.

"I saw refugees when I first came this way, during the famine in Henan. But they were peasants, not city people," she said. The three watched, mesmerized, as if a force of nature were passing in front of them.

"Where are the people going, Mother?"

"I do not know, my son. I doubt they do either."

A string of telephone poles alongside the dirt road was disappearing before their astonished eyes. One pole after another collapsed; not even their stumps were visible in the relentless migration of humanity. Like roving lumberjacks, bands of peasants with axes cut them for firewood at ground level before moving on to the next pole as soon as it was sectioned. Ellison blinked in amazement and started to run down the hill.

"Come on. Let's see what we can find out."

The whole spectrum of urban life churned along in a mélange of vehicles loaded with baggage, hauling all they could. Horses, mules and donkeys, beneath burdens meant for two, plodded in stoic submission, harnessed to carts heaped with the flimsy remains of households. Men bent parallel to the earth pulled rickshaws or pedaled the bicycle variety, piled six feet high or more, helped along by women and children who pushed in the rear. Others man-handled huge barrows with three-foot rough wooden wheels. The rich few drove cars that honked like busy geese. It did them no good. There was no room to move faster and the autos would run out of fuel soon in any case. Most walked, the precious remnants of their lives on their shoulders and backs.

Ellison looked around in a near panic. "The tracks! The bloody tracks are gone! We'll never make it to Xi'an, much less Paochi. Now what?"

"Wait." Su Li plunged into the crowd, hailed a black-uniformed policeman and returned a short time later. "The Nationalist army tore them up, he told me. To leave nothing for the enemy or the Communists. The Red army is massing for an attack. The Japanese are abandoning the city after routing the pathetic Kuomintang forces. The filthy dogs have taken all the food, destroyed the water system. "

"When did the Chinese army retreat?"

"Just yesterday."

"They may not be far ahead. They'll have to load up their supplies, field guns. We might be able to catch them if we hurry."

"Listen!" Su Li held up her hand.

Before Ellison saw anything he heard the unmistakable drone. Two black harbingers of destruction appeared above the eastern skyline. "Mitsubishi bombers! I bet they're headed after that train."

But to his incredulous eyes, the howling mechanical birds did not pursue the train; instead they swooped low toward the densest clusters of refugees. Within seconds bombs exploded a half-mile behind them, plowing up the earth in a relentless crazy-quilt pattern south of the railroad. Panic erupted as people stampeded, bereft of protection, with nowhere to hide, abandoning their belongings. The elderly, sick, young children — anyone too weak to flee — were trampled to death beneath the feet of their own countrymen. Ellison snatched the boy and Su Li along with him. They sprinted away from the panicked spray of escapees and threw themselves flat on the ground. Explosions rumbled past where they had just walked. Ahead of them the vanguard of the human tide wavered and buckled for an instant then charged onward and outward, driven by terror to escape.

Detonations roared up the road on helpless victims, indiscriminate of age, wealth, sex, and tossed them into the air, flopped them on survivors, drenched anyone near with the blood and gore of human flesh and bone. Gruesome scythes of shrapnel mowed anything close to the impact zones. Screams of agony, shrieks of the wounded, hysterical weeping and the braying of injured animals filled the intervals between the ear-splitting blasts.

The interminable bombardment finally ended as the planes climbed, banked and headed east. The craters stretched for a mile. Mixed with the tang of explosives, black acrid smoke filled the air from carts and bodies set on fire. The number of dead and injured seemed beyond measure. Frantic survivors picked up what they could and ran to catch up with the front of the line, terrified the bombers might return, but most sat or knelt and wept in despair or wandered aimlessly, stupefied.

"They did it just for the bloody hell of it," Ellison ranted in English. "No bloody fucking reason!" He shook his fist at the vanishing Mitsubishis. "Oh what I wouldn't give to see a squadron of Mustangs right now." Wishful thinking, he knew. The Chinese army had no air force and no anti-aircraft guns.

Those from the rear, who had been spared the butchery, pulled level with the carnage and detoured around it, like a stream that flows by a boulder in its center. They ran or drove their carts with feverish urgency, as if distance from the slaughter would put it out of mind, make it not have happened; and in spite of the hundreds who lay wounded, no one turned aside to give aid.

"What the hell is wrong with these people?" Ellison cried. A wave of helplessness swept over him. What could he possibly do? But instinct and memories of how his mother might have reacted kicked in. "Come on. We have to help." He ran to the nearest crater. Su Li inexplicably hung back, motionless, frozen in place.

"Su Li, I need you!"

His shout momentarily released her. Mangled bodies were scattered inside the depression. Near the edge a woman with her leg blown off at the knee was bleeding profusely and moaned in agony. Ellison took off his pack.

"A slave," said Su Li over his shoulder. "Leave her to her fate."

"What did you say?" Dismayed, Ellison retrieved his medical kit, took out scissors and cut two strips from the woman's dress, bound her thigh with a tourniquet as best he could and cleaned the wound. She groaned, opened her glazed eyes, a dying doe unable to make a sound.

"She is as good as dead." Su Li's voice was shrill, frantic. "There are too many. We cannot help them all."

"We can help one!" He roared, reaching into his med kit for the morphine bottle and syringe. When he turned to the woman again, she was dead. He let out a deep sigh, closed her eyelids and gave a quick frustrated glance at Su Li. She was still hypnotized, lost in the overwhelming indifference of her countrymen. "Su Li! Snap out of it!"

His command jolted her out of the persistent, creeping paralysis and she rushed to his side. He was ministering to an older man covered in blood, shrapnel wounds over half his body. Ellison injected morphine into his arm while Su Li tore bandages from strips of cloth, took Ellison's knife from its sheath and fished out pieces of metal from as many wound holes as she could. He daubed them with iodine before she bandaged them. They could do no more. A few weeping refugees approached, looking for wounded or dead relatives. Not finding any, they moved on. And there were signs that survivors were once more helping each other, gathering the scattered belongings of the elderly and loading the injured onto already overburdened carts.

"Maybe I'm wrong about them," he mumbled to himself out loud, surveying the sporadic pockets of help against the larger lines of cart-pullers and pedestrians who trudged through the carnage and whose faces pointed forward, as if nothing had happened. "Maybe it's not apathy but shock." Fright and bewilderment did disturbing things to people. Nevertheless, the widespread pell-mell panic continued to bother him.

At one point a dozen renegade Chinese soldiers approached. They were scavenging the craters for any valuables or body parts that might have jewelry. If anyone from the refugee stream drew near, the deserters threatened to kill them. "Bugger off, you bastards," he shouted at them, giving the robbers a black look. They turned to easier prey.

The two of them worked into the evening. Filled with adrenalin, he surprised himself at how deft he became. When the morphine and iodine ran out and light failed, they shuffled away from the road and camped in the open, weary of the groans of the injured, too exhausted to eat. The boy fell asleep as soon as his head touched the ground. Ellison propped himself on his elbow and stared at her.

Su Li, sitting with her elbows on her knees and hands clenched under her chin, avoided looking at him as long as possible. "You wonder about my actions at the bomb hole? For the Chinese, when it is time to die, one must accept it. To intervene is useless."

He kept staring at her, expressionless, refusing to judge her, trying to understand.

"You do not believe that, do you?"

To wait, to be silent seemed to him the only fit response.

"You realize what women are worth in China."

His eyes fixed on her like a homing beacon locked in place.

"Sometimes I forget I am one." She focused her gaze on the fire, her face a hard mask.

I sure as hell can't. Not since that night at the river. Her admission of weakness alerted him to how often that image had been playing in the back of his mind. The sudden arousal astonished him. *Get a hold of yourself, laddie. You don't understand her, but you ken well enough she would nae welcome your touch. A Shaolin one man commando squad. Hah!*

The craving, though, did not go away. He drew his blanket up to his neck as if it might cover his bewilderment when Su Li whispered, "Thank you, Big Tall."

He let out a soft breath, turned his back to the object of his perplexity, and closed his eyes.

CHAPTER 31

Not a tuft of grass below, not a single roof tile above — Zen saying

Hui tugged the dew-dampened blanket from Su Li's shoulder. "Mother. Come and see."

The sun had just risen over the horizon and the line of evacuees, halted beside the old railway bed, stirred like a long lizard feeling the new day warm its blood. The boy led them toward a heap of garbage where the caravan had discarded its shattered baggage, deposited its human waste and dumped some of its dead. A pack of snarling dogs fought over the corpses. Hui ran ahead with a stick to keep the mongrels away and stopped at a broken chair partly draped by a blood-spattered woman's dress, apart from the main pile. He picked up an object on the seat.

"Hui, you must not . . . ." Su Li cried as she drew near.

Eyes dampened with tears he handed her a baby, abandoned in the night, its cord dangling from its naval. She stared at the infant for a moment, eyes blinking, paralyzed by the sight. The stark memory of her own still-born child flashed like fire in her mind's eye. Ellison's knife found its way into her hand, igniting her spirit once more, but her response was mechanical, lifeless. The tiny girl, turning blue, whimpered when she cut the cord. She wrapped it in Ellison's flight jacket, pulled it in close and collapsed to her knees. Her soul plummeted into caverns of grief, not caring whether she lost her way or if she might ever find an exit. No sound came forth but her heart wailed as if every sorrow in her life, in China, in the whole world, lay centered in the small object in her arms.

The baby was dying of exposure. They had no clothing for it, no food, her own breasts useless. None of those fleeing would be willing to take such a one, desperate to save themselves. *I am all she has. I am all she has.* The thought — and the helplessness it implied — made her head throb. Part of her wanted to scream. Ellison touched her forearm, handed her his canteen. She poured water in the tiny mouth to no avail, then dipped her finger in the liquid and put a few drops between its lips. The sucking reflex was instantaneous. She repeated the procedure over and over. The dark eyes opened and moved back and forth as if pondering what chaos they had been born into.

Ellison helped her to stand and they resumed their trek on the fringe of the refugee flood. From time to time she gave it water but the infant's strength was failing. Nonetheless, her arms clutched it as if her body might lend it her own *chi*. By afternoon, the infant stopped moving altogether, but as the hours wore on, she continued to press it against her chest. Neither Ellison nor Hui questioned her, out of respect for the unspoken communion she made with the tiny bundle. Jaw set, focused on a distant emptiness, she ate nothing, drank nothing, and walked in a trance, her mind empty of words and thoughts. When the sun dropped below the western mountains, the train of refugees staggered to a halt. She stopped as well, turned and met Ellison's enigmatic yellow-flecked eyes that were filled with compassion. She vaguely realized how much she had come to expect that empathy; it offered a tentative way out of her despair.

Instinct drew them perpendicular to the road toward a barren meadow far from the multitude. The desolate field, pock-marked with craters from artillery shells and bombs, had been stripped of vegetation, but near an old wooden irrigation wheel she spied a cluster of faded purple iris sprung up among some equally forlorn weeds. Here she stopped and pointed. Ellison took out his knife and dug a shallow grave next to the flowers. She laid the infant in it, unwilling to depart, content to watch while Ellison and Hui covered it with soil.

For a reason she could not comprehend, the soldier hurled clods of dirt skyward over and over, mouthing angry words in his foreign tongue. Finally he stopped and looked down at the grave with deep sadness, arm draped over Hui's shoulder. She absorbed it—and what it told her about him—without thinking, fixated on the dying flowers.

She was not able to rescue this babe, unlike the Master who had saved her; and as she stood above the grave, a sharp disquieting sensation came with a rush—she must leave China or die.

CHAPTER 32

Float like a cloud. Flow like water – Zen saying

They took turns carrying Hui and stopped only to rest and eat, running far into the night before collapsing into sleep and arising each day before dawn. Ellison's chest heaved, his legs burned all day long and his feet blistered, but Su Li's example prodded him onward. She carried the boy on her back most of the time, arms around her neck, legs around her waist. Her stamina seemed inexhaustible. He wasn't surprised, not with the memory of his nighttime rescue from the Japanese camp.

"Why are we going so fast, Mother? Isn't haste wrong?"

"Not today, my son," she panted.

"Without the train, we'll be no better than those poor people we saw two days ago, Hui," Ellison wheezed, running alongside them, carrying two packs on his own back and one in his hand. "And never be able to reach your mother's Master. Or Shanghai," he mumbled to himself.

Not until evening of the third day did they catch sight of it, idle on a stretch of track amidst low, undulating hills east of fabled Xi'an, capital of the Qin dynasty that had unified China millennia ago, a China now broken apart. The retreating Nationalist troops had commandeered this last train to evacuate the shattered fragments of the army corps routed by the Japanese. Steam and caustic smoke wheezed from the old locomotive's elaborate red stack, a tattooed iron monster with a disease of the lungs and a yellow rooster painted on its long black belly.

Behind it trailed a coal tender and dozens of cars that swarmed with men hauling equipment inside. Crews winched howitzers up ramps onto flat cars or lugged crates of ammunition and supplies into boxcars. Behind the baggage car at the rear, squads ripped up the remaining rails and hauled them to another flat car, the steel too valuable to be abandoned. Meanwhile a sapper team laid explosives to blow up the ties and the roadbed, most of the work overseen by officers whose features told Ellison they were Europeans. Except for these pockets of efficiency, chaos reigned. There were no perimeter sentries anywhere and many of the infantrymen sat around unsupervised while others pushed and shoved to clamber aboard old stock cars, their transport away from the front.

"They look like lost bees returning to find their hive bashed in," Ellison said as the weary trio warily approached the encampment. "I'll look for . . . . Over there, by the carriage car. That's what we want." A mix of officers and civilians — not all Chinese — swarmed around an elaborate pavilion. "You and Hui had better hang back. I don't know what's going to happen."

Sentries barred his way. He reached inside his jacket for the Chinese flags. "I'm an American officer, attached to the Chinese government. Take me to your commander," he said to the soldiers.

They scrutinized him and looked over Su Li and the boy with appropriate suspicion. "We'll see what General Kuo wants to do with you," one of them replied.

They escorted him to the pavilion where a white linen table was spread with a banquet of food and warm *huangjiu*, rice wine. The pot-bellied General who presided over the feast took a bite of a peppery chicken from a variety of dishes and licked his fat fingers. He gave Ellison a cursory glance.

"Excuse me, General Kuo. My name is Lt. James Ellison, US Army Air Force. I'm on a joint mission for General Stilwell and Generalissimo Chiang Kai Shek. This document from him . . ." – he presented Chiang's letter given him by Stilwell – "orders you to give us a ride – ."

The General held up his hand, placed the paper alongside his plate, and continued to eat. Opposite him sat a thin man dressed in a rough field uniform with no indication of rank. He wore wire-rim glasses beneath a cap with a red star and puffed on a cigarette. His countenance blazed with fervor despite his relaxed pose, as dangerous as a viper ready to strike. Ellison glanced over his shoulder. Su Li and Hui were under guard ten yards behind him. He shifted uncomfortably, waiting for the General's reply. The longer he waited the more he worried his request for passage might lead to trouble.

"I commend your foresight, esteemed General. I see you're leaving nothing for the enemy to pursue you with," he said.

Kuo sipped the hot yellow wine from a glass goblet, holding up the document. "This says you can receive my help." He spoke in accented English and chortled. "But why? I ask myself. I don't have room for my own soldiers, pitiful as they are. My mission is to take as many of these demoralized buffoons out of reach of the Japanese as I can. Trying to save what remains of my army, you see, but the cowards keep coming in from the countryside, delaying us. I'm tempted to leave the lot of them out here." Kuo was bald and his eyes pinched by fleshy cheeks and a jaundiced-colored forehead. He placed Ellison's letter back on the tablecloth. "You have friends in high places, Lieutenant. That presents intriguing opportunities. Hmmm." He touched his finger to his lip as if considering a course of action. "The problem, frankly, is that Colonel Chou here, of the Eighth Route Army, has been trying his best to convince me to abandon the little landlord Chiang and come over to the Communist side. Haven't you, Colonel?" Kuo grinned.

The Communist officer made a mechanical grimace that passed for a smile.

"The Colonel, fervent fool that he is, believes in the people. Mostly in killing them." He laughed at his own joke. Another executioner's smile from Chou. "You must realize, Lieutenant, China in reality is divided into three parts. The north, ruled by Mao's Communists. Headquartered at Yennan, am I right, Chou? The south by Chiang's Kuomintang, the east by the Japanese. The Nationalists, which I have supported most of the war, are the official government of China. We're supposed to be allied with the Communists against the Japanese, but the two sides hate each other more than they hate the Japanese. They're maneuvering for strategic dominance after the war. Alliances depend on who is winning. A man must take care for his future." He gestured toward his troops. "These men are loyal to me, not Chiang Kai Shek. Of course, I pay them, not the little merchant. I suppose that is the depth of their loyalty."

"The heyday of the warlords has passed, General." Chou's voice was thin, reedy, and unpleasant but his implied threat unmistakable. "Do not underestimate our illustrious Chairman Mao."

Kuo made a contemptuous laugh, paused eating and looked up at Ellison, pointedly ignoring his companion. "Thus you will realize Chiang's safe passage means nothing to me," he said. "The Communists have offered me command of a whole province. And I have accepted. But you might be valuable in any negotiations that might occur. You Americans have no love for the Communists, I have heard."

He waved his napkin. Two soldiers stepped up and seized Ellison. An officer put a pistol to his head. The sentries outside had by then aimed their weapons at Su Li and the child. She pulled him in close, unable to resist their captors without risking his death. Ellison cursed himself for blundering into a major act of political treachery and putting all their lives in danger.

"Bind this man in the baggage car," Kuo ordered the guards. "The boy is comely, I see. Put him in my own personal suite. As for the woman, Colonel, I realize you

Communists tout yourselves as ascetic zealots but I'm sure you have time for recreation?" Kuo drank more rice wine, yellow drops glistening on his mustache, took up his chopsticks and resumed his meal. Chou threw a surreptitious glance at Su Li, puffed on his cigarette and blew a smoke ring while his captors led a furious Ellison away.

"Hui!" he shouted. "Don't worry. Tell your mother we'll find a way to escape. Somehow, I'll . . . ." A rifle butt slammed into his groin and he collapsed.

Chou excused himself. Kuo gave him a ridiculous leer but Chou didn't mind. He despised the effeminate general and his pathetic attempts at humor. To him, the corpulent warlord was worse than a slug. Besides, his crotch itched with anticipation. It had been months since he'd lain with a woman but he had little time. With twilight deepening, the train was scheduled to depart shortly. He walked over to several large boulders south of the tracks where Kuo's men had prepared the slave for his arrival. Not that he expected resistance. It would be an honor for any female to service a Colonel in the People's Liberation Army. The guards waited at the rock.

"All is ready?" he asked. They grinned. Chou drew his German Luger and brandished it in their faces. "Now, remove your smelly peasant toad mugs from my sight."

Chou navigated between the rocks and found what he had expected — a naked woman on a blanket. She had been beaten, he noted with approval. Good. Afraid. Fear was good. His crotch came erect and he panted with excitement. He tore off his pants and knelt over the prostrate captive, his pistol in one hand; with the other he grabbed her hair.

"Well, my terrified hen, let me see what you have here—."

Her eyes exploded with hatred, not afraid in the least. The Colonel's last thought was a question, how could a mere woman's hand strike a blow strong enough to break his neck?

In the deep twilight, Su Li put on her clothes and crept among the piles of debris the army had discarded. She edged closer to the tracks, soundless, invisible in the shadows. Small groups of conscripts who formed a token rear guard huddled around their campfires. In reality, their general was abandoning them because the train could hold no more. A shudder snaked through the cars as the air brakes released. The train lurched forward a few feet. She had to move faster, her attention fastened on the one car with oil lamps glowing through closed curtains, second from the end, Kuo's private car. An icy clarity of purpose covered the pool of rage inside and an even deeper fear of a parent for her child, not a feeling that paralyzes but a physical force that compels a mother, human or animal, to protect her offspring, no matter the cost. Save her son, kill the traitor.

The locomotive's whistle startled her. There was no more time for stealth. To reach the club car she had to pass through the line of campfires. She grabbed a box, held it on her head, stepped out of the shadows, intent on conveying the impression she was a camp follower on an errand. The steel wheels ground forward. Her heart thudded with fear. She was going to miss it. Tossing the box, she sprinted. A sentry called for her to halt as she sped by. A shot rang out. She raced alongside as the train gathered speed, an arm's length behind the platform between Kuo's car and the one in front. Chest heaving, legs churning, arms pumping. Faster. Faster, Shaolin. Faster, she told herself. The platform's handrail gleamed tantalizingly close in the wind rush of air.

The train rolled smoothly now. In a burst of speed, she leaned forward like a sprinter at the end of a race. One hand wrapped around the steel handrail, then the other. She hauled herself up to the platform where a startled sentry raised his rifle, took the simplest way and head-butted him over the side.

The baggage car served as a storage locker for tools, munitions and any miscellaneous equipment the Chinese were able to cram in. They had left a narrow access space in the middle where Ellison was secured, his hands in manacles and a chain fastened to an iron ring screwed into the wall. The aches in his body paled before his rage at Kuo and panic at the prospect of what might happen to Hui in the pedophile's private quarters. The boy had made him aware other affairs in the maelstrom of war needed attention, beyond his own narrow, selfish quest for righteousness. By chance, he had stumbled on a measure of human decency — maybe even love.

In the dim light from an overhead skylight he guessed the screws in the bracket might give. He tugged at the ring. Nothing. Using his legs for purchase, he pulled over and over but it wouldn't budge. For some reason he thought of his friend Buzz, so good at fixing things, figuring stuff out. *Your approach is all wrong, James. Use your head, not your brute strength, you hard-headed Scot.* Right. On a row of pegs on the same wall hung an array of large tools for repairing the train — open-end wrenches, bolt cutters, sledge hammers and a pry bar. Ellison seized the ring for leverage and leapt as high as he could, pirouetting so his boot nicked a large, open-end wrench and dislodged it from its peg. The maneuver threw him off balance. He fell to the floor and banged his head against a wooden crate. Momentarily stunned, he cast around for a way to secure the tool when he noticed the box: "Property of the United States of America. Dynamite." Holy shit, as good old Buzz liked to say. What irony, he thought. He reached out with his boots and inch by inch wiggled the wrench toward him, but the chain tying him to the wall did not have enough slack for him to pick it up.

"Balls!" he shouted. *Don't panic. Work on this.* A childhood memory surfaced. It had been years since he'd played football but he had learned a few tricks from those days. Still sitting, he grasped the tool between his boots, flexed his knees and flicked it up like a ball toward his hands. Not high enough. It dropped on his stomach, beyond his grasp. The next time he tried harder, put his gut into the kick. The tool flew upward enough for his right hand to catch it. He hammered the ring from the wall, grabbed the bolt cutters and cut the links of his bonds. Free, he squeezed through the narrow aisle to the exit. *Jesus, Buddha, Vishnu, somebody, protect the child. Huh! I'm actually praying. What the hell is that all about?* On the platform, a single, sleepy sentry slumped against the railing while the wheels droned hypnotic rhythms as they rode over the joints. Ellison whipped open the door, lowered his shoulder and body-blocked the astonished soldier before he could cry out. The next door led to Kuo's club car.

The General sipped his Scotch, filled with anticipation at his tryst with the child who sat bound and silent on the bed across from his desk. The ornate appointments in the carriage were old and shabby but the General did not mind. Better times were coming. Before he tested the child, he wanted to examine the contents of the American's leather pack and ponder a bit more the implications of this letter from Chiang. He put on reading glasses. Perhaps it might be altered, forged and made useful in some way. Of course there was the problem of how to deal with the Communists. Their single-mindedness did not preclude trickery. Chou thought him a fool. Kuo smiled. Another, possibly more lucrative alternative was to turn the fanatic over to Kuomintang intelligence. He placed the documents from Mao next to Ellison's letter.

Children always have such terror in their eyes at first, Kuo recalled, as he unbuckled his belt, approached the boy and stroked Hui's hair. "You'll come to enjoy it, child. They all do."

Hui pushed the molester's hand away and sat upright, eyes drawn to the front of the car. Kuo hesitated and glanced in that direction, shrugged his shoulders but before he could touch the boy again, the door splintered inward.

Su Li staggered in and paused to check on her son, time enough for the startled officer to draw his revolver out of its holster and send a fusillade her way. She dove for cover behind Kuo's desk. Her heightened senses traced the arc of the bullets as they hurtled toward her. One slammed into her chest below the shoulder blade, its trail searing her flesh as it burrowed through and emerged out her back. She slumped behind the desk. The firing stopped.

Her love for the child grew white hot inside her, a roaring furnace of will. She grasped the desktop, struggled to her knees, then finally levered herself upright. A frantic Kuo was re-loading with the spare cartridges in his belt. *Now. Now is the time.* She leapt over the desk and launched herself at the general who had turned at a new sound behind him. Kuo raised his gun to fire at Ellison just as the pilot slammed a steel wrench on his skull.

"Hui," she gasped, clutching her wound. Ellison untied the traumatized boy and lifted him in his arms. She hobbled near, her wounded arm hanging at her side. Weeping, Hui reached for her neck. His tight hug's simple goodness washed through her like the sun's warmth, momentarily masking the pain from her wound. It was not wrong to be grateful for that. She could still be Shaolin, even if she had a son, could she not? It hurt too much to return his embrace but any remaining doubts that the soldier had stolen her child's love vanished like mist.

"Christ, you've been shot. Let me look at that." Ellison took the boy from her, set him on the bed. "Wait here. I need to help your mother." He examined Su Li. "Can you lift it?"

"Have to go. Someone will come."

"Not before I stop this bleeding."

Ellison grabbed the whiskey bottle and poured liquor into the bullet hole, front and back. Su Li muffled a scream, closed her eyes and willed herself into a trance to slow her heart rate. He ripped a piece of cloth from a curtain and wound it around her shoulder. The bleeding slowed. She focused the power of her mind to clot the blood and flexed her muscle. The arm moved.

"Uhhh." She grimaced. She realized no bones were hit but her legs were about to crumble and her head was dizzy.

Ellison put an arm around her waist, grabbed the bottle of whiskey. "Drink this."

She shook her head vehemently. No!" she cried, "I .. . not hurt."

"The hell you aren't," he replied in English and managed to pour liquor into her mouth. She spat it out and coughed. The need to lay down and sleep was overwhelming. Take care of me, someone, her whole being cried. No one had looked after her for so long.

"Stay here by Hui," Ellison said, setting her tenderly next to the boy.

He gathered his belongings from Kuo's desk, including the letters from Chiang and Stilwell and stuffed them with his Browning into his pack. Another paper caught his eye — a letter with a red hammer and sickle at the top of a stack of documents, from Communist Party headquarters with Mao Zedong's signature at the bottom. *Bet this is important.* He folded them into the pack and handed an oil lamp to Su Li. He hoisted Hui and led them back the way he had come into the baggage carriage. When they reached the boxes of explosives, he set the boy down and ripped one open with the wrecking bar.

"I want to leave a gift for these traitors," he said. "Su Li, move to the back and see if you can open the rear door. And bring one of these lamps. Hui, you help her." He ran out a section of fuse and attached it to one of the sticks of dynamite. Buzz would have gotten a bang out of this, he thought with amusement. He could just see his old co-pilot's face. He set two sticks of explosives in Kuo's car, connected the fuses and trailed it out the last door where Su Li and Hui stood beneath a full moon. The train had increased speed, in open country on the final leg to Xi'an. Ellison held the oil lamp.

"We'll have to jump."

She blinked an acknowledgement, eyelids fluttering. Ellison checked the route ahead in the moonlight. They needed to wait for a curve, when the train slowed. Su Li's face was pale and haggard from the gunshot. He had never seen her this way. She had seemed invulnerable. Now he wasn't sure she was going to make it.

"It's going to hurt," he warned.

The train slowed. Ellison lit the fuse with the oil lamp and waited to satisfy himself it burned well enough. He looked ahead once more, the train's slipstream whipping his face. The best they could hope for. Su Li, eyes half-closed, tottering on the brink of collapse, suddenly lurched against him. Her arms wrapped around his waist with a distinct feel of desperation. Without warning he seized her in a bear hug with one arm, grabbed the boy in his other and launched himself backwards off the platform. They thumped onto the gravel of the raised track bed, the woman and boy on top, their fall cushioned by his backpack. He released them and they rolled down the incline to a grassy, level patch where they clambered to their feet, huddled together in relief and fear. The old locomotive showered sparks and cinders as it disappeared into the darkness.

In another minute, a thunderous roar split the night and the last two cars erupted in a ball of flames.

CHAPTER 33

I learn by going where I have to go – Theodore Roethke

Paochi was the western terminus of the single rail line in north China. The city was a mix of an old medieval core, a sprawling inchoate mass of buildings in disrepair that stretched to the west, and a newer, modern section in the east, hastily thrown together after the fall of Hankow. Near the Wei River, it had become a permanent home for thousands of migrants and a transit point for all sorts of nationalities. On the city's outskirts, Ellison and Su Li halted at a tent town. They had hitched wagon rides to Xi'an and miraculously found that the railroad to Paochi was still operating. Ellison's silver had bought them third-class seats.

"I imagine this place is full of Kuomintang informers," he said.

Su Li had hardly uttered a word to him since the train incident. On the outside she seemed almost normal. Her body's systemic wisdom accelerated her healing; in fact, her physical strength and endurance astounded him, but she kept her distance. Her spirit, he imagined, was wounded more than her body – the bullet, the abandoned baby. He did not know what to do or say to her.

"I'll find a market, get us some supplies, blankets, food, new shoes for you and Hui. I've still got some silver coins. Maybe you could find us a discreet route out of here." He handed her a packet of opium. She took it mechanically, without acknowledgement.

"Could I go with Big Tall, Mother?" Hui asked.

The brief flash of anguish on her face told Ellison that was not a good idea. "Your mother needs you. Stay with her. We'll meet here at dusk."

Ellison found a flimsy ad-hoc open bazaar in the tent city, set up to supply — and cheat — the downhearted, impoverished refugees. Trying to be inconspicuous, he turned his jacket inside out and quickly bought a hat to cover his hair. He was much taller than a typical Han Chinese but was not an anomaly among the mélange of equally tall outsiders, some with light, some with dark skin, from western and northern lands who wore fur hats and led caravans of camels. He procured new rucksacks and other supplies with his few remaining silver coins.

"Mother found the way south to Chungking," Hui said, later that evening when he returned to their make-shift camp site.

He nodded and handed out food. Su Li ate in stony silence, chewing on strips of dried fish. Even the boy sensed the tension, looking tentatively at his mother, then at Ellison. Near encounters with death had traumatized each of them — Ellison understood that. He had no particular inclination to talk about it either. He wondered if she blamed him for what happened. Yet something besides her withdrawal had changed, at least in him. On that train, he had taken care of her and she allowed him, reluctantly for sure, but in the end he held her and sensed a need on her part. Closer and farther, at the same time. *Try to figure that one out.* He lay awake a long time before sleep finally came.

The next morning they trudged up and over the same mountain pass Su Li had traversed in the opposite direction more than two years ago and crossed the bridge over the Chialing River, part of the Longmen Shan, the easternmost spur of the Tibetan range that separated northern China from southern China.

Like an endless serpent, the rutted road into the temperate Szechwan basin wound down a series of dizzying switchbacks cut into the steep mountainside, muddy and slick from recent rains. The trio was immersed in a caravan again. To Ellison's reckoning the whole damned country was uprooted. The able-bodied led donkey carts filled with bricks, coal, or gravel. Shaggy Mongolian ponies pulled wagons laden with wood and bamboo. The less prosperous bent beneath carrying poles with baskets of ducks and chickens, tools and goods of every kind; but hundreds more — sick with sores and tumors, scoured with wounds and mutilated faces — hunched alongside the roadway paralyzed with despair, their meager possession a clay pot, unable to comprehend a world fallen apart. Ellison, Su Li and the child wrapped cloth around their noses and mouths to keep out the filth as they marched past the derelicts.

Like the ground fog that blocked out the sun, the pressure of so many homeless people depressed Ellison, even as Su Li's presence continued to trouble him. Her vulnerability the past weeks had made her more attractive — or at least more perplexing — he was amazed to realize. Even more disturbing was the abrupt awareness that he had spent the last hour staring at her profile. How long had that been happening? The shape of her feet, her nose, her neck, the way her short hair hung coursed through his veins like a mildly intoxicating liquor. He couldn't determine whether it was simple desire from not having sex for so long or that he couldn't put together the pieces of her puzzle, which irritated like a pesky fly you kept trying to swat. She was more like a knot in a ball of string. The more threads you untied, the more you realized the difficulty of the damned thing; yet you can't tear yourself away from trying to figure it out.

He finally decided it had to be the first, plain lust. Memo to Lt. James Ellison from Captain Brain: Cease and desist. Order your restless gonads to return to barracks. Stop acting the village idiot and keep the mission in mind. Over and out. Time was passing and they were heading away from Shanghai. At this rate his mother would be dead before he ever got close to her. *What a half-cocked idea, going off on my own. Sheer lunacy. China is too bloody huge.* Yet, exasperated at himself as he was, he discovered he was still gawking at her, as bad as a moon-struck teen-age boy. *Pathetic haggis head.*

"Officer!" A man's voice bellowed in English above the swarm of travelers. The sound came from a car that had stopped on a stretch of road. "You'd better come here, young fellow." From the window of a gray Mercedes, a Chinese man motioned him over. The car was blocked by a bottleneck of pedestrians where the switchbacks ended and the route leveled and straightened.

"A guerilla merchant," Su Li said with a scowl. "A smuggler. The government toads in Chungking need the income — they control most of the smuggling. They have been selling the rice from our own famine-stricken territories to the Japanese. I heard it from that travelling monk who visited us. This one is rich. He will have connections. Go see what he wants." It was the most she had said since their escape from Kuo.

"Come with me," he said, waving to the man.

"You do not give orders to me," she hissed.

He paused, took a breath through clenched teeth and glared at her. "I wouldn't dream of it. Please, Mistress Su Li, accompany me?"

She bowed in mockery. "I must walk behind. I am your slave. Remember?"

"Then act like one," he muttered.

He elbowed through the crowd, Su Li clinging to his belt while the boy latched onto her shirt so they would not be separated. The Mercedes had four armed soldiers from the Nationalist Army at each corner. If this was a smuggler, he had official protection. Ellison reminded himself to be careful, aware of Stilwell's and Chiang's letters inside his jacket and Kuo's treachery.

"Can I give you a lift, Leftenant?" The driver spoke English with a Chinese/British accent. "You seem to be lost. I'm on my way to Chungking and you obviously won't last long in this rabble." He wore a homburg hat and a crumpled blue suit. A Gauloise cigarette dangled from full lips.

"And to whom do I owe this invitation, if you don't mind my asking?"

"Not at all. Fan. Wei-jing. At your service. And you?"

"Ellison, James. Lieutenant. US Army Air Force." He offered a tentative hand to the soft, ring-encrusted fingers held out the window.

"With *that* accent? What the devil brings you out here in this mess?"

"My transport broke down a ways back. Been out on a project for headquarters. Definitely would appreciate a lift."

"Please, accept my poor conveyance." He gestured to the passenger door. "I'm a great admirer of all things American. An innovative and profitable culture."

Ellison grinned. "Half-American and half Scots. But aye, thanks. I will." It felt wonderful to speak English again and there was something likable about this bloke who spoke it so smoothly. "What about my, uh, servants here?" He winked and gestured.

Fan made a face. "On the trunk by my guards."

"Actually, Mr. Fan, I'd appreciate it if they could ride in the—."

Before he could finish, the touch of Su Li's finger in the small of his back was a spike driven into his spine. He snapped forward and tried to pull it away.

"Uh, these are valuable. Paid a good price for them. An old friend of the Generalissimo's—Ho Ying Chin—asked me to look out for something special. She in particular can do incredible things." He couldn't resist turning around to cast a sarcastic smile at Su Li. The sting vanished. "You get my meaning."

Fan raised his brows and grunted. "You're connected to Ho and his gang of thieves? That carrion bird and the unscrupulous Chen brothers have made life difficult for a poor merchant like myself." He chortled. "Well, in any case, I'll allow it. As long as they don't stink."

Ellison piled in the front seat. In the rear, Su Li and Hui crammed themselves next to a stack of boxes and tin cans on the brown leather. Fan glanced over his shoulder. "A bit too tall and awkward for my tastes. But often treasures lie in ordinary containers. Perhaps a virgin. Worth real money. The boy even more." He focused his attention on the steering wheel again. His unbuttoned suit coat revealed a middle-aged, well-fed paunch that spilled over his suspenders. At his signal the guards in front jumped on the fenders and the two in back stepped onto the running boards. Fan put the car in gear and pulled even with the carts and humans that filled the road.

"At last someone who understands the Chinese. Undoubtedly a scholar before the war, no?" He held up his bejeweled fingers. "You don't have to admit anything. I know how such things work. You have this, shall I say, unofficial assignment along with your regular position. Which is?"

"Liaison. Communications. Sorry."

"Communications? Of course. Clever. By the way, Madame Chiang's brother-in-law has graced me with his beneficence." He turned to Ellison with a wide, plump face.

Ellison smiled. Behind the veneer of bonhomie, this manipulator bothered him. "A man of status."

Fan grinned with pride, revved the engine and leaned his palm on the horn. The soldiers in front shouted orders at the crowd who either ignored them or jeered. "Bloody fools. Most of them will lose all this before they arrive at the city."

At last the crowds thinned and the pot-holed road opened unimpeded. The Mercedes cruised while the voluble Fan attempted to impress the American with his contacts among the Japanese high command and his knowledge of the inner circle of the Kuomintang. He explained that he acquired his English in Shanghai, working for British exporters.

"You know Shanghai well?" Ellison asked, on edge, his heart racing.

"I make regular trips there. Pick up certain, ah, goods here, then sell them to Japanese intelligence." He shrugged. "Anyway, as I was saying, the Generalissimo's been toying with you Americans. Pretending he'll capitulate to the Japs. Let me tell you how the game is played here in the inscrutable East." Fan laughed. "Chiang's from the landlord class. Extort, extort, and extort some more. That's what he's doing to the allies. A master." Fan chuckled again. "We all have much to learn from him."

"The rich ye shall always have with you," Ellison chose his words cautiously. His chauffeur was a wily one with tentacles in both camps and needed to be cultivated with care, but he offered a first genuine connection to the pilot's ultimate destination. "I take it you're ambivalent about the Generalissimo?"

"He has enemies." Fan was dead earnest for once. "There are those who feel he has betrayed China."

"Are you one of them?"

"A humble businessman. What does my opinion matter? The Kuomintang is dead but not in the ground. And as we say in China, things not buried cause problems for the living. But such difficulties can be solved — and money earned." He tilted his head toward the rear of the car.

"The superior man's progress is always upward," said Ellison.

"Let me put it this way, Leftenant. I work the Japanese. I do not work for them."

The car rolled to a halt, as did the rest of the splintered convoy of emigrants, at an intersection of dirt roads north of Chungking. What appeared to be an army headed northwest to Chengdu barred their passage but it was like no military Ellison had ever seen. A peacock General mounted on a stallion, resplendent in a heavily decorated uniform, led the parade. Behind him, other high-ranking officers also rode on horses. Lesser ones marched on foot. Orderlies came next — peasants kidnapped from their villages — who carried baggage, field equipment, even furniture for the highest ranks. On each side of them, a line of veteran soldiers kept watch so no one would leave or steal anything.

258

Fan lit up a cigarette. "All for show. It's the Chinese style. Even if the country collapses. These riff-raff won't even make it to the base camp."

"No mechanized transport?" Ellison was flabbergasted.

"Not for this cannon fodder. They're headed for the Japanese. Chiang's real armies are held in reserve to fight the Communists while the Allies slug it out with the Japs. Just like the Generalissimo, to hoard his grain in the midst of famine. But what do I know? A mere seller of goods, ignorant of the higher counsels of power. "

"And yet I harvest such wisdom from the tree of your knowledge." The conversation now had Ellison's complete attention. This is the kind of information Stilwell or somebody in command might want. "Where are the guns?"

"Wait." Fan raised his hand. For the next ten minutes, infantry ranks shuffled past. They carried packs and tools but no rifles. After them, carts and wagons loaded with World War I vintage rifles, some pulled by horses or mules, others by groups of peasants roped to wagon tongues, rumbled by. Old, poorly maintained howitzers brought up the rear. "You're wondering why these 'soldiers' don't carry weapons. If they did, they would shoot their guards and escape. All they want is to go home. Then we would have no armies. Nobody fights for *China* or the homeland or your 'democracy.' Hah!" Fan blew a puff of smoke. "Abstractions bore the Chinese."

"But the artillery, anti-aircraft guns. That military aid the U. S. has been sending . . . ."

"Squirreled away in caves, my friend. For after the war." He stuck his head out and shouted at the guards in front. "Move them along, will you?" He leaned back inside, reverting to English. "Gifts from your country have a marvelous habit of transforming themselves into foreign bank accounts. You see, those who fight hate the Japanese or are afraid of being killed by them. Me? I don't hate them. Their money is as good as Chiang's. Better, in fact."

Fan's guards beat back the tide of human flotsam that had surged up from behind and hopped on the car. He pulled away, heedless of overturned wagons and bruised pedestrians.

CHAPTER 34

He who knows himself is unconquerable — Sun Tzu

Hours of hard driving brought them to the outskirts of Chungking, perched on a hump-backed peninsular ridge at the confluence of the smaller Chialing and the mighty Yangtze River. An incessant drizzle that invaded the whole Szechwan basin in winter and early spring shrouded the city in low clouds. Small factories — dismantled and transported piece by piece over hundreds of miles and re-built, many of them underground to escape Japanese bombing campaigns — and coal fires belched plumes of smoke and soot caught in a perpetual atmospheric inversion, a thick fog bordering on noxious gas. The yellow-gray air, palpable as dirty laundry water, swirled around the Mercedes as it passed through one of the old gates in the stone walls that surrounded much of the city and warily negotiated the steep, crowded, pot-holed streets.

"Have to be careful here," said Fan. "Chungking isn't friendly to autos. Did you know it only had its first road that could accommodate a car about fifteen years ago? And it's not easy to find petrol."

Ellison had previously noticed the side streets were far too narrow and steep for vehicles. Many were no more than series of wide stone steps. Where possible, rickshaws were the predominant mode of transport, hauling the odd expatriate European drawn to the city by business or diplomacy, high ranking government bureaucrats, or simply those rich enough not to walk. Up the hills, the

261

drivers stretched parallel to the pavement. Going down, they flew in front of the cab, tilted back so far the occupants were on the verge of falling out the rear. The lanes teemed with pedestrians from all over China and beyond, many dressed in native garb—Moslems from Afghanistan, Mongols from Manchuria, Tibetans, light-skinned natives from Viet Nam to the south and startling Uighurs from Xinjiang, a few with red hair like Ellison's own. Men and sometimes boys shouldering carry poles with buckets at each end stopped and gawked as the Mercedes passed.

"Most of the city has no running water," Fan explained to Ellison's curious look. "Those coolies carry it up from the river all day long. As for sewage, we won't speak of such unspeakable matters." He laughed harshly.

In topography, the city resembled the San Francisco Ellison had seen during his stay stateside, where hills of apartments and grand Victorians were surrounded by water, but in the temporary capital of China flimsy two-story structures often of bamboo crammed the hilly streets. Hundreds of them had toppled over, some into the river, victims of storms or the relentless bombardment the Japanese waged earlier in the war in an attempt to destroy the Kuomintang forces completely.

Fan pointed ahead to a steep, bare hill. "Those holes up there? Caves. Thousands live in them. They were bomb shelters at one point."

"It's like the Stone Age."

For Ellison, the sights embodied all the contradictions in China, an ancient civilization many of whose ways still persisted in a world that had passed them by. Su Li, or at least her Taoist ideas, was that way, too, he reckoned, noble but archaic. China had invented so many things long ago the West now took for granted but had gone virtually nowhere since. Worst of all, the distance between affluence and mere survival—these destitute, hard-working souls on the streets—was higher than the Himalayas and the Ganges plain. His modestly middle-class grandparents in Iowa would be princes here. America had got that part right. How could this vast country ever hope to be a modern power? he wondered.

"The most bombed city on earth." Fan scoffed and waved his hand. "Can you believe they boast about it?" He noticed Ellison's depression. "Don't be so glum. This is the Lower City. All is not lost. Up there," he pointed to the ridge that overlooked the river, "is the Upper City, where the respectable citizens live. The Kuomintang did a—what do you Americans call it—urban redevelopment project there some years ago. Electricity and the benefits of modern life. One of a few special districts that keep the riff-raff out." The car made a right hand turn.

"Unfortunately, we won't be able to see the Generalissimo's magnificent palace. It's worth the penny tour. The other government office buildings are those squat, gray rectangles of brick and concrete over there." Fan pointed a chubby finger. "More like bunkers, wouldn't you say? They don't deserve even a glance. Nothing like the Bund in Shanghai."

At the mention of Shanghai, Ellison came alert from his funk and glanced back at Su Li. She was trying to contain Hui's excitement at the sights of his first trip through a city. Don't get distracted, he reminded himself. This son of a bitch has contacts, information.

On the surface the city appeared to be hopeless, yet as they progressed deeper into the center, life's daily commerce blossomed, somehow managing to survive — even thrive — though crabbed and crimped by the sheer numbers of those who had fled there from other parts of the country. Small, two story buildings of shops and businesses, whose fronts were unpainted, weathered wood boards, lined the street, interspersed with some larger, higher tenements of tiny apartments whose laundry hung out the window. In front, sidewalk merchants hawked hairpins, key chains, fountain pens, slippers, rat poison. Food vendors sold peanuts or noodles with the sharp tang of Szechwan peppers. One cook-stand showed a dog's image painted above it on a wooden placard. Elsewhere along the shop fronts, professional letter writers offered their services above tiny desks with pots of ink and bundles of brushes. Once more Ellison marveled at the resilience of the Chinese.

"I presume you'll want check in at the American legation." Fan lit up another cigarette with a gold lighter, took a deep puff. "It's across the river on the south bank. Allow me to take you to the ferry."

Though the idea of being in the army had been fading since he parachuted out of the DC-3, Ellison still felt an obligation to Stilwell for what the General had done for him. The information he had gleaned from Kuo had to be useful to Army intelligence, he was sure. Fan dropped them off at the *Wang Lung Men* ferry terminal, the city's main river gate. A steep stone stairway led to the water's edge. On the hills opposite lay the American and other foreign embassies. He went to the driver's window to thank the smuggler.

"Honor me by joining me later for dinner? It'll be worth your while." Fan winked conspiratorially. "I enjoy having civilized conversation for a change. The Mandarin Blossom. It's not far from here — just a few streets away." He reached over to the passenger seat. "Don't forget your pack, Leftenant."

Ellison snatched it. "Thanks. I'll have to see." He gestured toward the opposite bank. "Orders, you understand."

Fan grinned knowingly and drove off. He left Su Li and the child to wait for him and boarded the ferry.

Two hours later, back on the north side of the river, a despondent, bewildered Ellison walked up muddy Yellow Tower Street, Su Li and Hui trailing. Stilwell had been recalled to Washington by the War Department, relieved of his position. Major Harris was transferred, too. His old outfit had moved from India to Burma with a new CO. Lieutenant James Ellison's very identity had fallen victim to the military's bureaucratic sinkhole. That was probably good, he told himself, after what had just happened. None of the Marines in the embassy cared about any report he might have; their sole interest was keeping their cushy jobs far from the fighting, and they refused to let him see any of the civilian staff. They sniffed at his torn, unkempt uniform, his lack of identification.

He made one more attempt. After an hour, an officer appeared in the lobby. Ellison produced the documents taken from Kuo.

"Listen, Major Fisher. The Communists are a wild card. They're siphoning off support for Chiang. Even in the south. There's serious treachery going on around him. It's right here in these letters from Communist headquarters. I've been on assignment for General Stilwell."

The intense Fisher, from the military intelligence team, listened with one ear while glancing at his watch. "We don't mention Stilwell anymore, here, Lieutenant. And I suggest you don't either."

"Wait a minute. You don't get it." Ellison said. "Half the Chinese army is corrupt and the other half couldn't beat its way out of a paper bag. General Stilwell — ."

"Are you some kind of wise guy? This is just bullshit to me." Fisher scowled at the papers and flipped them back to the pilot. "Nationalist China is our ally. Get that through your thick skull. Besides, you got no business butting into international politics. We got a war on here, buster." An ugly threat spread over the man's face. "And while you're at it, Lieutenant, you better get back to your unit. You could be facing a court martial. What'd you say your name was?"

"Bugger your ass!" Ellison spun around and stalked out of the embassy.

Out on the street he tore Kuo's documents to shreds. He ripped off his dog tags and threw them into a gutter. *Alone. I'm really fucking alone.* He had no identity now, one more fallen leaf floating on the war's river, heading nowhere. Trust in God, his father would have told him. *No, Dad, I'm trusting in this vision of a whore-queen of beggars in Calcutta – which would delight you no end.* He almost laughed out loud in sick amusement at the absurdity of it. *Forgive me, Dad. I'm not laughing at you. But your son is nuts.*

More depressing were rumors that Marine sentries at the embassy gate passed on, that the Japs might need to take some divisions out of China to fight the Allies who were advancing in the Pacific theater. If the Japanese General Staff were transferred, the war would swallow his mother and Lian. It had taken several huge bites out of him before now. Time and money were running out. A few silver coins left, a couple of opium packets. Seven hundred miles in the wrong direction. What the hell was he thinking? He had naively given his faith to this monk, guerilla – whatever the bloody fuck she was – who exerted a devilish magic over him, while a fiend of her own rode her back. The whole mess was her sorry fault. He cast a sullen glower at Su Li as they traversed the fog-dampened cobblestones. Why couldn't she act like a normal woman?   A plain ordinary woman. Hell, in another time and place . . . . Most of all he hated the smugness.

A stranger on a corner gave directions and the three travelers headed for the Mandarin Blossom. The afternoon light was fading beneath the deep overcast. Passers-by appeared and disappeared like phantoms.

The oppressive murky air heightened the hostility Su Li sensed emanating from the soldier. Tension between them had grown ever since the train episode. Before then, they had talked — argued mostly — night after night along the way, about China, Western values, religion, society, life in the monastery, men and women. The breadth of his knowledge surprised her; his skepticism of beliefs sometimes infuriated her, but her mind had been starving for any form of intellectual food, absent since her days at the Golden Sun; and though they disagreed, the foreigner paid complete attention when she spoke. In her world no one would respect — much less listen to — such opinions from a woman, at least, no Chinese man. His esteem filled her with an uneasy pride but she had not completely forgiven him for Hui's near violation by the Chinese general. The memory made her half-healed wound throb — that too was his fault. Yet they could not continue in this manner.

"In Tao, there is a principle, *wu-wei*. Not-doing. If you learned to follow the flow of the Way — to accept what life brings — you would be happier, soldier," she said, a clumsy peace-offering, unable to hit upon a better one. After all, she understood his doubts concerning her plan. Fear of the Master's rejection plagued her day and night.

"I don't need you to tell me how to live!"

"Did you absorb nothing from your life here?" she said, stung by his rejection.

"Just because I grew up in China doesn't mean I accept the shit that this country wallows in. Sometimes being a foreigner gives you a different perspective." He whirled around to face her, his mouth set hard. "You people could learn from us barbarians — if you weren't so bloody stubborn." He stalked ahead, shaking his head. "Look at this city," he grumbled in English.

"How to import *yang yien*, the foreign smoke? To force China to her knees by addicting her to opium?" She pursued him, her voice rising in spite of herself, despite her Shaolin discipline, despite the countless generations of Chinese women that had bred meekness into her bones. "Is that what we need to learn? Or is it how to bring Jesus to the *Lao Piu T'sing*, as your father did?" She could not control her sarcasm. She had misjudged him. He was as closed-minded as the others.

"Keep my father out of it! As for Jesus, well, what has Confucius done lately for these poor ignorant bastards who barely survive here? Not a hell of a lot as far as I can tell. You can't pull back enough to see your own culture's sicknesses, can you? Why don't you think for yourself sometime, instead of relying on your bloody Master?"

"How do you know what I can see and not see? You do not perceive the smallest part of what I have knowledge of, what I have been through." She sputtered with rage. "And you believe your education does not blind you?" She was shouting now. "How dare you attack a culture that was high when your ancestors lived in caves!" Pedestrians hurried past, pretending not to hear. Such public outbursts were impolite but she didn't care. Frozen in anger, neither spoke for a tension-filled moment.

"So." His voice was flat, matter of fact, as he looked her in the eye, then looked down. "Are you going to kill me?"

Her clenched fists were ready to strike. The sight took her breath away. "I . . . . I . . . ." Quaking with embarrassment and shame, she covered one fist with the other hand, a gesture of peace that did not begin to express her remorse. As much as she knew she should say something, words would not come forth.

In the next instant he turned on his heel and stalked away.

CHAPTER 35

If you don't want to be broken, bend – Lao-tze

Furious with the *kao pi tzuh*, appalled at her unconscious reaction to that anger, paralyzed by pride and revulsion at her conceit, stricken with an immediate, powerful regret at parting in a manner so unworthy of their previous time together, dumbfounded and unable to call out, she watched him disappear into the throng of pedestrians.

Hui, in a panic, tugged at her sleeve. "Please, mother," he pleaded. "Do not let him leave. He is a good man, not as you are, truly, but in many ways he is wise, and," he bent his head and continued in a cautious, low voice, "like a father."

It was the most he had said since the abduction. At another time, she would have slapped his cheek for such behavior. "I will not allow such disrespect."

He showed no remorse.

"Recall your manners! He is not your father. Besides, what kind of father teaches insolence to a child?" She yanked on his wrist. "Come!"

Hui dug in his heels. She frowned, uncertain of the proper response. The answer surfaced, hidden until that second, like a forest spring bubbles beneath the duff until finally it bursts through. She had always loved this child, even when she hated being his mother. The trickle of understanding became a rivulet, then a stream, then a river. Her life, her very essence had changed because of him. She hugged him to her breast. How were such

271

opposites able to exist? She never knew they could until this soldier came whom Hui loved so much. It was so clear but still she was refusing to believe it. It *was* the solider, and now the space where he had stood was empty, as empty as the hole in her *dan tian. He did not make me love you, my son – you did that – but because of him, I . . . .*

Hui pulled away and nodded gravely at her.

"Sometimes I forget you are a child." She knelt and kissed his hand. "Your soldier is a big monkey as well as a big tall." The child managed a smile. "Besides, it is he who is leaving."

He sprang from her, turning to shout. "Wait, Mother."

He spied Ellison a block away across the street on the sidewalk at the next intersection watching a funeral procession. Bearers in their best clothes carried the corpse wrapped in straw — there was no wood for coffins. Mourners clothed in white banged drums or held up red and yellow flowery paper wreaths cut in large circles, attached to bamboo poles. The procession's leader trailed a flowing white cloth, the soul of the departed. The sight unnerved him.

"Er . . . ris . . . son!" he called out but a heart-sick horn in the cortege blared, drowning out his voice. Up until that moment, the wondrous sights of the city had held in check the traumas inflicted on him during the journey. His attachment to the soldier had softened their impact as had his own peculiar psyche that floated mostly unscathed by and through the brutality of life everywhere they traveled, but the macabre tribute to the dead that he beheld finally broke down his defenses. Near panic with fear he might lose one of his two anchors in a hostile city, he dodged, falling and tripping, through the midst of the mourners and relatives who bore paper imitations of objects the deceased might wish in the more harmonious spirit world. Almost blinded by tears, he ran up to Ellison and threw his arms around the startled soldier's waist.

"What are you doing here, lad? You should be with your mother." He squatted to eye level. "And look at you, you're crying."

"Do not go," the boy pleaded in halting English, before switching to Chinese. "The mother is not this way." Tears continued to bubble out the corner of his eyes. "She needs you, Big Tall." He hugged Ellison's neck. "Stay with us. Please!"

"She doesn't need me, son." He wiped the tears with his sleeve, moved by the child's love for him. She didn't need anybody, he thought, that was for sure. But this little bairn did. What he really needed was a father. The insight startled him. The prospect of having children, much less caring for them, had never received serious attention in his life's plan which was resolutely — even obsessively, he admitted — focused on his solemn promise to rescue his mother. Ambivalence about his own father kept such speculation at bay. Oddly enough, his friendship with Buzz had led him to a state of partial forgiveness for the old man. Abraham Ellison as a young man would have been a lot like his co-pilot, a pain in the ass sometimes, but fundamentally a decent person. But James Ellison, a father? He had difficulty conceiving a future beyond the war, but someday, there would be no war, though hard to imagine.

"And how did you become so wise, Little Tall?" Ellison tousled his hair. "That spirit-father you speak of, the old hermit, must have been pretty special. Besides, who would teach you English?"

Hui smiled through his tears, took the reluctant man's hand and led him to Su Li. "You must be friends again, honored Mother. Big Tall," he said.

But the two refused to acknowledge the other's presence. The rest of the way, the child walked between them, holding a hand of each. A forced smile covered his apprehension whenever he glanced up at the surrogate parents he loved who faced stolidly straight ahead.

They turned the corner of Long River Street. Now closed behind steel shutters, the small intact shops lining the block had been spared from the Japanese bombardment. A dim glow from second-floor windows hinted at occupants in a desert of darkness. Outside the tea house entrance—an oasis of light—Fan waved to them. Ellison supposed he had delivered the goods hidden in the trunk, for his car and the guards were nowhere in sight.

"The scum deals in opium. Caravans for the Japanese pass through here. From the Shan state in Burma. Sometimes even around Emei Shan."

"Opium caravans?"

"Do not be so naïve, soldier."

"What the bloody hell?"

"Warlords sell to whoever pays the most. Kuomintang, Japanese."

"How?"

"He is coming." She backed against the wall of the restaurant.

"Leftenant Ellison! This insignificant merchant is made richer by your presence," said Fan in English, hand extended. "I notice you still have your little 'gifts.' I'll have my man see to them if you wish." He was accompanied by a single bodyguard, a huge, intimidating man with a drooping mustache and keen eyes. His scalp was shaved except for a small top-knot. Around his waistcoat he wore an emerald sash that held two daggers. Much heavier and at least six inches taller than Ellison, he exuded a restrained but highly lethal self-assurance.

"Thanks, but not necessary. They're not likely to escape. They have nowhere to go and I'm their source of food. Let's sit where I can keep an eye on them, though."

"As you will."

Fan escorted him through a wrought iron gate to a graveled enclosure. The semicircle centered on a stone fountain in front of a roofed pavilion that extended over the courtyard and covered the dining tables. Fan halted at a circular table and signaled to a waiter. The bodyguard sat apart with four other fierce-looking men. His daggers lay on the tabletop next to other weapons — swords, a club, fans able to rend and tear along with some unfamiliar items. The smuggler lowered the menu, noticed Ellison staring.

"Martial artists. Mostly from the north. Shandong or Manchuria. Or like my man there, from Mongolia. They're banned in Republican China." He answered the question on Ellison's face. "But they have their uses. And this," he made a gesture, "shall I say, is a special place."

A thick haze of cigarette smoke swirled around the tasseled paper lanterns hung from exposed rafters above the dining room. The hum of conversation mingled with the jangle of porcelain laid down by nimble waiters balancing overloaded trays. From the kitchen, open to the public and set at the back end of the room, the hiss of steam and the pungent smell of ginger and sizzling peanut oil suffused the air. Wispy-bearded scholars in blue robes with frayed hems smoked slender pipes and played *mah jong* in a corner beneath walls of red brocade cloth embroidered with gilded dragons. Thin spectacles creased their high, hawk-like noses. One wore a black skull cap tilted backward on his tufted bald head and scratched his nose with long, bent fingernails. A wealthy, older man in a traditional long coat held noisy court over relatives and friends at one large table covered with various dishes. A quartet of plump chickens snapped up the scraps on the floor boards. Overweight Chinese men in Western style clothes at three other tables were drinking heavily, heatedly arguing or else joking. Most had young females on their laps. The diners gave Ellison a quick guarded glance then returned to business. Similar young, heavily made-up women were descending the staircase from the upper floor.

Fan lit a cigarette. "Kuomintang bureaucrats. We Chinese love to mix pleasure with business. That bloke in the middle," he blew smoke toward one, "has made your humble servant's life difficult at times. He has friends even higher than mine. Sun Tzu, where are you when I need you?" He laughed and took another drag on his cigarette. "The young women? Sing-song girls sold into prostitution by their own families. They're capable of remarkable feats. I hope your ungainly slave is equally adept."

Ellison glanced toward the gate. "You have no idea."

Nearby, four Nationalist officers talked in quiet voices, intent on their meal. Soon another man joined them. His brown leather jacket and muddy boots spoke of a recent arrival from an arduous trip. An agent? Ellison had heard Chungking was full of spies.

"Excuse me, Leftenant. This acquaintance of mine has not eaten." Fan winked at Ellison. "A fancy way of saying I've not greeted him." He rose and joined the man in the dusty clothes. Take care, fool — Ellison could almost hear Su Li warn him. This smuggler is dangerous. He did not invite you here out of the goodness of his heart.

In the open courtyard on benches flanking the fountain, a quartet of women, dressed in diaphanous silk gowns performed on traditional instruments — the *ruan*, a fretted lute with a round back like a banjo; the *pipa*, pear-shaped, more like a Western lute; a wooden flute, and the *er-hu*, a two-stringed version of the violin not much more than a slender neck with tuning pegs at the top and a faceted base at the bottom. Willowy and tall with their heavy hair wound and pinned high on their heads, they performed with the utmost grace. Beautiful, he sighed to himself, his eyes refusing to stray from the striking musicians. *It would be good to be with a woman again, a real woman, not someone who could beat the crap out of you if you looked at her wrong.* His groin obviously agreed. When the music stopped, Ellison peered across the courtyard. Su Li and Hui had disappeared.

"Excuse me for a minute, Fan." He walked over to the gate. Nothing. When he returned to the table, Fan had ordered drinks. Ellison called the waiter.

"Will you please try to find my slaves?" he said in Chinese. The man glanced at Fan who nodded.

"I see you do speak our language after all, Leftenant." Fan eyed the American with an amused smile. "Deception. Part of war. Such matters exceed my poor comprehension. Are you a spy as well?" He chortled and offered the pilot a glass of yellow liquor, held up his own. "Dry cup."

Ellison gulped his wine. He had made a mistake. "Nothing but a poor student of your culture, caught in a war not his own." He laughed uneasily, thinking the while he wasn't sure of what he was now. "I was hoping to ask you about Shanghai." Fan was using him, of course, but the suave merchant might be his only chance for a lead. The smuggler knew how the Japanese hierarchy worked. Meanwhile the music twanged and plunked and sawed in a distracting, siren-like rhythm.

"Which do you admire most, Leftenant, the form or the playing?" Fan, who seemed to miss nothing, noted his fascination with the performers. "I could arrange for one of them to meet you. The owner of this establishment owes this simple dealer in goods a favor. And there are rooms on the second floor."

He found himself tempted. The make-up, the eyes, the gowns, all perfect. *"Huli jing.* Lovely. Exquisite." Something was wrong. His head.

Fan raised his brows. "Foxes in disguise. You're familiar with Chinese mythology. Hmm." He puffed on his cigarette and gestured to someone in the corner. "You know the Japanese have got it right, though. I mean for soldiers like yourself."

"What do you mean?" Ellison's tongue felt as heavy as a brick.

"The comfort stations at the camps. Women, lying around all day having sex. Wouldn't mind doing that myself now and then." He sucked on a *mi chu,* a mandarin orange.

Ellison's brain struggled to comprehend the thread. "You've seen these?"

"Seen them, yes. Been inside, no. There's one southeast of Hankow." Fan wiped his mouth with a napkin.

A soft hand touched Ellison's neck. A seductive Asian woman in a tight-fitting red dress leaned over him and smiled. Pushed up beneath the cut of her dress, her breasts brushed against his arm, her perfume intoxicating.

"Have you heard . . . I mean what sort of women are there?" Somehow the seductive vamp had managed to sit on his lap. His crotch hardened. She grinned, wriggling on top of him. He swallowed hard.

"Captives. Mostly Korean, some Chinese."

"Western women?" Ellison struggled harder to keep focused.

"Not in the camps themselves. There are rumors, though. Female missionaries, Europeans interned. Reserved for high officers. The Japs are fascinated by Caucasian females. Last delivery I had in Shanghai I overheard them brag about a red-haired Venus kept by General Okamura Yasutsugu. Probably the usual blow off." He eyed Ellison coolly. "What's your interest here?"

"I, uh . . . ." His head felt like a football. Fog in his brain. Yet Fan was saying something important. Shanghai. That was it. He wanted to ask another question. But the woman . . . .

"You are lonely, American." Her buttocks shifted.

"Aye." Her breasts were inches from his face. "Aye, I . . . ."

His head slumped onto the table.

CHAPTER 36

There are no areas in which one does not employ spies –
Sun Tzu

Outside the tea house, Su Li squatted on the damp cobblestones while a sleepy Hui dozed against a wall. Armed guards patrolling the perimeter to keep the innumerable beggars away gave them a suspicious look-over. She was growing impatient. This was the end, she seethed. He was still angry and intended to travel his own way. He could not say she did not warn him about this opium-dealing son of a turtle. Yet she wished she had made peace with him, parted as friends. They had traveled so far, survived so much danger.

The street was filled with human misery, shadows at the outer limits of the restaurant's lights, like the beggar and his young daughter who had appeared at the gate seconds after the guard moved on. The vagrants, on the verge of starvation, wept at the obscene amounts of food consumed within. Su Li pitied the man and offered him the meager portion in her pack.

"*Xie xie*, thank you." His gaunt face brightened. "But please come with me and share it with my wife and son. It is not safe here."

There were no better prospects. "Wait for one moment." Across the courtyard, Fan was drinking wine with Nationalist officers. Ellison was gone. Most likely with a whore in an upstairs room, she guessed. Let him take his pleasure. She did not care. "Come, Hui. We must find shelter and this man has offered refuge."

"But where is Big Tall?"

281

"He has abandoned us. We will go to Emei Shan without him."

Hui began to cry. "No, Mother. He would not do that. Evil has befallen him. Some spell by that wicked man. Please try to find him, I beg you."

"I refuse to be wet-nurse to a grown man."

But she hesitated. Even in the midst of her pique, she could not deny what she owed him: the attack at the river, his compassion for the refugees, his courage at the train. His laughter and kindness above everything else had filled their long days on the road like nothing she had ever experienced. And he walked under the sign of the tiger. That alone was why she agreed to take him to the Master, but he was no *laohuo*. He was flippant, cynical, stubborn. In any case why should she care what he was? To pretend to be his slave any longer was unworthy of a Shaolin. Solely because the boy loved him? But Hui hugged her and refused to let go. This fear was a message as clear as ice. Besides, he would give her no peace until she had made certain Ellison was safe.

"Very well. I will look once more. The fool is still my responsibility. My bond with him is not completely broken. But after this, we are finished." When she checked inside the gates this time, an attendant was about to shut the doors, waiters and towel boys were cleaning up and the customers had departed. No trace of Fan. Tocsins of suspicion sounded in her brain.

First, Hui. She handed him their packs, then pulled up her sleeves and showed her markings to the beggar.

His mouth opened. "Take my son with you. Protect him on your life. I have business here."

"Yes, Shaolin. An honor," he said.

"Go with him, Hui. I will return with Big Tall, I promise you." Hui kissed her while the man gave her directions to his hovel. "Hurry, before the guard returns."

Most of the windows on the second story of the teahouse were dark, but from two or three, lights behind drawn curtains shed a murky glow. If he were inside, it would be in one of those. In the narrow side-alley, a short sprint and leap launched her up to a window ledge near the house's rear corner. Spider-like she climbed the frame until one hand grasped the lion's-head corbel at the next level, then pulled herself up. A sentry with a rifle slung over his shoulder stopped directly below, leaned on the wall, lit up a cigarette. She clung to the building, stock-still, muscles quivering. The guard resumed his circuit. She pistonned up and to the right, managed to reach the next window sill, pivoted upward, lifted the sash and rolled sideways into the lightless room.

Ellison's forehead throbbed as if someone had hit him with a hammer. His eyes at first refused to open as his brain emerged from the drug. He tugged at his hands—tied behind a cane-backed chair—and shivered, realizing he had no shirt on. His eyelids cracked to see a dimly lit room but it demanded too much effort to keep them that way. Voices. The Asian vamp, speaking in a language he recognized but didn't understand. The other was Fan—he remembered that voice. His fog lifted a bit more. Wait. The officer who shot his father. Japanese! The haze vanished and he sat bolt upright. At a small table with a cheap electric lamp, Fan and the woman were examining the contents of his pack.

"Well, I see our spy has awakened," Fan said with a chuckle. "Just in time. Nothing personal, Leftenant. Business, you know. Now I'll leave you to the good graces of Madame Tenaka. *Zaijian*. See you again. Ha, ha. Not likely."

Ellison rallied. "Fan! Was it true what you said?"

Fan halted. "About what?"

"The red-haired Westerner, you bastard."

"We have a saying here, 'Never believe a thief,' Leftenant." He sniggered and closed the door behind him.

The woman ignored him for a while, intent on her inspection while he feverishly jerked at his bindings. A flimsy bed lay along one wall in the cramped space, one of the rooms used for paid sex. To the left, tattered curtains over a small half-opened window drooped in the humidity. The single door was opposite, on his right. His captor approached with a panther's grace, a haughty smile between rouged cheeks, long, jet black hair pinned up, stiletto heels, arms crossed below her breasts, perfect white teeth showing through red lipstick.

"Now, American," she said in accented English, "you will tell of this mission for General Stilwell and the poisonous toad Chiang."

"I am Lieutenant James Ellison. My serial number is —." Inch-long fingernails clawed searing trenches into his shoulder. They burned like a branding iron. Blood trickled down his chest.

"Do not waste my time! We have seen the papers. You are a spy. As such, you will be executed."

"I am not a spy!" He spat the words out in a low growl.

She grabbed a handful of hair and bent his head back. The cabled muscles of her arms could have snapped his distended neck. "Do not take me for a fool. No ordinary soldier gets a letter such as that." She brandished an ornate dagger and ran her thumb along its edge. "If you cooperate, I will let you die quickly." She dropped the knife, returned to the table and picked up a revolver. Ellison waited for the end.

The agent spun the gun's chamber but set it back on the table. "I think not. More subtle methods." When she faced him, her eyes had narrowed. "I've often imagined how it would feel to couple with a male of an inferior race. They say Americans are much larger than our own puny men."

"You are sick!" he shouted, filled with disgust, working at his bonds.

She swiped his cheek with her claw-like nails. "I will do with you what I please!" she screeched.

"You're insane, you sadistic bitch!"

"Now you will know agony," the spy announced. She reached for the dagger when she noticed him looking at the door.

"Stop, devil!"

The agent's body tensed as she turned with disbelieving, angry eyes. "How dare you enter without permission? Out of here or die, cur," she said in Chinese.

Su Li placed her fist against her palm, a sign of battle. In a fraction of a second the knife flew across the room straight at her head. Equally fast, the Shaolin ducked aside and caught the weapon as it thudded into the wall. She hurled it into the floor boards between the stiletto heels and assumed a fighting stance.

"So, a Chinese martial arts pretender." the agent sneered. "I will be happy to instruct you in true martial arts."

She kicked off her shoes, ripped the slit in her dress to free her legs, and with a battle cry snatched up the flimsy cot and flung it at Su Li before leaping to the attack. The bed crashed into Su Li's hard slicing palm and broke into pieces, Karate versus *kung fu*. Karate exploded against the intruder with piston-like strikes: reverses, scissors kicks, and double punches that rained like a meteor shower. Spins and half-spins morphed into vicious kick-punches, her body in a tee, her foot a ram to the mid-section where a hollow pit of fear opened in Su Li. Her core, her *dan tian*, turned to insubstantial vapor at the question that shot arrow-like through her mind: Am I going to die here? A volley of hammer-hard death-dealing fists bored holes in the plaster, missed by inches, and gave her a preliminary answer.

She ducked, dodged, parried, leaned back almost double, circling away, half-thoughts alternating with instinctual, neuronal commands: Flow like water. Yield.

Too late. Bone-breaking blows crushed her chest, drove her flat against the wall, emptied her lungs, tore open her wound. Worse than the pain was a paralyzing sense of dread at the force of the karate master, but she recovered enough to block, defend, retreat, all the while frantic to summon the zone she had attained against Master Zhao while a small voice in the back of her skull kept screeching at her: Stop trying, stop thinking.

But a bewildering tsunami of hatred from Karate rained against her faltering mental defense, overwhelming the voice. The sorceress had no weakness. No weakness. How could evil possess such skill, such power? She could not defeat her and the witch knew it. The poison of hate flowed in her veins now like a viper's bite; she could feel her limbs tiring, her response time slowing. Karate, relentless as a death sentence, somersaulted with ear-piercing cries and a blizzard of punches hard as battering rams. Dimly aware she had half-lost the battle by admitting her opponent's superiority, she stepped backward to make her adversary miss, miscalculated, and lost her balance.

Ellison, acutely aware of the whooshes, grunts and moans that punctuated the thump of hard fists on soft bodies, rocked his chair until it toppled over, still struggling with the ropes when a foot tripped over his calf. He twisted his head around—Su Li was on her back an arm's length from him, the she-devil's knees astride her waist. Out of the corner of his eye he spotted the knife. He hunched closer, feeling the handle, fumbling to get the blade right, sawing, sawing, until the last strand severed, then to his knees to see Karate clamp a vise grip on Su Li's throat and whip out a six inch steel pin from her hair. Unbound locks shrouding her face were an executioner's hood.

He lunged, plunging the dagger into Karate's side before the brooch descended. Her scream pierced Su Li's stupor. Karate released her choke-hold to pull the knife out, surprised, enraged when she spotted him, now frozen, stupefied at the woman's invulnerability. She hurled the dagger at him but Su Li locked on to her wrists and disrupted her aim. Karate twisted her hands free and raised a mortal fist aimed at her enemy's heart, still pinned beneath, but Ellison, finally unchained from his spell, grabbed a hunk of dark hair and dragged her off Su Li.

Karate punched his hand away with blows that nearly broke his wrists, leapt toward him, lashed out with a leg that thudded into his spleen. He howled and fell, knocking over the small table along with the revolver. He saw it fall as another brutal kick in his kidney slammed his face to the floor and nearly knocked the wind out of him. Karate turned to finish the dazed Su Li, but Ellison, still convulsing, clawed for the pistol not certain his hands would function, rolled onto his backside and fired.

The bullet burrowed into the wall, but its report, thunder in the small space, damped down the dynamo that drove the fighting automaton. Faced with the weapon, she backed off, panting, holding her side. Su Li scrabbled to her feet and moved alongside Ellison.

"You will never capture me alive, weaklings." Face contorted with venom, the spy's tongue shot out between her teeth; she bit it and spat out a piece of flesh. Blood squirted out the end of her tongue. She closed her eyes in a trance, then fell amidst a red pool that spread from her mouth. In five seconds she was dead.

Ellison and Su Li looked on in horror, petrified, each gulping the air, too dazed to move. When at last the adrenalin faded and their heart rates slowed, they faced each other. The sight of his shredded naked torso, strange and exotic, overwhelmed all she had just endured. His *chi* pricked her like a thousand acupuncture needles, his labored breath a faint echo from a land far away. His red hair, yellow-blue eyes, pale skin, trumped even her near death and undammed the reservoir of longing she had hoarded so tightly. She longed to weld her body to his.

He pulled her into an embrace. "How did you . . . ?" he asked.

The enchantment vanished. She winced, pushed him away. "We must leave. Now!"

"You saved my life—again," he mumbled as he threw on his shirt and gathered his scattered belongings.

"And you mine."

"Can we get out of here?"

"If you know how to jump."

CHAPTER 37

What immortal hand or eye, Could frame thy fearful symmetry – Blake

Su Li and Ellison hobbled their painful way through the sleeping city's slums, searching for the beggar's hovel, each street drearily alike – monotonous dunes of garbage and filth flowing up against mounds of rubble. Scores of residences had been leveled, twisted wood fragments and shattered bricks heaved into piles mixed with corpses. Beggars competed with the refuse, crowded around small fires or huddled against buildings the bombing had spared. The blind and the crippled congregated in the alleys, drawn together by their mutual afflictions.

Hui, though, was on the look-out for them beside a low-roofed lean-to of boxes with a flimsy sheet metal cover, light from a candle within wavering in the street's darkness. Inside, a boy lay on a bed of rags, sick with fever; his father sat on the bare cobblestones next to him, the scrawny daughter from the tea house on his lap. The mother, a sad-eyed woman who tended a pot on a brazier heated by two lumps of coal, looked up at the visitors. A tiny shrine with a doll-sized, tricked-up goddess and a red candle stood on a wooden crate. Their meager belongings lay piled in one corner.

"Kung's son is sick, Mother. They think he is dying. Can you help him?" Hui asked.

Su Li wiped her eyes with the back of her wrists, took a couple of deep breaths, then stooped to examine the child. He was severely dehydrated but would live. The fever would break before it killed him — if he had water.

"Get water," she said wearily. The man poured a thick mud-colored liquid from a jug into a cup. "Not that! Clean water. I don't care how you do it."

"Yes, spirit-woman." The father's eyes widened with wonder when he noticed Ellison. "Ah, your friend — the big nose! Your son told me of him." He rose to depart.

"Wait! We need your help in return. To go to Emei Shan."

He nodded and melted into the darkness.

"He will contact the beggar king," the woman said, her face pocked with scars from scarlet fever. "Or someone from the Red Dragon Gang. It owns this part of Chungking. If you have trouble with the law, they will help you — for a price."

In an hour Kung returned with a flask of water and another man, dressed in a gray coat, a tam pulled low on his head.

"Boil the water for tea, then put these in it." Su Li drew out a pouch of medicinal herbs she had purchased outside Paochi. "Give him more in the morning. He will be well soon."

"Thank you." Kung bowed. "I am in your debt, spirit-woman."

Spirit-woman. She arched her brows in frustration, looked at Ellison who nodded and handed the father a small silver coin. The trio left with the stranger who guided them through dark alleys where no Kuomintang police dared go. They came to a pier at the river's edge.

The guide paused, lit a cigarette. Su Li nudged Ellison who handed the man his last two packets of opium from his jacket pocket. The shadowy figure motioned them into a boat and rowed across. On the south side, his instructions led them through more deserted streets to a seedy warehouse district where a truck waited. She spoke softly to the driver who signaled the fugitives to hide under a canvas tarp.

The old stake-bed Ford, loaded with coal in burlap sacks, rumbled on through the night while the exhausted riders slept fitfully, racked by their near escape from the Japanese agent. At sunrise the truck passed through towns that serviced pilgrims who gathered each day at the eastern foot of Emei Shan, Delicate Eyebrow Mountain. When at last it halted, Su Li lifted the tarp. Hundreds of pilgrims were forming lines outside the Bao Guo temple where the journey up the cloud-topped mountain commenced. The travelers jumped out. Ellison handed the driver his last coin. The truck turned around and drove away.

To the north was a line of oak trees next to an orchard. Even further, a spiny ridge marked the start of the mountain's foothills. Between the two landmarks, Su Li knew, was a village where she once lived as a small child with old Mai, the midwife.

One day a monk arrived to take her away.

"I don't want to go, mama," she said and started to cry.

The gap-toothed crone gave her a hug. "You must, little one. You belong with the Master, not an old woman. He is a very great man. They say he has magic powers. I don't know why he wants a girl, though. He never tells his plans to such a humble slave."

"But why must I go?" she pleaded.

Mai set Su Li on her lap. "He said when he brought you that you were a child of destiny. I do not remember the whole story, but he told me your real parents were tigers. That they had given you to him as a gift. It frightened me."

"I'm afraid of him, mama." She buried her face between the old woman's breasts.

Mai kissed her and sighed.

When she stopped there the day after her exile, relatives had moved in. They told her Mai had joined her ancestors. The memory brought sadness at the passing of good things that happen in life's river, the comfort that physical contact imparted, a sensation not experienced for so long. No. That was wrong, she corrected herself. Especially in recent months, Hui's embraces fed her starved spirit, and the soldier, at the train, he held her and cared for her, too. But neither of them was gentle, healing ointment tenderly applied to a cut on the leg, or cool cloth beneath an anxious hand on a feverish forehead, or a reassuring hug for a crying little girl. The old mid-wife's affection had ignited a tight furnace of self-approval in her foster daughter, just as the Master had fanned it with the fuel of courage; and they both endured, despite the mountains of adversity she had climbed, despite how often she had lost her way. If she had not left the old house behind, would she have remembered these truths? Understood them? Without the Big Tall's arrival? It was his idea that prompted her to leave. His presence reminded her to believe in herself and confront the Master. She looked at him, standing beside Hui, a beaten expression on his face. *Why should I care about his opinion? Yet I do.*

Hui's hand had clasped hers. "Where are they going, Mother?"

"Up those stairs?" A steep stairway of stone treads worn smooth by innumerable devotees wound upward and out of sight. "To visit holy places." Pilgrims even now were ascending, encountering those who had spent the night at the dozens of shrines and temples that punctuated the mountain's slopes all the way to the top. "See those trees, my son? The ones that line the steps? *Nammu* trees. Legend says centuries ago the monk Hong Ja — from my order — planted 69,707 of them. And that temple, where the pilgrims are gathering, that is where the first Buddhist temple in China was built."

"Is the Monastery of the Golden Sun up there?"

"Our destination is beyond, on the other side. There are two main peaks on the mountain and we must travel to the far one. Come!" Some pilgrims were staring at Ellison, his uniform and features even more out of place here than before. "We need to leave."

A day of hard walking led them up a gradual slope to the last of the cultivated fields, dimpled by the ever-present shrines to the ancestors. Caps of what had once been boulders protruded meekly from the soil. The spaces between them, worn by centuries of wind and rain, had been filled by erosion. There was no hope of tilling such land; and the forest proper was yet considered haunted for the trees ahead remained intact. She took that as a good sign.

"There's the old path," she exclaimed, her heart beating with excitement. "I love this place," she said quietly, addressing her words to Hui. "Every rock and tree. Every flower and bird. No wonder it is called Beauty Under Heaven."

But the child was practicing English with Ellison and hadn't heard her. She rubbed her brow in dismay. The old doubts about his devotion to her returned even as the light from childhood memories darkened under the thick arboreal canopy of maple and bamboo that barred sunlight from the forest floor. Guilt and memories, almost forgotten in the hazards of the last months, tormented her once more.

At twilight, they stopped amidst a stand of pine trees and made camp. Ellison and Hui cleared brush and lit a fire while Su Li fetched water from a creek. She boiled it and cooked rice with herbs in a metal cup. They ate in silence, mesmerized by the flames. Eventually the child curled up in his blanket and fell asleep. In the fire's shadows, the soldier's head lay on his pack, his attention on the forest canopy above. He had spoken little during the whole time they had traveled from Chungking whereas before she sensed his eyes on her constantly. His spirit was wounded, she realized. He was ashamed. She understood that feeling well.

Night deepened and the flames burned low. Pines, alders and oaks circled the little camp in a mysterious curtain of uncertainty, but the mountaintop loomed visible above the canopy, flawless and indifferent in starlight and moonlight. Clarity and confusion. Mutual arising. The union of opposites. She glanced at the soldier — woman and man — and threw a bundle of sticks on the fire, unwilling to let it die. Listen to the stillness, the Master once told her. A bat skimmed overhead. A bird warbled its last futile melody. Small creatures rustled the brush. Insects flitted, the tiny buzz of their wings all but inaudible but not to her ears. They reminded her of the monks chanting in the temple. Attention, attention, attention they droned. The creek roared as loud as a mighty river. She whiffed the tar in the pines, senses alert, as if a mountain-shaking event were about to happen. The higher the flames flared the brighter the strange tiger symbol on the pilot's jacket glowed. The urge to handle it, to touch him, was irresistible and she leaned forward.

"Aaaah!" His cry split the silence.

She shook him. "Soldier! Wake up. You are having a dream." As he groggily came awake, an uncontrollable impulse moved her hand to his brow.

Ellison imagined for a second his mother was waking him. He rolled over on his side on the hard earth to find steady brown eyes above him, her palm as cool as starlight. High overhead the Milky Way's countless diamonds blazed in the cloudless sky. Outlined by the luminous stellar dust that arched in the inky firmament, she might have been a faery in the stories from his childhood, or an earth-spirit, a shape-shifter from old Chinese legends. What in truth was this creature beside him? he wondered for the hundredth time. He squeezed her hand; it did not resist. She was real, and actually touching him.

"Is it gone?" she asked.

"Yes," he lied and blinked.

"Will you tell me this dream?"

"Not now. Sometime."

"Perhaps it has meaning. Maybe I can tell you."

"No! Nothing has any *meaning*. Especially my wretched life." He took his hand away from hers. "I will never find them! I don't have time. I don't even know what I need." He closed his eyes. "Why did you return? You should have let them kill me."

"No." Her voice crackled above the forest's own sounds. "No, Ellison." She paused and smiled shyly. "You are impatient sometimes. You allow your feelings to govern you. But you are worthy of my concern. You have courage, compassion, intelligence. All the potential of a true man, as Lao-tze calls it."

She had smiled at him. He treasured that smile, it came so seldom; but her words were more surprising. He had imagined she disdained him. Potential? What did that mean? Chaotic images cascaded through his mind — the faded immature attraction for Lian, his devotion to his mother, resentment mixed with admiration for his father

297

coupled with remorse at failing to save any of them, and now the no-longer-deniable, growing ache for this enigmatic Shaolin, who defied comprehension and could never accept such weakness. But there was that hand — and she had called him by his name. The first time.

"That spy almost killed you because of me." He turned his palms up. "I have enough blood on my hands."

She stiffened, folded her arms tight across her chest, her hands beneath her elbows, out of sight.

"Were you afraid? I mean right then," he said.

"Each creature under heaven must die." She lowered her head in thought. "No, Ellison. I am not afraid of dying." At last she lifted her chin. "Sometimes, life frightens me more." She sighed. "Were you?"

"I was angry. At myself."

"When you are no longer angry at yourself you will be a wise man. Until that day . . . ," she breathed the last words to herself as if unwilling to share them, " . . . you are like me." Her fingertips touched his cheek where the Japanese spy had slashed him. They caressed his eyelids with the tenderness of a feather, the mystery and contradictions of life locked up in their touch. "I will have to look after you, I suppose."

The next morning they plunged into denser forest and mounted their ascent up the back slope of the mountain. Stout bamboo, dense and as wide as a stove chimney and reaching fifty feet high, stood sentinel above a trail, overgrown with ferns and brush, muddier the higher they climbed where the temperature was cooler. Sometimes landslides, loosened by the previous summer's heavy rains, blocked the way and they had to climb over or around them. They zigzagged up the mountainside over ridges open to the sun, then down shallow valleys where the forest ceiling closed in, then up again.

"Where are we headed?" Ellison asked. "I don't see anything but dense forest or sheer limestone walls."

"That outcropping about a third of the way up." She pointed to a landmark jutting out to the north before the incline resumed its upward thrust.

"Looks impossible to me."

"Trust me, Ellison. I know this way."

"I'll need to rest soon."

On a valley floor, the last one before the ascent steepened, the trees, now smaller in size and with less bamboo, thickened around thick undergrowth, but to Su Li's surprise, she and Hui stumbled across a well-beaten path perpendicular to their own upward direction. Someone had trampled the grasses and ferns along this section and cut down a few of the trees to clear the trail. It would function as a rest stop, wider and more open in the middle than at the ends, but she could not recall such a feature. Something about this place smelled evil but everyone was tired and needed a rest. The site would have to do before they mounted the more difficult slopes.

"Look, butterflies!" Hui waved then skipped along the trail before vanishing into one end of a tree tunnel.

Ellison, who had fallen behind, at length caught up with them, clambering through the brush, panting, glad to rest on one of the downed tree trunks. He wiped his forehead on his sleeve, drank from a leather pouch, then picked up a handful of pebbles.

Si Li came over and sat beside him, silent for a while, distracted, nervous. She took a deep breath. "Those women in the tea house—I mean the musicians . . . ." Words bubbled forth before she had a chance to think. His opinion of such women should not be her concern, she knew, but asked anyway, unable to help herself. "Did you find them desirable? And this Lian you speak of, was she beautiful like them?" She ran her hand self-consciously over her dirty braids of hair. Her tattered tunic and trousers seemed shabby.

"She was . . ." he paused, eyes closed, as if the act of speech were painful, ". . . a girl."

"Chinese."

He nodded.

"In truth I do not believe a Western man can love a Chinese woman."

The pebbles fell from Ellison's hand.

Her pulse quickened. A hollow channel of fear opened in her stomach. "You still love this girl?"

"It was a long time ago."

She pondered his reply. "This love. How is it different from coupling? Merely another word for a man to use when he wants to lie with a woman." She scowled. "I am not ignorant."

"No."

"I do not understand you."

He made a slow, hardly perceptible shake of his head. "Nor I you." He stared straight into her eyes.

300

"Who taught you to look that way?" she snapped.

"What way?" he answered.

She tossed her head sharply. "Do you want to find this slave or not?"

Ellison gathered their packs. "Where's Hui?" The opening in the tree tunnel to the left now looked ominous.

"Not far, I hope." She had no more spoken when a cry echoed from beyond the tree line — her son's voice. In the next instant two bandits emerged from the opposite side of the clearing. They carried Japanese Arikawa rifles with bandoliers of ammunition across their chests. One plunged into the forest in the vicinity of the sound. They had not yet noticed Su Li or Ellison.

"Moon flower convoy," she said in a low voice. "That guard is after Hui. He must have panicked and fled into the woods. Find him. I will lead the other one away."

"No!" he protested.

"Protect him!" she commanded and shoved him into the underbrush.

Ellison winced with indecision at Su Li's command. No doubt, to try to help her would end it for them all, and she had ordered him to protect the boy. He crawled on his hands and knees in the vicinity of the first outlaw, hacking through the thick undergrowth, hoping to hear some sound that would lead to Hui, when another noise stopped him dead. Male voices were singing the tune to "Onward, Christian Soldiers" in a language he did not recognize. The world in fact had gone completely bonkers, he thought. He dropped behind a tree stump when the rest of the caravan marched out from the tree tunnel. Their leader was armed with a rifle and mounted on a horse, followed by a dozen mules and donkeys, outfitted with specially built wooden yokes that carried crammed burlap bags. Most of the bearers, though, were not animals but wizened men, laden with wide bricks of opium lashed together and piled five feet, roped to their backs on top of a stout T-shaped stick which reached inches above the ground, and when planted acted as a backrest. The column paused to finish its chorus and rest.

Something was moving twenty yards ahead but he heard a rifle crack not far behind him. He stopped in his tracks, fearing Su Li had been shot. In the next split second, a growl as loud as an airplane engine blasted over the whole plateau. He had heard that earsplitting roar in India.

Su Li stepped from her hiding place long enough to make sure the second guard glimpsed her, then withdrew into the trees. The barrel-waisted bandit, who wore a Western style bowler hat above a stringy goatee, waddled toward what he had seen, but the convoy leader, who had by then ridden into the clearing, wanted no more delays.

He gestured scornfully and called out a command. "Leave her alone. She's too puny to carry a load."

"She should not be here. Maybe she is a spy. From the Kuomintang," the guard hollered. "Besides, she has other uses."

"Leave her! She is a crazy woman."

But lust had deafened him. The bandit poked his rifle into the bushes and took a step. Su Li was about to flee further when the fat man slumped dead, a bullet through his ear. The leader's gun barrel was smoking, he and his horse ten paces away. Then a roar thundered off the mountainside. Everyone including Su Li stiffened, not daring to breathe.

The caravan's leader sniffed the air. She smelled it too, something wild and terrifying. He was young, not much older than she was, with a scar on his forehead, covered partly by a red bandana above an eye patch. His one good eye twitched.

"I know you are in there and I know you are Shaolin," he said. He wore a shirt cut off at the shoulders and on his forearm was the tiger scar. "We are one with the spirit-tiger, you and I. Even if I have strayed from the Way. He is near. That is why I let you live." He fired his rifle in the air. The caravan resumed its song and faded into the forest.

Ellison's chest thumped with fear for the child's safety. Straight ahead a snarl preceded a bloodcurdling cry. Let me not be too late again, he prayed and rammed through the bamboo and brush, elbowing aside the low branches that whipped his cheek.

"Hui," he called. No answer. Then at long last . . . .

"Here!"

In a narrow opening between the trees, Hui held his palm upright at arm's length, warning Ellison to stop. In front, two paces away, an enormous tiger straddled the body of an outlaw whose head was attached to his neck with a few tendons and strips of skin. Tail twitching, the animal turned toward Ellison; its wild scent filled the enclosure. He blinked. When his eyes opened the tiger was gone. He blinked again. Hui was safe. That was no illusion. He heaved a sigh of relief, stepped over the dead man and lifted the child into his arms.

"I have a hundred questions but there's no time. We have to hurry and help your mother."

"She is well, Big Tall. Nothing can hurt her. Not here."

"How do you know, Hui?"

"I can see things. Did you see it? The magical tiger?"

"I don't know what I saw. Your mother needs me."

They found Su Li near a felled tree, eyes closed, in the lotus position. The outlaw lay sprawled face-down a few feet away. Filled with wonder, Ellison fell on his knees. He wanted to comfort her, hold her but she had withdrawn to a place to which he had no access.

Far above, a hawk screeched.

CHAPTER 38

Why did the wise ones of old love the Tao? Because when you seek, you find. And when you sin, you receive forgiveness — Lao-tze

"Enter."

Su Li sensed the command not as a voice from inside Po's chamber but as an awareness, an illustration of the mystic communion she once shared with him. She opened the door, entered and closed it behind her.

"You have returned, tiger-daughter."

His greeting, so indifferent it might have described a clear sky on a summer day, floated above the storm of emotions inside her. The soul-wrenching round of hope and despair that had cycled for more than two years — but seemed much, much longer to her — had come down to this one confrontation. She called upon mind-control training, received in this very room, and threw her shoulders back, determined to rein in the quivering that threatened her whole body. *I will be here and now. And wait.*

"Chuang-tze's humor still astonishes me after all these years. A sage who could laugh at himself."

His white beard flowed below his chin over a gray robe while his finger traced the symbols on a venerable wooden slip or *jiandu*, narrow pieces of bamboo with ideographs painted from top to bottom, tied together with thread. A repository of Taoist lore, he had used it for many a lesson. Next to the old book, on a low table where he sat, the same sea-green jade bowl of perfumed ink she herself had replenished so often wafted its potent aroma across the room. The simple bed, the brown storage chest and the ancient re-curved bow that hung on the wall, even the mysterious hawk on his shoulder — all was as she remembered.

"We could all do well by not taking ourselves so seriously," he said, rising and moving to the window that overlooked the garden. She was about to speak when he held up his hand.

"The monastery is failing, tiger-daughter. Only the very old and a few young novices remain. It survives because it is remote and offers no threat. The Red Brigades, if they win, promise to destroy the old religions of China." The voice, always vibrant and energetic, now resonated with weariness. "It is time for me to pass on also."

"No, Master, please do not say such things." She cringed at her impulsive, inexcusable boldness.

He turned, eyes as fierce as the bird's. "What claim do you have on this place?" he demanded after a time.

"Master, this unworthy one, begs you . . . ." She bowed her head. *Here and now,* a voice reminded her like a distant echo.

"Who are you to judge who is unworthy?" The air crackled with the tension of lightning about to strike. "Even the Buddha cannot tell who is worthy," he continued in a quieter voice. "Have you eaten sufficiently? Of the bitterness?"

The gathering storm was losing momentum but only dark clouds were visible to her traumatized mind, not the sunlight breaking over the top. Tears streamed down her cheeks. She wiped them on her sleeve.

"I believe you have had a full cup," he said.

"Forgive me, Master, for my transgressions." She choked on the words.

"It is not for me to be angry. Or to forgive you."

He moved away from the window and as he did the hawk flew from his shoulder and landed on Su Li's. It screeched but to her mind it spoke as it had so long ago. *Here and now.* Afraid, she glanced at it out the corner of her eye.

Po's eyes widened. "You alone can truly forgive," he murmured.

What had he said? Her mind floated without direction, spinning like a branch caught in the rapids of a mountain stream. So deep were the old feelings of shame, she could not acknowledge what her own eyes had seen, ears had heard. "I have tried to follow your teachings, Master. But the world is hard and I am a woman." She hung her head. Even the word tasted bitter to her tongue. Who was she deceiving? That was no excuse. No excuse for anything. Why couldn't she think straight? Now, of all times.

"Listen to the hawk, tiger-daughter."

He took two sudden steps toward her, seized her wrists in his hands, and lifted her arms above her head. The mystic symbols of tiger and dragon on her forearms, emblems of power, badges of knowledge, deepened to red. Po's own sleeves dropped to his elbows as well. Arms raised, intertwined with his, her limbs were on fire once more, burning like the time she had lifted the iron brazier. Her knees threatened to collapse, the memory's sensations were so intense, but Po's grip gave her strength. Past and present flowed together in a new way, as sunlight pours through a window into a dark room when the shutters open. Some parts linger in shadow; others are startlingly clear. Once again she stood tall. *He is testing me once again. I see it now. I have saved lives and taken them. Fought evil. I am raising a son, worthy of a master. And now a strange man who stirs powerful feelings has altered my life.*

"You have done these and more," he said. "And I trust you will never again use your gender as an excuse for failure or success. Such was my teaching to you. You have made mistakes, errors of youth, not femininity." He returned to the table, rolled up the scroll and set the brush back in its bowl. "That is human."

Her ears burned. The inevitable rejection had not occurred. Instead the Master had given her a gift, the gift of new understanding. She could declare herself a woman without apology, now and forever. When she first entered the room, a part of her had wanted to fall to her knees and beg him to take her back. *How childish. The final test was to see if I had changed enough to forgive myself, to always remember I am a Shaolin monk. I have passed. I am free.*

"You remember the story of the farmer who lost his horse?" He stepped over to the brown chest, knelt down and opened the lid. With utmost care, even reverence, he lifted a yellow cloth and laid it on his lap. She nodded. "Your favorite, not so?" He gestured for her to speak.

"One day a certain farmer's horse escaped. It was his prize possession. His jealous neighbors, who came to console him, told him how unfortunate his life was. The farmer simply said, 'Maybe so.' The next day his son went out to search for the horse, found three more and brought them back to the farm. Seeing this windfall, his busy neighbors returned to congratulate him on his good fortune. 'Maybe so,' the farmer replied. The next day his son fell off one of the new horses and broke his leg. The son was his only help. Again the envious neighbors descended and berated the farmer for his bad luck. 'Maybe so,' was all he would say. The following day the Emperor's agents arrived intent on conscripting recruits but they passed over the injured boy."

"And what was the point, tiger-daughter?" Po asked while he examined the cloth.

"Not to make judgments, Master. At least not until the end of the story."

"Oh? And when does a story end?"

One final time the hawk screeched. The Master had forgiven her and now she could go on with her life. Not in the monastery, she realized with finality. That piece of the tale was over, but the rest of her story was what she would make it. "Master," she went on with newfound confidence. "I have come to ask for your help. Not for myself, but for others." For the first time since she left the old house the words carried the weight of honesty because of the man with the tiger symbol on his jacket.

"To help others is a task worthy of a Shaolin." He held up a finger.

She caught her breath, filled with amazement, as the boy entered, just as she had, with no verbal invitation. Hui stood next to her, not awed in the slightest at the presence of the greatest Master in China. The boy smiled at her, noticed the bird on her shoulder and held his arm out. It flew to his forearm where he stroked its neck feathers. The Master blinked hard, mouth open in amazement.

"Esteemed Master Po, forgive me, but you were wrong about my mother. The Tao sent me here to correct your mistake," Hui said.

Su Li gasped. Po's countenance vacillated between astonishment and anger. "And how do you know this, child?" he asked.

"The bird told me, Master."

Po took several long deep breaths, pondering what the boy said, then burst out laughing. He walked over to Su Li and put his hand on her head. "Rest easy. It is my own folly that amuses me, not yours." He addressed her in the familiar tone she remembered. "Though males are yang and females are yin, both sexes have a measure of each, mutually arising. Unlike most women, you always had plentiful yang, tiger-daughter. Now you are finding your full measure of yin, which females have by nature and most males lack. To attain such balance needs no forgiveness." He kissed her forehead in blessing, drew out the ivory and onyx disc around her neck, then tucked it back beneath her tunic. "Only praise." A twinkle in his eye, Po glanced at the boy. "Leave us now. I must draw insight from this new source of wisdom. After that I will meet your companion."

Ellison noticed that afternoon Su Li seemed elated and yet nervous while she explained over and over the protocol for his interview with the Master. Of the myriad baffling qualities about her, the hardest to work out was her devotion to some ultimate font of authority whereas he had prided himself, ever since his father's death, in rejecting every received so-called wisdom. He acknowledged the good deeds various religions inspired in people he had known—his father, mother, and grandparents among them—but the content of their beliefs struck him as little more than attempts to rationalize stories akin to the Greek myths his mother had forced him to read as a boy.

The object of Su Li's awe, on both knees, was planting a sapling, a frail old man who liked to putter in his garden. The blossoms at his feet were as forlorn as the story he had gone over so many times. Once more, though, the lessons of Calcutta lent him courage to plead the case for Mary Ellison and Lian. After all he was Shiva, right? Creator and destroyer. He laughed inwardly but still carried the paper scrap from India. No doubt the smuggler's tip, which had the ring of truth despite the man's glib denial, sounded preposterous, but these flimsy pointers were all he had. Po listened to his tale while he dug a hole but looked up when Ellison mentioned the name of General Okamura and his headquarters in Shanghai.

"So, I am asking for your aid, Master Po."

Po set down his trowel and leaned back on his heels. "Let us speak in your tongue, Lieutenant. It has been many years since I have practiced, though." His English was understandable and like Ellison's own, tinged with soft British "r's". Po placed the tree in the hole and patted the dark earth around the small tree's roots; a half dozen pencil-thin twigs, its sole branches, were studded with buds.

"China is collapsing. Perhaps our land will destroy itself. To arise again, like the phoenix, or like this seedling. I do not know. One thing I do know. This peace," Po waved his hand at the garden's expanse, "has seen its day, like the passing of autumn. Winter awaits." He nodded sadly. "It will not survive this war." He paused then resumed mulching. "This is a dogwood tree. When mature its foliage and blossoms will be most beautiful. I am trying to grow it here, even though the elevation makes it difficult. We will see. It takes time for seeds of nature to bear fruit." He poured water from a wooden bucket onto the ground. "I have listened to your story out of my regard for tiger-daughter. Interesting. Sad. And your devotion is worthy. However it has no special claim for my help."

Ellison's body tensed. Po was dismissing everything he had clung to during the past five years. "Yet I have heard for those that follow the Tao, compassion is a great virtue, Master Po."

Po arched his eyebrows. "I care nothing for missionaries. They are the enemies of the Tao — and yet part of it as well." He grinned mischievously

"My father was a man of integrity. He followed his way with honor — even though I myself do not follow it."

The Master adjusted the sapling. "No one can fight successfully against the Tao. But they can pretend to. You feel you are responsible for their fates, your parents, this girl. That their death and misfortune are your fault. No one is answerable for anyone else's fate unless you save that person's life. I am surprised you have not learned this truth from your time with tiger-daughter." Po brushed the dirt off his hands. "In any case, I am old."

Ellison's impulse was to defend himself, his last chance for redemption flitting away like the rose petal wafting to his boots. He bent to pick it up. Its withered delicacy retained a trace of fragrance, a faded dream. The Master took the blossom from his hand.

"Many years ago, a man — a soldier, as you are — lost a wife and two children to brutes not unlike the Japanese. He struggled long and hard to avenge them, but was unable to. Once a member of the Imperial Guard, he became an outcast, a blood-thirsty mercenary, until a monk stopped him on a road. In his arrogance he tried to thrash the holy man, but the Shaolin defeated him easily, this strong fighter. As he lay on the earth humiliated, he decided to let go of the vengeance and anguish and guilt that drove his life and to follow the monk wherever he went." Po looked straight at Ellison. "That is what you must do also to attain peace. Learn to use the perverse devastation of this hellish enemy — this war — for your own ends. Forgive yourself. Let the burdens you carry fall away. And whether you find and rescue your mother or not — or this girl — do it without regard to the ultimate result."

Po went over to the stone bench and sat next to a small carved wooden chest. He opened the lid and drew out two folded pieces of paper. "Did you know the old General Matsui was a martial arts enthusiast? This is a standing invitation — a challenge — to do battle with his Japanese champions." He thumbed through the papers. "Sent eight years ago. He is long retired. In fact, it is an insult. He claims the Chinese are weak, cowards. I have ignored it. I do not accept challenges, particularly from beasts." The Master seized the pilot's wrist. "Are you prepared to risk everything, including your life, on the skills of a tired, old man?"

The question's simple clarity startled him. White or black. Death or life. Yet to know his mother was alive and not to try was unthinkable. "Su Li thought you alone could help us."

"Us? You care for this woman?"

Again, simple and clear. Yes or no. Ellison hesitated. Not so simple.

"She cares for you. You do not perceive it? She would not have brought you here otherwise, despite whatever she says. Whether she herself knows it or not." Po smiled, then set Matsui's challenge back into the chest. "Let us walk for a while."

They strolled out through the portal and exited to the exercise yard. A bow in her hand, Su Li stood in the midst of a semi-circle of a dozen apprentices and Hui. The onlookers cheered as arrow after arrow buried itself in the bulls-eye of the target. A few older monks, arms folded inside their sleeves, nodded in approval. Ellison and Po stopped next to the mighty stone pillars that supported the portico of the temple proper. Stylized bronze statues of two fierce lions guarded each.

"You know her story?" He recounted the tale of how he had found the cast-off, briefly alluding to the circumstances that surrounded her banishment from the monastery. "Thus the heavy burden she bears. She has never admitted who the father was. But I believe it was dragon-son."

The man at the forest clearing, Ellison realized. Now it made sense—the demon of shame haunting her, the edge of guilt that hung over someone otherwise so accomplished.

"This symbol on your jacket," Po continued after a long pause, "I am not familiar with it." Ellison explained how he had received the special Flying Tigers emblem. The Master nodded. "I have certain friends in Shanghai. I intend to send to them and see if your mother is indeed in Japanese clutches. We will travel to Hankow and await their report. If they confirm she is in Shanghai, I will confront the current General so that everyone will know. He cannot decline such a challenge."

For a moment, Ellison felt as though his brain was spinning from the same drug the spies had given him back in Chungking. The Master had in fact said "yes." How their exchange led to this outcome he had no idea.

"You are surprised, Lieutenant?"

"No. I mean yes, Master Po." He bowed. "I am deeply honored."

Po cut him off. "Here is the price. If I win, you must promise to protect her."

Ellison stiffened. Another promise? To agree to Po's bargain amounted to a staggering commitment; such a pledge would change his life forever, dwarf even his vow to rescue his mother. He was afraid even to think about Su Li. "I doubt she needs anyone to protect her. Least of all me."

"Whatever you may have witnessed you have drawn the wrong conclusion. She is headstrong, true, but in many ways the best of what is good in China. And that alone makes her unsuitable to live in her own country."

"I don't understand."

"You have lived here. You have seen the hills deforested? The tiger parts sold in the medicine shops? Yet trees and tigers are supposedly sacred to us. The truth is, for most Chinese nature is a philosophical ideal or a purposeless impediment to survival. Thus my people destroy the best the Tao has given them. Add to that she is a woman. And to the Chinese, a woman is soil, to be plowed and fertilized and trod on. That will not happen to my gift from the tigers." The Master set his jaw but unexpectedly laughed out loud. A hint of amusement, of self-irony, played around his utterances. "Her journey will take her elsewhere," he went on, "where her talents can thrive. Strange places where you will guide her. She trusts you." He placed the blossom in Ellison's hand. "Will you agree?"

After the initial wave of refusal swept by him—an open-ended obligation? No way, not the plan, he bristled—he found himself in a still mode, took a breath and thought some more. He had to admit nothing that had occurred in the past months was part of what any rational person would be kind enough to call a plan. Neither was Su Li. Despite their differences, what they shared together was deeper, more primal than most people found in a lifetime, and he was by this time responsible for her according the rule of honor. Hell, he had saved her life twice. But, her caring for him? Where did Po get that idea? Because she had touched him, called him by his last name a few times?

And did he care for her? A guy was supposed to find an adoring, classy brunette, brown eyes, nice tits and ass, preferably one who had learned how to cook, take care of a house, produce a couple of kids, bring your slippers at night when you got home. That's what the blokes at the university were chasing; that's what the rest of the single pilots back in India all said they were looking for when they got back from the war. The notion made him want to puke. Okay, he admitted, he did care for the woman. But nay, could he love her? Why was love so damned complicated? Everything about her was full of twists and turns. What would his Father say? His Mother? "Dinna make a promise ye cannae keep, Jamie." She wouldn't want him to risk his life for her. *Tough, Mother.* That was irrelevant; he had made that commitment since the day of her abduction. But the price for the mere chance of rescuing one woman was a commitment to another. He couldn't bring himself to do that unless, unless he at present did love Su Li. *Shit. I can't figure this out.*

"Lieutenant?"

"Master Po, I'm not so sure."

"You are a seeker — a hunter. And yet you give up so easily in this chase. I perceive your feelings for her."

"You know more than I do, Master Po. You would entrust her to me?"

Po shrugged. "It is up to her. You have been sent."

The unblinking eyes of the exotic bird unsettled Ellison. No sympathy there. So be it. He exhaled a long breath. "I promise to do my best," he replied. "If the Tao carries us that way."

"You learn quickly, young man." Po's face hardened. "I cannot help you with your lost young woman, however. That is not my affair."

Later, Po knelt before the three Pure Ones in the temple. Hundreds of candles burned amidst braziers of incense along the hall and in front of altars. Painted on the ceiling, an intricate zodiac of the heavens beckoned the observer to unite with the Tao, but this night Po came not for comfort but forgiveness. The one he had been waiting for, the one to carry on his wisdom, was this precocious boy, not his foster mother. What a fool he had been, acting too much like a god with the tiger's first gift, overconfident of his knowledge of the Tao. The girl who departed had returned a warrior, a priest, a mother, transformed through the suffering he had set in motion, and the Tao had given her a replacement for the child she had lost. And so he had been wiser than he knew. How fortunate, he thought wryly. Now the encounter with this foreign soldier. Yes, he must help this man. He opened his eyes. Buddha gazed at him with compassion. Lao-tze with the cold eye of reason, and the Eternal One with unfathomable mystery. By and by he fell into a trance and a vision opened in his mind's eye.

He stood on a grassy knoll on an island surrounded by a vast ocean. The day was warm with the radiance of gold. He looked up and saw that the light came from the face of the Eternal One, who sat on a puffy cloud that floated above. On the knoll, a young woman and a man, arms around each other's waist, sat and watched two children play. He looked closer – the man was himself, the woman his long dead wife. They were circled by a halo. Where the children played their game on the grass, a white and gold-striped tiger rested and guarded them, a few yards away, as if the children belonged to it and not to the parents. The young Po called their names but they did not respond. Finally they turned. They were not the boy and girl he expected, his offspring, but Han and Su Li. At last the tiger rose and walked away. The children followed. Po called out again, but they waved and continued on until they disappeared. He wept, and when he turned to his wife for comfort, she too was gone.

He emerged from his trance with tears in his eyes, shaken by emotions not felt for fifty years, yet his wife's loveliness lingered as if it were yesterday. She had been poisoned by conspirators who resented his rising position in the Forbidden City because he came from commoners. His children, a boy and a girl, were sent to his parents' house for safety. He raced to save them but the house had been burned to the ground by his enemies. He should have been there in time. Was that the real reason he had rescued the child on the mountain, to recapture the long ago?

He had wished tiger-daughter to be more than she could be. Buddha forgive me, he prayed. Suddenly an insight hit him with a blow to his *dan tian*. He had one more task to do. Back in his room, he retrieved from his chest the gold cloth. Memories of sadness and joy swept over him. The woman who left the babe, who was she? He never bothered to inquire. Perhaps he had not wanted to find out. Now her unknown origins consumed him. Had he missed a clue? He would send the cloth along with messengers to all the monasteries within fifty miles of Emei Shan and ask them to search, wait for their answer at Hankow, before he proceeded to Shanghai.

CHAPTER 39

He who speaks, does not know. And she who knows does not speak – Lao-tze

The unruly Yangtze was swollen with the annual melt-off from its source in the distant Himalayas. Each spring it swelled into an out of control monster that sometimes towered a hundred yards above its normal depth in the narrow gorges, bringer of sustenance as well as death to those who touched its power. Downstream, destruction reigned for miles on each side, and yet it left a legacy of rich, life-giving silt deposited along its shores. Upstream, the Chang Jiang — or Long River — thundered and twisted through endless canyons like a caged dragon. At Chungking it flattened out, as if resting from its headlong dive from the roof of the world. It rocked between the hills, almost gentle for a while, almost sad, though not as sorrowful as Su Li who stood near the prow's great yellow eye while the ancient avatar of the Tao swirled under the junk's stern, propelling them toward Shanghai.

Over the last week they had retraced the route to Chungking, their departure point for the journey to eastern China. The wharf where she had said farewell to her adopted son receded as life fades into memories, memories that would never repair the aching void inside.

"This is where I need to stay for a while, Mother," he told her when they parted, looking so small and grown-up in Ellison's jacket. "I will learn from these Masters and make you proud of me." His face was calm, sober, brave, fighting a losing battle to hold back his tears.

She sighed, again and for the last time inwardly thrilled and amazed at his maturity. "I am already proud of you, my son. You will be a great man someday. But I do not know when or if I will see you again. And my heart is so heavy." Yet he was not *her* child, she thought, but the Tao's. She wiped her tears first, then his, her hands lingering on the boy's cheeks. She took the tai chi disk from her neck and placed it around his. "Take this and remember me."

"You are my mother. How could I forget?" He reached up to kiss her cheek. "You will stay by *laohuo baba*, tiger-father Ellison? Teach him as you taught me?"

She nodded.

"And fulfill your destiny. As I must mine."

He walked over to the soldier and hugged him. "I will practice my English," he said in his new language, took the hand of the old monk who attended him, turned and disappeared into the crowd.

My destiny. The boat shuddered past a monstrous whirlpool that, to her astonishment, moved upstream, a yawning mouth eager to devour anything foolish enough to come near. The boatmen called it *xuanwo*. An omen, she thought. Like the junk, her own existence now floated on a raging flood of war. Try as she might, she foresaw no good ending ahead, but no one could know for certain, not even Da Shi. Like the farmer who lost his horse, she would have to wait for the story to unfold.

"The war will end some day. But you will endure, for you are stronger than whatever evil men can inflict on your brother, the earth, or each other," she said to the water. "May I be like you."

My destiny. Her son's words washed over her like spray from the current dampening her scalp, not shaved this way since she first left the monastery. Once again she wore the orange tunic and black leggings of a Shaolin monk, dressed for battle. Once again she traveled as a male. The disguise, her life for so long, felt natural. Part man, part woman. Male, female, did it matter? But it did, because she was tied to the soldier, now part of her Tao.

"I'll miss him," said the enigma that always seemed to confound her. He leaned on the rail, inches away, dressed as she was, his head shaved. The Master had done wondrous magic to his face and especially his eyes—those wild eyes that fascinated her so, pinched back to appear Chinese. Not true Han Chinese, but he might pass for a member of those strange tribes who lived in the far West, descendants of barbarian invasions long ago.

"He loves you," she said

His sad eyes nodded as the boat lurched sideways from a wave. Stout cypress upriver junks—*fanchuan*—had been used for centuries, and in the hands of an experienced pilot were well adapted for the treacherous Yangtze. This one had two masts with bamboo lattice sails of canvas. Broad-beamed for stability, the flat deck rose toward the stern and the living quarters which lay mostly below where the owner had provided for Po to stay. Su Li and Ellison slept on deck with the crew under a shelter near the bow. Deep in the hull the ship carried a cargo of wood and bricks—ballast—in compartments separated by bulkheads.

Seething currents pushed them along with breakneck speed and before long the Yangtze again became an uncontrollable beast. Water spouts appeared out of nowhere, roaring towers that threatened utter destruction. At other times the splash and roar of rapids filled the air. Spray swept over the deck as tons of water shattered against, then swirled by, rocks as big as temples that protruded out of the surface.

"Look!" she called out in excitement one afternoon, pointing. "They call it the Pillar of Heaven."

"My god, it must be nearly half a mile high," Ellison said, apprehensive, as the behemoth loomed near, but the pilot steered past it.

"Shrines like that one," she gestured toward a pagoda jutting out of a rugged outcropping and niched into a sheer wall of green limestone, "are tributes to a hero or god. Who knows?"

"Looks as if the deity itself had simply set them there, fully complete. I can't imagine how else they were built. I wish my friend Buzz could see this."

A few miles farther on, far above the drama of the water, whole towns peered down as if spectators from a balcony above a stage, the river's high level.

"I'm presuming human hands, not gods, built those. But how do you get up there when the river's low?" he asked.

"Look more carefully," she said and pointed. Hundreds of stone steps soared from the water's edge to a town they were passing. "We can see only the upper part, with the river so high. But the stairs descend much, much lower, so when the level drops later in the year, there is access to it."

He nodded and said, "The Chinese!"

On the third day they sailed through the first of the legendary Three Gorges. Qutang Gorge, a crewman called it. Emerald mountains and cliffs plummeted headlong into the stream, forcing its course to their will.

"Magnificent," he said to her. "It's like kneeling before an ancient emperor. Power that's indifferent to us ordinary human beings." And a dragon that will never be dammed, he suspected. But I bet engineer Buzz would say, "Hell, yes, it will. And by Americans."

A sailor, who looked the same age as his former co-pilot, was regaling them with stories about the other, lesser known gorges with names such as Yellow Cat and Windbox that whipped the current faster as they sped on toward Wushan. Rapids once again spread across the water's surface.

"Those men, up there on the slopes?" he asked the crewman. A line of a hundred small, men, naked except for a loin cloth, crawled through narrow open-sided tunnels cut into the rock too low to stand upright. Bent over double, they pulled on long hawser ropes attached to a junk headed west, against the current.

"They are called *qian fu* — trackers," he said. "In certain places on the Yangtze towing is the only way to make headway upstream. The men on the bluffs coordinate with the pilot, the man near the bow . . . ." The young sailor, bare to the waist, pointed at a figure in the other boat, who was dressed in a loose-fitting robe and a conical hat, then opened his eyes wide, made a foolish gesture and laughed. "He is a magician who fearlessly confronts the wicked eddies and evil whirlpools of the treacherous current." He exaggerated his words with a straight face and motioned a mock magic sign. "He shouts his incantations to the men up there. That man next to him with the drum, he gives rhythm to their pull. Watch. He's starting. Prepare to be amazed!" On cue the drum sounded above the water's roar and the trackers shouted out a chant each time it boomed.

The deckhand reached into a pouch and drew out an antique clay pipe, stuffed with tobacco. With a set of tongs from the cook's fire, he took hold of a sizzling ember from the brazier, and lit the pipe, took a puff or two, a serious look on his face.

"As I see it, life's a lot like sailing on this river. A person has to know the water, its moods, its quirks, the dangers. Oh yes, the many, many dangers. Like those rocks you saw and the whirlpools. You have to know your boat, too. What it's capable of. The weather. All that stuff. Then, after a while, you start to get the knack of it. Don't you think?" He nodded his head solemnly. "A very wise man instructed me in this." He burst out laughing. "Look at me, giving lessons about life to some monks."

"How did you come to be a sailor?" Ellison asked him.

The man winked. "The wizard on this boat is my father." He laughed and walked away to another part of the ship.

"Why would those men risk their lives like that? Is that following the Tao?" Ellison asked Su Li. "The hardship, the danger of falling or being caught and twisted in the ropes. Every day? It's hard to fathom."

Su Li shrugged. "Perhaps it is no more or no less than what you yourself did when flying your airplanes. Or what you are doing now."

He fell silent for a moment, smiling whimsically at her. "I've been thinking about you the past few days. Trying to imagine you with hair pinned up like those beauties in the tea house."

Su Li was taken aback, momentarily breathless, confounded once more by his maddening unpredictability. She ran her hand over her smooth scalp self-consciously. "You sound worse than a mandarin in the old stories, scheming to have his way with a concubine. I have no desire to dress like those prostitutes." She spat out the word. "Do you judge a person by their appearance?"

"Of course not." The current's spray rose to the gunwales. "I'm sorry. I was just trying to," he managed to laugh at himself. "to, ah, umm . . . to say you are pretty." The last word was in English.

"Plitty." She tried to imitate the sound. "What is that?" A puzzled smile took shape despite her best efforts to suppress it. "You . . . you are an uneducated man." She moved closer to him. Their arms touched. Ellison let his hand fall against hers on the wood rail. His touch was a jolt of static electricity. She could smell his body, his strange breath, feel her own heart beating faster.

"I am awed at your wisdom, Su Li. Your inner beauty."

She jerked back her hand, turned her head and found his eyes fixed on her. Again, she flushed, helpless. "You mock me."

"No!" he protested. "I would never do that. I could not love women like those." His air turned uncharacteristically, completely serious for once. "Su Li, you are the most extraordinary person I have ever met."

"You know nothing, foreign devil." With an amused grin she rolled her eyes upward in embarrassment. "At Hankow the Master will stop and prepare himself," she announced, still non-plussed by his directness, "and wait for news. There is a temple there."

"Who are his friends in Shanghai?"

"The Green Circle Gang. They practically run the city. Their leader, Duo Yueshen, is a promoter of the martial arts. He and Da Shi knew each other before the Master became a monk. So he once told me."

Ellison remained silent, lost in thought for a minute.

"That man," she lifted her chin toward a crewman hauling on a rope, "said there is a Japanese camp down a tributary, not far from our stop. People say it houses women for their soldiers. Mostly Chinese. Anyone from your old village will probably have been taken there."

"Lian?" Ellison was excited. "Would we have a chance to go there? Maybe ask the local people. If Lian were somehow alive."

She exhaled in dismay. How could she make him face the truth that Lian was dead? The answer was to show him once and for all the power of the Shaolin way. Afterwards, let him choose, the present or the past. All of a sudden the boat rocked as it plunged ahead into a limestone chute that soared to the sky. Ellison and Su Li flew apart, losing their balance. A huge rock narrowly missed the junk. The moment had fled. She turned away, unable to retrieve it.

The next day they docked at Hankow's harbor where the twentieth century jostled with the fifteenth. Junks and sampans brushed sterns with modern steamers which traded goods up and down the river, plying both the Japanese and the Nationalist territories. Stalls selling straw sandals and cheap kitchen ware competed with food vendors frying tofu in charcoal-fired woks in a kind of boat bazaar on the wharf, as they had for centuries.

Po led them through the crowded waterfront. "I visited here often in my mercenary days. A city notorious for its wickedness. One of its famous sights are those blackened ruins of the Yellow Crane Tower." He pointed to a hill above the docks. "They say a great Taoist sage launched himself there and flew away to become an immortal. Why would someone want to do that?" He laughed out loud.

"Conceivably the sage wasn't seeking immortality, Master," Ellison said with a sly smile. "Maybe he was trying to escape Hankow."

Po halted for an instant and laughed heartily. "Come. We must hurry. Hankow is full of Japanese agents and sympathizers. The Nationalists run a covey of criminal gangs along with their predictable network of spies and informants. I am told the Communists have an underground of cadres as well since last I came. We don't want to be noticed by any of these. That is why we take the back streets."

Su Li kept alert for any signs of being followed as they hurried through drab streets of two-story buildings, shops below and living quarters above. Beggars, gangs of young toughs, opium addicts and prostitutes thronged the cobblestones, as pervasive as ordinary citizens going about their business. The constant sight of women and children bought and sold into prostitution according to their weight, like pieces of meat, sickened her.

"How can the Communists ever hope to change such as these?" she asked Ellison. "Just as there will always be sages, there will always be criminals."

"I think Hankow is their capital," he said.

On the outskirts of the Hanyan district, where the streets gave way to cultivated fields stood a monastery, their destination. The Guiyan Temple resembled the Golden Sun but was much larger and grander, with towers and roof tops rising high above the outer wall of cut stones.

"The temple here is dedicated to the Goddess of Mercy, Guanyin. Its Master is a friend of mine, allied to the Shaolin order," Po announced when they stood in front of the gates. "I expect an answer from my contacts in Shanghai regarding Ellison's mother in two days. If all goes well, we will hear from the commandant, General Okamura." He stroked his wisp of a beard. "We are all in need of mercy."

"Master," Su Li said. "I was told there is a special place, a day's journey away. The sailor told me. I wish to show it to this foreigner."

Po arched his brow in surprise. Tired, distracted, he made no comment and rang the entry bell.

CHAPTER 40

The ox is slow, but the earth is patient – Chinese proverb

"There's a bounty on monks like you," said the driver of the donkey cart who wore a flat wool cap, short pants and leather sandals held together with rope thongs. Behind him Su Li and Ellison clambered onto a stack of bricks. The day was mild with scattered clouds floating overhead. "I won't betray you, though. The devil-dwarves money has shit all over it." He took a puff on a long-stemmed pipe then spat derisively. "A barbarian camp with women? Hmm. Not here but about a day's ride on this rutted piece of beetle dung that passes for a road there's a big beehive of the Jap devils. There's a small river near it. I can take you most of the way." His mouth was missing several teeth. "Deng is my name and it pleases me to see young monks who follow the old ways. People like me need to have some sign the world has not gone completely mad."

Following a long, gently sloped plain, Deng prodded the donkey deeper into Japanese-occupied territory along a dirt track past a few villages and a larger township. Above the lintels of the mud brick huts lining the road, occupants had painted yin/yang symbols and the Eight Signs to lure the spirits to grant prosperity or ward off death. Outside a walled town, they passed crowds of peasants who squatted alongside the roadway, meager tools neatly rolled up next to threshing baskets. Smoke billowed from fields higher up where fires had been lit, as if the flames had driven the vagrants out of the hills like wild animals.

"*Mangren lioulonghan*," Deng called them. "Blind drifters. They once had farms up there but their food ran out and they lost their land. Now they live out in the open. I was once a farmer too. I was born here and grew up on these plains. Now all I have is this poor beast and this cart. I haul bricks made in the villages to the towns, sometimes as far as Hankow. I'm alone now. My wife, my children, are all murdered by the invaders. The looms are empty." He puffed once more on his pipe. "My parents sent me to a missionary school in a town for a while so excuse me, learned monks, but I know things. Not enough though. My ancestral land was stolen by cheating collaborators." He jabbed the donkey with a bamboo stick. "There has been little rain. No food. Famine has led many to devour their seeds instead of planting them. Clay and bark. All that most have to live on. The looms are empty."

Ellison cast a quizzical glance at Su Li who whispered to him, "It means the times are very hard."

"They say the desperate are devouring pieces of dead bodies. I would never stoop so low," Deng continued with a sad shake of his head. "Our government army added its share of those in these very fields after the barbarians defeated it. Four years ago, I think it was. The soldiers who died no abacus could count." He looked up at the sky. "The gods must be angry. Very angry."

"No wonder the Chinese despise soldiers," Ellison mumbled to himself as they passed lines of desiccated, eyeless corpses. "What an eminently sensible attitude." Frequently the wagon had to swerve around a rusty tank or transport truck abandoned in the rutted track. To the east, shattered field guns, cars and other military gear littered the landscape.

"I could do this myself. You didn't have to come," he said to Su Li.

"I should have defeated that witch. She was not that skillful."

"Is that why you insisted? To show me how expert you are. Because if that's . . ."

"You would be dead before you got there, Ellison." She managed a little laugh despite herself. The cart's gentle sway rubbed his shoulder against hers. She found the unfamiliar tingle between her thighs more than pleasant.

"So you came to protect me?" His eyes danced with their familiar humor.

She paused before answering. "Someone must enlighten you. The Tao has cast the task on me." She shrugged.

"I suppose I should feel grateful."

"I sympathize with your feelings about this girl," she admitted. "My own mother abandoned me to die. I never knew her."

"I am sorry, Su Li."

"Sorrow?" she snapped.

Her dead mother was a hollow part of her spirit, like an empty stomach that could never be satisfied. Never to know her love, not even her identity, was not to know herself. In spite of her training in the present, she found herself wondering, questioning, desiring answers written on the winds of time. *Would she be proud of me now? Love me? Approve of how I have reared Hui? I cannot remember you, my Mother, but I miss you. I need you. Did you care for my father as I am beginning to do for this man? And did he hate me enough to send you to the mountain?*

Without warning his arm found its way around her waist. She cast a puzzled glance at it, moved to dislodge it then decided to let it stay. The warmth of his touch penetrated her skin like an updraft of warm air that meets a cold ceiling of clouds, generating a lightning spike of awareness. She wanted him, whether or not her mother might have approved, not as she had desired Han, different this time — and right. She watched him out with her peripheral vision. What her mind perceived was his half-clothed body in the Japanese spy's lair, his courage at the bridge, his gentleness with Hui, his listening, questioning eyes.

He withdrew his arm. "You think I'm deceiving myself about Lian?" He was distant once more, preoccupied. "It was my fault she got captured. I should have protected her. I told her I would."

"You spend too much time on what might have been instead of what is, Ellison." Her tone was flat, depressed. How could he not see? That she let his arm stay? That she was calling him "Ellison," not "soldier"? "You seek and seek but you do not see because you search so obsessively. The Master has taught us not to seek for it is all here. Right in front of your big Western nose." She paused, waiting for him to look at her and respond to the feelings she struggled to comprehend, but he was intent on his own thoughts.

"Ah, yes. The Master."

By late afternoon, dark thunderheads billowed over expectant hills to the west where sheets of rain marched in ranks, first over the distant peaks and in due course into the valley. Lightning flashed and thunder boomed along the ridges. Ahead of the front, a rainbow arched over a fertile plain that now stretched before them. Thin gray formations, mixed with denser black clouds, spread a mottle of shadow and gold on the land. The drought seemed ready to break at last.

"You're almost there. I travel further on to the next town," Deng said.

"These towns and villages look more prosperous," Ellison remarked.

"They chose to cooperate with the occupiers. Most do not care whether the Japanese or the Kuomintang rule. One day the sun shines; the next it rains. To the farmers who survive, the fiends are sometimes preferable since they take less of the food in taxes. For the rest of us the looms are empty."

"It sets the teeth on edge," Ellison said. Deng grunted.

Farmhands were finishing their day's work, unhooking plow mules or belled donkeys harnessed single file. Pigs grunted. Roosters crowed. Deng most likely came from a village like the one he had known. A wavelet of regret swept over him, and not merely the loss of his mother, his father, and Lian. He had not paid enough attention to those days. Gone was the sense of awe of his boyhood, the belief that life was a mystery waiting to be discovered. If there were a way to catch up each memory, put them in a book that would never age, where he could call up every day of wonder . . . . He shook his head. That world was gone forever. His world was war now. But that wasn't exactly right, he realized. It also included this confusing link to the person beside him, and because of her he was able to remember the joy as well as the sorrow, and today might be a wee chance to redeem his carelessness that made so much of it go away. The sun was setting behind the weather front when they jumped off the cart and said farewell to Deng.

"You must be careful. The people around here are treacherous."

"We need a place for the night," Su Li said.

"There." Deng pointed. "You'll see it in a while." They turned to go when he called out. "Wait! If you would, a blessing for a poor man."

Su Li rested her hands on his bowed head, just as she had seen Po do dozens of times. "May the goddess of mercy grant peace and prosperity for the good deeds you have done." A grin of delight spread over Deng's face. With new-found liveliness, he flicked the donkey forward and waved farewell.

Not far away, across a field of rapeseed, a low structure nestled amidst scrub pines. As they approached in the twilight, its red tile roof rose as high as her head.

"We will stay here tonight. Tomorrow we will see if we can find out what happened to this Lian of yours."

"Why do you say it that way?" he asked.

"What way?"

"Never mind."

Square, squat and as big as a small sleeping quarters, the shrine had a low door of carved wood and one empty window, the outside walls as dusky as the evening. Ellison had to crawl on all fours to enter. The smell of incense pervaded the tiny room. Half-burned joss sticks were scattered on the dirt floor. Two figurines fashioned of clay, the size of large dolls, held court on a mound of hardened dirt, male and female, dressed in a comic version of royalty, with red paper for robes, gilt for a crown. Offerings had been left behind quite recently — bits of food, pieces of cloth, rice paper with calligraphy prayers for plentiful crops.

"So these are what the gods of the earth are supposed to be. We had one of these near our village but my father never let me go into it. Claimed it was pagan superstition." He picked up a cloth sack filled with beans and tiny buns, popped a couple into his mouth. Su Li looked horrified. "Hey, I figure this place is a monument to earth, to life. And something brought us here so we could eat. And drink." He pulled out the stopper, took a swallow from the leather flask and laughed. "Do I sound like a Taoist or what?" he said in English, mostly to himself, and gave a little laugh.

She could only roll her eyes. "The river is due east. I intend to leave in the morning and find the camp, while

338

you wait here until sundown," she announced. "The deckhand spoke of a bridge. Meet me there at twilight, on this side. Hide near the front entrance."

"No. I don't like you going alone. Too risky."

"It is nothing for a Shaolin." Her mouth was set. "I will enter with the workers. They — the women — will know whether someone such as Lian came through."

"There has to be another way."

"You are not my master. You may not command me."

He sighed. "Never. But what if . . . ." He choked on the words. "I do not want to lose you."

"Lose me?" Her heart raced faster. What did that mean? Was it possible he did understand after all? She laid out a makeshift bed on a piece of tattered cloth. "You are worried you will be left here alone. Fear not. I will return. And if I do not, you will know one of your searches is over, Big Tall." A quicksilver smile quickly disappeared.

"Don't even say it. Not return?" He lay down an arm's length away. "No. That's not — ."

"Do not go out until evening. Someone will see you and report it."

"Anything else, master?" he asked with a mock bow.

They lay back to back. Before she fell asleep she was aware of his warmth against her. *I will remember this night. Always. No matter what happens.*

CHAPTER 41

Where armies camp, weeds and thistles grow – Lao-tze

As dawn broke, Su Li crept past a sleeping Ellison and set out in the direction given them by the wagoner. Despite Deng's warning, she was confident she could pass unchallenged through the open countryside. In fact, the peasants, by now at work in the early morning harvesting a meager wheat crop, paid her no mind, more interested in their own affairs than in a shaved head in a faded robe. Stealth through boldness, she told herself. She was Shaolin. Ellison would appreciate what that meant when she was through. But second thoughts nagged her the farther the undulating terrain took her away from the shrine. Even if this is reckless, she assured herself, the lesson from Master Zhao was to be unafraid of folly. That settled it.

By late afternoon she crested a rise in the land where an orchard, neglected and overgrown since the occupation, overlooked a ribbon of water. Across lay the Japanese army base. To her left, north of the grove, a wooden bridge arched into the camp's busy main portal where sentries stood guard while armored personnel carriers and officers in scout cars passed through. Forgetting her instruction to Ellison, she decided to make her way downstream for a less dangerous point of entry, following the water's curve in a lazy semi-circle not far from the base's southernmost limit.

She squirmed forward on her stomach in the thick cover of weeds. Opposite, a bedraggled line of women and two armed guards shuffled through an open wood gate set in a high barbed wire fence, along a bramble-covered path toward the stream. Barefoot, scalps shaved, dressed in cotton shifts with holes in the top and sides for neck and arms, the prisoners walked in silence, heads bowed. At the water's edge, they stripped and waded into the slow current. Lesions, purple and yellow bruises, and swollen red patches of skin plastered their torsos. They began to clean their sores and wash their bodies in the shallows. Now and then one or two moved downstream to relieve themselves. Two infantrymen, rifles on their knees, sat on the bank, smoking cigarettes, ignoring their captives. The current's swirl punctuated the unnatural silence from the human beings.

She discarded her robe for the pants and long-sleeved tunic beneath, hid it along with her shoes in the tall grass, slithered in, and swam underwater a short distance upstream. Her head popped above the surface, but the few vacant eyes who noticed paid no attention. She wriggled out of her pants and let them float away. Her tunic would have to serve as a substitute for the shifts the other women were wringing out. The guards blew a whistle. The prisoners put on their wet clothes and congregated on the path where Su Li stole into the grisly line unnoticed. The women radiated an unsettling aura of despair, far worse than she had imagined. They longed for death.

The procession passed a cleared space where a corpse — female but long dead and rotting — hung tied by hands and legs to a pole stretched between two trees,

341

trussed like an animal over a fire. Skewered between its thighs, a stake of bamboo angled menacingly at the sky. A sign in crude, red calligraphy — blood, she guessed — was nailed to a tree: "For those who disobey."

Her mouth filled with bile. Her mind refused to accept what her eyes beheld. This could not be. Human beings did not defile one another in such a manner. There could be no good to balance such horror, no yin for this yang. In the face of such outrage, the Master's teachings on life's sanctity, on detachment, harmony, inner peace were no more than meaningless ashes. She fought an impulse to kill the guards on the spot. The column moved across the barren, packed earth of the compound while the soldiers closed the gate behind them. She had entered the mouth of the ten devils. Rage gave way to a dread deeper than any she had ever felt.

Inside a converted warehouse, rows of head-high wooden stalls divided the long rectangular room into sections. One set lined each of the outer walls while a double row back to back paralleled them in the center with space for a corridor on each side. On boards above each stall a number or name was painted that matched the backs of the sack dresses. Floating above it all, the raw stench of male lust — sweet, acidic, fetid — assaulted her nostrils. Her group filed down one of the passageways where each woman entered a compartment with the curtain pushed aside. In one she glimpsed a half-dressed soldier urinating on a naked prisoner who lay on a woven mat. Soldiers in dirty uniforms or short pants waited in a line that stretched to the door. Some joked and swaggered with their comrades. Others moped, heads down, or mumbled under their breath. A few smiled shyly. The sole female sounds were moans or an occasional squeal of pain. Male grunts and sighs echoed above the partitions along with the slap of flesh against flesh.

A heavily-built sergeant who carried a small crop waddled his way down the opposite passageway. The overseer stopped to joke with a couple of the men, clapped them on the shoulder good-naturedly, gestured and peeked inside the nearest curtains. His comrades burst into laughter, the obsequious merriment of subordinates before one who wields power.

She neared the far end of the building. There were no soldiers here yet. She surmised these women must be the least popular. The woman in front of her slipped into an unoccupied partition, a crude metal bucket, a pile of bloody rags and a stool the only furniture. She followed and closed the curtain. The sex slave turned in alarm but Su Li clamped a hand over her mouth.

"Do not cry out! I will not harm you. Do you understand?" The terrified woman nodded. Su Li released her. "I am trying to find someone," she said quietly. "Will you help me?" Oozing sores covered the lower parts of the woman's mid-section. Dried yellow pus stained the inside of her thighs. No wonder no one came to this end, Su Li thought.

"What are you talking about?" she said harshly. "You want the whip? Go to your own stall!" Her appearance bordered on insanity.

"No. Listen." Su Li grabbed her shoulders and shook her. "How long have you been here?"

"Are you new?" The disease-riddled captive's eyes rolled in their sockets. "You see this?" She lifted her shift to reveal a distended, discolored pubis. "Still some come, when the lines are long and they cannot wait any longer. For this!" She grimaced. "They will not come today. Not many. But the brute, he will." She pushed Su Li's hands off her. "Leave me alone."

The sergeant at the front of the room was ready to make a circuit of the cubicles. Su Li squeezed the woman's shoulders hard. "Listen to me! A girl. Her name was Lian. From Plum Blossom village west of Shanghai. Maybe five, six years ago. I need to know her fate."

The woman's eyes, tinged with madness, shifted uncontrollably up and down. "Lian? Lian? I don't remember names."

Su Li shook the woman again. "You have been here a long time. You must know!"

The woman cringed. "No. No. Let me go."

"Try!" Su Li ordered.

The captive squeezed her eyes shut. "I don't . . . . There was a girl. Here when I came. I remember because she sang songs. Then she was with child. No good anymore. That awful thing on the path? That is what they did to her shortly after I got here. My turn now." She began to sing—more like a moan—but loud enough to attract attention.

"Quiet!" Su Li commanded in as high a voice as she dared. "Have you heard of a foreigner who might have been here? A red-haired high nose."

The woman was powerless to keep her own voice low. "She never stayed here. She passed through the camp they say. The soldiers still speak of her. That is all I—."

The curtain ripped open.

Ellison awoke, the heat of her body still palpable on his back. Uneasy, he sat up and leaned against a wall. She had seemed different yesterday, cocksure of herself. He should have paid more attention, not have allowed her to go alone. As much as he stood in awe of her, she was entering a minefield of danger for his sake. If he had to see this through, it should not be at her expense. *Damn it!* A deep longing for her filled the shrine and he fingered the gilt-clad goddess-doll as if it had the power to allay his foreboding. The more he looked at it the more its features changed. *Su Li, I love you.* The insight exploded like a mortar round. *Su Li, I love you.* He dropped the figurine in amazement. *I love you.* The words resounded in his brain. *I love you.*

He bolted out of the shrine and ran toward the risen sun. He estimated he was no more than an hour behind her. He tried to recall bits and pieces about the camp's location. The river was the key. What to do if and when he got there, without a weapon, in a strange land, dressed in a clumsy robe, enemies everywhere—he put those thoughts out of his mind and avoided contact with the farmers or their families who labored together in the fields. Whenever he drew near anyone, he pretended to limp. If someone called out, he bowed and gave the blessing of the Buddha, to his mind the supreme irony for the son of a Christian minister. By mid-afternoon he found the river.

He knelt in the tall grass, took off his robe, folded it under his arm and crawled toward the bank to reconnoiter. The bulk of the Japanese encampment stretched upstream, to his left, surrounded by a fence that followed the narrow, slow-moving river from south to north where it curved out of sight. To his right, the barbed wire took a ninety-degree angle to the east, at the southernmost extent of the enclosure. No sentries patrolled the perimeter because no enemy should have been within a hundred miles or more. Further in, rows of howitzers and neatly arranged crates of shells and munitions were stockpiled next to lines of half-track transport trucks and *Shinhoto* tanks parked alongside metal-sided warehouses. So, a supply dump and logistics depot, he realized. The headquarters would be up north. But where was Su Li? Did she get in somehow?

He crept upstream and paused, curious about the activity at a wooden single-story warehouse-style building where a ragged procession of soldiers in casual dress were entering and exiting. He crawled further along for a better vantage point when he hit upon a place where the grass had been trampled. Two small shoes and an orange robe lay hidden in the brush.

"What you do here? I not know you. Go your place," the Japanese sergeant growled in broken Chinese. His lips curled in anger, his eyes wide in disbelief at the affront to his authority, he rained two lashes on each of them. One huge hand gripped Su Li beneath an armpit and lifted her out of the stall as easy as a child and set her next to an empty cubicle, the last one in the line. His thick finger pointed for her to go in. She weighed her options. Too many soldiers, too visible to resist. The heavy man followed her in and drew the curtain closed.

He gestured with the lash at her tunic, indicating she should take it off. She pretended not to understand. An angry grunt and a powerful hand pressed her to her knees. She submitted, calculating it was not yet the right opportunity to kill him. *Wait until no one else can see.* The sergeant dropped the lash and unbelted his pants, his erection awaiting the expected response. When she did not comply, he leaned over and pulled her head toward him. Her left hand slid behind the soldier's kneecap. Forefinger and thumb found the tendon and snapped it. Before he hit the floor she leapt on top of him, drove a knee into his chest and with one short jab of her knuckle shattered his windpipe. The brute thrashed his arms and legs in panic before his life drained away. She allowed herself to savor his death only for a brief second. The comfort station was as busy as a market and someone would find the dead soldier soon. Despite its nauseating smell, she unbuttoned his shirt and put it on, pulled on his fatigues, tightened the belt and tucked the shirt in. She slipped on his sandals, drew his hat low over her forehead and walked past the other stalls and through the door.

Outside daylight was fading. A few more soldiers approached from the main barracks, half-drunk, laughing among themselves. She quick-stepped in the opposite direction, hoping to round the corner toward the gate. Someone shouted at her from behind. She walked faster. They called again. Her heart pounded, unsure what to do. She pointed to her rump and squatted. They laughed and turned back toward the comfort house.

As she approached the row of parked tanks, two guards turned a corner and met her head on. Their first impulse was to salute. Startled she bent low and returned the gesture. They parted to let her pass but something aroused their suspicions. They shouted a warning and unslung their rifles. She lashed out with her foot and crushed one soldier's sternum. Air exhaled from his collapsed lungs as he fell dead while she seamlessly spun and drove her fist straight between the eyes of the second soldier. The strike shoved splintered nasal bones up into his cranium but did not prevent a reflex convulsion of his finger curled around his rifle's trigger. The gunshot shattered the evening quiet. Crows protested and rose into the sky from the orchard, tantalizingly close across the stream. By now the same group of soldiers who had hailed her piled out of the warehouse in pursuit. She fled for her life across the parade ground but the baggy trousers slid from her waist to her ankles and she tripped, five paces from the fence, the gate and freedom.

Crazy with rage, the soldiers pounced on her and began to punch her head and ribs. Su Li took slow breaths and waited. Given a chance, she might even defeat eight unarmed men with only one small opening, but they gave her none. They turned her over and ripped the trousers off her ankles. A soldier grabbed her pubic hairs and hoisted her pelvis so all could see; their eyes widened in amazement and they babbled with excitement. Two of them spread her legs apart while another drew a knife and pulled up her shirt. The knife jabbed into her skin above her nipple and drew blood.

She absorbed each detail like a wild animal captured and prodded by tormentors who want to see how it reacts. These were the barbarians. Death would not be easy or quick. Her hips were able to twist a little but no more. The men laughed derisively at her futile resistance. One took off his shorts, knelt and pressed against her but his repeated thrusts could not penetrate. When his comrades mocked him, he became angry and ripped her apart with his fingers. At that instant, she ceased to struggle. Her spirit withdrew from the body and fled to a realm of shadows.

Ellison heard the shot at the same time as the crows. Across the river a Japanese soldier was running toward the fence, a half dozen or more in pursuit. The fleeing man passed the ranks of trucks, heading for the tanks. Fumbling with his pants, he finally tripped like a comic from a silent movie. He lashed out at his pursuers for a while until they pinned him face-down, one at each extremity. He knew it was her.

Their backs were to him but he could see them waiting to take their turns. He swam furiously, their laughter echoing above the swirl of the water around his neck. *I will kill you all. I will kill you.* He scrambled to the bank and sprinted up the path. Another shot rang out. He stopped at the last line of bushes and hid. An officer had approached the rapists with his pistol drawn. The startled soldiers threw on their clothes and stumbled to attention. He snapped an order and gestured. They turned her over on her stomach, face pressed into the earth. The officer yelled another command at the soldiers who saluted and left. He pulled out a knife, laid his gun belt on the ground and undid his trousers before he knelt between her legs.

Ellison crawled along the fence, tearing his fingers on the barbed wire in a desperate search for an opening. At last he found a post where the staples had come loose, pulled the wire far enough apart to wriggle through and sprinted for the row of tanks.

Her last vestige of sanity faltered as the steel tip ran along her spine. Despair brought a cry from a swollen tongue and a mouth filled with dirt. "Master," she managed to breathe, "help me." A voice uttered harsh, unintelligible words in her ear. Right when she thought the horror had reached its limit, the knife point neared her crotch. She shrieked.

Ellison damped the fire of anguish to the cold, calm cunning of a predator, a single-minded tiger on the hunt, suppressing a nearly irresistible howl of rage lest he alert his prey. His feet flew across the ground as if they never touched the earth, eyes ablaze with hatred and fixed on the pistol holster a yard behind the torturer. He dove headlong and rolled to his stomach. The Japanese officer turned in disbelief before two bullets burrowed through the side of his skull.

CHAPTER 42

When you reach the top, keep climbing – Zen saying

There was no time for grief, no time for outrage, no time for comfort in the typhoon of raw emotion that blew his mind to the edge of reason. He knew these things unconsciously as he lifted her in his arms, in the same way a father might lift an injured child, swiftly but with infinite tenderness. How light she felt. How fragile. Not superhuman at all. The eye of the great storm allowed him this briefest second of detachment, then resumed its malevolent fury. Move now, flee for your life, his central nervous system screamed.

Shouts from other parts of the camp were echoing in the deepening twilight. Klaxons sounded and flood lights switched on. Orders were called out and soldiers mobilized, but he had by that time raced for the gate, unhooked the chain and started running down the path to the river, plowing through brambles, stumbling on stones. *Move. Concentrate. Do it right. Watch your bloody, fucking step. Can't fall now.* The commands to himself gave a temporary order to the chaos in his mind. Their survival depended on the same cool detachment he possessed when he killed the rapist.

Sunlight bathed the underside of massed high clouds on the horizon with its last faint glow, lengthening shadows painting the river gray. He hesitated. Cross the way he came and try to find his route back to the shrine or go downstream? There would be more cover in the water as the light failed, he calculated, and the Nips might be fooled for a while and assume he escaped by going straight across. He was an indifferent swimmer but the river was shallow, manageable at that point. Yet he did not know where it would take them.

Nevertheless, he plunged into the sluggish current, his chin inches above the surface, Su Li alongside, her shirt forming air pockets to keep her on top of the water. Still, he vacillated; the stream kept tipping him off balance, prodding him to his left. Okay, he decided, go with the river. Swim as long as he could then walk on the bottom. He pushed off and drifted with the flow, keeping to the middle, side-stroking to conserve energy, allowing the current to do most of the work, towing her by the collar so her face was just enough above the surface to breathe. He steadily put distance between himself and the shore, the water level a foot or so above his height. When his arms tired, he took a breath, dropped to the mud beneath and propelled himself forward into a dead float. After a while, more shots rang out, but none toward them. As he had hoped, they were aiming across the river, the obvious escape route, shooting at phantoms in the twilight. He had made the correct choice — or the river had done it for him.

The remaining sunlight winked out. Dusk shrouded the banks in front of the approaching weather front. At that point he was walking in water up to his neck for he no longer possessed enough strength to swim. He hoped it was safe to stop and edged toward the shore at the southern end of the abandoned orchard. Breathing heavily, he hoisted her, slogged up a gently sloping bank of crumbly soil and laid her in the weeds. Beneath the Japanese soldier's shirt the cuts and deep black bruises on her skin threatened his fragile self-control once more.

"Hang on, Shaolin!" he said and touched the hurts as if his hands could draw out their suffering. An ear to her chest told him her heart was beating. A forefinger to her lips felt the faint flutter of exhaling breath, but her brow was cold. He remembered his mother had diagnosed symptoms like these. She was in shock and needed a blanket. "You'll be fine, Su Li. You'll be fine. I'm going to take care of you," he told the unconscious woman.

Far upstream a searchlight crisscrossed the water's surface accompanied by the low growl of an outboard motor. He slung her over his shoulders in a fireman's carry — his own body heat would keep her warm, he hoped — and settled into a steady dog trot perpendicular to the river. Far to the west, a dim outline of hills rose in moonlight filtered through threatening overcast. There might be cover there. They had come through hills. It must be the direction.

And so he ran and walked and hobbled through the darkness, trotted until his strength ebbed, rested, walked, limped, ran for a few minutes, over and over, in a marathon race against inevitable pursuit, each cycle slower, more labored, shorter. Over and over he tripped in furrows, fell to his knees and grunted back upright or blindly banged his legs on rock walls that lined the fields while clouds threatened to shutter the last faint backlight of the moon. Neck muscles too weary to lift his head, he bumped into a house, all but invisible in a shadowy cluster of mud brick homes closed up against the night, but no one stirred. He righted himself and plowed onward. After uncounted hours, he dropped to his knees in exhaustion, laid his burden next to an irrigation ditch and lapped a few drops of water into his mouth. If he could only rest a while. His lungs sucked in great gulps of cool, damp air in the soundless night. He needed to stay awake. Had to.

A bell rang.

Bugger! Fell asleep. Idiot. The bell rang again followed by a lowing sound. Just an ox stirring in its stall. They were safe for now, but sleep meant death. With a groan he summoned the strength to pick her limp body up and lurch ahead, still protected by the cocoon of darkness. Burning sensations pulsed in all his limbs, each one howling in protest: make it stop. *You're not gonna make it,* a sinister persona in his head shouted above the screams of pain in his muscles; but a different inner voice began to sing counter melodies, songs of valor and heroism his father had taught him, and for a while his feet marched in step to their rhythm. *Give me some men, who are stout-hearted men,* it sang. Other times wild, manic thoughts cascaded through his brain. He speculated about the Chinese constellations, counted the bullet holes in the Dragon Lady's tail, promised himself he would learn to play his father's violin someday, resolved to see Buzz again and tell him that joke he couldn't remember. *You're quite batty, old man.* His legs shook uncontrollably when he shifted Su Li onto his other aching shoulder. *It's very simple, you see. One foot, then the other foot. It's called walking, laddie. Any child can do it. But, wait is this the right direction? Hard to make anything out in this damned moonlight. Pretty sure I'm moving away from the river. That's good. Where the Japanese are. I hope.* Su Li never moved or made a sound, as if her spirit were somewhere else. *Just as well.*

When the first tint of dawn bleached the leaden sky, he was a mud-splattered wild man alone on a desolate field. His thoughts teetered on incoherence, his body hardly able to move. Open space stretched out behind him. A pitch-black band of rain clouds looked poised to strike the hills he once aimed for. Now, he realized, they were much too far to reach. He had no idea what to do except hide-out before they were discovered. A faint rise in the terrain offered a slim hope. There was nowhere else to go. But his legs trembled with the simple effort of standing and his knees resisted the mind's command to bend. Shoulders slumped, he pitched forward. Su Li who once seemed so light weighed as much as a mountain. He was reduced to carrying her like a small child, splayed on his chest, legs around his waist. Forward, not sideways, man, his nearly delirious brain ordered. One foot in front of the other. Hut, two, three, four.

Scattered raindrops fell on a string of boulders from an ancient volcanic blowout that littered the rocky soil where the land swelled upward then sloped away into a swale. He staggered to the edge. Through a break in the clouds his sweat-blurred eyes made out a copse of trees surrounding a dim four-story tower. He teetered, crumpled, let her fall on the ground and collapsed beside her, his mind, feverish with exhaustion, unable to string two thoughts together. He lay there taking in deep breaths for a while. Finally, with a roar that devoured his last ounce of energy, he wobbled to his feet, took hold of her wrists with both hands and dragged her the rest of the way to the old pagoda. He hauled her through an ornate door half off its hinges, its partner swaying freely in the light winds, onto a broken tiled floor alongside an immense statue of the Buddha.

He crumpled next to her as the rain came down in earnest in the gray morning light.

CHAPTER 43

Military officers should observe their duties gravely – Lao-tze

Lieutenant Ahiro Hideaki of the 3rd Imperial Regiment cursed his luck. His platoon was awarded the worst of the operation, a search for fugitives who had somehow infiltrated the base and killed three men and an officer. For two rainy days they had slogged through muddy countryside when he should have been preparing himself mentally for the next battle. His patrol had checked every damned hut and house from the river to the farthest end of the plain – in vain. In truth, such crimes needed to be punished. But why him? He joined the army and came to China to fight, not to be a policeman. The account from Colonel Sadduharu was unclear. Some story about a woman, one of the sex slaves. Presumably someone had wanted the wretch enough to snatch her away. But to break into the base? There wasn't a Chinese vermin within a hundred miles with such courage, except those fanatical lunatics, the monks; and they cared nothing for women. If it were not for the orders, he could not believe it had happened.

Multiple rapes. Those were the rumors among the men. Sickening. The Major who died had been a participant. Had discipline fallen so far? Ahiro asked himself. To let soldiers run wild like animals over something so despicable? Had morale sunk that low? "Comfort women," the War Ministry called the captives. Disgraceful. Where was the honor?

"Move your sorry asses, toads! I don't care how wet you are. Our orders are to find the criminals." He kicked the spurs into his horse. The soaking, hungry infantrymen swore under their breath.

When Ellison awoke a gentle rain was falling. He forced his eyes open. Gray outside. Evening? Where was he? He tried hard to recall the previous day. His aching muscles reminded him — inside a pagoda. His last memories were the blurred image of blood-shot eyes and a dulled brain. He crawled over to the big doors, afraid he would be unable to walk. It took all his strength to close the warped wood portals before he hobbled back to Su Li who was curled up on the tiled floor against one wall, near the seated Buddha, pale as death, coma-like.

Artillery shells had blown holes in the shrine especially on the upper floors where the tower sagged. Jagged splintered beams along one wall supported a staircase that circled up and around an immense, thirty-foot high statue dominating the center of the room. Its ancient bronze finish still maintained a coppery sheen but the priests or monks who manned the temple had long since fled and any object of value had been looted. Yet the lack of attendants had not prevented the common people from seeking the Enlightened One's blessing. Whatever the poor could manage as an offering littered the hexagonal ground floor — clumsy images fashioned out of bamboo and clay, painted scraps of paper, odds and ends of cloth, furniture.

He placed a roll of frayed unbleached silk beneath her head for a pillow and covered her with a tattered tapestry embroidered with what were at one time colored birds and flowers, now faded and indistinguishable. The river had removed most of the blood from her skin but she was filthy. He ripped off a piece of cloth, held it out a window to dampen it and cleaned her face, arms and legs. Weary beyond belief and cold to the bone, he squatted and kept watch over the comatose woman before falling into another sleep of exhaustion, close beside her.

After what seemed mere minutes, a steady rain drumming on the curved eaves of the pagoda's multi-tiered roofs awakened him. Through the shutterless windows, the light grew brighter, penetrating thick overcast. He had slept for twelve hours. Her eyes were open. In a wave of tenderness, he cradled her head, pulled it to his chest and stroked her cheek over and over, like a mother might comfort a sick child.

"Water," she gasped.

He laid her back down, found two wooden offering cups and filled them with rain water. She drank greedily. When she lay back against the statue to rest, he went outside once more to slake his thirst and take the measure of his own body — covered with dirt and mud, splotched with blood from her wounds and from his own skin ripped by the barbed wire. He stripped off his clothes, oblivious to the temperature, and held them under the stream that poured off the roof tiles. The rain brought cleansing and time to think. How could he possibly save them from the Japs? The storm may have slowed their pursuers but those bastards never rested until they got vengeance. He could find no answer. Shivering from the damp he wrung out his wet clothes and put them back on. Inside, she had propped herself up against the Buddha's base, legs drawn up against her chest, arms around her knees. Her eyes were brighter, clearer. Her spirit had returned.

"I have much to tell you."

"Su Li," he stammered. "We need to leave."

She placed a hand on the cracked floor tile next to her, indicating he should sit. Her face was puzzled, as if searching for the right words. "I traveled to a place. When I was away. Saw things. Light." She looked up at the Buddha. "Brighter than I could imagine. And darkness. Black as black can be. And I was one with all things." She breathed deeply. "I cannot explain this."

"You were in a coma, Su Li. The mind does strange things."

Her voice grew stronger. "I cannot describe it, but when I turned back to the light, I saw you, Ellison. And when I looked into your eyes, *laohuo* was looking back at me, the eyes of the tiger. And I have been fearful of those eyes. For they are fierce, yes, but gentle at the same time." She nodded her head slowly. "And I knew I could never again be afraid of them. Or of you."

"Afraid of me?" His forehead creased with anguish.

Their eyes hung on each other's. "Where are we?"

"I don't know. An old temple. West of the river. As far as I was able to run in one night." He glanced at the battered doors. "The enemy will be looking for us. We're lost and no one knows where we are. And it's my fault, what happened to you."

She gripped his wrist. "We will not speak of the past, for who can judge whether it is good or bad, or both?" She sipped a little water. "Every Chinese would have left me to die in my disgrace. Yet you saved my life. Why?"

"How can you ask that?" He frowned in disbelief. "I love you."

She uttered a moan and leaned back on the plinth. "Love me? You cannot love such a vile wretch as me. Not after what they did to me."

"Su Li, you are my master, my teacher." He took her in his arms. "I have learned how to live again from you."

She nuzzled against his chest and lay there, drawing his *chi* into her own. After a time, she murmured, "Lian is dead. I am sorry."

"How?" Ellison asked.

"You would not want to know."

He closed his eyes and summoned everything he could remember of the girl he had loved in what seemed another life, tried to hold her image in his mind long enough to say a final good-bye. All the grief and happiness from those days surged like an incoming tide and he thought his heart would crack. She placed her palm on his chest. Have no fear, yes, but what about sadness? Not even the rain outside had the power to wash away that sorrow.

"Now I must sleep," she said.

When she awoke gray clouds had deepened into twilight. He was sitting there, keeping vigil, patient, filled with trust and hope in her capacity to heal herself. The light in her eyes told him how far on that journey she had come. "I believe your mother is alive. A trophy for the Japanese commanding general. The smuggler was right."

"A lot of good that's going to do us." The rain intensified, pounded the roof tiles, roared like a rock slide. They sat in silence, mesmerized by its force. Just as quickly it eased into a steady downpour.

"Thank you for saving me."

"Aye." He spoke in English, then in Chinese. "You should hate me. I have brought this on you."

She placed her hand on his. "It is not for my life that I am most grateful, Ellison. No one has ever held me as you just did. Or told me what is in his heart, as you have. This love you speak of has no room in the Master's lore. It has been absent in my world — until now." He tried to interrupt but she put a finger on his lips. "It makes one do foolish things." She coughed. "It brings sorrow and joy, yin and yang. That is Tao. Because of it, I know I can never be a Shaolin monk in the full sense, worthy or not. I cannot fight against this other force, this love-*chi* that is also the Tao. No, I surrender to it. I wish to learn the Tao of love."

He forced a smile. "Can we return? To the Master?"

"He will find us. First, though, you must be the master and hold me again the way you have done, so I may study how to do it to you."

"Su Li, I am a poor teacher."

"You are wise in your own way, James." She touched his cheek. "If there is good in this world that might balance the evil I have suffered, you are it."

Ellison wrapped his arms around her. "Sleep, Shaolin. Sleep," he murmured.

CHAPTER 44

Spiritual power! Supernatural activity! Hewing wood, drawing water – Zen saying

"Hello in there! Time to awaken!" A roar of laughter sounded outside the door to the pagoda. "The rain has ended."

He awoke from a troubled sleep. Was that a voice or was he dreaming? His first clear thought was the Japs had overtaken them. His second was that Su Li still lay nestled in his arms, now tingling from lying all night on the hard tile floor. He unwound his arm and looked around for a weapon. She roused herself and held her hand up to signal silence.

"Do not be afraid. We are friends." More laughter.

Ellison peeked through a narrow crack in the double doors. Outside beneath a sky of broken clouds stood two old men in faded saffron robes carrying bamboo walking sticks. With a sigh of relief he pulled open one of the heavy, sagging doors.

"Aren't you going to invite us in?" said one with a broad smile.

"It's the least you can do," said the other. "After all the time we've spent searching for you two."

"For us?" Ellison felt as if he were half-asleep.

"Da Shi sent us. We're, ah, friends of his, you might say," said the taller one.

"No time to explain," said the second. "The Japanese patrol is close behind and you and tiger-daughter must hide."

"Hide? Where?"

"Will you let us in so we can show you?" asked the first monk. He followed Ellison and glanced around. "Ah! There she is." While the smaller monk circled the statute of the Buddha, the other examined Su Li, a pained expression on his face. "Wing, the child is hurt."

"Time for that later." Wing ran his hand along the bottom of the huge Buddha's pedestal "Ah, here it is, Wang. Behind the Enlightened One, a wart, near his rump."

"A very enlightened location," said Wang with glee. He was thin and bony, with a full top knot of snow white hair. "Do as my friend Wing says."

"Master Wang? Is it truly you? My Master's old teacher?" Su Li asked. "When I last saw you, I . . . ." The old memories welled in her eyes once more.

"Yes, Tiger-daughter. Da Shi has a special place for you, it seems." He winked at her.

Wing gestured. "Touch the wart and a door will slide up. Hide in there until they leave. Hurry."

"We'll deal with the barbarians." Wang's eyes twinkled as he brandished his bamboo staff in a martial arts stance.

Still not quite believing what was happening, Ellison carried Su Li to the rear of the statue, groped the smooth bronze until he found a small bump, touched it and a slab of metal slid upward. He placed Su Li inside then joined her. The door slid shut.

"What's that ahead?" Lieutenant Ahiro asked his sergeant. "A building in those trees?" He took out a pair of field glasses. "Surround that damned thing. Move out!"

The infantrymen spread out in a ragged line and rallied to the lip of the swale then staggered into the bowl of land. Ahiro drew out his pistol. The bedraggled soldiers fanned out in a half-hearted semi-circle, rifles ready, and closed in on the dilapidated pagoda. He scowled at his men's disarray. Nothing showed a man's honor, his *bushido,* more than war itself, and here he was, stuck with ignorant farmers — mules — for soldiers and an assignment for an idiot.

"Prisoners, Sergeant?" He dismounted and confronted two wizened old men who stood outside the doors, guarded by his men. He recognized from their robes they were priests, but these sorry clowns were too old and too frail to be any threat. Worn out. Like the temple. Typical of the Chinese, to let their holy places go to the devil. The whole culture was rotten. He gestured to the soldiers to lower their rifles.

"Priests, we're looking for fugitives. A man, maybe a woman." Ahiro had learned Chinese as a contribution to the war effort but he hated it, full of double and even triple meanings. He never knew if someone were mocking him or not.

"You speak our language well, sir." The oldest and tallest bowed.

"That's because it's such a simple one," Ahiro said.

"Indeed," agreed the smaller man. "That must be the reason your country learned its own language from us."

Ahiro was tempted to shoot them on the spot but the general had issued strict orders against any more disturbances. The camp depended on local farmers for food and these might be revered holy men. "What are you doing here?"

"We needed to get out of the rain," explained the talkative one. "We're on a journey to Wushan. They say if you perform the pilgrimage to the Golden Temple this year, it counts for twelve other years."

"And Wing is quite lazy," added the tall one with a guffaw.

"Enough! I have no time for this nonsense. Have you seen any criminals, a man and woman? They have committed murder."

"Murder? You'll find no murderers in this sacred place," said the taller monk.

The one called Wing pursed his lips, clasped his hands behind his back and looked at his feet, as if deep in thought. "Now, the day before yesterday — when we were heading this direction — I saw someone," he said and raised his forefinger, "by the river, south of your camp. Remember, Wang? It was early in the morning and you were taking a shit and it started to rain and — ."

"Idiots!" shouted Ahiro.

"There were dead bodies floating in the water, sir."

"Hmph," he grunted. "I don't believe you. I intend to search this temple."

"Just make sure the spirits of the dead are not disturbed, sir. I wouldn't want them to bring bad luck to you and your family," said Wing.

Ahiro hesitated, gestured to his men to go in, but they glanced uneasily at each other and refused to move. "Superstitious bumpkins," he yelled at them. "There's nothing to be afraid of here! Sergeant!" But no threat could motivate them to enter the temple. Ahiro glowered. This was not the place to make a scene about discipline. Besides the general had warned the officers not to desecrate sacred places. He said he did not mind fighting the Chinese people but did not want their angry gods and ancestors against him.

"Chi Wan thought thrice before he acted. When Confucius was informed, he said 'Twice will do,'" chimed Wing with a sly smile.

"I'll go in myself," the officer fumed, steadied his pistol and walked cautiously toward the entrance.

"No violence is allowed in this holy place." The voice of the older, taller monk rang out like a command from on high.

Ahiro returned the gun to his holster despite himself. The room was empty, in any case. A waste of time, just as he suspected. He knelt before the Buddha, folded his palms together and recited a prayer, a hope the war would end soon and he could return to his family, then rejoined his platoon. "There is a reward for the heads of these criminals if you see them, priests."

"Indeed," said Wang, with a solemn face. "I could use extra money."

"Move out, Sergeant. Enough of this circus." Ahiro scowled, turned on his heel and mounted his horse. The sergeant shouted an order and the patrol stumbled up the rise the way they had come. Wing monitored until they disappeared then nodded to Wang.

"You can come out!" Wang shouted, back inside.

Tiny rays of light shone high above Ellison and Su Li through the eyes of Buddha but it was too dark to see much. He banged on the door with his fist. "I can't get out," he bellowed.

Wing hurried around and pressed on Buddha's wart. "You forgot to tell them how to exit, Wang. I swear you've lost your mind."

The secret door slid up. Ellison returned Su Li to the crude bed while Wang started a fire with pieces of furniture and bamboo. A brazier intended for burning charcoal soon became a pot of boiling water for tea.

"I was beginning to fear we'd never find you." Wang's eyes sparkled with humor above a wispy white beard. "You made a stir at the Japanese camp. A hornet's nest. But we'll escort you back to Guiyan. After we attend to tiger-daughter there." He bobbed his head toward Su Li.

"You know about us?" Ellison was still having a hard time thinking straight.

"Po sent word. He believes General Okamura's reply will come soon," said Wing. "Your little adventure has complicated things." Unlike Wang, Wing was beardless and his skull ready to burst from the taut wizened skin of his bald head. Four inches smaller than his companion, he moved and spoke with the vitality of a much younger man.

"You know Da Shi also, Master Wing?" asked Su Li in wonder. She was stronger, feeding off the vitality of the old monks.

"We both were his teachers when he came to the monastery," said Wing who ambled over with a cup of steaming liquid. "Here, drink this, child. It should help you feel better." While she sipped the medicine he drew salves and ointments out of a pouch and applied it to the cuts on her breasts and inner thighs. "My poor dear." He touched her brow in genuine sympathy. "You will recover. In time."

"We must return you two to Hankow and our former pupil. Can you travel, tiger-daughter?" Wang asked.

"It has been a long time since someone other than the Master called me that name, Master Wang," said Su Li, brightening as she struggled to her feet. "I can try."

"No!" insisted Ellison. "You can't walk. I'll carry you on my back."

She pushed his hands away and made a feeble attempt to stand upright.

"I carried you before. I can do it again."

"I am not an invalid."

The old monks looked at each other in amusement while she took two steps before her legs collapsed and Ellison caught her. They eyed each other in mock disbelief. "What do you suppose, Wang?"

"Indeed. She makes a perfect bride." He opened a bundle wrapped in silk and drew out a red bridal gown.

"Put this on and let us be on our way. You will be a bride being escorted to a wedding by two old priests and your brother."

"A bride?" She groaned.

"But it is the color of good fortune." Wang laughed. Both monks raised their eyes to the ceiling as if the roof might cave in.

Faced with stronger wills than her own, Su Li took off the Japanese soldier's shirt and threw the red embroidered dress over her abused body, grimacing with each movement. The men discreetly turned their heads. Wing put out the fire and gathered the food and water pouches they had carried with them. The motley entourage saluted the Buddha, walked through the door of the abandoned pagoda and set out in an unfamiliar direction, one monk in the lead while the other brought up the rear. Ellison carried her on his back, her legs around his waist and her arms around his neck, chin resting on his shoulder. She clung to him with fierce desperation as if afraid he might let go of her. He fancied his own strength flowing to the urgency of her need, somehow healing her inside.

Wang and Wing marched onward inexorably at a pace Ellison, burdened with Su Li, found difficult to maintain. He had made it two nights ago, he could make it now, he told himself. A worn dirt path looped around the foothills of the stony peaks northward toward Hankow and the Yangtze. When they broke at nightfall to rest and eat, the monks reminisced about their former student.

"He was, shall I say, unique." Wang nodded sagely. "It was impossible to keep your precious master in the monastery. He would leave for months on end sometimes, wander all over China."

"You mentioned, Master Wang, Da Shi spoke of me," said Su Li.

"Did I? I may have. He often tends to be dramatic."

"To me, it seemed he was never satisfied. I have no complaints. I was honored to be his pupil. But at times I supposed he made it harder because — ."

"Indeed." The old man held up his hands before the fire. Each of them fell silent before the primeval magic of flame. "Claimed you were his best student, though. Most in tune with the Tao. Some such nonsense."

"And now he's on this mission to teach the Japanese what they cannot learn," added Wing shaking his head. "Headstrong to the end, that one."

"Talk wisdom to a fool and he calls you foolish," Ellison laughed. "I should know."

"Good, young man!" Wang clapped him on the back. "Lao-tze should have written such a thing. But Da Shi is a wise fool. His knowledge of the Tao is great. And no doubt what appears to be a foolish quest to us is the flow of wisdom to him."

Ellison said nothing of what he supposed was the reason for the Master's journey — the rescue of his mother. Perhaps the monks already knew. Little escaped them. Then again, maybe he himself didn't know the true motive Po was helping him. There were many currents roiling this river.

The next day they arrived at the Guiyan monastery.

CHAPTER 45
From caring comes courage — Lao-tze

Po met the exhausted travelers at the gate. "I will attend to her," he commanded, a quaver in his voice and anguish in his mien. He caught Su Li in his arms and carried her off toward a dormitory room, Wing and Wang trailing behind, leaving Ellison to wander the monastery alone.

The place had a hollowed out, empty feeling, with few monks and only a dozen students. Clearly it had once been magnificent and prosperous with its large, elaborately decorated buildings connected by covered footpaths, its statues of bodhisattvas and Guanyin presiding over formal gardens and grottoes in various locations, but war or some other scourge had left it in disrepair. Weeds choked untended paths and bare patches dotted the flower beds. Tiles lay on the ground, fallen off the curled eaves of the temple roof, and paint was peeling from its wood columns. One space largely intact beckoned to him, a striking, circular moon gate that opened to a legendary garden in the private style with a lake at its center, flanked on opposite sides by two pavilions. A roofed walkway led to the nearest one where several openings framed vistas of trees or shrubs. He absorbed the sun's warmth on a stone bench, rapt at the swans paddling among huge lotus leaves near the water's edge. After a time the serenity of the scene enveloped him.

An outbreak of influenza in the countryside swept through the region around their village. Infants and the old were particularly susceptible but no age group was immune to the death-dealing epidemic. People were frightened.

With his father back at mission headquarters in Shanghai to beg for more medical supplies, it fell to his mother to rally the bewildered villagers. She enlisted the aid of her ten year-old son to help minister to the sick in the course of which he witnessed his own friend die. Wu's death was one of dozens over the next weeks, most of them fading anonymously into each other, except for one. While he held her bag of instruments and medicines, Mary Ellison was sponging a prostrate woman's forehead when suddenly she stood upright and banged an angry fist on the bed. Her patient was dead.

"God damn it!" she hissed, gazing at the ceiling.

He was scandalized. He had never heard his parents curse.

When at last those intense blue eyes peered over the surgical mask at her scandalized son they told him there were no medicines capable of combating what confronted them. She covered her face and wept, then knelt to hug him. "Nay, Jamie, you dinna' hear me say such."

But he did. And he never forgot it.

For a month she nursed tirelessly, against hopeless odds, day and night, from house to house. All the villages within walking distance became her wards and he went along on her visits. He sensed how much she suffered, aware her medicines and skills could do little more than separate the well from the sick. She made sure those who had a decent chance were hydrated with clean water. Her very presence gave them hope.

At night mother and son slept on mats outside. Exhausted, she lay sobbing, her back to him. Wanting to comfort her but not knowing how, he listened until it became unbearable, stared up at the stars and cried silently.

A hand rested on his shoulder. He reluctantly pulled back from the memory. He had not experienced such serenity for many weeks—nor such resolve. "Master Wang."

"My apologies for the interruption. You reached a stillness. Like the water."

Ellison nodded

"The Pavilion of Meditation has that effect." Wang paused. "Balance and harmony reign in the garden. Unfortunately, not so in the rest of the world." His eyes twinkled above a thin smile. "So. There is news, young monk. Your mother is indeed in Shanghai, as we suspected. And General Okamura has renewed the challenge to Master Po. You must leave tomorrow." He gestured behind himself. "Behold, they come."

She could have been a bodhisattva, with the same hermaphroditic smile from an inner calm beyond humanity's mindless circle of waking and sleeping. Neither spoke, but the last knots in Ellison's troubled spirit unraveled. War, the great enemy, was confronting someone, something, it could not vanquish. Their eyes

377

locked together. *If you look long enough and deeply enough into your beloved eyes, you will see the whole universe looking back at you.* Suddenly, he recalled not only the words but who had conveyed them to him, like a throwaway comment that means nothing at the time and yet is always on the perimeter of attention. Inexplicably the mind both desires it and resists it, so after a while you give up trying to retrieve it; and only when you let it go, some unexpected event releases it from deep in the ocean of memory and it floats instantly to the surface of awareness. He was fairly certain the ambiguous oracle of Calcutta had not spoken those phrases aloud — impossible to say for sure — but implanted them in his brain somehow, perhaps during the moment they were entwined; and he knew someday, if they survived the war, he would take the time to stare long and deep into Su Li's eyes and see for himself what the universe looked like. His hand folded around hers as they walked, oblivious to the monks.

"Events have not unfolded as you anticipated," Wang said. He and Po strolled through the vegetable plots in a warm afternoon. "She has recovered her yin and her wholeness, though. That is well." The older man paused. "Strange that yin should elude a woman so."

"She is no ordinary woman, my old teacher." Po carried the leather case given to Wang by the courier, the Imperial Seal of Japan, a red Rising Sun, emblazoned on its cover. It contained a letter from General Okamura that renewed the challenge to Po, the contest to be conducted in Shanghai, the location of his headquarters.

"I suspect only old men appreciate yin."

"She has learned lessons I could never teach her. Eaten more bitterness than I could have imagined." Po rubbed his palm on his forehead and breathed deeply. "Without the foreign soldier, I think she would be lost."

Wang halted and glanced archly at his companion. "Most gracious of you to admit your mistake. I was not able to curb your tendency to believe you possessed all the answers. My failure as a teacher, no doubt. You have gained wisdom in your dotage."

Po laughed softly. Memories of his young manhood and time with Wang flashed through his mind, the best part of his life. Even he did not know Wang's age. One hundred? One hundred ten? "You were more than a master to me."

The two old monks' eyes met in recognition — they would not meet again. Wang bent at the waist and poked at the ground. "Look at this bok choy. I think it's ready to cut, don't you?" His bones made an audible creak as he came erect. "My eyesight isn't what it used to be."

"Will you return to Emei Shan, Wang?"

"I am well past my hundredth year. Why should I go back there? It doesn't matter where I die." He turned sharply to Po. "Ah, you wish me to look in on the boy. Speaking of which, I have one other piece of information for you."

CHAPTER 46

When you speak it is silent. When you are silent, it speaks – Zen saying

After leaving Hankow, the junk plied the Yangtze for two more days. Although a hundred miles inland, it dueled with ocean tides as the majestic river widened, burdened with the freight of China's heart. The travelers passed modern steamers as well as sailing ships whose design spanned the country's history, even an occasional antique with the distinctive red and white striped sails of empire-era government. Largest in the lake-sized channel were huge rafts of cypress and cedar logs lashed together, self-contained vessels with living quarters and an outdoor kitchen constructed amidships.

Nearing Shanghai, they turned south into the mouth of the Huangpu River, the narrow, polluted tributary of the Yangtze, threading through ferries, tugboats and hundreds of other vessels, some destined for the Pacific Ocean. Nimble sampans skirted passenger steamers and lighters that ferried cargo to the wharf from larger ocean-going freighters. Other junks, laden with goods from western China, dodged barges with double tows headed north. Japanese patrol boats proclaimed the occupiers' control of the port, a major Chinese economic asset.

"I always thought the gateway to hell was on land," Ellison said. He and Su Li stared in revulsion at an interminable minefield of dead bodies on the water's surface as they neared Shanghai's harbor. Throughout the last part of the voyage, she clung to him whenever she could, usually when they were at the gunwale and no one was watching them. He would find her shoulder touching his or her hand slipping over his own, but she seldom spoke.

The boat hove to along the Bund, south of Su Wan Creek, which opened on the Huangpu after a sinuous course through the city's center and was covered by a solid platform of thousands of small boats that would never sail again, permanent abodes for families with no real dwellings. While parents scrambled for survival, little children, with slits in their pants, were left tied by ropes to older siblings to keep them from falling into the water, the common sewer for the floating inhabitants.

On the waterfront stevedores and longshoremen from around the world worked alongside a hive of Chinese dockworkers. Hand signals and the bellow of white foreign supervisors magically overcame the obstacle of dozens of mutually unintelligible languages so the port functioned in the midst of apparent chaos. Heavy steel cranes, driven by noisy gasoline engines, lifted the bulkier cargo out of the holds of the larger ships. Bells, loud whistles and the deep roar of freighter horns drowned out crates of pigs, ducks and geese. The din was deafening, despite the muted effect of the fog that blended with the pervasive scent of salt water. Ellison tried to remember how it looked when he and his parents first arrived: people, unending waves of them, heaving against each other, surging by the neoclassical edifices of the Bund, the run-down symbol of the hated foreigners. "Pearl of the Orient," his mother had called it. He remembered her radiant smile and himself holding her hand as they watched from the steamer's railing. He was unable to see much more than dense throngs, pushing and shoving to their destinations, but he recalled his father's words, "city of sin."

The frantic tides of humanity had not changed, but unlike the Bund's former colonial overseers who had extorted as much wealth as possible, his parents had not been pampered French or British who leeched off the Chinese. They were humble people who had tried to bring a vestige of the modern world to a backward village. He could be proud of that, but as far as he was concerned, an ironic circle had closed. Now in the guise of a humble Chinese monk, he had become one with the country he once took for granted.

The crew tied off the hawsers, making the boat secure, and ran out a gang plank. Two men waited on the landing stage, one of them a tall, muscular fellow who wore a beret and a blue waistcoat and was trying to make himself heard over the babel of the dock's languages and the blare of ship sirens. Ellison noticed a bulge underneath his coat.

"Grand Master Po! Welcome! I am Chung, sent by the honorable Duo Yueshen. He sends his highest respects and invites you to his residence. He honors you for his father's sake."

Po nodded. "We are pleased to be his guests, even in this cesspool of a city."

Chung grinned. "Yes, Master Po. As you say. Still, it's our cesspool." He gestured. "Please follow me to our car.

It's not far from here. The competition is tomorrow," Chung continued as they walked, "and General Okamura has asked my boss to dine with him this evening. Duo cannot refuse but intends to receive you later tonight as his guest of honor and instructed me to inform you the woman you spoke of will be in attendance at the contest. He gives his word."

Chung and his man pushed and shoved and hacked through a thick forest of coolies bent double beneath massive bales of cotton, jostling passengers loaded with trunks and suitcases, headed the opposite way toward waiting steamships. At an intersection a man in a fedora, smoking a cigarette, leaned against a black Mercedes limousine. Chung nodded and the man opened a door.

"We will walk for a while," Po demurred. "I have not been to Shanghai for fifty years. I want to see for myself how degraded it has become."

"But Master Po," Chung pleaded, "the streets are full of Japanese puppets and traitors, and of course, hordes of beggars." Po held up his hand. A sulking Chung climbed into the back seat of the car and emerged with gray cloaks and skull caps. "If you insist, at least wear these. Everyone in the city has to have an identification card so we better not be stopped. Besides, the Japanese military has standing orders to arrest monks." He handed out cloth face masks. "Keep your heads and mouths covered and wrap yourselves with these. Catching a disease might be worse than being captured." Po donned the cloak and drew the string snug around his neck; Su Li and Ellison did likewise. Chung yelled to his driver, "Ling, follow us with the car. We cannot let anything happen to them."

"Who is this Duo?" Ellison shouted above the pandemonium as they elbowed forward.

"Head of the Green Circle Gang, *Qing Bang,*" Po replied. "The most powerful criminal organization in China. The older Duo fled to Macao four or five years ago. Now his son handles his affairs. People say Duo single-handedly props up the Chiang regime." Po gestured at the grand Bank of Shanghai and the Bank of Hong Kong. Though the Japanese conquerors had boarded up many of the old buildings or occupied them as command centers, these two neoclassical structures built by the British were still imposing. "They are beholden to Duo."

"A very rich man."

"Potentially in all of Shanghai."

"And yet he collaborates with the Japanese?" Su Li interjected.

"Business. Shanghai is about money. And for Duo and his son all that matters is money. Except martial arts. Of that he is a great patron, especially now it is banned." Po laughed. "Something of an adept himself, too, in his youth."

The owners had abandoned most of the shops and businesses that lined the narrow side street, the movable shutters cannibalized for firewood, their storefronts empty mouths. The resistance had painted slogans on the walls: "Death to the occupiers of China," below signs with fanciful names such as Celestial Fragrance or Good Luck Forest Tea House. Legions of rats ran rampant in open daylight through the bricks and rubble of crumbling apartments, bombed and shelled in the battle for the city between the Japanese and Nationalist armies, but never re-built. Close by, the sweet smell of opium, commingled with the stench of human excrement, spilled from gullies into the alleys. Merchants, who once lived with their families in rooms on the second story of the derelict buildings, had swelled the throng of beggars who hooted and hobbled and stumped with missing limbs in the crowded street.

"The beggars are without end. Many of them organized into packs. And they have levels — apprentices, journeymen, and masters. You can hire the whole damned lot of them if you need a diversion or to lay an ambush," Chung said. "My boss is on good terms with the Head Beggar. He's practically on retainer, I think they call it."

On one block a squad of Japanese soldiers, led by an officer and driver on a motorcycle and sidecar, filed down the avenue. They guarded a prisoner bound with thick ropes, stripped half-naked. He had deep gashes on his head and a huge gag stuffed in his mouth.

"Assassins are constantly killing Jap officers, even sentries. Usually they escape." Chung shrugged. "The police look the other way, naturally, because they're paid by us." He smiled but his eyes were cold and hard as steel.

Ellison hunched lower and brought the cloak collar high over his nose. He motioned for Su Li to do the same. It was no time for their disguises to fail. The throngs grew denser when the entourage entered the Nanking Road, the wide avenue flanked by smaller, two-story shops, still intact but dominated by multi-story department stores with huge flags flying in front. Rickshaws and pedicabs angled through soot-belching autos, smoking, rickety trucks and street cars. On the sidewalks, water carriers pushed their wooden boxes with a spout on wheelbarrows. Their calls competed with the noisemakers of cobblers, repairmen, barbers, and every kind of itinerant vendor of food and drink. Cripples, the blind and seriously ill, the starving, the old and feeble bunched together along the great thoroughfare, as if sharing their infirmities might bring comfort.

"They're simply waiting to die," said Chung, answering a mystified Ellison.

"And those?" Ellison pointed. Dead bodies lay every few yards, frozen in place or propped against the shop fronts. Dogs tore at their flesh, fortunate they themselves had not yet been caught and eaten.

"Some from the Japanese. Some from other Chinese. Who knows how? Most are simpletons who have no idea what's happening, much less what to do about it."

Nearly as numerous as the beggars, rouged women in gaudy clothes or peasant dress, approached them incessantly. They swarmed like bees in front of the Wing On Tower building, the tallest landmark on the street. Chung angrily waved them off. "One of twelve females in Shanghai sells their bodies for money, it's said." He grinned. "But that wouldn't concern a bunch of monks!"

"A city of whores," Su Li muttered.

"They're trying to survive. I feel sorry for them," Ellison said. The sheer tonnage of misery and infirmity weighed as heavily as his memories of Calcutta's streets. No, he reconsidered, this was a lower level of the Inferno, but his father and Buzz, they would have understood. Shanghai was undergoing divine retribution for its debauchery. The women stirred a cauldron of anxieties in Ellison, forgotten in the hubbub of arrival. What if Okamura's red-haired woman was not her? And what if she were? To see his own mother a high class courtesan or slave? His mind could find no rest.

"Come, Master Po. I beg you. You have seen enough of this hell hole. Please ride the rest of the way," Chung said.

The car eventually turned onto a side street to a neighborhood near the Shanghai Race Club and the Military Police station, a gray stone building where Japanese bureaucrats, dressed in Western-style suits, climbed stairs beneath a large flag of the Rising Sun. The Mercedes halted before a formidable portal of bars and plate steel, set in a wall made of cut stones. Chung rang a bell. The gate swung open. Before them lay the compound of the underground ruler of Shanghai.

CHAPTER 47

When an ordinary man attains knowledge, he is a sage;
when a sage attains understanding, he is an ordinary man –
Zen saying

Chung closed the massive bronze and iron gates, shutting out the ruined city as if did not exist. Immediately inside, the visitors confronted an elaborately-carved stone spirit-wall, the *yingbi*, protecting the compound from evil spirits who were powerless to move around corners. Beyond the ghost barrier, a brick-walled courtyard opened on a realm of fountains and artificial waterfalls whose water spilled into a circular pool in the center of the tiled-floor enclosure. Lotus leaves spread over its surface; barefoot women in short filmy robes giggled and laughed on the honed granite bench rimming the pond, absently feeding golden fish that swam beneath the purple blossoms. Around the perimeter, exotic plants with stupendous spear-shaped green foliage spilled over plastered planters. Scented red and orange ginger blossoms and fragrant sprays drooped from trellises or cascaded over stuccoed partitions. From other containers sensuous orchids of white and yellow bent their long stems inward. Overhead brilliant paper lanterns dangled along with gilt cages that held birds with plumage of red, gold, blue and green; their calls filled the air.

"Some are blinded to sing louder," Chung proclaimed proudly.

"It's hard to tell a flower from a bird," said Ellison. "Like a summerhouse in a mountain valley. Paradise."

"Built on corruption, opium, prostitution. It turns my stomach," Su Li said.

Chung led them through a set of double doors into a wide, long hallway, a colonnade adorned with tapestries, scrolls and paintings from the Chan period, vases from the Sung dynasty on ebony pedestals and ancient suits of armor and weaponry that reminded Su Li of her dream about the ghost army. Great mandarins lived in this manner, she imagined, recalling her hours of Chinese history under the Master's tutelage, at the cost of many lives, a ruthless contrast to her haven of peace in the old house. They halted before another pair of high doors of filigreed mahogany, guarded by blond, fair-skinned, stone-faced men with arms crossed over their hard-muscled chests, guns beneath their coats.

"Bodyguards. White Russians, I'm guessing," Ellison whispered to her.

"I will wait inside the room until the younger Duo returns," Po announced. "After that I must ready myself. You will not see me until tomorrow but I will send instructions. You must prepare as well."

"Prepare for what, Master Po?" asked Ellison.

He laughed. "Perhaps to die." Ellison blanched. "We must live each day as if it were a good day to die on."

"You will win, Master," Su Li said.

"Even so."

"You are the greatest master in all China," she insisted.

He shook his head and turned toward the door.

"Master Po," Ellison said. Po stopped. "I . . . I wish I could have been your student."

Po bowed slightly. "And I yours." His eyes twinkled in a manner Su Li had seldom seen.

CHAPTER 48

One joy scatters a thousand sorrows – Chinese proverb

After a simple meal shared with the house staff in the kitchen, a servant led Su Li and Ellison down a hallway to a small room, their quarters for the night. Inside, two narrow beds flanked the lone window opposite the door. Taped newspaper sealed the glass panes against the black-out imposed on the city. On a teak chest of drawers a single brass electric lamp cast a dim light over a statue of a pale green dragon twelve inches in height. The artist had so finely wrought the jade figure that each individual scale evoked the pebble-like texture of the dragon's skin and had captured all of the creature's mythic power poised to strike in blessing or punishment.

"By Lao-tze," he exclaimed with a wry grin, "this thing is flawless. It looks like it could just fly away." He held it up to examine it.

She climbed on one of the beds, intending to meditate, but his presence distracted her. She continued to marvel at how Chinese he presently appeared, powerless to take her eyes off him while he admired the dragon; the current of her feelings flowed as powerful as the Yangtze. His visage, even his Western aroma, fed her desire but he was oblivious to her longing.

"I've been thinking about my father tonight. I never told you about him." He sat on the opposite bed, bent at the waist, hands clasped between his knees, eyes on the floor. "Hard on himself. Me. The world was a bad place. Sin, you understand." He looked up and smiled at her puzzled expression. "No, you wouldn't. The Chinese don't have that concept, do they? But we Westerners love our idea of sin. Anyway, he didn't approve mixing races. Caucasian Christians are allowed to save the Chinese, not marry them." He laughed. "So he and I, well, we didn't get along. To say the least. Never really talked to me — as a man. As a preacher, yes. The Reverend Abraham Ellison. So unlike my mother." His face had a faraway look. "Ah, she was a queen, Su Li. In another life, maybe." He paused. "I think I'm a lot like her." He went to the dragon once more. "In another life!" He chuckled.

She sympathized. He was afraid to fail after coming so far, but she did not fathom his constant return to the distant past to comprehend the present. For their time together had laid bare his courage and his commitment to her, markers that scoured away the memory of the horrors at the Japanese camp. The here and now were him, her. As for the future, it did not matter. There was nothing to be fearful of, even death. She wanted to speak but hesitated.

"I remember when I was a boy," he went on. "She would read to me Lamb's *Tales of Shakespeare*. Or Tennyson. Romantic stuff. Then I'd see that dreamy look. 'Ye'll surely marry a lovely girl one day, a bonnie fine woman.' I guess she was hoping for a Scottish lassie." He spoke mainly in English, unable to find Chinese equivalents, aware she understood no more than bits and pieces.

"James."

Throughout the journey, she had listened to his language lessons with her son and learned much in secret, waiting for the right occasion to surprise him. The word produced its desired effect. Startled, his whole body grew calm, as if a thunderstorm had blown itself out. He had his eyes fixed on hers in that probing, curious way she had at first hated but now had come to treasure.

"Su Li . . . ." A startled look metamorphosed into a serious demeanor. "What I'm trying to explain is that five years ago I became convinced there was no goodness left in this world. The war had destroyed it all. But because of you I know that's not true. I believed in nothing, trusted no one, certainly not myself. But you . . . ." A thin smile of delight crossed his face, ". . . are far more than anything I could have ever imagined. I believe in you, Su Li. I trust in you."

As she looked at him, time stopped. He had not been talking about the past at all. In a flash of insight her inner self opened like a blossom ready to be pollinated and she felt and understood, in every fiber of her being, everything that existed, deeper than conscious speech or thought, awe and horror, joy and sorrow, life and death, love and hate, mutually arising, just as the Master once taught. The Tao—stars, planets, sun, moon, water, wind, earth, fire, all she had endured, her breathing, the freckle on his chin below his smile—had led to this single moment, this instant, where there was no time, no past, no future. The feeling pervaded her nerve endings, her blood cells. No words could express it. Yet it was so simple, the universe contracted to a single point embodied in this man right here—and utterly perfect. He was perfect. Beyond time. Like the jade dragon.

"Su Li?" His words snapped her awake. He was kneeling before her, brow furrowed with concern. "Did I say something wrong?"

She was aware of tears rolling down her cheeks, of happiness and of sadness that the vision had to finally fade. She touched the dragon and shook her head. To cling to a vision was to betray it.

"I was telling you I love you, Su Li."

Her face lit up. "Say the words in English, James."

His head cocked in puzzlement. "I love you."

"I . . . love . . . you." She repeated softly and took off her tunic.

CHAPTER 49

Oh, you followers of the Way. If you meet the Buddha along the way, kill him. If you meet the Master along the way, kill him. If you meet your parents along the way, kill them. Kill everyone. Stand above them, pass by and be free – Li Jin

It was time.

A servant escorted Su Li and Ellison through the maze of Duo's mansion to an exit at the end of a back hallway. Ellison rippled with excitement and dread, aware all he had striven for during the last five years was about resolve itself in the next few hours, possibly in his own death, just when a new motive for living had appeared, as one dream fades into another. That reason had slept peacefully in his arms the night before and now walked beside him. In the alley a black limousine idled, a small Japanese flag mounted on the hood to signify official business. Po, seated in the front passenger seat, was preoccupied, cloaked in the shadows of the late afternoon sun. The car pulled away and threaded its way through the war-torn streets of Shanghai.

"Ling's the name. We're heading for the old Shanghai Gymnasium." The garrulous weasel-faced driver kept turning around. One eye wandered in its socket; the other focused on the tall passenger in the back seat. "Where the match takes place. You know it?" He seemed oblivious to the danger his inattention presented to pedestrians and cyclists, bent on their destination before the curfew fell. Most denizens of the street, though, had nowhere to go, lost chickens looking for a roost.

"Scum," Ling leaned on the horn, sneering at them while lighting a second cigarette with the butt of the first. The vehicle swung out of control as he took both hands off the wheel. At last he decided steering might be worthwhile, but after a moment thought better of it and twisted his neck around as if the rear view mirror did not exist. "The boss says whatever you need will be there. He's taken care of it. Couldn't come with us, though. He has to kiss the Japanese asses a little. In return for leaving us alone. But what do monks like you know about business or politics?"

Ling resumed actual driving in time to jam on the brakes. A Japanese military convoy blocked the intersection and the limousine had to let it pass. He cackled and torqued his head around again. "The whole damn city's betting on this fight, see. The Japs want it to be a big propaganda deal. You know, the superiority of the high and mighty conquerors over us simple-ass Chinese. Me? I slit a few Jap throats every night, just for fun." The car stuttered forward. "Part of me wants the monk to squash those pieces of turtle shit. As a businessman," he shrugged and laughed, an ugly grating snort, "I bet on the Japs. The Master here, pardon me, he's pretty old. It won't matter anyhow. Money says you'll all be dead."

Ellison was having difficulty comprehending Ling's heavy Shanghai accent when Po interrupted the driver's blather in a voice so understated yet powerful it sent a chill up Ellison's spine. "Quiet, dung." The chauffeur hunched his shoulders and sat lower in his seat. Po turned around to face Su Li.

"Tiger-daughter, something I must tell you. I learned the truth at Hankow before we departed. You were weakened and I have been distracted, unsure how I might best say it. This may be my last opportunity." He held his hand up before she could protest. "You were the child of the war lord Xing-tu's concubine. He ordered you killed but she refused. When he threatened to kill her, she escaped and took you to the sacred mountain. Old Wang found out the story for me. He spoke to those who once knew her. I do not know if she abandoned you or was on the way to the monastery before I. . . ." He paused. "Whatever the reason, the Tao gave you to me. Your soldier prompted me to find out the full story." Face drawn with sadness he glanced at Ellison. "What happened in the past was meant to be." He sighed. "I sent messengers to Han. He has been near Zhengzhou, I understand, with the underground. I hoped he would join us. He once fought alongside the Green Circle Gang so he knows Chung. I intended to tell him also, what I told you. But, sadly, there has been no word of Han." He turned his face to the windshield.

Su Li closed her eyes and dropped her hands to her lap, her ears on fire. The earth seemed to shake beneath her as she tried to grasp what she heard. A lowly concubine had defied her lord and master, unheard of and lethal. Where did her mother find that kind of courage? In forfeiting her own life, she paid a price, against all reasonable hope, that Heaven might in some way intervene so her child might live, and so it came to pass. She allowed her heart to fill with love for her long-dead parent one final moment, not to forgive her but to thank her, thus laying the past to rest. She, too, was a mother, filled with gratitude for the presence of Hui in her life, the gift the Tao had given her though she did not deserve him. Her spirit called to her son across the miles. Suddenly a hand squeezed hers. *And you, my soldier. I once was afraid you would change my life. How wrong not to trust you. Because of you I learned to love. Because of you I myself am free though today might be our last.* She sent him a silent message, uncertain he was capable of receiving it: *If we survive, I will tell you the whole story. If we die, it will be a good day to die, for we die together.* To her astonishment, he nodded.

The car turned down a boulevard manned by policemen behind wooden barricades that held back a huge throng of curious on-lookers, for in this part of the city the curfew had been lifted for the night's event. Even the side streets had been blocked off with armored vehicles to maximize crowd control, so vast was the multitude descended on the scene. The limousine pulled to a halt before a tall rectangular brick building with an arched roof that extended a quarter of a city block. To its immediate right were athletic fields where another mob who hoped to gain entry into the heavily guarded venue swarmed hawkers selling fake tickets and vendors of food and goods who took advantage of the temporary freedom to form an impromptu street fair. Japanese sentries patrolled the sidewalks to keep the most

398

disreputable vagabonds away; closer-in, a ring of evenly-spaced soldiers surrounded the gymnasium. At each corner of the structure a line of people was making its way inside a set of double doors.

"This is where you exit. I have to go back." The driver pulled his flat cap low and glanced suspiciously around as if he expected a trap. Su Li and Ellison exited and stood alongside, waiting for Po to lead them. "Walk to the side entrance over there." Ling ground a cigarette butt beneath his sole. "Where it's cordoned off. Someone's ready. It's been arranged." He grinned, fidgeting with the keys. "Don't be afraid of the soldiers. Not yet, anyway," he snickered, slithered back in the car and sped into the gathering twilight.

An officer and guards manned a private entrance. The officer snapped General Okamura's letter from Po then eyed Ellison suspiciously. "Lieutenant," Po insisted in a voice that compelled obedience. The officer scowled, jerked his thumb at the door, and handed the papers back to Po, but kept his eyes on the tall, odd-looking monk.

Inside an attendant ushered them into a small room. "Duo hopes everything will be satisfactory, Master Po. It gives him great honor to provide these humble tokens." He pointed to items on a bench, bowed then left.

A small triptych with the figure of the Eternal One painted in the middle and Taoist saints alongside rested on a wooden table. From a bronze brazier, burning incense wafted upward and filled the room. Po stood before the small shrine, eyes closed. On the boat Su Li had explained to Ellison that the Master worshipped no gods, but that images helped him concentrate his inner strength. Whoever had the most powerful *chi*, she told him, would defeat an opponent, not the one with the better technical skill.

Outside, an incessant drumbeat and a menacing buzz of voices assaulted the door like a fortress under siege. Inside the room, no one spoke, the tension as thick as the perfumed air. The Master nodded at Su Li who retrieved an elaborate ceremonial robe and assisted him as he put it over his gray tunic. The green silk's patina gleamed with intricately stitched overlays of gold dragons and phoenixes of purple and red embroidered on the wide sleeves. On the front an orange tiger reared. After they dressed Po, she and Ellison donned plain yellow robes folded on a bench. One had a hood for Ellison to cover the sandy fuzz now apparent on his scalp. The garments seemed like shrouds for burial. The pulse of a huge drum grew louder.

Su Li tugged on his sleeve. "Pay attention."

He whispered to her. "What are we supposed to do?"

"We are his escorts." She handed him one of two white silk banners hung on thick walnut staffs with red tassels. Chinese calligraphy emblazoned the pale cloth. "We walk behind him. Follow me and do what I do."

"What do the signs mean?"

"One says 'The power of water is supreme.' The other, 'The hills of Emei Shan kiss the morning.'"

"Bound to get the crowd excited," Ellison mumbled in English. Yet the Master and Su Li had come to this point for him, an extraordinary gift. He could sense their power flow into in his own being. Outside was the ninth level of hell; but with these allies, he had a chance to make amends, to recover something sacred and true that was stolen. Even if only in a small way, even if he failed, he had come. Like the day he had out-flown the Zeroes, he wanted to shout a battle cry: providence was on his side!

A drum sounded. A door opened for them. The monsoon noise of a thousand people blew in. The attendant returned. "If you please, Master Po, it is time." He opened a side door. "I apologize for these barbarians. You realize most of them are Chinese traitors and Japanese sympathizers. Waiting for you to be sacrificed. Birds fly south when winter comes. Only a few dozen are patriots."

Po nodded. "Then we must feed the ones who remain lest they starve."

The little procession filed through an aisle between two sets of bleachers and waited for a signal. Wooden grandstands along all four walls, filled to capacity, rose from chest height to rows of clerestory windows just below the roof line. Bright carbon arc lights dangled from the ceiling. A hush fell over the assembly for a second before a roar swept up to the rafters as the trio marched into the arena proper. Po's jade-green multi-tipped hat, symbol of his high place in the Taoist hierarchy, bobbed above them all. Erect and regal he led them single file in a circular route across the hard-packed white sand floor while a brass band played martial music.

A small dais had been erected before the grandstand proper on the east side, a huge Japanese flag draped over its railing. Presiding over the event, Lt. General Okamura Yasuji, the Commander of the Japanese Expeditionary Army in China, was flanked by other Japanese flag officers, in dress uniform. Each wore an ornate samurai sword. Okamura was a slender, older man rigid as a steel pipe whose glasses matched an expressionless, weather-worn face. A bespectacled junior officer stood at attention just behind the general. Behind them and to the left in the auditorium seats, Japanese high-ranking civilian officials in formal diplomatic regalia — pince-nez's, top hats, striped pants — peered down, stiff and haughty. The right end of the row held a Chinese contingent, including Zhou Fohai, the mayor of the city, and Wang Ching-wei, the occupiers' puppet ruler of Central China; but the most striking Chinese, in a neck-to-toe, sea-green over-gown, tilted his head at Po so no one would notice — Duo, the boss of the Green Circle Gang. Heavy set and uncomfortable, his reptilian eyes darted nervously. Rings with enormous emeralds adorned each of his fingers. But the self-important dignitaries shrank into insignificance at the creature who lay on the ground, in front of the Japanese flag — a mammoth tiger with a wide, thick leather collar attached to a chain.

The Master stopped ten feet from the platform, a few steps from the animal, who turned its massive head toward him. Unlike the tigers he had seen on Emei Shan, this one with a mane around its neck had pale black stripes and was much larger. An Amur, he realized. From the northernmost reaches of China and the Russian border. Such huge beasts were supposed to be the stuff of legends. He took it as a sign of hope. A great gong sounded. Remember me, spirit tiger, in my need, he prayed. The onlookers quieted and the young officer rose to introduce the proceedings.

"On behalf of General Okamura, I welcome you to our evening's demonstration of marital arts. As you know, the Japanese race has perfected such skills. They have become a symbol of our fighting prowess. Still, at times, we encourage the participation of lesser known figures."

He spoke in a belligerent, arrogant tone, pausing to allow an interpreter on the loudspeaker to translate his remarks into Chinese, but Ellison wasn't listening. Out of the corner of his eye he spied a group of Japanese women, dressed in kimonos, sequestered well up and behind Okamura where a flash of orange and gold in their midst caught his attention—hair, pinned and twisted in the Japanese style, the red once his mother's pride now streaked with gray. Except for the hair color, she appeared as much Japanese as he now did Chinese. But as he focused more intently, a lump rose in his throat. The taut, freckled skin on her face had a sick yellow pallor. Her empty face registered no emotion whatsoever. His mother was an opium-addicted concubine.

He squeezed the banner staff until his knuckles turned white while the officer droned on, his words an irritant throb in the eardrums. Yet how could he blame her? How else could she endure the humiliation? Opium was her escape. He called out silently, hoping somehow she might see him, recognize him, moved by the sheer force of his will, but her face was a mask.

At length Okamura spoke to the officer who relayed his words in Chinese to the audience and the Master. "General Okamura welcomes you, Grand Master Po. But he did not expect the champion of China to be so old and feeble." The audience laughed.

"Age has taught me fighting is a waste of energy." Po's strong voice resonated in the arena. "My code does not condone inflicting wanton suffering — as others do. I do not normally accept challenges from barbarians." An angry murmur buzzed through the spectators at the direct insult.

The officer translated for the clean-shaven General who glared back and responded. "Nevertheless you are here. To test yourself against the talent of the superior race. As you see before you, the Chinese tiger is captured. Like you, your country is old and worn out and needs the infusion of modern Japanese discipline and hard work. So, therefore, what stakes do you propose?"

"Her!" Po's voice rang out strong and clear above a low murmur that turned silent. He pointed his finger at Ellison's mother. "The foreign woman you have abducted."

The whole stadium threw its attention on the woman with the red hair pinned above her head while in their special viewing box behind the dignitaries, the other Japanese geishas gawked at a bewildered Mary Ellison. The General glanced over his shoulder then narrowed on Po, dark with anger. The Master had put him in a corner, with the assembly's eyes on his exotic red-haired trophy, but he could not deny the challenge without loss of face in front of his fellow officers and countrymen. He laughed and spoke directly to Po. The officer translated.

"You are rather old for that, are you not, priest?" The Japanese sycophants howled in amusement; the Master folded his arms. The General again spoke through his translator. "And what you do offer in return?"

"My life," said the Master, "and that of my attendants."

A stunned silence settled over the crowd but Ellison could feel the tornado of hatred around him threatening to suck the very air out of his lungs, to vacuum up him and his friends and spit them out like bits of debris. What in the bloody hell are we doing? he asked himself, his previous enthusiasm short-circuited by currents of panic doubling in amperage. When the uproar subsided, he was able to find his still center once more. After all, Po had warned him. He knew all along it would come to this, find her or die, but not necessarily both at once. Nor had Su Li figured into it. If only they could have had more time. Because of her he was not afraid of death. Because of her he didn't want to die. Her mouth was tight-lipped and intense, eyes fierce; and on her forearm, her sleeve fell slightly but deliberately as she held the banner's staff to reveal the Shaolin markings. She tilted her head forward. *Watch the spirit-tiger,* she told him silently.

Okamura nodded.

Ellison took his position along the opposite grandstand, holding Su Li's banner while she helped Po remove his ceremonial robe. For this challenge he wore the same clothes as on his mountain treks, a gray tunic with wide sleeves and leather leggings. In the middle of a thirty-foot black ring painted in the sand, the boundary of the contest, he began a tai chi exercise of supple grace and beauty. He appeared younger and stronger, suggesting the outlines of the powerful, intimidating manhood he must have possessed in his prime. She realized he had entered the state of *wu hsin*, no-mindedness, free from thought or emotion, open to all energy within himself and without, a condition of great *kung fu* power he had often described to her but which she had never experienced.

The gong rang.

A mountain of a man emerged from a corner aisle. The Japanese dominated throng cheered. Su Li had never seen one but the masters had spoken of them. They were called *sumo* by the Japanese. Taller than Po, the monster lumbered into the ring, his sole garment a thick leather belt wrapped down over his genitals and up again between his buttocks. He was three times the size of an ordinary man in girth with massive arms and legs. His body glistened with rubbing oil, his hair tied behind his head in a knot. The sight of the Master brought a laugh to the behemoth, who raised his hands with a comic puzzled grin as if to ask the spectators, "Is this a kind of jest?" The onlookers roared with delight.

Su Li's heart beat with a sudden fear that made her body shiver. The other instructors in the monastery spoke with awe of Da Shi's skill but she never witnessed his style of *wu shu*, and he was old. Find a way to defeat this giant, she prayed.

The behemoth bowed to the dignitaries and lumbered forward, an unstoppable juggernaut, his tree-trunk thighs waddling against each other. Po stood unperturbed, arms folded inside his sleeves, his expression quizzical, as if the huge man were not real but a phantasm from a mythological hell. The wrestler was surprised his opponent made no move. He paused, held his hands out and raised his brows in mock perplexity playing the crowd, shrugged, pressed in for the kill, his arms spread wide. There would be no escape from the massive human vise he was about to close. The brute would snap his challenger like rotten wood.

When the sumo was close enough to touch, Po shifted his feet. In the same instant his right arm exploded from the cavernous sleeve like a bolt of lightning from a great ominous cloud, before it disappeared back inside. It happened so fast few could have seen his fingers flatten and thumb fold to make a spear point. The tip drove deep into the mass of flesh just below the wrestler's left nipple. The giant stopped in his tracks as if a bee had stung him, grinning, but when he tried to take another step he faltered. His leg would not lift. The vast mass began to sway like a tree that has been cut but refuses to topple. His visage screwed up and grew pale, unable to comprehend the ugly crimson tide spreading across his chest beneath the skin. Disbelief turned to terror before he toppled. The tiny Chinese contingent sent up a cheer. The Japanese sycophants booed the fallen man as attendants ran to the wrestler. After a brief examination, one of them stood, faced the General and shook his head. It took six men to haul out the dead sumo.

The officer spoke into the microphone. "General Okamura says, 'Now that the comedy has ended, the tragedy must begin.'"

One fragment of Su Li's consciousness had remained on the tiger, which stood and stretched when the saucer-shaped bronze bell sounded again. While three shirtless men, each wearing a black cloth belt around loose white trousers paraded out of separate corners of the gymnasium, the tiger's eyes met hers. In that meeting, reality shifted for her once again. The animal's growing impatience and pent-up anger, the hatred the new Japanese adversaries exuded, Ellison's mounting anxiety, the hostility of the viewers—all joined together like a discordant symphony of emotion. She could identify all the raw energy around her, even her own rage at the Japanese trickery, but with the detachment of an observer on a mountain top who watches a fierce thunderstorm sweep over a valley. Only the impassive Po and the third Japanese master, who stood apart, stayed immune to her transformed receptivity.

The two fighters' warm-up routine was a display of acrobatic ability designed to impress the audience and cow their opponent. When they finished, they took positions along opposite points of the circle, not bothering to bow but closed with a dizzy array of kicks and chops that only appeared to rain on Po. His fighting stance transmuted into a sail as he floated through gaps between his adversaries, his slim body bent and twisted at minute angles. The sleeves of his garment acted like a moving target, deceiving the punches aimed at his body and head. In her state of heightened awareness, Su Li observed the duel like a judge of high art, evaluating skill and technique within a hailstorm of blows and blocks and turns from three antagonists intent on death.

She could see the energy of his opponents flow over or around Po as his hands struck out and drove one or the other of his two challengers back, stunned by a punch not quite witnessed. As the whirlwind swirled longer, his aura grew dim. Many more of their kicks and blows landed. At last, when Po's attention was on the other fighter, the karate master launched a spiral kick in the exhausted Master's midsection. Po faltered. The second fighter pounced in the gap, throwing quick strikes to the kidneys. The Master stumbled to his knees. He was finished.

The spectators howled. The fighters backed off, strutting in triumph around their pitiful opponent, working themselves up for a spectacular finish. They had expected an easy victory and were angry at being thwarted by an old man. All the while the component of Su Li's attention monitoring the tiger observed the animal become increasingly agitated as it paced back and forth the length of its chain, while everyone in the building focused on the impending defeat in the ring.

The karate masters charged from opposite directions, each intending the honor of victory for himself, but before they reached the Master, a thunderous growl erupted. The roar drowned out every other sound in the hall as the Amur launched itself, snapping the chain from the collar and intersecting the fighters, overcommitted and unable to flee, as they neared Po who knelt in the center of the ring. Its mighty forepaws spread wide, claws extended like knives in a slaughterhouse, the tiger ripped open the men simultaneously, disemboweling them. Organs and blood squirted on the sand while the alarmed spectators recovered enough to shriek and rise from their seats. Japanese guards raised their rifles, but before they could fire the tiger bounded for the dark passageway.

The Amur's charge unfolded in half the speed of normal perception for Su Li. Its eyes, incisors, claws, the rich colors in its luxuriant fur coat washed over her in a wave of terrifying splendor, heightened by its death-dealing fury. The spirit-tiger was overflowing with implacable wrath, she realized, dumbfounded at how completely the animal's emotion had filled her mind. After the cat vanished, her point of view switched to the Master. He was near his limits. One bushy eyebrow oozed a trickle of blood. One arm hung limp. His eyes were glazed, his breaths rasping in heavy wheezes. The bright yellow glow of his former energy had turned pale.

Su Li's cocoon of preternatural awareness burst when the band began to play marches to calm the assembly while attendants cleaned up the bloody mess. Afterwards the junior officer made his announcement.

"Remain in your seats, ladies and gentlemen. Our troops have the situation outside under control and there is nothing more to fear." He leaned over to listen to Okamura. "The General says now that the interlude is over, the drama must continue."

Throughout, the third and last Japanese fighter stood apart. His mind had been hidden from her, shielded by his mental discipline. Was it from a sense of honor or to study his opponent better? Or to let the others wear the Master down? Her questions were answered when a bright sliver of metal flashed—a samurai sword. A murmur swept over the audience. Ellison's face was an enigma but his body was tense and he leaned as if he were on the verge of racing to the Master's aid, what she herself wanted to do, but a voice of power spoke a single word inside her mind: *Wait!*

The confident, relaxed kendo master walked calmly toward Po, elbows spread high and wide, the hilt of the ornate weapon held off center at face level. Then the katana burst into a dance, a whirlwind of arcs and slices, back and forth, up and down; the very air seemed to sing and sigh in admiration at its speed. Even the monks of the Golden Sun had told stories of the great samurai of Japan. His skill was beyond awe.

The fighter closed. The Master backed away. The Japanese leaped in pursuit. Soon the weapon was ripping the Master's sleeves and tunic, his leggings, even his sandal straps. The swordsman was playing with his foe, threatening to carve him into pieces, limb by limb. Close, so close, the blade was a whirring blur of annihilation, but over and over the Master in a trance-like state eluded the lethal strikes by a hair's breadth. At long last he staggered. The game of hunter and hunted stopped. Blood flowed down his shredded arm where the blade had landed deep in flesh. Slumped over, Po covered the wound with his hand and took rasping breaths. The confident Japanese paused, let his sword dangle, and glanced around the arena, basking in its adulation.

Po, stooped over near the black-painted perimeter of the ring sideways to the swordsman, seemed resigned to defeat. The kendo master gestured to the audience for approval. The sword crested high as he leaped in for one final, dramatic mortal strike — to take off the old man's head in one cut, but the Master, who had appeared insensible, took one long swift step, seized the man's wrists and swerved the sword aside. Momentum pulled both their hands to the sand where the sword disappeared halfway to its hilt. Both men tugged and grappled. The Master, too tired or too dazed, could use no moves. The Japanese fighter lashed out with his leg and tripped Po with a kick to the ankles. He wrested the sword free. Po stumbled and fell. The samurai pounced, knelt and straddled the prostrate, exhausted monk, sword held high. He looked up at Okamura who turned his thumb down. Japanese partisans roared their agreement. The Chinese hooted. Like a dagger, the sword plunged downward. Su Li squeezed her eyes tight.

CHAPTER 50

If you believe that life and death are the same, you are wrong. If you believe that life and death are not the same, you are wrong – Buddhist saying

The audience held its breath.

Su Li opened her eyes to a sight that defied belief. The sword had descended half way then stopped. Palm up, Po was blocking the point and pushing it steadily upward against the strength of his opponent, re-directing the force of hatred to its source, classic *wu shu*. Blood flowed from his hand; nevertheless, the blade moved higher, inch by inexorable inch. Then, suddenly, Po's palm fell away The Japanese master's jaw dropped in astonishment, his downward momentum burying the steel in the sand once more, a slight hesitation that made him vulnerable, off-balance, within reach, exposed. Before he caught himself, the Master's uninjured hand exploded from his last reserve in a punch that crumpled the left of the swordsman's rib cage. He screamed and clutched his side. In the next instant Po seized his wrist. A sharp twist broke a tendon. The weapon slid from his grasp.

The samurai rolled off, desperate for a counter-attack, fought to come erect but the left side of his body would not comply. He eyed the katana and made an excruciating motion to retrieve it, but Po, crawling on his knees, reached it first and threw the blade behind him. Still the crippled fighter advanced, determined to uphold his *bushido,* his left arm hanging useless, his right forearm twisted unnaturally. The way of the warrior demanded he fight to the death. Po, who had staggered upright a few steps from his nearly doubled-over opponent, shook his head and frowned. He did not want to kill this man. He covered his fist in peace, but his suicidal adversary refused to yield and tried to lift his legs for a kick, a futile effort that lurched into a sickening fall onto one hand and knee. Nearly paralyzed, still he glared with unrelenting hate. Po grimaced in frustration. Finally out of pity he limped over and touched a certain spot on the man's neck. The kendo master collapsed in a soft heap. Po picked up his sword, examined it, then broke it over his thigh and tossed the shards toward Okamura. The Master drew himself up before the dais as the crowd quieted in anticipation. Blood ran down one arm and stained his shirt. More had spread across his forehead.

"I claim my prize!"

A cheer erupted from the band of loyal Chinese. The General glowered at his fellow officers and the frenzied crowd. He had no choice. He lifted a hand. Two soldiers escorted a confused Mary Ellison to the arena floor. Da Shi nodded. Su Li helped him don his tri-tipped hat and draped his ceremonial robe over his shoulders. She and Ellison took their places behind his mother as Po led them past an enraged throng on its feet, hurling insults at them.

CHAPTER 51

The sage is not sentimental. She knows that all beings must pass away – Lao-tze

The prize we sought is won. The prize we sought is one. His mother's favorite poem cycled through Ellison's giddy, exultant mind like a schoolboy proudly showing off his winning contest entry. A part of him wanted to raise his fist in triumph and shout to the heavens but he clamped his jaw shut, subdued by fear something might yet go wrong and snatch victory away.

They followed the attendant through the frenzied crowd milling in the vestibule. Japanese sympathizers hissed and spat at them but most in this small space were Chinese loyalists, delirious with joy, who wanted to touch the Master's garment. In the dressing room Po and his entourage paused long enough for Su Li to bandage his bloody arm and to change into their original clothes, hidden beneath the gray cloaks provided by Chung.

Arms crossed, hands twitching inside the kimono's wide sleeves, Mary Ellison's submissive, mystified eyes darted around the small room for a clue to her fate, like a prisoner being moved to a new jail. Ellison wanted to assure her she was in safe hands but it was no time to abandon his disguise. His mind called to her not to be afraid but she was beyond reach. He gently pressed her toward the side door where she exited behind Su Li and the Master to the wide esplanade in front of the gymnasium.

415

They edged uneasily toward the curb, anxious for a hoped-for rescue. The city was now in complete darkness, but a pale moon high in the sky cast ominous shadows on the street, electric with tension, like heavy clouds hovering over a valley. At checkpoints, fires flickered in steel barrels where soldiers, warming their hands, eyed the little group with sullen hostility. More threatening, an officer had started to circulate quietly among his men, whispering commands. Out of the dark, the limousine thundered up to the curb and squealed to a stop, windows curtained, headlights a slit through the black-out tape. On cue, thousands of shouting beggars poured onto the streets. One second, there were none; the next minute, they submerged the Japanese soldiers and surrounded the armored cars on the side streets in a controlled, cacophonous chaos. Except for the tight circle around the car, no one could move.

Chung jumped out the passenger side. "Get in. Right now."

The four piled into the back. Su Li and Ellison sat on the extra fold-down seats across from Po and Mary Ellison. Ling gunned the accelerator while the sea of beggars parted to let them through as the powerful Mercedes inched its way forward then sped away through the darkened streets. "I told you the damned beggars are useful. Now we have to squirrel you out of the city before the General changes his mind."

"General Okamura has no intention of letting us go," the Master replied to Su Li's questioning look.

"He's right," Chung added with a crooked grin. "But don't worry. My boss knows the Japs are double-crossing shit-eaters. He's prepared a little surprise for them."

Ellison registered the crisis like a faint echo, as if he had heard it all before and no longer cared, still in a warrior mode, confident now he had freed his mother no one had power enough to take her back. Gradually, though, he descended from the exhilarating heights of triumph to the hardscrabble landscape of a broken woman, ghost-like in the dim dashboard lights. He could barely imagine how desperate she was, twirling the rings on her nervous fingers and biting her lip. Go slow, lad, he reminded himself. This is harder for her than you.

"Mary Stuart Ellison. Mother." He took her hand in his, "It's me. James. Your son. I've come for you." He switched on the roof light. "You're safe now."

She lifted her head and squinted. "James? Jamie?" Her voice quavered. "How? Good God." Her hands shook as if they had a case of palsy. She ran her fingers over his features to make sure this strange monk was indeed her son. Finally she nodded. "It *is* you." She leaned forward and hugged him fiercely. Great tears squirted down her cheeks, then she pulled away, moaned and covered her face. "Turn it off!" A wave of tenderness and pity swept over him. He leaned to comfort her.

"Nay! Dinna' touch me!" She lurched backward and pushed him away. "I want to kill myself. Ye should ha' let me die. Ye should nae ha' come."

He swallowed hard. Her words reduced his triumphal joy to a plaintive whimper, not the liberation he had imagined. Untold times he had gone over in his mind the speech he wanted to make when he rescued her but now the ideas struck him as ridiculous and puerile. She was in essence a stranger to him. His impressions of her sprang from the perceptions of a self-preoccupied seventeen-year old or, even less reliable, from dim memories of his childhood. He had never interacted with her as an adult, had no clue as to whether in truth she was as emotionally strong as he once believed. She was a depressed, crushed woman. That was undeniable. Yet he remembered soldiers, ex-prisoners he had met, who were also liberated from the Japs. They were far more broken than she. Su Li could help her recover. Maybe take her to a monastery, let the Master apply some of his magic power.

"I had to. How could I not try to rescue you?"

"Who are these other people?" Her voice was shrill.

"Friends. They helped me find you. We're going to take you away from here."

The limousine screeched to a halt. Bright lights blazed through the windshield. A bull-horn bellowed over the engine's noise. Chung turned around.

"A gun's mounted on that armored car. They've cut us off." He drew his revolver. "We'll have to make a run for it. Everybody out!"

A fusillade from the Nambu machine gun ripped into the limousine. The windshield shattered but Chung and Ling had already rolled onto the pavement. With the open doors as shields, they returned fire at the Japanese. Ellison pulled his mother out where they huddled on the cobblestones behind the rear door. Po and Su Li crouched behind the other door. Another burst. Chung screamed, fell dead. Ling was next.

The bull-horn blared again. Ellison put his finger to his lips, motioned for his mother to stay low. Chung lay sprawled out on the stones, riddled with bullets, a smile frozen on his face, his hand still clutching his gun. Ellison on his stomach crawled below the door and retrieved it, took aim. Two cautiously advancing soldiers in front made perfect targets for two quick rounds. By that time the machine gun had reloaded, its thirty-five caliber shells blasting holes into the heavy steel of the Mercedes. This time Ellison aimed at the scout car's headlights.

On the other side of the limousine, Ling's raked body lay slumped on the running board in a pool of blood, a cigarette still glowing next to his shoe. The Nambu chattered into the night once more, then stopped.

Su Li scrabbled after a plan. The soldiers would be coming soon to finish them off. She would circle behind and slay them as they closed. They would never expect it. Shots erupted from on the opposite side of the car. Cries of dying soldiers. The tinkle of broken glass. The searchlight winked out. That would be Ellison.

"Now I will kill them, Master," she said and made a move to steal away.

"No!" Po ordered. "This is no time for —."

Crouched low, she moved beyond the door's protection. From the blackness a new searchlight flared and caught her in the open in front of half a dozen soldiers. The light blinding her, they raised their guns but the Master lunged and knocked her off her feet. Their volley missed. Another shot from Ellison took out the light. Su Li tried to rise but something held her ankle.

"Master?" she cried, frantic to wriggle to herself free, but his hand did not release its grip.

Another hail of gunfire erupted, this time from the attackers' rear. Probably Duo's men, she thought. Chung's surprise. The Japanese returned fire and retreated to the cover of the armored car but not in time. The firefight lasted thirty seconds.

"Master!" She knelt over the fallen Po whose chest was damp with blood. Ellison heard her cry, grabbed his mother by the hand and pulled her around the car. A light swung out of the darkness.

"Chung?" A voice called out in Chinese. "The rats are dead."

"So is Chung," Ellison hollered back. "Who are you?"

"Han. Duo sent us. He knew the Japs would try something. Are you hit?"

"The old Master is," Ellison replied.

Black clad figures with flashlights circled around a distraught Su Li. From their midst, a tall man stepped up and knelt beside her. He took his hood off.

"Is it the Master?"

Su Li nodded, too distressed even to greet him. She pressed Po's tunic tight against the wound in his chest. Blood oozed through her fingers.

Mary Ellison leaned in to bend over the dying man. "I . . . I'm a nurse. At least I used to be." She spoke in halting Chinese while making feeble attempts to tear strips of cloth from Po's tunic, gave up and examined his wound. Her fingers probed the bullet hole, expert at first but as the seconds passed more and more without purpose. "I cannae help him, Jamie. The wound is too deep." Her face was haggard in the flashlight's glow. "Who is he?"

Su Li, on her knees, wept. "Master, I brought you here. I—."

The Master raised a hand. "No. The Tao brought me—us. My time is at an end. I wish dragon son Han . . . ."

"Here, Master. Old Master Wang sent me. I wanted to be your attendant but I see to my shame I am too late. Forgive me."

"Do not say so, *long er*. We triumphed for all of China before her enemies." His eyes closed. "Ah, I have made mistakes . . . . So long ago. *You* must forgive *me*. And forgive yourselves."

Forgive him? Su Li failed to understand what he meant then realized with a jolt her teacher had in truth not journeyed to fight for Ellison's sake, but for hers. It was his folly, his act of atonement, just as her venture to the Japanese base had been her folly. Now her final chance to tell him what she had known all her life and what Ellison had taught her how to say was slipping away. She was much more than tiger-daughter. She was *his* daughter.

"Master, I love you." The words were an anguished sigh. "You have been a father to me." Her tears fell on his forehead.

"Not always a good one." His voice sounded as if it came from far away. "Know this, child. Any man, even a Grand Master, would be proud to claim you as his daughter, as I do." He folded his hand around hers. "A sage is not supposed to have love influence his life." His voice grew weaker. "I suppose I have failed in that respect. Now your destiny lies with him who has the eyes of *laohuo*." He squeezed her hand. "Hold firmly to the Tao . . . ."

". . . and you may go anywhere and not be afraid." Han finished the words of ancient wisdom.

Po managed a smile. "You remembered." His eyes turned to Ellison. "Your promise." A somber Ellison nodded.

Grand Master Po Lin was dead.

Han closed the dead man's eyes and folded his palms in prayer. "Amituofo," he chanted. His followers did likewise. Praise be to Buddha. At last he lifted Su Li and pulled her into his arms. Her once dry spring of emotion, dammed up for two long years, burst forth in deep sobs. After a while Han pulled away, held her shoulders and looked into her eyes. "Courage, Su Li. Remember what he used to say, 'Heaven and earth are impartial. They let all people die.'" She nodded and wiped her tears.

Han gave quiet commands to his men. "We must go. Now! There will be others. Take the Master's body with us."

The next morning, under low clouds and a cold steady rain, a car plowed through the broken streets of

422

Shanghai. Small Rising Sun flags fluttered off the front fenders. Curtains hung over the rear windows. It stopped at various check points, where the driver showed papers to soldiers more intent on staying dry than prying into the business of a senior officer. It was not a true Japanese staff car, however. The Green Circle Gang had its own fleet of stolen vehicles.

In the back seat, Su Li sat between Ellison and Han who was dressed as a Japanese colonel. The driver, with a sergeant's insignia, was also one of Duo's men. Ellison wore an old US Army Infantry uniform, rank of major, and someone had found a lieutenant's uniform for Su Li, a little large but close enough. The fugitives were disguised as prisoners, part of an exchange, the gear provided from the gang's wardrobe of stolen goods. So Ellison was once again a soldier. The wheel had come another circle.

He fumbled for a folded piece of paper in his shirt pocket. Inside lay a lock of red hair. Mary Stuart Ellison had disappeared before the sun had risen. In her empty room they had found her hair cut off and lying in a heap of the floor. On a table was a note.

Jamie, I always knew you would be a hero. And I am very proud of you. You rescued me from an awful existence. But now you must let me make you proud. You must allow me to die, as befits a Stuart. Don't try to find me. At least give me that bit of victory. Save yourself and your beloved. Remember me as I was.
Your Mother.

They had talked the night before while Japanese patrols scoured the streets. He wanted to hear the whole story.

"I tried ta kill myself many times," she explained. "But Okamura always ha' someone watchin'. But the opium . . . . It was the only wa' I could stay sane." She paused on the verge of tears. "The thin's I ha' to do just to live." She closed her eyes and shook her head. "Ye should ne'er ha' seen me like this."

He wanted so badly to explain what had happened that day and ever since. How hard he had worked. How he had spent so much of his life for this reunion.

"After I left China I went to Uncle Alan in Rangoon."

"Alan?" She spoke dreamily. "You saw my brother?"

"Then to the states. I'm a pilot—or was—for the U.S. Army. I've been trying to find you since that day. And Lian. You remember Lian? She's dead."

"Alan is a knight of the air."

"Along the way I met a woman. She and I traveled half way across China and back." Above all he wanted her to understand, to approve, the last living link to that scarred past. How could he reach her? "I made a promise."

"Promises." She hissed the word. Her voice and mood changed.

"I did the best I could." He covered his face. "I'm sorry. I'm so damned tired and sorry."

She cut him off. "Promises are for stories. The stories are o'er, laddie." Abruptly her mood softened. "Nay, dinna be sorry. There is nae a place for sorry. Your story,

Jamie. That's a' that matters now." She sighed, leaned over and kissed him on the forehead. "Ye were such a good boy. Your father so wanted ye to play the fiddle. But ye bein' so stubborn." She paused, her mind far away in a vague, distant past, calm once more. "Queen Mary, he named me. An' I called him Abraham the Patriarch." She laughed, and in that sound the remarkable woman who had loved him and inspired him and taught him so much, even his sense of humor, blossomed one final time. "So bloody sure o' himself and his gospel. He died tryin' ta save me. Do ye remember that? I looked for ye then. Hopin' I wouldna' see ye. Hopin' ye ha' the sense ta hide."

"I should've been there. Kept you from all this."

'Nay! I wanted ye safe." She twisted her sleeve with trembling fingers. She looked twenty years older rather than six. "You're so angry at your father. Aye, I've kenned it a' this time." She touched his face with a thin smile. "Ye probably cannae believe the man could laugh. Ye ha' ta forgive him, ye ken. To forgive yourself. An' me."

Eventually, she collapsed in his arms. He held her like a child until she went to sleep, laid her on the bed. When he came to fetch her in the morning, she was gone.

He folded the hair inside the paper and returned it to his pocket. What did explanations or excuses, real or imagined, matter? There was only one way to embrace the now: forgive. *That I will. Your last gift to me. I'll forgive you and Father and myself. And maybe someday I'll forgive this whole stupid world for this fucking war.* She would doubtless be nursing lost ones in an opium den, or immersed in the illnesses of an infinite throng of beggars, their queen. That's how he promised himself to remember her. Music ran through his mind, the songs she had sung to him when he was a boy. "Speed, bonnie boat, like a bird on the wing, O'er the sea to Skye." He hummed the melody, her favorite. He had never been to Skye. He would go there when the war was over and take Su Li with him.

Her hand covered his. "You are a good man, James. You kept your promise, just as the Sage says. And now she has regained some of her dignity."

Ellison curled her fingers through his. Once again he marveled at how a hand could be a lethal instrument of death and a solace for sorrow at the same time. Two-edged, he thought. Like everything in China. Hell, everything in his life. One of many things he was beginning to appreciate. Why he loved this woman beside him. Through the curtain, the blurry outline of the city passed before him. Somewhere out there, the source of his original being, the spring whose water would always course through his veins, would cease to flow.

Han checked his watch. "The plane will take off in thirty minutes. We should be there in time. Good that your heads are shaved. And your uniform makes you look like you have shrunk, Su Li. Also good. They starve their prisoners." Earlier they had talked quietly, recalling their time at the Golden Sun Monastery. She told him the story of their prematurely dead child, about Hui, and her anguish regarding the boy's safety until the war ended. They vowed to each other to carry on the Master's teachings. Despite the grief and loss, she sensed a kernel of wholeness growing inside, much as an embryo might develop in her womb, certain it would come to ripeness in the course of time and tip the balance of life firmly to one side.

At the airfield perimeter the car passed through the last check point, flanked by bunkers with machine guns. In the distance on the tarmac, the tail end of a line of GI's was climbing into the passenger section of one of the newer C-49's. A Japanese platoon stood guard. The dark car pulled up alongside.

"I will go see the boy," said Han. "Tell him of his brave mother." He prepared to exit. "But first I intend to kill this Okamura."

"No, Han," Su Li said. "Do not waste your *chi* on one so vile." She kissed his cheek. "You will always be in my heart."

He nodded and got out, growled an order in Japanese at the supervising officer while Su Li and Ellison exited the car. Han boxed her on the shoulder and shoved Ellison. He shouted in nasty sounding English, knowing the Japanese soldiers did not understand. "Look after her, foreigner."

They filed past the young American co-pilot with a clip board, who was checking the prisoner manifest, and started up the ladder. For a second, Ellison imagined he might see his friend Taylor.

"Hey," the officer said. "I thought I was getting thirty. Where'd you guys come from, Major . . .?"

"Ellison. It's a long story, Lieutenant. Just get us out of here."

"Yes, sir."

Two days later, at the Allied air base in Kunming, a Mr. James Ellison, British citizen, and his Chinese wife, refugees who had escaped from Shanghai, boarded a transport plane to India. Han had arranged for clothing and new identities. Every trace of Lt. James Ellison, US Army Air Force, had disappeared. A few hours after take-off, mountain peaks came into view out the small window, the eastern end of the Himalayas.

Ellison put his arm around her. "We'll come back, after the war. We'll find him."

THE END

THE AUTHOR

Eugene McCreary has lived on both coasts as well as in the Midwest and South. He now surveys the human condition with his wife from their home on Sonoma Mountain, north of San Francisco. There he practices mindfulness, studies Chinese philosophy and history, plays Scottish and Irish music on his piano and guitar, and grows amazingly delicious raspberries.